Destiny's Denial
The MacLomain Series-
Book 2
By Sky Purington

Sky Purington

Dear Reader,

Thank you for purchasing, *Destiny's Denial* (The MacLomain Series- Book 2).

Destiny's Denial was a labor of love. For those of you who have read Fate's Monolith you will instantly recognize the hero, Ferchar, in this novel. While you knew him before as a courteous medieval teenager from Scotland, in this story he's grown into a brooding man with the weight of both a powerful highland clan and the ability of prophecy on his shoulders.

Who better to keep Ferchar in his place than a twenty-first century woman. I loved writing about Caitlin. She surprised me at every turn. We modern day gals are fairly strong but watch what she goes through and how she turns out at the end.

I still 'tip my hat' to Caitlin and Ferchar for coming as far as they did when all the odds were against them. Amazing couple!

Be sure to keep an eye on a certain deceptive time-traveling youth in this book as he becomes the hero in the next tale, Sylvan Mist.

For those of you who are new to this series, don't forget to pick up your copy of *The King's Druidess* (The MacLomain Series-Prelude), *Fate's Monolith* (The MacLomain Series-Book 1), and *Sylvan Mist* (The MacLomain Series-Book 3).

Best Always,
Sky

"If you like romance AND time travel you will love this book!... The sexual tension snaps and vibrates through the entire story. Caitlin manipulates her 21st century womanhood in such a way that at one time she has three Scottish chieftains after her! I loved the language, I loved the men, I loved the descriptions of a Scotland that I have never seen...Did I mention I read this story twice?"

~The Long and Short of It

"There is so much packed into Destiny's Denial the story is gripping. I couldn't put it down until I finished the last page but don't take my word for it, you really need to read these books. If you have the slightest interest in time travel, Scotland or magic you will be pulled into this story hook, line and sinker."

~Simply Romance Reviews

"Beautifully put together, the images that Sky Purington leaves you with will have you wishing that you were of the Broun clan and that your own MacLomain would pull you back through time to be with him yourself. Take some time during this hot summer to cool down in beautiful Scotland and see just what will have you wishing you could find such a destiny of your own."

~Night Owl Reviews

Previous Releases Include:

The King's Druidess- The MacLomain Series- Prelude
Fate's Monolith: The MacLomain Series- Book 1
Sylvan Mist: The MacLomain Series- Book 3

Highland Muse

Darkest Memory
Heart of Vesuvius (Sequel to Darkest Memory)

The Christmas Miracle (FREE read)

The Victorian Lure (Calum's Curse- Ardetha Vampyre)
Coming Soon- The Georgian Embrace- (Calum's Curse: Acerbus Lycan)

This is a work of fiction. Names, characters, places, and incidents are either the product of the author's imagination or are used fictitiously, and any resemblance to actual persons living or dead, business establishments, events, or locales, is entirely coincidental.

Destiny's Denial

COPYRIGHT © 2011 by Sky Purington

All rights reserved. No part of this book may be used or reproduced in any manner whatsoever without written permission of the author in the case of brief quotations embodied in critical articles or reviews.

Cover Art by Tamra Westberry

Published in the United States of America

This book is dedicated to my grandmother, Mildred. May you forever gaze upon the sea. 1922-2003

Sky Purington

Prologue

"Don't be afraid, I'm not."

He laughed and dove after his nephew. Cool mist sprayed his body as he descended within the waterfall. Cold, mountain born water sheathed his hot skin when he hit the river. The lad's legs retreated ahead in a sea of underwater foam.

"'Tis glorious," he bellowed as he surfaced. The tall and mighty pines basked their needles in the springtime sun.

He turned to his aunt, who sat on a wide rock. Her knees were bent. She leaned back on one elbow.

"You should join us," he urged.

She sat forward and wrapped her arms around her knees, "Nay..."

Blatant alarm shot from her green eyes.

"What is it?" Fear trickled down his spine.

She jumped from the rock and scanned the water. "Where is William?"

He spun.

The lad was nowhere to be found.

Impossible! *He was right in front of me.*

He scanned the river then dove. Surely the lad jested. He pushed his way back to the waterfall's base. White bubbles and river current pushed at him but he kept his eyes open and searched until black flecks threatened his vision.

When he finally surfaced for air, his aunt tugged anxiously at his arm. The octave of her voice chilled him to the bone. "Where is he? Tell me now, where is he!"

He again scanned the river then dove. *This isn't happening. There's no way.* But William was nowhere to be found. Panic rose.

He searched and searched, desperate.

Still nothing.

Out of breath and about to resurface, he spied something. With renewed strength he kicked his way down to the piece of fabric caught on the rock below and yanked it free. His aunt grabbed his arm the moment he surfaced.

They stared at the scrap of bloodstained, blue and green tartan in his grasp. Please, this can't be real. *This has to be a nightmare.* But he knew it wasn't.

Her face turned white.

"No. God no," she whispered.

He caught her just before she fainted. For the scrap of tartan belonged to her son.

Chapter One

*North Salem, New Hampshire
Present Day*

"No! He's not dead!" Caitlin sat up, rolled off the bed and fell flat on her face. The hardwood floor turned slick with tears as she pressed her cheek against its cool surface. Breathe. Just breathe. Would this horrid nightmare ever leave her alone?

She released a deep breath and rolled onto her back. Falling out of bed in the morning was a common occurrence. She sat up with a growl and worked to untie the knot of sweat soaked sheets from her legs. As usual, both her down comforter and pillows were scattered around the room.

"Damn dream." Caitlin sat on the bed and held her head in her hands. She didn't know what to make of it. For three years now she'd been having the same dream, well, more of a nightmare. The worse part of it? She was inside this stranger. That he was a man she had little doubt. Caitlin felt the horrible agony he experienced in losing his cousin. She spent every night locked inside of him, replaying the same excruciating moments over and over.

His pain tore through her and broke her heart every single time. She kicked away the balled up sheet, walked over to the window, whipped it open and stuck her head out into the fresh spring air. The ancient oak tree outside her window was full of new, green leaves. She reached out and fingered one of the soft stems.

"You're going to be late for work."

Caitlin disregarded Shane's words as they floated up. Her brother had just walked out the front door and was heading for his car. As usual, he was reading a book with one hand and drinking a cup of coffee with the other.

She shook her head and yelled down to his retreating form. "I've got plenty of time."

He ignored her, jumped into his silver Acura and peeled off down the drive.

Caitlin glanced at the clock. Half an hour to get to work. She grabbed a shower and threw on a pair of khaki colored pants and a navy blue polo shirt. God, she needed a cup of coffee. Grabbing her apron, she rushed downstairs.

The house was empty. Amanda must've left for work. Her best friend held a job as a social worker and she was never home anymore. Caitlin and Shane's mom and dad had died in a car accident when they were twelve and Gram had taken them in. When they turned eighteen, she agreed to let them live in the old colonial house on her property. They paid a small rent just to cover the taxes and paid for their own utilities. She knew Gram was a wealthy woman and didn't need the money. Charging them rent had more to do with instilling a sense of responsibility into her grandchildren.

A couple of years ago, Amanda moved in with them, desperate for a cheap place to live while she got her career going. Gram had always liked Amanda so there was no problem.

Her horse whinnied from the adjacent barn as Caitlin flew out the door. "Morning baby, I'm leaving for work. We'll go for a ride when I get home."

Destiny's Denial

C.C. offered no response. She would've preferred spending time with her horse rather than going to work, but at some point she needed to continue her college education and the only way to do that was to make money.

"Ah, good morning to you as well sweetheart." This time she was talking to her Ford Explorer Sport. Though only a 2004, she looked pretty in red with silver trim. Caitlin jumped in and cranked the radio. Rolling down her window, she waved to her grandmother as she drove down the dirt lane that connected to the main road.

Lucky for her, Dunkin Donuts was quiet. She was out of the drive-thru in thirty seconds flat. Record time. Medium French Vanilla iced coffee in hand, Caitlin swung into the parking lot of the restaurant where she worked. She really did love working here. Weathervane Seafoods stood like a silent ship on Route 28 at this hour and she enjoyed getting here before it filled up with hungry customers.

"Hey girl, you made it," Rick said as she entered through the back door into the kitchen, slid her timecard and plunked her purse down on the ice cream cooler.

She glanced at the clock and winked. "I'm on time today, so relax."

Rick laughed and pushed a box of donuts her way. "Care for something sweet? Or maybe a donut?"

Caitlin rolled her eyes and entered the dining room through the swing doors. She switched on both coffee makers and stretched.

What was up with her dream? It was all she could think about lately. The glimpse of a young boy diving off a cliff in front of her. The love of the man who dove after him. The woman on the rock and the pain that flooded her face.

"There you are."

Caitlin jumped at the sound of Jessie's voice. She turned and smiled at her manager. "I'm right on time. Aren't you proud of me?"

"Of course." Jessie placed a hand on her shoulder and issued a wide smile.

Caitlin slumped. She knew that smile. "Oh no, really?"

"You know me too well." Jessie gave her the puppy dog eyes she couldn't refuse. "We're in a tight spot."

Jessie needed her for a double shift. It was Friday after all, not such a surprise. Time to bargain. "Can I lose my day shift tomorrow?"

Even though she needed the money, doing a double today would rob Caitlin of her Friday night with her grandmother. Her gram was her best friend and Fridays had always been theirs. She would spend Saturday with her instead.

Jessie's eyes softened. She knew. "I'll see what I can do. No promises."

Caitlin smiled. Whenever Jessie said that it meant: *Don't worry, I'll get it covered. You do me a favor, I do you a favor.*

Five hours later, Caitlin took her break. It was three o'clock and a perfect day to sit out at the picnic table situated behind the restaurant for employees. Regrettably, there were three other waitresses plus two cooks already on break. Not that she minded the company but there was nothing better than solitude after four hours of waiting on tables. Not going to happen today apparently.

"Caitlin, I've got a spot all warmed up for you," Rick said as she approached the table.

She slid in next to all six feet of him, well aware that he didn't move over much. She slid her tray of fried chicken tenders with honey mustard sauce down, wishing it were a plate full of whole bellied clams and sea scallops. What was the point of working so hard if you were going to waste it on a fourteen-dollar plate of food when you could instead order a seven-dollar plate of food?

She hated her reasoning as she gazed at the plate of fried oysters across from her. Damn. Her gram said it was the Scottish in her. Frugal to the bone. She shoved a piece of chicken into her mouth and pretended it was a delicious piece of Haddock. In short time, everyone began to filter back inside until it was just her and Rick.

"Good money today?" He'd managed to make five french fries last twenty minutes. She knew why.

"Not bad. It's been better," Caitlin said.

He pushed his plate away and folded his hands on the table. An unruly light brown lock fell forward over his forehead as he seemed undecided as to what to say next. "You make me nervous, Caitlin. I don't get nervous."

She stopped eating and focused on twirling the claddagh ring on her finger. He turned his head slightly and gave a slow grin. Sexy...definitely sexy. Was she normal? This guy should have her sweating all over.

"It's just me, Rick." They'd worked together for at least a year now.

He pushed back and swung one of his legs over the bench seat of the picnic table so he straddled it in her direction. His dark-blue eyes grew serious. "Yeah, I know."

His position was more intimate...erotic somehow. A picnic table behind a restaurant. She was just about to laugh at her thought process when his hand slid down her forearm and covered her hand on the table.

The air vibrated and her vision blurred. Then it cleared. Transfixed, she watched his hand change, become tan and lengthen. The palm widened, became stronger, more sure. A burning sensation started beneath her fingernails and slowly crept over her hand as though first fire and then scorpions clawed the delicate skin.

Caitlin tried to talk, tried to tear her gaze away from the hand covering hers, but couldn't. Something was wrong. Everything around her hand and his was wrong. The air compressed and it felt as though tiny bolts of lightning zapped every inch of skin on her body.

The restaurant vanished. The traffic pulling into the parking lot faded away. The trees were gone, the nearby post office, the dumpster. Everything. Not even the sky above remained. A rush of heat rushed over her and sucked the air from her lungs.

That's what made her panic. She couldn't breathe.

"He's not dead. He can't be." A deep voice saturated her eardrums.

Pain ripped through Caitlin. Fresh, pliant, raw pain. Physical, psychological, mind-blowing pain. Rick was gone. She was with *him*. The person she became late at night, under the cloak of sleep, year after year. But where was he? Her eyes couldn't find him. The hand tightened over hers. She felt so exposed. Possessed.

"Let me go." My voice doesn't sound right…it's far too distant. Panicked, she screamed. Nothing came out.

"Who are you?" His question held incredible rage. Blatant accusation.

Fresh fear bombarded her. Shards of ice streaked up her arm until her chest seized. Was she having a heart attack? I'm too young to die. A horrible, hot wind blew over her and she turned away. She tried to get away.

A strong arm seized her from the back before she could flee the bench. Bare and muscled, it squeezed tightly across her ribcage just below her breasts.

Caitlin was pulled back against the phantom man until he straddled her backside on the seat. His anger poured over her.

"Who are you?" He breathed against her ear. His resolution dripped into Caitlin. Her body began to shake. He squeezed tighter still. His free hand came up to her throat. Though it didn't squeeze her neck, the power beneath his fingers was palpable. Ready to easily take her life.

"Rick?" The word was a week squeak of hope through clenched teeth. Though she knew it wasn't Rick, maybe he'd get spooked if he thought her "boyfriend" was nearby. Her sense of reasoning suddenly seemed ridiculous. Whoever this tyrant was she had the very distinct impression that he feared no man.

His breathing shifted, became abstract, as if her question incited him to switch tactics. His hand slid from her throat down through the top of her polo shirt to skim the top of her bra.

Caitlin meant to scream but purred instead. Literally purred. Electricity traveled from his hand straight down to her throbbing womb. Sweet pleasure scorched her, burning a tunnel of need straight through her that only he could satisfy. Caitlin's body quivered. Then, before she could comprehend what was happening, a sharp orgasm raked her body. *Ohhhh!* Though her lower half arched off the bench in pleasure, the arm locked beneath her breast held tight.

"Will you tell me now?" His soft words teased her, tickled and aroused places he couldn't possibly be touching.

For all the violent, hateful things she wanted to do, her body was putty. What was going on? Thankfully, when all else failed, one emotion always seemed to take over. Anger. Caitlin had just been used. In the worse way possible. That's all it took.

"Get away from me!" She did the only thing she could think of from this angle. Clawed. Never one to keep long nails, she used what she had and dug deep, then raked with all her might from his wrist to his elbow.

The minute she did it his other hand caught her chin and whipped her head sideways. "This isn't over. I'll find you."

Before she could jerk her head free he attacked her with what he knew would work. The dream. The horrible pain of loss. Death.

Caitlin bent over and threw up. She felt as though every person close to her had just ceased to exist. Bastard. What a tormented, horrible soul.

"Caitlin?" Someone was shaking her. "Caitlin, are you okay?"

"Rick?"

"Yeah, you okay, hon?"

Caitlin opened her eyes. Though cloudy, the day was painfully bright. The soft wind blowing up behind the restaurant hurt her skin. If she never ate again, it would be too soon. She raised a shaky hand and nodded. "I'm all right."

"Are you sure?" He kneeled down beside her. "One second, I was telling you that you made me nervous, the next second you're over here by the fence all curled up and shaking. I didn't mean to...well, I don't know. Did I scare you that much by telling you I was interested in you? I'm sorry if I did. God, you look horrible."

Caitlin brushed away his hand. She needed to be alone. "Thanks."

He sat beside her and brushed the hair away from her face. "Come on, you know what I mean. Just because you just threw up fifteen shades of green doesn't mean you're any less fine to look at."

Caitlin sat back against the fence, pulled up her legs and wrapped her arms around her bent knees. This guy still found her attractive after she'd just lost everything she ate for the past twelve hours? That should mean something. Right now, it meant less than nothing.

She lifted her head and offered him her best attempt at a smile. "You're a good guy, Rick. Thanks. Mind if I have a few minutes alone?"

He studied her face. "You sure? You want me to tell Jessie you're sick?"

"No." She shook her head. "Just head on in, I'll be right behind you."

Rick rose to his feet. "If you're not inside in two minutes, I'm coming back out."

Caitlin tried to smile at his retreating form. What was the matter with her? Taking deep, steady breaths, she leaned her head back against the fence, closed her eyes and tried to relax. Something strange was going on and she couldn't begin to comprehend what. Then an odd revelation hit her. In her dream, she understood the verbal exchange on some subconscious level though she never actually heard anyone speak.

Her mystery man had just spoken and with a thick Scottish brogue.

"Caitlin? You coming in?" Rick asked.

She got to her feet and retied her apron. "Yeah."

He stood at the backdoor and waited. As she passed he touched her elbow. "You sure you're okay."

Caitlin nodded and pulled her arm away. Wow, was she sexually charged right now. Men beware. She headed for the bathroom. It wasn't that she didn't like sex. What experiences she'd had were okay. The problem was they didn't even come close to what just happened to her outside. Caitlin rubbed her temples against a newborn headache and stared into the mirror.

As disturbing as the whole nutty experience had been, it agreed with her. Her cheeks were rosy and her eyes shone a lighter gold than usual. She looked like a sated woman. Leaning over, she splashed cold water on her face, reapplied some lip gloss and went back to work.

An hour into the dinner rush, Caitlin realized how grateful she was to still be here. Keeping busy kept her from thinking too much about how insane she felt.

Was she cracking up? It wasn't as if she was under pressure. With a steady job, great friends and a growing savings account, Caitlin led a fairly stress-free life. About the only thing that bothered her on occasion, besides the reoccurring dream, was her uncanny ability to foresee things. It happened on rare occasions and was usually as simple as dreaming about what parking space would be available when she went to a crowded shopping center the next day. Gram told her it was just heightened intuition and it ran in the family.

As always when waiting on tables the evening passed quickly. There was nothing like stepping out the door after a busy shift with two hundred and fifty dollars wadded up in her apron. Caitlin looked forward to a hot shower and a good book.

"Hey, Caitlin, wait up." Sean the busboy ran to catch up with her halfway across the parking lot.

"Oh no, I didn't tip you? I could've sworn I did." Caitlin reached into her apron pocket.

"No, you tipped me and if you didn't I wouldn't chase after you for it. You always tip me too much." Sean smiled and blushed.

"What's up, then?" Caitlin fished around in her purse for her keys.

"Well I was wondering if maybe your grandmother was looking for some yard help again this year. Maybe some spring clean-up."

Caitlin opened her door, threw her stuff onto the back seat and jumped in. She started the vehicle and rolled down the window. "I'm sure she is. You did a really great job for her last year."

"Thanks." He rested his arms on the door. "Actually, it wouldn't be just me this year. I've got a new foster brother that wants to help too. He's only twelve but he's a big kid and really nice."

"Sure, I don't see why not. I'm hanging with Gram tomorrow. I'll let her know you're interested."

"Great." Sean ran his hand through his light blond hair. "We could take care of your yard too, if you want."

Caitlin let her hair down. Not such a bad idea. Between her and Amanda working so much and Shane pursuing his literary career they could use the extra help. "That sounds good. Let me talk to Shane and Amanda and I'll get back to you."

"Alright." Sean headed for his car. "Have a good night."

"You too," Caitlin said. She was about to pull the shift into reverse when someone knocked on the passenger side window. Startled, she jumped. It was only Rick. She pressed the button on the side console and the electric window rolled down.

"Hi, sorry, didn't mean to scare you." His face broke into a not-so-sorry grin.

He looked tired. It'd been a hard night in the kitchen and Rick was the guy that always kept his cool. He handled stressed managers, frenzied wait staff and emotional cooks like a pro. That's why the restaurant was going to hate losing him at the end of the summer.

"What's up?" Caitlin asked.

"My brother just called and can't pick me up. You think I could grab a ride?"

"Sure." Caitlin unlocked the door. "Hop in."

"Thanks." He jumped in, filling up the Ford's interior. They made small talk as she took a right hand turn onto Route 28, then onto route 97.

"You want to swing into Sam's for a drink?" He said.

"No. Not tonight, I'm too tired." They drove by Samantha's Restaurant.

"That's cool." He leaned over and turned up the music a little.

He lived a half-mile from the Salem library so they didn't have to go far. Rumor had it Rick's family was wealthy but he lived in a fairly small house. As Caitlin pulled into his driveway she felt the tension rise within the truck.

"Here we are." Caitlin shifted into park.

"You're the best." Rick had his hand on the door handle but hesitated and cleared his throat. "Caitlin, I never got a chance to talk to you earlier."

She held back a sigh. For a confident guy who was recently accepted into Harvard Law School he appeared pretty nervous. Maybe she should give him a chance. After all, he would be leaving in a few months and she could use a casual fling. Actually, she could really use some male companionship.

Caitlin decided to make it easy on him. "Yes, I'd love to go out with you sometime."

The breath he'd been holding blew out of his lungs and he turned to her. "Really?"

"Really." She smiled. "You have my number, give me a buzz."

He leaned over and brushed the top of his knuckle across her cheekbone. "You got it."

Caitlin watched him enter the house and then pulled out. She felt pretty good. Maybe, if he played his cards right, she would make it a summer to remember for him. She smiled ruefully to herself as she drove through the back roads of Salem into North

Salem. Maybe, he might be able to make her feel like she did today at the picnic table with a Scotsman at her back.

****

Mildred awoke at 9:00 a.m. sharp, just like she did every morning. She let Remington, her Lhasa Apso, out the back door and sat down in her favorite reclining chair beside the huge, multi-paned window that overlooked her front yard. Sunlight streamed through the glass and lit up the colorful array of blown glass fixtures she had hung.

Birds flitted around a feeder that hung near a round temperature gauge attached to a nearby maple tree. It read fifty-five degrees. Not bad for an April morning. Mildred had just grabbed one of her hard candies when Caitlin pulled into the driveway. She set the sweet aside when she saw the coffees her granddaughter had in hand.

"Morning, Gram." Caitlin came through the door behind her and gave her a kiss on her cheek. "I brought your cinnamon donut and coffee just like you like it, small, cream and two sugars." She set her own ice coffee on a coaster and went to let Remington in before his incessant barking drove all the birds from the forest.

"How are you feeling?" Caitlin asked as she plunked down in the chair beside her and took a long sip from her drink.

"Horrible," she said and smiled.

Her granddaughter ignored the response because it was the same one Mildred gave everyone. Not that she was a pessimistic person, she wasn't. Just sick of being in a body that didn't get around quite like it used to. She eyed Caitlin and sipped her coffee. Beautiful to the bone, that's what Mildred always thought. Her long, wavy chestnut hair was her crown of glory. All full with streaks of flaxen and gold.

They chatted a bit. Mildred figured she did well to talk casually as long as she did before finally asking Caitlin what was wrong. The girl was a ball of tension and fidgety to the point of distraction.

Her granddaughter was silent for a time, appearing to contemplate her next words. When she did speak, it was with a light sheen of tears in her eyes. "I promised myself I wouldn't say anything but the truth of it is, Gram, you're my confidant. I just can't not talk about it anymore."

Mildred placed her hand over the curved top of her cane and leaned forward. She couldn't remember the last time she had seen Caitlin cry. "What's going on dear?"

"I've been having the same dream for three years now and if that isn't enough, yesterday at work my dream started to infiltrate my reality. I think I'm losing it, Gram." Caitlin sat back and wiped a tear away.

"Tell me about your dream." Mildred handed her a box of tissues. She didn't like the sound of this.

Caitlin let out a puff of air and then told her about the dream. Detail by painful detail. It was obvious her emotions were all wrapped up in it.

When she finished, Mildred sat back. Her mouth felt dry. Her heart beat a bit faster. "So, you don't know where you were?"

Caitlin stared down at the inch of coffee left in her cup. "No. I suppose after what happened yesterday I could speculate."

That bad feeling Mildred had was getting worse. "Go on."

Caitlin told her about the man in her dream accosting her at the restaurant. Theirs had always been an honest relationship so when her granddaughter told her about the sexual interplay Mildred was neither shocked nor embarrassed. She knew well that the blush flooding Caitlin's face had more to do with remembering the event than telling her grandmother about it.

"I take it he must have had an accent and that's how you know where the dream might have taken place." Mildred met Caitlin's eyes and knew for a fact she wasn't going to like what Caitlin said.

Caitlin shrugged. "He had a very thick Scottish accent, so perhaps it was Scotland."

Coffee forgotten, she reached over, unwrapped a caramel candy and popped it in her mouth. That is exactly what she was afraid Caitlin was going to say.

Chapter Two

Caitlin rolled her head around on her neck to ease the knots of tension. Gram appeared overly disturbed. She waited while her grandmother vigorously sucked half the candy in silence. She gave up smoking years ago and had replaced the habit with any melt-in-your-mouth sweet she could find. Suddenly, she stood. Not an easy task for a woman with a bad hip.

"Gram, what are you doing? I can get you whatever you need. Sit down." Caitlin stood.

"Relax child, I'm just walking to the kitchen table." She waved her off and shook her head.

Caitlin bit at her lip. She knew her gram wasn't feeble and had all her faculties in order, but those facts did not ease the worry. Four years ago this December she had suffered a minor heart attack and since then Caitlin had been a vigilant watchdog over her gram.

She walked over to the linen closet just at the start of the hallway and opened it. "How old are you now? Twenty-three?"

"Yep. Why?"

Gram ignored her question, removed the stack of neatly folded sheets from the second shelf down and handed them to her.

Caitlin set the sheets on a chair and watched in amazement as her grandmother unlatched and opened a small hidden door, about a foot high and two feet long. She peeked over her shoulder. Caitlin thought she'd known every orifice of this house. It seemed she was not nearly nosy enough as a child.

Gram reached in and withdrew a package wrapped in plastic. "Go on over to the table. Sit down."

Caitlin did and waited patiently while Gram set the package down and went to retrieve another hard candy. At last she sat down next to Caitlin. As though this were a major affair, she rolled up first one sleeve, and then the other. With great care she untied the aged faded green ribbon that bound the package. With the precision a brain surgeon would give his first surgery, she removed the plastic.

Caitlin gasped. "What a beautiful book."

"This," Gram said, as she delicately ran her finger across the title, "is very, very old."

The hardcover book was deep maroon with one-inch tall gold letters embossed across the front. She leaned forward and read the words. *Fate's Monolith* by Beth Luken.

Gram opened it to the first page and Caitlin read the words aloud. "Dedicated to my dearest friend, wherever and whenever you may be, Arianna Lilius Broun MacLomain."

Her grandmother closed the book and handed it to Caitlin. "I want you to read this."

She tested the weight of the thick book. It was cool and smelled new, though it was obviously old. Caitlin didn't know what to say. For some reason this book was very important to her grandmother.

Then Gram proceeded to answer a few of the questions formulating in her head before she had a chance to ask them.

"It was published in the year 1802. The book is written about my distant aunt who disappeared in the year 1800."

Caitlin set the book down and sat back. "That's incredible, are you serious?"

"Very."

"Why do you want me to read this now?"

"Because knowledge is power and historical ammunition is underrated."

Caitlin couldn't contain a burst of laughter but cut it short when she saw the seriousness in Gram's blue eyes. "What are you talking about, Gram?"

She stood and looked down at her granddaughter. "I'm talking about you sitting down and reading a good book."

Remington started barking and ended the conversation. Caitlin stood and walked over to the window. A red S-10 pick-up truck had just pulled up to the top of Gram's driveway. "It's Sean."

"Who?" Gram walked up beside her and peered out the window.

"Sean, you remember, the kid who took care of your yard last summer. He's a busboy at my restaurant. He asked me last night if you'd be interested in hiring him again this year. I completely forget to mention it to you."

"Oh yes, nice boy. Did a good job. Who's that with him?" Gram's brows drew together.

A boy with short black hair jumped out of the passenger side and followed Sean up the walkway. "Sean mentioned a younger foster brother that he was hoping could work with him this year. That must be him."

They walked over to the door and opened it as the boys arrived at the threshold.

"Good morning, Mrs. Seavey. I hope I'm not popping over at a bad time," Sean said.

"No, no, come in boys. Would you like something to drink?" Gram said.

"No, we're good, thanks." Sean and his foster brother stood in the living room, looking rather uncomfortable. "Hey, Caitlin."

She smiled and nodded.

"You're ambitious," Caitlin said and gave him a mock punch on the arm.

The poor kid's face turned as red as a tomato. "Yeah, well, it occurred to me, coming in person might be more appropriate."

"Who's your friend, Sean?" Caitlin said.

"Oh, I'm sorry. Mildred and Caitlin, this is Gordon Bain, my foster brother. Gordon, this is Mildred and Caitlin Seavey."

"Nice to meet you, Gordon." Caitlin reached out to shake his hand. Handsome kid.

"Hi," Gordon said, his voice cracked. Puberty.

Ten minutes later the details were worked out. The boys would work for Gram over the summer and Caitlin would let Sean know about her house as soon as she talked to Shane and Amanda.

Caitlin spent the rest of the afternoon playing cards with Gram. When she got into her SUV to leave, she noticed one missed call on her cell phone. She always left her phone behind when visiting Gram. No modern day interruptions necessary, thank you.

She went straight to her voice mail. It was Rick. He didn't waste any time. His message was short and to the point; he wanted to get together tonight. Sounded good. Caitlin called him back and made plans. He'd pick her up at eight in his new car and they'd go to dinner.

She looked at the clock on her dashboard. It was only five. That gave her plenty of time to spend with C.C. After parking her truck, she hopped out, stretched and headed for the barn. When she opened the door, her horse stood waiting, head hung over the stall, eager to welcome her. Caitlin had named her C.C., short for Celtic cross, because of the small black mark on her neck that looked exactly that, a Celtic cross.

Gram had given C.C. to Caitlin for her twenty-first birthday and she'd been in love with the horse ever since.

"You're looking exceptionally gorgeous today, baby." Caitlin rubbed her cheek up against C.C.'s muzzle. With a white body, black mane and tail, the horse was a prize.

C.C. whinnied her agreement and swished her tail back and forth, preening.

Caitlin laughed. "Vanity becomes you, girl."

Time flew as she first took C.C. out for a trot and then groomed her. All the while, Caitlin could only think about that book. For some odd reason, she was both eager and wary to read it. As though once she did, her life would never be the same.

Eight o'clock came fast but Caitlin was ready when Rick arrived. They'd decided that the Ninety-Nine Restaurant sounded good so she had opted for low platform heals, boot cut jeans and a form-fitting white sweater. She wore her hair down and applied a darker shade of pink lipstick than usual. Good to go.

She met Rick at the front door of her house and followed him out.

"Very nice. How can you afford this on your salary?" Caitlin said, running the tip of her finger over the glossy black hood of his 6 Series Coupe.

"None of your business. It was ready at a good time though, eh?" He held the passenger door open and eyed her up and down with appreciation. "You look great, Caitlin."

"Thanks, so do you." And he did. His hair was cut, his designer jeans were tight and loose in all the right places and the slate-blue shirt he wore did wonders for the muscles she had had no idea he possessed.

He slid behind the wheel and reached down behind her. Whatever cologne he had on wasn't half bad either— a sporty, citrus scent.

"This is for you." He pulled a single long stemmed red rose forward and handed it to her.

She held the flower to her nose and inhaled the heady fragrance. "Thanks. You're so sweet."

"Hey, I've been waiting for this night for a long time. The other eleven roses are in the back." He shot her a killer grin.

Rick turned on the radio and they were off.

A few minutes later, he bypassed their intended destination and jumped onto Route 93 Southbound. She quirked an inquisitive brow in his direction.

He smiled back at her, the devil in his eyes. "We're city-bound, babe. Boston bound, to be exact."

She lifted her shoulders once and relished the sweet feeling of the BMV eating up the pavement. From zero to sixty miles per hour in five point three seconds, the V-8 engine left Salem behind. "Whatever you say, nowhere too fancy though. I'm not exactly dressed right."

He ran a stray eye over her jean-clad thigh. "You look dressed right to me. You like to dance?"

She bit back a smile. "Love to."

"All right, we'll grab a bite and hit Landsdown Street, sound good?"

"I'm all yours." Caitlin hadn't been to the street next to Fenway Park since she graduated from high school. It hosted a variety of nightclubs and bars.

"That's what I hoped you'd say."

They had a great night. By the time he pulled back into her driveway it was 2:00 a.m. A gentleman to the end, he walked her to the front door.

"Thanks, Rick, I had a really good time." She pulled the house key out of her purse.

"You're a great dancer, Caitlin, I had no idea." He placed a finger beneath her chin, tilted back her head and kissed her. It was a nice kiss, feather-light at first.

Forget this. If we're going to start something, let's go. She stood on her toes, wrapped her arms around his neck and deepened the kiss. He definitely didn't resist but he didn't maximize its possibilities either, as if he were holding back. She pulled away and frowned a little.

"I have to go, gotta work tomorrow," he said, his eyes full of compassion and something else...

She nodded. "Okay, I'm working the day shift. I'll see you then." Caitlin pulled away but he grabbed her hand.

"I don't want to rush things with you, Caitlin." He released her hand and left. She watched him drive away and sighed. Rick wanted a serious relationship. She went upstairs and flopped down on her bed. Too bad she didn't. He was perfect in every way. What was wrong with her? It wasn't like her to only want sex from a guy. Caitlin closed her eyes and drifted off to sleep.

The dream swelled up fast; the dive into the river, the feel of the cool water, searching desperately for the boy. She held the scrap of bloody tartan in her hand, staring down at it in horror.

"He's not dead!"

She sat up abruptly, and was forcibly slammed back down.

Not again.

A long, hard, wet body covered hers.

"No, he's not." Caitlin stilled as the Scottish burr flooded her senses. Blackness surrounded her but he was there. Right on top of her in her bed, swallowing her form with the sheer size of him. His body felt on fire where it touched hers. She knew he was holding the bulk of his weight off of her, though that didn't last long.

He gripped her wrists and slammed them down on either side of her head. She froze. There was no mistaking the heavy, swollen erection pressed against her thigh. Caitlin should be petrified, screaming, something. But no, instead, as she struggled in desperation to see his face, her body went into overdrive.

Scorching desire drove steaming blood through her veins. She felt like an animal in heat and inhaled sharply. He smelled like the outdoors in fall. Spicy and sweet. Somewhere between warmed maple syrup and fresh cut grass.

"You're only a figment of my imagination." Caitlin pushed the declaration past unsure lips.

He leaned in close, until the corner of his lips rested next to her eardrum. "I can assure you that your imagination is not nearly that creative."

She narrowed her eyes. Whoever this stranger was, he wouldn't get another rise out of her like he had before. Caitlin focused on staying as calm as the earthquake within her heart would allow. Her room was too dark and he was too close. His hair brushed against her face.

"Who are you? What do you want from me?" Though petrified, her words were level. She gave herself a mental pat on the back. Good girl, Caitlin.

He didn't seem impressed by her bravado. His next statement came out on a hiss. "You know exactly what I want from you."

"I have a good idea and you're not getting it." Caitlin made her best attempt to knee him where it counted but was pinned down in such a position that the attempted action was completely futile.

"You flatter yourself, woman." He wedged his knee between her legs instead.

Caitlin might be able to control her words but her body had a mind of its own. Fire scorched through her limbs like a freight train. Sweat trickled down her forehead. Not only her thighs, but every muscle in her body tightened almost painfully.

She pushed her words through clenched teeth. "Get off of me."

The sound he made was half laughter and half growl. Then he was gone.

Caitlin couldn't sit up, her body shook so badly. The arousal was so intense her thighs trembled violently. It took many minutes before a logical thought formed in her mind. This was nuts. When she finally sat up, blood rushed to her head so fast the room spun.

She switched on the bedside light and checked the time. Three o'clock a.m.. Caitlin surveyed the room. Of course it was empty. What did she expect? She knew that no one had walked away from her bed, yet her disbelieving eyes still looked for a man climbing out the window or hiding in a corner. Ridiculous.

Water. I need water. Caitlin wasn't surprised to find Shane sitting at the kitchen table downstairs, laptop open, typing away.

"Hey," she said and grabbed a glass. Caitlin turned on the sink faucet and had a sudden urge to immerse her whole head under the icy, cold water. Instead, she filled her glass and gulped it down, then refilled it again.

"Hey," Shane said absently, an intense scowl directed at whatever he was writing.

She plunked down at the table across from him. Shane was older than her by two years. His hair was as black as the night and his eyes an arresting turquoise. Absolutely every female that had ever been in his presence fell instantly in love. It was disgusting. Thankfully, he was oblivious. Like herself, he'd been serious a couple of times and that was it. His writing was always, by far, his first passion.

Caitlin finished her water and began tapping one finger on the table. That was the cue and Shane knew it. One eyebrow arched as he looked over his laptop at her. The man continued to type even as he gazed at her.

She shook her head and wagged one finger back and forth. "Not legit. You have to stop typing to make this a bonafide brother-sister moment."

"That word annoys me." He pushed the laptop away and sat back.

"What word?"

"Bonafide. It's overused and reeks of an Internet scam sales pitch."

Caitlin laughed and shook her head. Shane always became picky about words when the ones he was trying to write, or type, were not coming together well. "You just get stranger with age, huh?"

"You bet." He offered that smile that had women falling at his feet and took a sip of beer.

When he set down his bottle, she leaned over, grabbed it and gulped down the rest. This is what she probably should've gone for instead of a glass of water. No doubt she needed it.

"How was the conference?"

He shrugged. "No good agents there...or editors for that matter."

"They probably saw you coming and ran. You have to be a nuisance at this point."

Shane shot her his best wounded look. "Take it easy, sis. Only the persistent make it in this field."

"You are that." Caitlin bit her lower lip. "What are you planning to do if you can't sell your book?"

She hated to ask. He'd given up a great bartending job almost a year ago to write this book and had to be close to sucking his savings account dry.

"I've got some ideas," he said.

Shane was great at hiding emotion but Caitlin knew him too well. He had no idea. He'd counted on this book.

"You're going after the right people, yes?" she said.

He sighed and turned sarcastic. "No, I've decided to search out the comedy agents to help me publish my war novel."

"Take it easy, buddy. You know what I mean."

Shane grabbed another beer and for a flicker of a moment looked deflated. "Yeah, I do. I'm on the right track but I'm beginning to think medieval Scottish stories are becoming a hackneyed subject in the twenty-first century."

A lightning hot shiver ran through her. "I doubt it."

"You okay?" Shane hit the save button and shut off his computer.

She wasn't about to break down on her brother like she had Gram. Enough was enough. Instead, she nodded and stole his beer.

"So, what's going on with you little sis? We haven't had a chance to chat lately."

Uh, oh. He was on to her. The two of them had been through a lot together. Besides Gram, he was her rock. Should she tell him the truth? That his sister was crazy? A little lost in the cookie jar...

Nope. Not tonight. "Not too much. I went out with Rick. We had fun."

Shane shook his head. "That guy's not for you. You'd control him in no time."

"What are you talking about? You don't even know him that well."

Shane yawned. "Don't get me wrong. He's a nice enough guy. You forget, I went to school with him."

Caitlin narrowed her eyes and pursed her lips. "That's right, you did. And if I remember correctly, you both had a thing for the same girl. The one he ended up with."

He flinched. "Not one of my better attempts."

She laughed. "Most likely the only attempt you ever had to make."

"I think you might be right about that. She really wasn't my type anyways."

Caitlin groaned and stood. "Wasn't she the homecoming queen and class president? All good looks and feminine wiles?

"All right, that's enough. All that loss of female flesh to your current beau doesn't change the fact that I don't think he's right for you."

Time to switch topics. "I was at Gram's today and Sean stopped by. He'll be taking care of her lawn again this year and wondered if we were interested in hiring his services."

"Heck, yeah," said Shane. "I hate raking. That old oak sheds like an Akita in the fall."

Caitlin frowned. "No doubt. Speaking of Akitas, where's Nakita?"

"She's upstairs sleeping on my bed."

She grimaced. "Her hair is going to stick to your bedspread."

He shrugged and grinned. Nakita was the one girl that had made it into his life and stayed there. The ninety pound American Akita was the queen bee of dogs. And Shane was hers.

"Well, I'm crashing. See you in the morning?" Caitlin said.

"I would imagine." He gave her a small smile and sat back down at the table, laptop back in position.

The last thing Caitlin wanted to do was sleep. She needed answers and had nowhere to turn to get them. What she did have, however, was a book to read. A book that Caitlin suspected was related to her current set of circumstances—if they could be called that. She was still convinced she'd gone off the deep end without a life preserver.

Six hours later, she did a very naughty thing. She called in sick to work.

This was no average book and she knew putting it down to go anywhere, period, was not an option. History had never held any interest for her—for Shane, yes, but definitely not her.

Now it did.

Fate's Monolith was about her distant aunt who had lived in the very same house she lived in now. Caitlin didn't need to picture what the author described in her mind. All she had to do was look around. The woman, Arianna, whom the book was about, had even called Caitlin's room her own. Amazingly enough, the oak tree outside her window had been there two hundred years ago. Unbelievable.

But what had her calling in sick to work had little to do with reading about her distant relatives. A couple of times while reading the book, Caitlin almost hopped in her SUV and flew down to Gram's to question her until she was blue in the face. The end of each page, though, kept her turning to the next and she stayed right where she sat.

This had to be a joke…

"Caitlin." A knock resounded from the other side of her bedroom door. "Are you awake, girl?"

Page one hundred and sixty. Caitlin made a mental note and closed the novel. "Yeah, come on in."

Amanda swung open the door, swooped across the room and drew back the curtains. "Do you know what time it is?"

Her Amanda: always bright and sunny—amazing, considering her occupation. Social workers saw what existed at the bottom of the barrel in decent society. As far as Caitlin was concerned, the Vatican should grant them all eternal sainthood.

She squinted and threw back the covers. "Shut the bloody curtains."

Had she just used bloody as an adjective in a sentence? She gave Amanda three, two, one...

"Did you just use the word bloody? What, are you from England?" Amanda said, unable to contain a snicker.

Caitlin grabbed a clip and secured her hair. "Very funny."

"Skipped out on work, ha? Tsk, tsk. We're not teenagers anymore Caitlin." Amanda's gray eyes shone with a teasing glint.

She ignored her friend and padded down to the bathroom. When she came out, Amanda was leaning against the wall of the hallway.

"So, what are you doing with the rest of your day?" Amanda asked.

"Do you mean you actually have the day off?" Caitlin was incredulous.

"You bet, want to do something?"

Caitlin walked back into her room. She had a whole slew of things she wanted to do and they all had to do with the book. "How about Mystery Hill?"

"Mystery Hill?" Amanda looked confused.

"Yeah, you know, our little local Stonehenge. Are they open yet?" Caitlin got out of her sweats and threw on a pair of jeans and a dark green T-shirt.

Amanda's mouth hung open and she shook her head slowly.

"What?" Caitlin said.

"You're serious?"

"No, I just wanted to get a reaction out of you. Of course I'm serious." Caitlin put on her sneakers.

Amanda looked dubious. "Caitlin, you don't do anything woodsy or historical if you don't have to."

"Well, now I do. Are they open?"

"I don't think so. Not until May or June," Amanda said. "Besides, I was thinking more along the lines of shopping."

Caitlin headed down the stairs, looking at everything in a new light, the banister, the foyer. Descriptions of things that had happened here in the past flooded her mind's eye.

"Let's go." She flung the order over her shoulder and headed outside. "You can ride Shane's horse."

Amanda was right behind her. "Oh, that's ripe. He'd love that."

"What he doesn't know isn't going to hurt him," Caitlin said, as she entered the barn.

The barn. She looked around at it in a whole new way, too. In fact, according to what she had read, C.C. was in the same stall that Fyne had been in. Arianna's horse. Too cool. The oddest thing was that Fyne had apparently had a Celtic cross on her as well, except that it was on her forehead. Like Gram had not made that connection. She was sly, very sly and the whole thing seemed more than a little bizarre.

Amanda was no stranger to horses and had ridden Shane's horse before. Caitlin knew her friend would have no problem riding him now. She'd do anything to irritate Shane. Caitlin had always admired the love-hate relationship that her brother and Amanda shared. Neither one of them backed down, but when push came to shove, they were there for each other.

Caitlin swung up onto C.C.'s saddle and steered her out the back of the barn. "Ready to go break the law?"

Amanda came up beside her. "Oh sure, let's just not get caught. I need to maintain a certain amount of credibility in this town."

Caitlin laughed and urged her horse into a gallop. Springtime had made its mark in North Salem. The air was mild and varied shades of verdant leaves textured the woods. Maples, birches, oaks and pines silenced the outside world. How many more would there have been two hundred years ago? Were some of these trees mere saplings when Arianna had trekked to what was then, Pattee's caves, now called Mystery hill?

"Hey, wait for me," Amanda said.

Caitlin was already off her horse and striding for the centrifugal map point once they reached the Stonehenge. Shane had been here and she had a basic idea of what the place was all about. Multiple rocks situated at different points in the wood, marking astrological points. Where was the stone she was looking for?

She studied the worn map encased beneath the glass. Where was the rock that was aligned with the Northeast horizon? Ah ha, there it was. She bounded down and headed in the given direction, Amanda hot on her heels.

"Did you know there used to be a house and barn built here?" Caitlin said. She walked along a path until she reached the rock.

"No, I didn't Caitlin and I can't imagine how you would know that," Amanda said.

Caitlin shot her friend a sideways look. "You think I've lost it, ha?"

Amanda bit the corner of her lip and smirked. "I didn't say that."

"You didn't have to." Caitlin ignored the platform that described the rocks history and walked right up to the stone. A long path of treeless earth lie before her until it reached the horizon. She closed her eyes and placed her hands on the spear-like stone. According to the book, this was where Arianna had experienced her first unusual occurrence.

Caitlin opened her eyes slowly. Nothing. No change of season. No other-worldly vibration emanating up her arm from the rock. No whisper on the wind from an unknown, mysterious lover.

Then again, what did she expect? Sweet words of passion from a flippant tyrant? This was ridiculous. What was she thinking anyway? That there existed some sort of parallel to the story she was reading now just because she was related to its heroine?

Not likely. If anything, she was chasing after the enemy. To think she was even entertaining the fact that he might be from—no, stop. This was all nonsense.

"Let's get out of here," Caitlin said and turned away

Amanda rolled her eyes. "I thought maybe we came here to sightsee. My bad."

Caitlin stopped. "God, I'm sorry. Do you want to take a look around?"

Amanda ushered her toward their horses. "Actually, no. I've never been one for woodsy things myself, that's why we get along. Remember? We like to make money and spend money."

Caitlin laughed. "Good point. Let's return to civilization."

Today, civilization meant returning to her book. Amanda was more than glad to let her off the hook and headed to town by herself.

Caitlin should've felt bad for blowing off her friend but she knew Amanda wasn't one to get offended easily. By nine o'clock that night, she had not only finished the book, but had reread many parts.

There's no way that this book was not at least ninety- nine percent fictional. Come on. Magic? Time-travel? Yeah, okay.

The problem was Caitlin felt discontent. She lay in bed, running different scenes over and over again in her mind; Scotland, warriors, Highland clans, romance.

Magic.

Not that she was entirely opposed to the concept, especially considering her most recent encounters with a mysterious stranger. From her dreams, no less...just like Arianna.

It made her feel a little saner than she had.

But, then again, magic? Please. She might be a fan of paranormal movies but Hollywood was Hollywood. Better to leave it there, behind a rolling camera and a talented director.

That would be her last thought before she fell asleep.

Sky Purington

Chapter Three

Caitlin woke to the sound of her alarm clock. She reached over and slammed it. That didn't work. Keeping her head under the blanket she patted and slid every button or switch of the blasted thing but still it beeped.

"No more." She mumbled, leaned over, grabbed the cord and yanked it from the outlet. Quiet settled over the room. Blissful quiet.

Too quiet.

Caitlin bolted upright. What was wrong? She looked around the room. Everything was in place, from her laptop to her mahogany framed picture of Mom and Dad.

Then she figured it out. The alarm clock had awoken her. Caitlin's alarm clock hadn't awoken her before her nightmare in three years. Why now? Her chest tightened, caught somewhere between elation and morbid curiosity.

She didn't have the dream last night!

Her blankets lay on the bed, covering her from head to toe. There were no twisted sheets or bands of sweat. Better yet, she was still in her bed, not laid out with sore muscles on a cold, hardwood floor.

How exciting! Caitlin jumped onto the floor. She whipped open the curtains and did a little dance. It was over. She had read the book and was released from...from...whatever. Thank you, Gram. Two thumbs up.

Caitlin sailed through her day at work like she'd sprouted wings and knew how to fly. When she got home that afternoon, Sean, his foster brother and Shane were standing in the driveway.

She hopped out of the vehicle and all three turned her way. "Hey guys."

Shane spoke first. "It appears Sean was eager to see if we needed his help this summer."

Caitlin put her hands on her hips. "I see a future in sales for you, kid."

Sean grinned and executed his now famous blush. "You don't get ahead if you don't shove."

Shane cocked his head. "Though not eloquently said, you've got my vote."

"We talked two nights ago and decided we'd love to hire you, Sean," Caitlin looked at Gordon. "And you as well."

"Thanks." That was it. The kid was all monosyllables. "You're welcome." Caitlin eyeballed the yard. "This lawn is larger than Gram's. What do you say we go inside and haggle on a price?"

"Sounds good to me," Sean said. His narrow shoulders pulled back as though he was ready to go to battle.

Shane led them inside and tossed each boy a soda. "So what are we talking here? Spring clean up, mowing the lawn, watering the flowers and fall clean up?"

Caitlin snorted unintentionally. "And what flowers will they be watering, pray tell?"

"You could plant some flowers," Shane said.

She was about to tell him what she thought about that idea until she caught his expression. He was serious. Mom used to plant flowers. Petunias. She loved dark purple Petunias. That's where his mind was at. Caitlin knew it instinctively.

"Sure, I suppose I could." She looked at Sean. "Perhaps with a bit of help."

"I'm your guy," Sean said. "In fact, I was thinking some Rhododendrons would look great along the front. Maybe some Clematis planted to climb the front porch. They can handle half shade, half sun. A few English Boxwoods along the side of the house. Of course, we'll need some fresh loam, fertilizer, Miracle Grow and mulch. Not the cedar mulch, too pricey and the wrong color for a colonial hou—"

"Stop man." Shane held up a hand. "You're starting to give me a headache. One step at a time—a few flowers, some water, that's it."

Caitlin patted her brother on the shoulder and gave him her most sympathetic look. "I'll plant. You water."

One side of his lips shot up. "Careful."

She looked at Sean. "Aim high in life, kid. You're a die-hard salesman and I appreciate that but today we're talking about the basics. Depending on the weather, you'll be mowing every one or two weeks. I'd say we have an eighty dollar lawn. Spring and fall clean-up looks to be about a hundred and twenty five."

Shane's slight ripple of posture told Caitlin his savings account was getting really low.

Sean nodded and peered out the kitchen window. "Big lawn. You wanted the backyard done too, right? How about ninety for mowing the lawn, the rest sounds good."

Caitlin nodded. He was sharing his proceeds this year after all and he'd only really upped the amount by about a hundred and twenty dollars over all. "Done."

They shook hands and sealed the deal.

Shane was sitting on the counter now and wore a slight frown. He looked at Caitlin. "Any idea where the yard tools are?"

"They should be in the barn."

He clucked his tongue. "You would think. But they're not."

She hated when he did that tongue-clucking thing. It always either preceded or followed a statement that made her feel like she'd mucked up. Right now, it meant that when she put the tools away last fall she had not put them where they should be, in the stall at the end of the barn.

Caitlin rolled her shoulders and headed outside. She knew she'd put them there last year. It's where she'd put them every year since they moved in.

Yet, they weren't there. In fact, they were nowhere in the barn that she could see. She flipped open her cell and dialed Gram's number. When Caitlin hung up two minutes later she was shaking her head and walking back toward the house.

Shane sat at the kitchen table with his hand suspiciously close to his laptop when she walked in. He looked at her and smiled. "Any luck?"

She glared and offered a dainty snarl. "No, oh ye of infinite wisdom. I called Gram. She said that they're in the attic."

His black brows drew together. "Why the attic?"

"My question exactly. According to her, she was worried about them rusting out in the elements and so she had her plumber bring them in," Caitlin said.

Shane burst out laughing. When he had himself under control, he gave his opinion on the matter. "Inside the barn is out of the elements and her plumber?"

Caitlin bristled slightly at his tone.

He wrapped his arm around her shoulder and became serious. "I meant no harm, Caitlin. It's just that it all sounds a little weird, don't you think?"

"No." She stood up straighter. He kept his eyes locked on her until she relented. "All right, a little strange."

He continued to stare her down.

"Okay, a lot strange. But, whatever, let's go get them. Gram is allowed to have her eccentricities."

Shane looked at Sean. "You're familiar with the layout of the barn. Why don't you run out and see if you can't pull together anything else you might be able to use. There are still some things out there—the lawn mower to start with. There's a seed spreader somewhere, too. Gordon, you mind helping us?"

Gordon nodded and followed them upstairs as Sean headed outside. Caitlin ran her hand along the top edge of the molding above the door until she found the small key that would unlock the attic entrance. She slid it into the old fashion keyhole and pushed the door open. Reaching up, she pulled the string overhead and a single bulb turned on.

The wedding dress.

That's all she could think about as they made their way up the steep stairs into the attic above. The magical wedding dress handed down generation upon generation to the women in her family. According to what she read, it was in this very attic that her distant aunt had given Arianna the dress to wear when she was to marry Edward Huntington, a childhood friend. Supposedly, the dress was loaded with emeralds and hand selected pearls from the North Sea. It sounded like it would sell for millions on the open market.

Cool, musty air surrounded her as she reached the last stair. How many times had she played here as a child? There were never any emerald encrusted trunks with rose petal handles.

Suddenly, Caitlin felt guilty, as though her thoughts were disrespectful.

"I'm not seeing them," Shane mumbled.

"Me, either." Caitlin frowned and climbed over a stack of planting pots. She looked at Gordon. "Would you mind grabbing those? They might come in handy."

He gave a slight nod and picked up the plastic pots. She continued to peer into the shadows of the attic. There were multiple racks of clothing, three pairs of snow skis, four pairs of boots, an old armoire and multiple other odds and ends.

"Caitlin, come take a look at this." Shane's voice held a touch of awe.

He stood on the opposite end of the attic with his hands on his hips. Caitlin saw clearly what held him so intrigued.

"Where did this come from? Did you see this when we walked up?" Even as she asked the questions, Caitlin's heartbeat increased. No. It can't be.

An incredible black piano stood alone, facing outward, in the corner of the room. It was sleek and polished and smelled like lemon oil.

She walked around to where an old bench sat pulled out as if someone had just been sitting at it. The lid over the keys stood open. Nervous excitement fluttered in her stomach. This had to be the piano described in the book. Back in the year seventeen ninety-nine it sat downstairs in the parlor. She hit a key.

"Sounds good," Shane said. "This must be a gift from Gram."

His assessment sounded unsure. After all, why would Gram buy a piano for them and have it brought up here? She walked over to the top of the stairs and looked down.

"There's no way this piano fit through that narrow door. No way," Caitlin said, and turned back. "This is weird."

Gordon and Shane now stood behind the piano, interest apparent on their faces.

"Look at this." Shane lifted a copper bucket filled with what looked to be antique canes. He was just about to set it on top of the piano when Caitlin lurched forward.

"No, don't put it there. You'll scratch the wood." She took the bucket from him and set it on the floor.

Shane came around and crouched down beside her. "When have you ever been worried about scratching furniture?"

Since I read the book. "Since we found what must be a valuable family heirloom."

"Heirloom? How do you know that? You don't know that." He scoffed.

Gordon sat on the floor across from them, crossed his legs and said nothing. It appeared he was no stranger to brothers and sisters debating. She could only imagine the bickering he heard living in a foster home.

Caitlin started to sift through the interesting array of canes. "Mmmm. Whatever you say. Still, it's old and it's upstairs in a house that's been in our family for hundreds of years. It seems a logical conclusion to me that it would be an heirloom."

"So now you're suddenly a sentimentalist?"

Caitlin tuned him out when she spied something that was about one third the lengths of the surrounding canes. She carefully pulled the stick out. It couldn't be...but it had to be. According to what she read, this could only be the stick that Arianna's Uncle Liam had carved into a wand for his seven year old daughter, Annie. She'd dressed up for Halloween as a fairy and this was her magical wand.

She leaned in closer to study it. About two fingers thick, the foot long stick was carved with tiny leaves and rose petals. A small star made out of corn stalks adorned the top. The workmanship was exceptional.

"Mind if I take a look?" Shane leaned over and wrapped his hand around the stick.

That was a mistake.

Instantly, tiny bolts of crimson static electricity sizzled up and down the stick. They illuminated the rose buds into tiny points of fire. Caitlin and Shane released it at the same time and fell backwards. Holy hell! Terror seized her as the bucket of canes flew across the room and the wand whipped to the center.

The three of them froze.

The windows smashed inward and sent small shards of broken glass everywhere. Hot wind surged through, lifting and flinging things furiously. Meanwhile, the stick hovered in the air about three feet above the floor, not moving. Then everything stilled. No wind. No heat. Nothing but their ragged breathing.

Caitlin was afraid to move as she stared at the suspended stick. "Shane?" She whispered.

He shook his head slowly and put up one hand.

"Don't move, Caitlin."

Gordon remained silent, his eyes round and fearful.

Don't move? Instinct told her to hightail it out of there, and she was just about to when the stick made its move.

It started to jerk in different directions though its center remained in the same spot. Within five seconds it swirled so fast it became a blur. Within ten seconds it spun at such a speed it created a shape through optical illusion. She was reminded of those flip books she had as a kid. On each page a different picture was drawn but when you flipped the pages really quick the picture came alive and moved.

What blazed before them all now was clearly a star. It blazed sapphire and steam rose around its points. The steam started to circle the star and stem out until it held all three of them in a tornado of humid heat.

"Shane!" Her lungs burned and air became sparse. She could no longer see Shane or Gordon. All she could see was thick, twirling sheets of gray. The star became a distant beacon of fuzzy blue and heavy dew drenched her skin. A sweet burning odor overwhelmed her and she choked on the scent as though she could taste it.

Pain slammed into her head when a massive crash resounded like a clap of thunder but a hundred times louder. Her body was either pulled forward or pushed back, she couldn't tell the difference as she'd lost all sense of gravity.

Then she fell, of that she was sure, so fast that panic turned her body completely numb. Caitlin searched for a coherent thought, anything to keep her mind intact. There was nothing for her to grab on to, nothing to think about but death. At this speed, it would be quick. That should have reassured her...

It did not.

****

"Man, my head." Eyes closed, Shane raised his hand to his forehead. His head pounded. Just keep breathing. He coached himself and took deep, steady breaths. Within seconds, the feeling retreated. Nice. His eyes felt heavy when he pried them open.

Trees? How is that possible? He bolted upright. Tall pine trees towered far overhead, their grayish red trunks were a layer of sporadic columns that chopped the forest into roomy hallways as far as he could see. Clusters of ferns dotted the golden pine needles on the woodland floor. The sun shot long stripes of light at intervals throughout the forest.

Caitlin! Where was she? "Caitlin?" He looked around, frantic, until he spotted her about twenty feet away. She lay face down, her hair a tangle of dark brown locks around her head.

"Caitlin." He shot to his feet and ran to her side. He didn't move her. She could have a broken neck or back.

He placed his hand on her shoulder and leaned down. "Caitlin?"

Relief flooded him when she groaned in relief.

"My head feels like an elephant is sitting on it." She mumbled the words into the pine needles beneath her.

He sat back. "Just give it a sec. It'll pass."

She did and eventually rolled up until she was sitting beside him, spitting a pine needle or two out of her mouth. Caitlin blinked a few times and took in her surroundings. He had to give her credit. Most women would be freaking out right about now. Not Caitlin. She'd always kept cool under pressure. It took a lot to get her riled. Not to say she didn't have a temper, she had a bad one, but she didn't show it often.

"What's going on? Where are we?" She pushed back her hair with a shaky hand. An indication she was more frazzled then she let on.

He looked around. "I have no idea."

"Where's Gordon?" She looked at Shane, concerned.

"I'm here." They turned at the sound of the boy's voice. He stood, braced against a pine tree. His skin looked as green as the pine needles above him. Tears shone in his eyes as he inhaled deeply.

Caitlin stood. "Are you all right?" Poor kid. He looked horrible.

"Just take deep breaths." Shane clasped his shoulder.

"In through the nose, out through the mouth."

Gordon nodded and did as he was told. Thankfully, his color gradually returned to normal and he was able to stand without the support of the tree.

Shane looked at his sister. Her golden eyes appeared contemplative and she was nibbling on the corner of her lip. The hackles went up on the back of his neck. Caitlin only did that lip-chewing thing when she was holding out. She knew something he didn't.

"Caitlin?" He drew the word out and crossed his arms over his chest.

Now she just looked downright curious as she sniffed the cool air and spun slowly around. "Yeah?"

Shane wasn't afraid of an adventure but this particular set of circumstances—an attic that turned into a forest—petrified him. Why wasn't it scaring her? "Aren't you a little nervous that we don't appear to be in the attic anymore?"

She stopped biting her lip immediately and set to wiping pine needles off of her T-shirt. "Ahhh...a little."

"A little?" Shane stopped her incessant exploration of a clump of purple heather. "Just a little?"

"Maybe a lot." She nodded her head in agreement, as though she was humoring him.

Humoring him! He blinked down at her and tried to make sense out of all this. "Have you completely lost it?"

She seemed taken aback. "No."

"Then why aren't you curious where the hell we are?"

"Hey guys," Gordon said.

Caitlin looked at her brother and pulled her arm away. "I am curious."

"Hey guys," Gordon repeated.

Shane ground his teeth. She was stubborn to the bone and deceptive to boot. "Wrong word. Let's try scared. Why aren't you scared?"

"Hey guys." This time Gordon's interruption was a yell over his shoulder while he ran in the opposite direction.

Shane had three solid thoughts before a fist crashed up against his head and sent him reeling into darkness.

Kilts. Weapons. Bad.

Chapter Four

Scotland 1210

Spring growth ravaged the land. It licked the grass more green than any had seen in years and promised a summer harvest likely to revile the one back in the year 1199.

Flowers were bold and burst early and full. Trees grew their leaves weeks earlier than intended. The bird's overhead came louder and sooner. The fish in the loch were more swollen and plentiful.

Everyone rejoiced in good fortune.

Ferchar did not. He'd stopped believing in good omens a long time ago.

"Just be done with it." Though he spoke softly, his words were not lost on his first in command.

He turned his steed back toward the castle and disregarded the laughter behind him. The gray stallion beneath him broke into a run at his command. A child hunkered down by the far right prong of the outer portcullis. With white-blond hair, she stood out like a full moon on a cloudless night. When she saw him approach, her little legs turned into wagon wheels and rolled her forward. She looked so fearful and eager. This should have affected him.

It did not.

"Laird Ferchar? Is he well? Will he come home?" she asked.

He gazed down at her mournful eyes, so full of regret and hope, youth and awe. Ferchar searched for an inkling of compassion that must surely exist somewhere within him. He found nothing. He did, however, give her an answer. "Aye."

He urged his steed on and longed for a smirk...a chuckle. Neither came. At least the little girl had her goat back—a goat that'd wreaked havoc throughout the entire castle and village. Even the cook could not stop the errant beast from plowing through every corner of the vicinity, including the armory.

Then Ferchar became involved. For the goat had managed to dislodge a dagger and carry it, hilt in mouth, out of the armory, under the portcullis and halfway over the first moat before it caught the hem of a servant and threw her into the water beneath.

The little girl with white-blond hair, then screamed at the top of her lungs that her great warhorse had gone astray. She ran like a banshee over the first drawbridge after the goat, which scuttled away from her at an impossible speed.

Matters got far worse at the second portcullis where the goat, with dagger still in mouth, nicked the guard whose job it was to warn the others to drop the outer portcullis. When they heard his indistinguishable yelp, they did what they were trained to do.

They lowered the second portcullis.

This, after all was said and done, would have been fine, if the hundreds of people within its confines had any idea why the portcullis was being lowered in the dead of afternoon.

However, they did not and pandemonium ensued. One would have thought the castle was under attack and for all the people knew, it was. Wives were seeking children and husbands alike in hysterics. The clan's warriors were drawing their weapons and rushing to the positions in the castle designated for potential attack.

"It's but a goat." The yell emanated from somewhere on the wall-walk shortly thereafter and all calmed within a matter of hours. The animal was caught. Many chuckles ensued and the portcullises were raised again. All was well.

Ferchar shook his head and dismounted his horse. A bloody animal ignited his clansmen to frenzy.

Humorous.

He worked at a wry grin. It hurt his face. Instead, he noted the miniscule piles of dirt collected at the edges of the stone steps as he climbed them. The second he walked through the doors of the castle, he wished he hadn't. No one was in the hall, save his aunt. She sat before the great hearth which hosted a low fire at this time of the year. Her head was bowed, her hands folded in her lap. She uttered useless, voiceless words to herself. He crossed the room and knelt before her, taking her hands in his.

"Aunt Muriel, 'tis Ferchar. Is there anything I can get for you?"

She raised her head. Her once brilliant green eyes were dull and full of sorrow. Though her lips moved, nothing came from her mouth. Beneath thick lashes her eyes pleaded with him. Begged him.

As always, he had nothing to give her.

Long ago, he had tried to offer the sanctity of peace within his eyes. The truism of reality. The ability to let go.

It had not worked. It would not. She was lost to him. Though not insane, his aunt had retreated within herself. Gone to a place of safety. He could not hold that against her. Most likely, he would've done the same thing.

He bent his head and held it against their entwined hands.

"Iain?"

Ferchar kept his head in place. "No, Aunt Muriel. 'Tis Ferchar."

He felt her smile before he saw it and lifted his head. Her eyes were round and clear and met his gaze. They shifted to the low embers briefly before they met his again. "He's coming back, isn't he?"

He wasn't sure how to answer. Though of late she often confused him with her long lost brother, she'd never appeared so acute, rational. Her brother, Iain, former laird of clan MacLomain had vanished eleven years prior. For her to think of him now, in light of all she had gone through, was odd.

Or magic.

Ferchar was careful with his answer. She didn't know of his vision. "Mayhap. I know naught. What would make you ask such a question?"

She started to shake her head with vigor but he caught her chin gently and met her wild eyes with compassion. "Aunt Muriel, 'tis just you and I, and the logs on the hearth. Have no fear."

Muriel's eyes drifted down until they rested somewhere on his chest. Then they closed. Her top lip curled over her bottom lip before her eyes opened and locked on his.

"What will he make of all this when he comes back?" She stood abruptly and looked down and around her as though she may have forgotten something. Obviously content she had not, she went up the stairs.

Ferchar sighed and sat before the flames. Muriel and Iain had been close. Besides her younger sister, he had been the only one left of her immediate family. How Ferchar wished he could put Muriel's mind to ease, but he could not.

A servant handed him a cup of whiskey. He took a deep swallow and set the mug aside. As he leaned back in the chair, his gaze wandered to the chiseled features poised over the hearth. In it he saw his relatives of past and perhaps future. Many he didn't recognize. And, as was his way, Adlin poked his face through them all.

"Why bother?" Ferchar said.

The face above could only be described as mock-terrified.

Ferchar crossed his arms over his chest and closed his tired eyes. "I'm in no mood for your games."

"You're never in the mood for my games," Adlin replied. Ferchar knew that the wizard sat beside him now but kept his eyes closed nonetheless. "What do you want?"

"Open your eyes and address me with respect, lad."

Ferchar did so but looked at the fire instead of the wizard. The old man might have been his Uncle Iain's mentor but he wasn't his. He would give him enough respect due his station and no more.

Slowly, he swung his gaze Adlin's way. "What do you want?"

"A moment of your precious time." Adlin's fingers curled over the top of his walking stick.

Ferchar grunted. "Sarcasm doesn't suit you, wizard."

The blue veins in Adlin's arms bulged. "What you've become doesnae suit me. Luckily, how we feel about one another is irrelevant. What is relevant is the year."

"Ah, yes, the year." Ferchar leaned forward and rested his elbows on his knees. "And the prophecy. How could I forget? After all, 'twas my prophecy, was it not?"

"Aye, 'twas," Adlin agreed.

"And you feel the need to remind me?" Ferchar wanted to throttle the old man. He stood and walked to the fire.

"What are you going to do?" Adlin said.

Ferchar turned and glowered. "What do you think I'm going to do?"

"I think you're going to fulfill it." Adlin's eyes began to glow their icy blue.

Ferchar looked away. "Don't even try it. If I wanted you in my head, I'd invite you."

He began to pace in front of the fire. Adlin had a great way of reading people's minds under the cool influence of magic. His eyes could both soothe and rip apart a person. Ferchar was in no mood to allow the wizard to divine neither his feelings nor his heart.

Adlin sighed. "Farewell, then."

"Farewell. Those are your words of wisdom?" Ferchar swung back to find the chair empty. He ground his teeth in frustration. Leave it to Adlin to leave before things became confrontational.

Ferchar sat back down. Would his life ever be his own? In all honesty, how well was he doing at the life that had been given him? Aye, he had done fine as laird of the MacLomain clan since Iain left. However, none of that mattered in light of his greatest failure. The loss of William. But he wouldn't dwell on that right now. His thoughts remained focused on Iain.

Adlin had told him little of his uncle's fate, save he was safe. He explained it was not his place to divulge information that was Iain's alone to give, that both himself and their clan knew all they needed. To offer more insight would be to change the course of things, or not. Ever vague, the wizard would offer no more.

How had Iain fared in retrieving his one true love from a different time? Had he found her? If so, where did he find her?

These questions had plagued Ferchar since he last saw Iain disappear in the war of the clans back in 1199. Since he had become Chieftain of one of the most powerful clans in Scotland. It had been a long road earning the respect of not only his own clan as a leader, but the fellow chieftains of their allied clans who were raised with his uncle.

Men clamored into the hall behind him for the noontime meal. He rose to join them.

"Nay, sit with me a bit."

Ferchar looked down at the petite blond in front of him. He could never deny his mother.

"What brings you here at this hour?" Ferchar sat with her.

"A mother's intuition." She had two goblets in hand, one of which she handed to him.

He offered her his best attempt at a grin. "You've always been good at that."

She shrugged and gave him a sad smile. "Aye."

Ferchar eyed his mother, Helen. The years had been kind to her. With pale blond hair and gray eyes, men still sought her favor. Regrettably, since she had lost her husband, his father, twenty-one years earlier, Helen had not remarried. He had little doubt she took full advantage of men's favors; she was under the protection of the laird and was not obligated to marry. Nor had she been under Iain's rule.

"And what does your mother's intuition tell you today?" Ferchar sipped from the goblet. Whiskey, of course. Helen was known for her ability to deliver the spirits when they were most needed.

"That change is coming," Helen said.

Ferchar met her eyes for a long moment. "Aye."

Helen took a long swallow of whiskey and set the goblet aside. "Am I going to lose you?"

He closed his eyes and ran his fingers along the stem of his cup. "I dinnae know."

When he opened his eyes she simply sat with her hands in her lap, staring at the fire. Her shoulders were back and her chin jut forward in defiance. He waited for her to speak but she did not.

"You willnae lose me," Ferchar tried to assure.

Helen's head snapped around. "Won't I?"

He had a thousand comforting words in his head to soothe his mother's fears but none would come. "What would you have me tell you? You know the way this family works. I know that you lost Da and now you're preparing to lose me. If I could tell you not to worry I would. I cannae. I willnae. You must cope with it, Mother."

Her nostrils flared briefly in what could've been either anger or defiance. "What have you become?"

Ferchar didn't look away. "Me."

Helen stood abruptly and walked over to him. When she spoke her voice was low. "That's where you are wrong. I gave birth to you. Watched you crawl, toddle and then walk. Babble and then talk. Grow from a boy into a man. That man had emotion. That man was you."

She placed a hand on his shoulder and squeezed. "This man has my son locked somewhere deep inside."

Instead of watching his mother depart, Ferchar kept his eyes on the fire. She was right. He saw her pain only through the flame riding low in the fire, weeping on the hackneyed logs.

It was then, lost in the dire contemplation of his fate, that he felt magic stir. Faint at first—a slight hum in his inner ear. Like a storm in the distance. Before he made it to his feet, it was a roaring ocean against the walls of his mind.

Was it time?

"Arthur." He called out to his first in command as he strode from the castle.

"He's in the armory," Michael said. His head servant was efficient.

"Good." Ferchar headed for the armory. Arthur must've heard his bellow because he was walking to intercept with one battle-axe strapped to his shoulder and one in his hand to pass off to his laird.

He didn't ask any questions as they mounted their horses. Arthur was good that way. Trust was the only thing he knew when it came to Ferchar.

Once the two of them were well beyond the castle gates and halfway across the field beyond, Ferchar slowed his horse to a canter and spoke. "We'll maintain this pace. Whatever is amiss, all is well now. Our men are there."

Arthur nodded and offered him a small smile. "Is there fun to be had?"

Ferchar gave a loose shrug. "Could be."

The men rode in silence along the western shore of Loch Holy until they veered off in a Northwesterly direction into the wood line. A cloudbank had rolled in from the east and obscured the sun. The wind blew cooler and gave the forest a near sinister look.

"Do you smell that?" Ferchar reined in and sniffed the air.

Arthur did the same. "Nay. What am I supposed to be smelling?"

Ferchar didn't answer but continued forward. His friend was well used to his bouts of silence and his unfailing ability to leave questions unanswered. He was grateful to have Arthur. The man was a rock and had known Ferchar his entire life. Originally, he'd been third in command to his uncle and then the same to him when he first became the Chieftain. When Hugh, Muriel's husband, left, he took the position he held now.

The scent started to seep into Ferchar. The wind carried it and teased his senses. Cinnamon? Apples? No, much more potent yet evasive. Musky sweet. Tempered spice. A strange burn started in his stomach. His muscles tightened.

"Let's go. Now." Ferchar urged his steed into a steady gallop and swung his horse due west.

Something was happening.

Chapter Five

Caitlin had never spit in anyone's face before, but she did now. It was the only defense left.

"Damn you," she seethed and wished she were brave enough to implement a head butt.

The man swung her around and lifted her. Her hands were tied behind her back so Caitlin kicked at the air. She'd put up a good fight so far. Though she didn't have any training in combat, she had ten years of dance lessons under her belt. She knew how to move fast, kick high and turn on a dime. The only problem was she had no idea when or where to apply such talent.

"You little—" Before the man who held her spoke his next word, which she knew was going to be a nasty one, Caitlin arched her back and jerked her weight down as hard as she could.

That made him mad. The next thing she knew, Caitlin was slammed up against a nearby tree trunk. Luckily, she turned her head or her nose would have been broken.

When they had first arrived here, Caitlin was mesmerized. Had she traveled through time like Arianna? Was she in Scotland? The woods were beautiful, so silent and hypnotizing. She could almost picture her distant relative running through this very same forest, eager to escape her one true love yet heartbroken at the same time.

For just a moment, Caitlin thought she was in some sort of multi-dimensional paradise. That is, until they knocked her brother out. Bastards! She saw red and retaliated. In all reality, she'd seen red and defended herself because what came at her was beyond her wildest imagination, though it should not have been—six men on horseback with enough weaponry to put a Roman gladiator to shame, all well-muscled and well trained. Their blue and green checkered kilts were the only thing she could focus on at first, as though her mind saw the weapons as less of a threat than the reality of long-haired men wearing kilts.

Kilts! Caitlin had freaked out. There was no doubt she caught these men off guard. They'd managed to take down what they considered the most immediate threat, Shane. Poor Gordon was already bound, gagged and astride a horse. Yet in her they had not a submissive female, but a berserker.

Until now, not one of them had managed to get a solid hold on her. Even the man who held her long enough to tie her arms back had lost her.

This guy had her. Not only because of the pine tree she was wedged up against but also because of the cold metal she felt pushed against her throat.

"Dinnae move, lass. Do you ken?" He had his front to her back.

She nodded her head as much as she dared while he continued to talk to the other men in a foreign language that had to be Gaelic.

In less than a heartbeat she was pulled back, and lifted astride a tall, chestnut horse. The man glared up at her. She almost smiled when it became apparent that he was less than thrilled with the idea of riding his horse with her.

Suddenly, one of the men gave a low whistle that sounded like a bird and everyone stopped what they were doing to wait for something. Caitlin wished she could reach Shane and make sure he was okay but he was at least fifteen feet away and unconscious. She hated that they'd thrown him over the back of a horse like a sack of potatoes.

Caitlin sighed and tried to move her nearly numb arms. What were they waiting for? An uncomfortable vibration ran through her as she looked into the forest. It was not bright and sunny anymore but dim and spooky. The day was getting later and spots of murky twilight skirted around the bases of the trees.

Just before she spoke to break the monotony of the stretched silence, two men on horseback materialized from the shadows of the forest. The front man unhorsed and walked the remaining distance.

Caitlin tried to swallow but found it impossible. She tensed and made a solid attempt to breathe. The man was bloody gorgeous. His hair was a deep, blue black. His body was long and lean with broad shoulders and tight muscles, so very many tight muscles and in all the right places.

And he was focused on her.

Not dead weight Shane. Not timid, scared Gordon.

Her.

"Get her down," he said.

Caitlin's heart stopped dead as she was pulled from the horse. That voice! It was the same voice that accosted her at the picnic table and in her very own bed. She gained her footing, stood up as straight as she could and met his eyes. Whoa! Big mistake. Her muscles went weak.

His eyes were amazing. Like icy sapphires caught in the sun, they glared down at her. A muscle jumped just beneath one of his high cheekbones, above his strong jaw and wonderfully sensual lips. He was all model material and Wall Street corporate hunk wrapped into one. The cleft in his chin, deep-set eyes beneath straight eyebrows and the small scar on his temple added military man to the whole package.

"Who are you?" This question came from her. Caitlin was amazed her voice worked. Doubly amazed at the fact she spoke first.

His eyes held hers, and analyzed. Caitlin suddenly felt dizzy but kept her stance. She wasn't about to look away. That would give him the up. God forbid he give her an answer. Instead he turned away, looked first at Shane and then at Gordon.

His gaze stayed on Gordon and Gordon's on his. Caitlin gave the kid credit, he had courage. What happened next she didn't expect. Her mystery stranger barked out sharp words in Gaelic and she was immediately tossed back onto the horse. The clansman who'd held her at knife point jumped up behind her and urged his horse into a run.

"Wait a minute, what's going on?" She couldn't see a darned thing but knew that other horses followed. After some time they broke free from the woods and entered a massive field. The cloud cover had retreated and a vivid sunset swallowed the sky to her right.

"Wow." That's all Caitlin could say. Forget the majestic mountains in the distance or the endless serpent of loch, all she could see was the enormous castle that rose up before her.

It glowed bronze as it bathed in the light of the setting sun. Centrifugal in design, it was all harsh angles and soft curves. Towers shot to the sky held together by wall walks; two tall walls with portcullises and moats wrapped around it in protection.

They passed multiple thatch-covered huts while they approached the mammoth dwelling. There were hundreds of people and most of them cast curious looks her way as they passed. Kilted warriors mingled throughout.

She knew she wasn't out of her mind. This was real. Of that she had little doubt. In fact, she had a good idea what she would see when they passed beneath that second portcullis. The armory would be to the right, the kitchens to the left, the stables and more cottages. What she didn't expect was how different everything looked in reality. When pages from a book materialized right before your eyes it was, at best, unsettling. Foreign. Every reader saw something different and no reader ever saw what the author did. How could they? The imagination was a beautiful place.

The man behind her swung down and pulled her after him. He grabbed her arm lightly and led her up the steps to the tall doors of the castle. "Come on."

Caitlin looked back and tried to locate Shane but couldn't see him anywhere in the throng of productive, if not curious, people passing by. "Where's my brother?"

"Sleeping it off." He led her through the doors.

She stopped short and gawked. A massive chamber surrounded her. Caitlin tried to compare it with any other room she had either read about or stepped into and could not. It was enormous; wealth at its best, tasteful, comforting and totally medieval. Somehow, all of her thoughts seemed like one big oxymoron. Even though this place was laced with Scottish clansmen, trestle tables and endless rock, it was elegant.

"Sit." He sat her into a wooden chair close to the behemoth fireplace. She looked up at the faces carved in place of the mantle. She looked away just as fast. Kind of creepy.

"Hello." Even though the place was swarming with people, the woman's voice startled her. It was at that moment that Caitlin realized how tense she really was.

A woman sat across from her who looked to be fairly close to her own age. Her light brown hair was long and full of soft curls. She wasn't beautiful but attractive in a subtle way. Feminine. Peaceful. She was working on some sort of tapestry.

"Hi," Caitlin responded. It would be nice to talk to someone half-civil.

"Hi." The stranger repeated the word and said it in such a way, Caitlin knew that she was unfamiliar with it.

The woman's face broke into a smile. "I like that. Hi."

All right, moving on…

"Do you live here?"

She stopped her weaving and set it aside. "Aye, I'm so sorry. I was being rude. My name is Catherine. Ferchar is my nephew."

Her smile widened and she waved at a passing servant.

Caitlin couldn't help but smile in return. "Nice to meet you, Catherine." She had read all about Catherine and knew that she was Iain's little sister. Caitlin frowned. If Catherine was ten years old in the year eleven ninety- nine, what year was it now? She wasn't about to ask the woman her age.

Catherine took two pewter mugs from the servant and handed one to Caitlin. "Where are you from?"

Caitlin was tongue-tied. Another time perhaps. She said the first place that made any kind of sense. "England."

"England?" Catherine's eyes went wide and she looked Caitlin up and down.

"Yep." Caitlin crossed one leg over the other and sniffed the liquid in the cup. Beer? Good. Maybe England wasn't the best choice but she spoke English and she was from New England so it was the best she could do. Yikes, the Scottish hated the English.

Again Catherine seemed interested in Caitlin's word. "Yep." She repeated.

At least she seemed to hold more concern for words than the discomfort of having an Englishwoman sitting across from her.

Caitlin made a mental note to speak as articulately as she could from now on. No slang. Nothing twenty-first century. Because as she looked around and took full measure of the place, torch-burning wall sconces and all, she figured it would be best to fully comply lest save future confusion.

When in Rome, do as the Romans do.

Except this was Medieval Scotland, of that she was pretty sure and something told her it was around about the thirteenth century.

Catherine interrupted her thoughts. "My nephew is the clan's Chieftain. I take it you have already met him."

Caitlin took another sip. That's right. After Iain had disappeared into the future, Ferchar was said to have taken his place. Oh no. It couldn't be. Her heartbeat kicked up a notch.

She sat forward and set down her cup. "I may have. Tall man, piercing blue eyes. A bit on the arrogant side?"

Catherine laughed and nodded. "That description sounds about right. Except he's no' just a bit on the arrogant side, but a lot on the arrogant side."

Caitlin sat back and gave her a small smile. This was her opportunity. "Excuse my curiosity, but how old is he?"

"Let's see, if I'm twenty one now, he must be twenty six."

Her face dropped. If Ferchar was twenty-six that meant the year had to be twelve hundred and ten. If the story was right then that meant that—

All thought ceased when Ferchar entered the great hall. Not because he was so head-turning good-looking with a smile on his face but because of whom he had his arm around.

Catherine screamed in delight and Caitlin nearly fell out of her chair when the woman shot out of her seat and flew across the room. What was going on? Why was Gordon looking up at Ferchar as if he was some sort of god? Why was Ferchar looking down at him as though he had found his long lost son?"

She stood but didn't move. Nothing made sense. Then she heard a woman's cry from somewhere above. "William!"

Caitlin's legs gave out and she fell back down into the chair. William?

A woman nearly stumbled down the stone stairs that ran along the far wall. "William!"

The stranger was a blur of gray dress and long black hair as she reached Gordon and pulled him into her arms. They both started to cry as Gordon wrapped his arms around the woman.

This was absolutely unbelievable. Her dream. It had to be. The woman on the rock...Muriel. This had to be her. And Gordon? Gordon was William? The lad who had supposedly died at the base of the waterfall? Gordon, the kid that was going to rake her yard for some extra cash? The foster kid without a trace of a Scottish accent...

He had an accent now and a thick one at that!

She continued to sit there while the family reunion took place. People were flooding through the door as word spread that William had returned. After a time, she couldn't see them through the haze of well-wishers. Thankfully, a servant brought her another mug of beer.

What now?

"You have my thanks."

Caitlin tore her gaze from the fire and looked at the chair across from her. An old man sat where Catherine had sat before. He wore a long white robe with a blue and green tartan wrapped over his shoulder. His hair was alabaster white and his eyes were, well, the exact same color as Ferchar's.

She tried to act nonchalant and failed miserably. Her hands shook. Thunder drummed in her ears. It couldn't be...but had to be. "You must be Adlin."

His face erupted in a smile as wide as the Atlantic Ocean. "Aye. I am he."

Then she did something that she'd never done in her entire life.

She passed out.

Sky Purington

Chapter Six

Damn blackguard of a wizard.

Ferchar had been keeping an eye on her. Whenever Adlin appeared something was bound to happen. He shoved his way through his clansmen until he reached the lass's side. She was passed out cold.

With an irritated glance at a very innocent looking wizard, he scooped her up and brought her upstairs. Emma stood at the top of the stairs. "Go fetch some water and bring it to my chamber."

He passed her and ascended another set of stairs.

"Aye." Her eyes strayed to the woman in his arms before she scurried off to do his bidding.

Ferchar carried her into the chamber and laid her down on his bed. Turning away, he walked over to the window. He certainly wasn't going to stand over her and stare at her until she awoke. He wanted to but he wouldn't. She nearly sucked the life out of him when those golden eyes of hers were open. He would not make the mistake of standing anywhere near her while she lay there looking so vulnerable and innocent.

"My laird." Emma entered the chamber. She set a pitcher of water and a mug on a small table near the bed.

"Thank you." He flicked his hand and a fire roared to life on the hearth.

"Who is she?" Emma sauntered his way.

Ferchar placed his hands on the sill of the window. "I dinnae know." That was a lie.

Emma bit her lip and pulled away the hand she was about to place on his shoulder. "I see."

He continued to stare out the window rather than look down at Emma because if he did his eyes were likely to travel right over her shoulder until they found the stranger lying on his bed.

The lass moaned and sat up. "Where am I?"

Against his better judgment, Ferchar went over to the bed. "You're in my chamber, lass."

She looked around. He could've sworn he saw a flicker of recognition in her eyes. She swung her legs over the side of the bed. Her leggings clung tightly to her thighs. She looked first at him and then at Emma.

"Where's my brother?" She attempted to stand.

He put a hand on her shoulder and pushed her down. She needed to gain her bearings. He didn't want her passing out again. It took every ounce of willpower he had to keep his eyes off her sweet little body and on her face. She was easily the most beautiful lass he'd ever seen. Her full lips frowned, drawing her fine eyebrows together.

Before he could pull his senses together, she'd whipped up her feet, crawled across the bed and was standing on the opposite side.

Eyes fixed on the anxious woman, he said to Emma, "Go find Catherine. This lass needs something suitable to wear."

Panic flickered across the stranger's face. "She stays or I scream."

Ferchar actually felt laughter bubble up but contained it. This woman had brought William back. "I'm not going to hurt you."

"I don't believe you. Nope, she stays."

He couldn't really blame her. He had, after all, done his best to terrorize her quite recently. William had disappeared three years ago and up until three nights ago his cousin had been completely lost to him.

He owed it to Hugh, William's father, to find his only child. Hugh had left two years earlier to find a son everyone was convinced had died. But because no body was ever found, Hugh left. He said he had no choice. If there was a chance William was still alive, he had to find him.

"Emma, go," Ferchar repeated and she did, none too happy about it. He looked back at the woman. "Do you have a name, lass?"

She was pressed back against the far wall now. Though her posture spoke of a woman preparing for rape, her eyes were defiant and angry. "No."

He sighed, turned away and walked over to the fireplace. Just like he knew she would, the silly chit made a dash for the door. Ferchar moved fast and grabbed her.

Pain rushed up his arm and knocked into his chest. Not pain in the common sense but a pain born of carnal pleasure. Lust raced through him even though she struggled to pull her arm away.

"Let me go. Now." Her words were low but he could feel her rapid heartbeat fill his body. He'd never experienced anything like this.

Not even when he'd tormented her previously.

He drew forth his magic and tried to separate her from him, inside out. If anything, his urgency became worse. He gritted his second request through clenched teeth. "What is your name?"

She stilled. Ferchar suddenly knew that she was feeling the same thing. Her lips opened slightly and she shivered. He worked hard to keep his gaze off her tightly pebbled nipples. Fresh arousal flared and his groin tightened. Bloody hell.

"Caitlin," she whispered and met his eyes.

"Caitlin." The single word tasted like Heaven on his tongue. Like a spring morning leaden with wildflowers and fresh, cleansing air. He released her and stepped back.

She didn't move. When she spoke her voice was strong and determined. "Where is my brother?"

He released breath he didn't realize he was holding. "Resting."

"Where?"

"In a chamber below." He walked away from her. "He'll be fine."

"I want to see him."

He let the fire warm his face. "That's not a problem."

"Now!"

He turned. She stood beside the doorway. Her high cheekbones had a tint of red blooming on them.

"Pushy lass, aye?" He stayed right where he was.

"Yes."

She wasn't going to let up. Better to give her what she wanted. He owed her that, at the very least.

"Follow me."

He strode by her as fast as possible because he knew if he did not she would be screaming for dear life.

From his bed...

****

Caitlin sat alone on a cot in the small, stone chamber. Two pewter wall sconces held torches that spit fire at the ceiling. An arrow slit window offered a peek at the darkness outside.

Within ten hours her life had turned upside down. She wasn't sure what was worse. The fact that she had traveled back to a time that didn't have basic plumbing or that the man from her dreams was here and so enticing she was almost sick with desire for him.

Snap out of it, Caitlin. Condoms haven't been invented and her birth control pills were roughly eight hundred years away.

Tonight they were holding a feast below in honor of William's return. No waiting around while the poor kid became acclimated. Not here. She glanced at the dress lying on the cot next to her. Were they serious? The garment was long and cumbersome. What she wouldn't do for the perfect little black cocktail dress right now.

Tap. Tap. There was a light rap at the door. She'd politely refused any help from a servant earlier. Caitlin opened it cautiously. When she did, she almost burst out laughing. Shane pulled off a kilt as well as any picture she'd ever seen.

"What do think?" He smiled and breezed past her into the room.

She did giggle a little. "I'd like to say you look like a movie extra in a Scottish movie, but hon, you definitely look more like the star."

He nodded in avid agreement. "My thoughts exactly." Caitlin watched her brother study the torches and run his hand through the slit of window. He was in writer mode. Excitement and intrigue swallowed his handsome face.

She shut the door and sat back down on the cot.

"Well, at least one of us is taking all of this in stride."

He was kneeling now, fingering the animal skin carpet. "This place is amazing. I can't believe time travel is possible! At first, I was petrified, then angry when I woke up here in this castle. But all and all, you're okay, I'm okay and we're celebrated heroes. Who would have thought our little landscaper was an important medieval clansboy."

"Clansboy?" Caitlin rolled her eyes.

"What? Medieval, Scottish pre-teen. Is that better?"

He sat next to her.

"Technically, he could be next in line for the Chieftain position," Caitlin replied.

"Right." Shane leaned over and grabbed the crème colored gown from the bed. "Wow, this is really nice. Are you supposed to wear this?"

She snorted. "Yeah. Can you believe it?"

He studied her for a moment and looked at the dress in his hands. "Somebody knows what would look good on you. This color is perfect. Come on. Get dressed. We'll go down there as a team, sis."

Caitlin slumped in submission. "If you say so. Stand outside until I get this thing on."

As she slid into the dress she was suddenly grateful for the poor excuse of a bath she had had earlier. A small tub had been carried up and filled with water that was tepid at best. She had unsnarled her hair with an odd looking comb. No conditioner. Thankfully, her hair responded well to whatever they put in the water because it was soft and full.

"Are you dressed?" Shane asked from outside. When she answered, he came back in.

He didn't say anything, just stared at her. "Well?" She asked.

"Well," he said. "You might just catch yourself a burly Scotsman tonight."

"That's the last thing I want to do." Caitlin ran her hands down the front of the dress. The bodice was cut low, the waistline snug, and the arms flowing and delicate. Little copper colored beads ran in a v-shape from her hips, lined the bodice and the ends of the wide mouthed cuffs.

"Damn, you can pull off medieval attire, that's for sure. Love the shoes! Made using the turn shoe method and designed more for comfort than appearance."

She looked down and grimaced. Luckily, the hemline of the dress covered them except when she walked. They were hideous, reminding her a little of socks turned inside out. "I'd die for a pair of heels at the moment."

"Even if they were invented in this time period they'd be highly impractical on this terrain," he said.

"How observant of you. C'mon, let's do this." She walked to the door, surprisingly loving the feel of the skirts brushing her ankles.

Caitlin stopped outside the door. She'd not had a chance to really look around earlier. They had just exited a door that brought them onto the second landing in a gigantic stone chamber. Two separate staircases descended from both ends of the long stone walkway they stood on. Only a waist high wall kept one from stumbling and falling an easy sixty feet below.

Large tapestries hung everywhere, brought to life by the hundreds of torches that burned along the walls. Her eyes passed over the depictions of landscapes, past the behemoth Viking tapestry and went straight to the twenty-foot tapestry of a woman and man entwined. Her belly clenched and her legs jellied. Shrug it off, Caitlin, or else.

"Come on." Shane grabbed her hand and pulled her after him. They walked down the stairs together. "Do you hear that?"

She did. The sound of bagpipes filled the hall. The sound saturated with the soul of pride and wars won. Caitlin had heard the instrument only one other time, at her parent's funeral. Except then, the sound spoke of two souls being pulled away and returning to a better place. Now it spoke of the heart and essence of the people below them.

The woman who could only be Muriel, William's mother, met them at the bottom of the stairs. Her long, dark hair was swept back and she wore a gown of silver. "Caitlin?" She reached out her arms.

Caitlin stepped forward and found herself all wrapped up in the woman's arms. Muriel, Iain's sister, had played a big part in Arianna'a acclimation to this society. She would have to be in her mid-twenties now.

Mental thanks to Gram for giving her the book.

Muriel pulled back, tears in her eyes. With fine bones and ivory skin, her sparkling eyes were captivating. "Thank you for bringing my lad home. I am indebted to you eternally," Muriel said.

"You're welcome." What else could she say? I had no idea your lad was lost because he never told me and even if he had I would not have believed him. No, best to say nothing.

William stood beside her and looked nothing less than sheepish. He stepped forward and nodded. "Thank you, Caitlin."

She patted him on the shoulder. "No problem kid. How about you and I have a little chat later?"

He smiled at his mother and nodded at Caitlin. "'Twould be my pleasure."

Caitlin kept a straight face. The kid was good. Versatile to the end.

Ferchar came next. It appeared that formalities were being honored for the rest of the clan to see and the Chieftain had just stepped up to the plate.

He reached down and took her hand in his. Caitlin tried to relax as he lifted the back of her hand to his lips. Don't kiss it. Please don't kiss it.

He did. His lips burned her skin and sent ripples up her arm. Her chest tightened and her breasts ignited. If she could rip this dress off now and remove the abrasive weight of the material from her sensitive skin, she would. His kiss lingered too long and as he released her hand his finger skimmed along her palm.

"Caitlin. Thank you." His deep voice made her name sound almost erotic, as though he'd spread her thighs with that one word. She closed her eyes and turned her head. Damn him, closet tyrant. Caitlin hadn't forgotten how evil he'd seemed at the picnic table or in her bed late at night.

"Caitlin?" Shane glanced her way, a look of speculation on his face. "You okay?"

She opened her eyes and scowled. "I'm fine."

"Are you sure sis?" They smiled at a multitude of gracious faces as they filtered into the welcoming crowd. "Because you didn't seem okay just now. In fact, you seemed flustered when that guy kissed your hand. Did you know he's this clan's Chieftain?"

She stopped short at the first of at least twenty or thirty trestle tables lined with food. Had she died and gone straight to heaven? Seafood! So much seafood! Plates of pink salmon and sea scallops. Her mouth began to water when she spied the large bowls of mussels.

"Caitlin? Are you listening to me?" Shane wasn't immune to the slew of food either and grabbed a scallop.

"Yeah. No. What were you saying?"

Before he could speak the giant who had accompanied Ferchar in the forest earlier approached them. They were both speechless with apprehension. With long, blazing red hair, a massive barrel chest and biceps as large as Texas, he stood at least eight inches taller than Shane.

He handed them each a mug. "A wee dram for you both!"

They received their mugs, each remaining silent.

"My name is Arthur and you have my thanks for bringing our boy home," he said.

Caitlin spoke first. "You're welcome, Arthur. I'm Caitlin and this is my brother, Shane." She'd read about him as well. He was a burly giant with a heart of gold.

Arthur cocked his head and studied her momentarily. "You look like you could be Arianna's sister, are you?"

She choked for two reasons, the hot whiskey searing her throat and the first real connection between the book and herself.

Shane patted her on the back and directed his question at Arthur. "Who's Arianna?"

A brief cloud passed over the man's features before the sun came out again. "She was...is the former MacLomain Chieftain's wife."

Caitlin had herself under control again. It occurred to her she probably should've told Shane about Gram's book immediately.

"Really?" Shane said. "Where is she?"

Arthur drained the whole of his mug and wiped his mouth with the back of hand. "Damned if I know."

Shane frowned. "She's disappeared then? What of the former Chieftain?"

"Disappeared as well." Arthur hailed a servant.

"I'm sorry for your loss, then," Shane said.

"They're not dead, just missing." Arthur grabbed another mug and polished its contents.

Caitlin decided to change the subject, lest it incite the Scotsman. She would fill Shane in later. "This is good whiskey, may I have some more?"

A boom of laughter broke from Arthur's chest and he wrapped an arm around her shoulder. "Och, 'Tis Scotland lassie, if there's one thing you can have more of 'tis whiskey."

Caitlin felt as small as a flea next to the man. She handed him her cup and shot him her sauciest smile. "Well then, fill her up."

Destiny's Denial

Shane's eyes widened but he made no remark. Smart man.

"I see you have made yourself a new friend, Arthur." A petite woman with pale blond hair said and smiled at Shane. Catherine was with her.

Arthur nodded and squeezed Caitlin's shoulder. "That I did and a mighty bonnie one at that. Helen and Catherine, this is Caitlin and Shane."

Caitlin eyed Helen. This was Ferchar's mother, a woman described to possess strength and dignity as well as a streak of hellion. A good girl with a touch of bad girl.

"Aye, I met Caitlin earlier. Shane, welcome." Catherine said after Helen had greeted them. She smiled and curtsied in his direction.

Shane smiled in return, took her hand and kissed the back of it. "It's a pleasure to make your acquaintance."

He showed Helen the same courtesy.

Caitlin smiled. Medieval Scotland just happened to be Shane's passion, which would undoubtedly prove to be a boon for them.

"I see you both have met my aunt, mother and first in command." Ferchar had approached unseen, an indefinable expression on his face as he looked at Arthur with his arm around Caitlin.

Helen beamed with a mother's pride up at Ferchar and Arthur removed his arm.

Shane responded before she could. "Aye."

"Aye." Caitlin repeated the word, pronouncing it as Shane had, *I* instead of a long *a*. Shane was definitely going to come in handy here.

Everyone had started dancing to a merry mixture of string instruments and bagpipe. Caitlin kept her eyes anywhere but on Ferchar and knew for certain he wasn't doing the same. If he dared to ask her to dance to this music, she was going to develop a sudden case of sprained ankle.

Shane turned to Catherine. "Would you like to dance?"

She blushed and nodded. The two disappeared into the throng of dancing clans-folk. Leave it to Shane to jump head first into a daunting situation. Caitlin swallowed down a shot's worth of whiskey from her cup. Only under the direst of circumstances did she drink hard liquor and was already feeling the effects of the first cup.

Fresh air. That's what she needed, the perfect escape from the inevitable. "Excuse me. I think I'll step outside for some air." She waved her hand as if to fan her face.

"I believe I'll join you," said Helen.

Caitlin smiled. Perfect. No Ferchar feeling the need to accompany her. She glanced at him briefly and saw that he and Arthur were already heading into the crowd. It seemed she was worried for nothing. Something about that annoyed her. Get over it Caitlin, it's not like the guy is smitten with you or you with him.

Helen walked out the tall, wooden doors with her into the cool night. Caitlin could see little beyond the blaze of torch lit dwellings within the immediate vicinity. Men swaggered and women flirted. A young boy sat on a barrel, his legs swinging back and forth as he chewed on a piece of bread.

"Come, let's sit here." Helen sat on one of the stairs that led to the activity below.

Caitlin sat next to her and said nothing.

"Tomorrow, I'll have Catherine show you around. I'm sure this all looks very foreign to you." Helen took a sip of whiskey.

Caitlin figured that this was the opening she had been waiting for. "No one believes we're from England, do they?"

Helen laughed. "Lord, no."

"What is everyone thinking? We show up with foreign clothes on, with Gordon...William dressed the same as us after having disappeared so long. Why aren't people giving us the evil eye and throwing rotten vegetables at us?" Caitlin knew less than nothing about medieval people but what she did know is that humankind had developed into a more civilized unit in her time. So far, these medieval Scotsmen were proving her high school history books wrong.

Helen laughed louder this time. "Evil eye? Rotten vegetables? We're not barbarians."

"I didn't mean to—"

Helen placed a hand on hers and shook her head. "Have no worries, lass. I took no offense. This clan has seen many strange things in its numerous generations. It has lost too many loved ones to this country and its wars. Too many." She sighed.

"This clan is devoted to its members," Helen continued. "And would never see the return of one of its own unharmed as anything but cause for gratitude."

Caitlin nodded but said nothing more. She was uncomfortable with Helen on a level she didn't understand. Not merely because she was the mother of the man Caitlin was having...thoughts about but because there was a minuscule level of animosity radiating off of her.

But why? Deep inside, Caitlin knew that it went against the woman's character to dislike anyone. It was almost as if Helen, without realizing it herself, resented her arrival here.

It also struck Caitlin that Helen knew a lot more than she was saying.

A little old woman hobbled up the stairs, her shoulders bent with age. Helen patted Caitlin's hand and stood. "Enjoy the eve, lass."

Before Caitlin could respond, Helen disappeared into the castle. She swung her gaze back to the gray-haired woman approaching her. Why had Helen left so abruptly? She waited, curious.

The little old woman was forthright. Two stairs down and eye level with Caitlin, she held her hand out. "Greetings lassie, I'm Iosbail."

Caitlin reached out and took the frail hand offered. Not one person in this century had offered her a hand shake thus far. Did they even do that in this time period in Scotland? She didn't think so. Caitlin wished she knew her history better.

"Hello." Caitlin shook the surprisingly strong and decisive grip.

The woman's eyes were such a dark brown they appeared black. She drew her tartan closer around her shoulders and sniffed with derision at the intrusive breeze. "Have ye a wee dram of whiskey on ye?"

Iosbail's Scottish brogue was so thick that Caitlin had to concentrate. She smiled and held out her cup. "What's mine is yours."

"Aye, 'tis good." Iosbail took the cup and took a hearty swig. "Bloody Beltane's not nearly warm enough for these ol' bones."

Caitlin noticed the mug of whiskey was not returned to her. "You have a beautiful homeland."

Iosbail shuttered. "If ye think so."

Caitlin looked past the old woman to the lit huts beyond. Many Scotsmen filtered in and out of the armory where others stood in conversation. Women did their best to distract the men. One was successful enough to have two rambunctious men chasing her into the stable.

Destiny's Denial

"What do they do in the armory at this hour?" Caitlin was eager to make conversion.

"'Tis what the highland men do." Iosbail hackled a crisp bite of laughter. "They raise their feathers like a bird and see what sort of lassie's they'll catch."

Caitlin swung her attention back to the woman. "Their feathers?"

Iosbail drank down the rest of her whiskey and smacked her lips with relish. "Aye, like a male bird, these MacLomain men. All pretty colors meant to entice their mate, aye?"

Caitlin got the idea. She didn't quite know what to make of this woman. "How are you related to the clan?"

Iosbail set the cup down and continued to climb the stairs. At Caitlin's step she stopped and looked down, her dark eyes shrewd and intelligent. "I've often wondered that meself, lassie. Often wondered that meself."

Caitlin turned as she made her way up the stairs. "It was nice to meet you, Iosbail."

The old woman didn't stop but nodded. Her response a wayward throw over her shoulder. "Aye, lass. 'Twas nice, wasn't it?"

Before Caitlin could attempt to continue conversation, Iosbail disappeared into the celebration within. What an odd little woman. Caitlin leaned back and drank in an old civilization as it unraveled at her feet, praying every minute that Ferchar would not decide to join her..

Chapter Seven

Arthur sat, legs spread, with a wide grin on his face. A good distance of new grass lay between him and his laird. "Bloody hell, that was close!"

"I guess I'll never throw an axe like Hugh did." Ferchar shrugged, offered a hand to Arthur and helped him up.

His first in command rubbed the back of his neck in contemplation. "You willnae hear me complaining. Och, I let you know my intentions toward Caitlin and you whip an axe at me." He shook his head. "Training exercise, my arse!"

Ferchar slapped him on the back. "Aye, 'twas only a simple training exercise. You avoided well, my friend."

He dislodged his weapon from the ground, re-secured the battleaxe and looked to the middle of the field. Large logs were being dragged into two large piles for tomorrow's bonfires in honor of Beltane.

"I take it you want her for your own." Arthur kept pace with him as they headed back toward the castle.

Ferchar sniffed in derision. "Who?"

"You know who. I saw the way you looked at her last eve." Arthur shook his head. "She'd be no good for you. She's got a sense of humor."

This made him stop. "I'm not without humor."

Arthur quirked a thick, red brow. "You are."

Ferchar clucked his tongue. "Well, I was. But not now that William is returned. Mayhap a bit of the old me will return."

"Maybe." Arthur looked dubious. "But then, you didnae have a sense of humor before he disappeared."

"Of course I did."

"Nay. Never."

Ferchar was getting irritated with the conversion. "I have no interest in Caitlin. She's all yours."

The big man roared with laughter. "Good."

"Good." Ferchar continued walking.

Besides, he had Emma to entertain him. Ferchar comforted himself with this knowledge as they crossed over the first moat. Emma was beautiful. Her willowy body was nothing to guffaw at. Though she wasn't voluptuous, she was firm. Though her hair was not streaked through with flaxen and wheat, it was an even light brown. Steady and dependable.

When he passed beneath the second portcullis, he stopped, as did Arthur, who released a low whistle. Caitlin stood outside the armory. The lass looked too bloody good. She wore a light green dress and her hair shone in long, chestnut waves down her back. It was less the beauty she depicted that stopped him dead in his tracks, but more what she was doing and with whom.

Caitlin held a simple, steel sword with a black leather encased wooden handle in the air. It had been Iain's favorite. She stood, legs in combat position, with her arms straight out and held the weapon high. Behind her stood a man, his front to her back. His arms over hers, teaching her how to cut the blade down.

Alan Stewart, Chieftain of the Stewart clan.

Ferchar swore and strode forward. When had he arrived? Ever a stout ally to clan MacLomain, the Stewart clan had increased their land substantially back in the war of clans in eleven ninety-nine. The enemy, clan Cochran, had been alleviated. In that the Stewart land bordered to the north and they had lost many good men in the battle, it was only right that they take a portion of the Cochrans' land.

Alan Stewart had grown up with his Uncle Iain and had remained faithful in his ties to Ferchar and clan MacLomain in his absence.

"Ferchar, good to see you lad," Alan said at his approach, making no move to remove himself from Caitlin.

"Aye." Ferchar struggled to keep his tone light. "I see you've met our new guest."

Alan smiled down at Caitlin and then stepped back. "Aye, a wee bonnie lass she is."

He took the sword from her, lifted her hand to his lips and lowered his eyes. "'Twas a pleasure teaching you about the finer points of swordsmanship."

A pretty blush stained her cheeks. "The pleasure has been all mine, Chieftain Stewart."

He leaned in close. "Alan, please."

Ferchar nearly snarled as she smiled and nodded in return. It appeared his little foreigner was doing just fine amongst his people.

"What brings you our way at Beltane?" Ferchar kept his gaze firmly on Alan.

"Oh, not now." Alan waved his hand in a dismissive gesture. "'Tis too early in the day and I am weary. We'll speak this eve about it, with a warm fire, whiskey and beautiful women, aye?"

He slid a pointed look at Caitlin with his last words.

Ferchar looked her way as well. "If that suits you." It was one thing to know that Arthur was perusing her but an entirely different thing to know that Alan was.

"Caitlin?" She tore her gaze from Alan and met his with less enthusiasm. "May I have a word?"

She returned her golden eyes to Alan, shrugged and shot him a look that could only be described as a distressed resignation to Ferchar's request. "If you insist."

"If I insist?" Bloody lass! His temper started to flare. "No, I merely request and that should be enough considering you are partaking of my goodwill in my castle."

Her eyes swung his way, incredulous. "I guess being considered a hero doesn't last long around here." She planted her hands on her hips. "Remind me in the future that if I come across another one of your long, lost relatives, that I should turn away and not assist them. After all, if I were to do the right thing and return them to you, within twenty-four hours I'd surely have it thrown in my face that I was merely partaking of your goodwill, in your castle."

Ferchar narrowed his eyes. "The blade?"

Alan handed him the sword. Clansmen didn't question clansmen. Not when it came to their women. And while Caitlin was with the MacLomain clan, she was a MacLomain.

She took a step back even though her chin thrust forward.

"Come with me," Ferchar said.

"No." Caitlin stood her ground.

"I merely wish to speak with you."

"Then why are you holding a sword?" She pointed at the blade in his hand.

"Because I'm returning it to the armory. Please join me."

She shook her head. "Absolutely not."

The last of Ferchar's patience snapped and he stepped forward, grabbed her before she could flee, swung her up over his shoulder and headed for the armory.

****

She didn't kick and flail, though she wanted to. Caitlin merely stared at the ground and the back of his hard body all the way into the armory. Kilts were bad that way. No defined behind.

Not that she was interested in that part of him or any other part of him for that matter. Between last night and his adamant display with Emma and what he'd just pulled now, he could jump off the nearest cliff for all she cared.

She tried not to picture Emma across his lap before the fire. Their lips locked for minutes on end. The display was cheap and reminded her of after hour parties in Boston. All entwined people impervious of others. It was disgusting and inappropriate. Blasphemous and outrageous.

Erotic and mesmerizing.

She squeezed her eyes shut against the lust that the last two words awoke in her. It was a good time to think other sorts of thoughts. How would the Red Sox do this season? Who was going to make it to the White House in the next presidential election? Would she return to the twenty-first century?

He swung her down in the midst of a hundred swords and turned away. She ignored the way his muscles moved beneath his tanned flesh as he returned her sword to its place on the wall. Ignored the way his long, muscled legs swung him back around to face her.

"I didnae expect you to be so much trouble," he said, his deep Scottish burr rolling the words out at her like a whip.

Caitlin bristled. "Define trouble and I might be able to defend myself."

He crossed the small distance between them and stood mere inches from her. "Trouble means your innate ability to flirt with multiple men, hence one way or another, causing problems for me in the future."

"Problems for you?" Her heart missed about ten beats.

"Aye, 'tis one thing to do what you're doing within my clan, another to involve men outside it, especially a Chieftain."

Caitlin purposely looked away from his broad chest. He was worried about Alan, and he should be. Though he had to be somewhere in his mid-thirties, the man was beyond fine with his dark hair and deep brown eyes.

She wondered, however, was it really because Alan was not of his clan or because Alan was so good-looking? Not as good-looking as Ferchar, but pretty close, and suave as well. Too suave. Caitlin had a word for men like Alan back home. But right now, Alan was a card in her hand and she wasn't ready to give him up.

Especially not to this lout.

"I didn't realize I was doing anything to your men or otherwise." She took a step back as he took a step forward. Thump. Thump. Her heart beat into her throat. God, he was tall and so incredibly sexy.

"Unlikely," he said.

"Why do you doubt me? You don't know me." He had her backed up another step.

"I know enough about you just by watching your actions."

Both his tone and assumption annoyed her. Blast his ice blue eyes. She wanted to look away from them but that would just be giving in. "And I you."

"It's unwise to compare us." He almost had her against the wall between the room of claymores and battle-axes. "But if I were to humor you, what do you mean by that?"

Ah, she'd gained ground. "Just that my appreciation for the male species is obviously equivalent to yours for the female species."

One corner of his lip pulled up and his eyes flickered over her face until they landed on her lips. "You could only be referring to Emma."

Caitlin willed the fire from her face. She was as transparent as a newly cleaned window. "I'm referring to the fact that I have as much right to entertain a man as you do a woman."

His hands fell to the wall on either side of her head. Her breath caught. What was he doing? She could duck beneath his arm and escape. But she didn't because that would, again, give him the upper hand. He leaned in close enough that she could make out the little flecks of silver caught in his eyes.

"Our situations are very different," he whispered.

His luscious mouth was within inches of hers and the nearness of his heat began melting the muscles so crucial to holding her legs up. She suddenly rethought things. It'd be best to move away from him. Caitlin sprang into action and dipped to move under his arm.

Too late, the skin on their arms touched. That was all it took. A feral gleam lit his eyes. He pushed her back. His hands had hers pinned against the wall and his lips came crashing down. Not sweet and cautious like a first kiss, but deprived and needy like a kiss between lovers separated for too long.

Wow! She relished his tongue when it delved into her mouth. She'd kissed men who used their tongue to twirl with hers, lapped, gone back and forth, but she'd never had one consume her, take her past the point of coherent thought and dislodged joints she didn't know she had.

"Caitlin." He pushed her name into her mouth with the vehemence of a warrior, the passion of a ruthless lover trying to be gentle. His hands left hers, traveled down, grabbed her backside and lifted her in the air. His long, thick erection pressed against her stomach.

Holy heck! Her groin burned hot. Fluid pooled between her thighs. Now, please. She needed this... him. Nothing was real anymore. Fire and heat tunneled a path from her belly to her outermost extremities. Her heart ached and her breasts grew super sensitive. She floated someplace surreal and unobtainable, someplace wicked and heavy.

"This is." Her words were swallowed by his mouth. He ate them and changed them. What she was going to say was that this was wrong but she didn't say that. Instead she breathed something else against his ear as he pushed against her. "This is unbelievable."

He drove his mouth against the top of her cleavage, making sweeps with his tongue that had her moving against him with desire.

"Ferchar? Are you in here?"

That soft, feminine inquiry brought Caitlin right to the floor. Literally.

Ferchar took a step back and looked down at her as if she was the one who had accosted him. He held a hand down and she took it. She didn't want to but she did. Some part of her wanted Emma to catch them together. As soon as she was standing she felt differently.

A woman didn't deserve this from her boyfriend and that is pretty much what she figured Ferchar must be to Emma. Unless they were married? The thought made her sick to her stomach. In fact, whether they were married or not, Caitlin had mistreated another woman's relationship.

Emma rounded the corner to find them that way, hand in hand. Her dark blue eyes rounded. "Ferchar!"

He made no move to release Caitlin's hand. "Emma."

"What? Why?" She glanced down at their hands.

"What, *why*, what?" Ferchar's tone sounded unrepentant.

Caitlin pulled her hand away and looked at the other woman. "I'm sorry. This isn't what it seems."

Emma looked first at her and then at Ferchar. "I thought we had an agreement?"

Caitlin frowned. An agreement?

"Not anymore." Ferchar stepped away from Caitlin. "Find someone else to make him jealous."

She ground her lips together. "Fine." She stomped out of the room.

Caitlin was stumped. Make who jealous? She looked at Ferchar's back as he headed for the door. "Hey!"

He didn't stop but strode decisively back into the village of people outside. By the time she made it into the castle, the direction he had headed, he was gone.

"Here." A mug of beer was shoved into her hands by Emma, who appeared from nowhere. "Come join me."

Caitlin was mystified. What was with these people? Emma plunked down in a chair in front of the fire and gave Caitlin a courtesy glance.

"We are not together, so dinnae go thinking Ferchar is some kind of blackguard," she said.

Actually, Caitlin had just officially classified him in Alan's category. She kept her mouth shut and waited for the other woman to speak.

"We're just friends."

Caitlin swallowed her laughter. Ah ha. There was a word for their sort of relationship back home too but she wasn't about to voice it even in her head. After all, didn't the book say that certain MacLomain clan members possessed magic and could read minds?

Emma shook her head and offered a wry smile.

"We've only ever kissed, nothing more."

Sure. Whatever she says. Just smile and agree.

Emma twisted her lip, a twinkle in her eye. "You can talk, you know."

Better to be straight and to the point. A fool's a fool as long as they play the part. She took a sip and leaned forward. "I'm a perfect stranger caught alone with your...friend that wasn't your...friend yesterday, according to what I saw. Based on that alone, what is the most appropriate thing for me to say right now?"

Emma's countenance was one of pure speculation. "What can I say to you, Caitlin, to make you understand?" She ran a finger over the top of her mug. "Ferchar is...was a means to an end knowingly. He's guilty of helping a friend with her problems and I am guilty of returning the favor. My man sought another woman a fortnight ago and Ferchar was lonely. We have been close since childhood so he agreed to entertain my plea to help me bring my man to heel."

Caitlin eyed her over her cup. "So you mean to tell me that the two of you have been doing what you did here last night for a fortnight and haven't taken it any further. Don't be ridiculous."

The woman's eyes met hers. "Dinnae get me wrong, I would have gladly taken him to bed, but Ferchar wouldnae have it. He counts me as one of his friends, regrettably. That allows me the benefit of a few kisses and nothing more."

Caitlin arched her brows. "So he merely kisses his female friends?"

Emma shrugged and laughed. "No. Just me. Ferchar doesnae stay with any one lass too long. Those he does take to his bed know not to expect much more than a brief physical relationship."

"Isn't the laird supposed to take a wife, to make an heir and all?" Caitlin asked.

"Aye. My thought is that if and when he does seek a bride it will be outside the clan. It wouldnae surprise me if that might have something to do with why Chieftain Stewart is here."

Something twisted inside Caitlin. "I don't understand."

"There has been some talk for a while of Alan's younger sister marrying Ferchar to thicken the two clans. Our laird has been finding one reason or another to put off the inevitable for some time." Emma's tone was bland. "In my opinion, he shouldn't have to marry if he doesnae want to. He has devoted his life to this clan and served it well. The last thing we need is one more tie to another clan."

Caitlin set aside her cup. Her heart felt sluggish. "Does he get along well with Alan's sister?"

Emma chuckled. "Aye, he's already had that one."

Caitlin rolled her eyes and her heart resumed a steady beat. Why, she couldn't imagine. Him having slept with the woman did not lessen the threat. It may make her a little less enticing.

What was she thinking? What was the matter with her? If he'd just taken her, out in the armory, would that have made her less enticing? Her thought processes were that of a cave woman. Shape up Caitlin or you're going to start wishing you were a fresh virgin for him. Figure the odds.

"She's a bonnie lass but I can tell you he'd never be happy with that one," Emma said.

Caitlin couldn't help but smile. "Why?"

Emma tapped her forehead with her finger. "There's not a lot up here to keep him entertained long."

"She lacks intelligence?" Caitlin said.

"Nay, she's smart enough. She just doesnae use it to engage him. She's too compliant and lacks common sense. Two things Ferchar detests."

Caitlin crossed one arm over the other. "By compliant you mean quick to jump into his bed."

"By compliant I mean she does nothing to thwart him but laps at his heels like a dog. She doesnae use the mind God gave her to contradict him when she disagrees with something he says. That one is all formidable flesh around our laird," Emma said.

No matter what Emma said to her, Caitlin's sense was that Ferchar would, as he had always done, do what was right for the clan. Compliant twit of a female or not.

Not that it was any of her business but her mind locked onto something Emma had said before.

She was too nosy for her own good. "So, Emma, you said before that you were returning the favor to Ferchar when you two put on your show yesterday. Who did he want to make jealous?"

Emma smirked and stood. As she sauntered away she offered the only answer she was going to give. "I think you know the answer to that question."

****

Shane plunked down next to his sister. She looked lost in thought and uneasy.

"Hey." He leaned over and waved his hand in front of her face.

"Hey." Her response was, at best, distracted.

"Are you okay?" He frowned, worried. Caitlin's features were drawn and she appeared stressed.

When she met his eyes, her expression was carefully guarded. "Yeah. Just overwhelmed by all of this."

"I would imagine. It would probably be best if you avoided the kitchen, there's this cook—"

"Euphemia." Her expression visibly lightened. "That woman is the best."

Shane raised his eyebrows. "If you say so. She reminds me of a ship's captain that just lost the blip on the screen that signals an incoming nuclear warhead."

Caitlin laughed. "Vivid description. She reminds me of a woman who could run a ship of five hundred crew members for six months without more to eat than moldy bread and still manage to keep them from ripping each other's throat out."

"Well, then, I'll give you points this round for being more optimistic than I." He leaned forward and took her hand. "Really, you're good?"

Her smile was wistful and different. "Don't worry about me, I might not be good with change at first, but once I accept it, I excel."

She was okay. Shane could see it in her eyes and relaxed. He was glad she had shared Gram's book with him last night, it shed a lot of light on all of this. He wondered, though, if she had told him everything. A novel had the ability to obtain so much information and the smallest details tended to have the biggest impact.

"It's beautiful here, don't you think?" she said.

He nodded. Beautiful was an understatement, what with the choppy, enchanting loch and spiked, grayish- white mountains. The castle was built high, affording it an overview of the water on three sides and a forest of pine, birch, and larch beyond. The air was sweet and salty, the texture of the landscape whole and natural. Just like he had always envisioned this Scotland— Medieval Scotland.

"Tomorrow they celebrate Beltane," he said. He wished that she understood more about the culture and could get excited alongside him but her mind was elsewhere.

Shane watched his sister gaze at the fire. What put that look on her face? He didn't recognize it, had never seen it. Whimsical, was that the word? No. Reflective? Maybe...

Whatever she was thinking would not stay locked within her long.

It never did.

"How are we going to get out of here, Shane?"

The question startled him. They'd just arrived and the amount of raw material for a historical writer was staggering. He needed more time.

"I have no idea," he replied. "I wonder what happened to that stick. Annie's fairy wand."

Caitlin looked speculative. "Do you think it's the only way home?"

Shane shrugged one shoulder. "It stands to reason."

"Not in Arianna's case, she came here through the rock at Mystery Hill." Her eyes grew wider. "Do you think we'll meet her?"

Shane rested his elbows on his knees. "Now, that would be amazing. She would be younger than us, huh?"

Caitlin smiled. "Yes. Nineteen. This is the year, according to Ferchar's vision, that Iain was supposed to return."

"Who would be laird then?" Shane asked.

"Good question, I have no idea. What I wonder about most is if they return from the future this year and they're the same age they were when they left, how are they going to explain the fact they haven't aged a day in eleven years?"

He had no idea. The concept of time-travel still baffled him. "Magic?"

Caitlin finished her beer and set it down. "And who is always at the heart of all magical transactions?"

They looked at one another and spoke simultaneously.

"Adlin."

Sky Purington

Chapter Eight

Wind whistled through the pinstripe window and ushered in the crisp tang of sea salt. This marked the second morning she'd awoken here. Yesterday had been a blur of activity while she became acquainted with an extinct civilization.

It was early and Caitlin was unsure of not only the very low cut forest-green dress she had on but of the circle of pink and white flowers encircling her head.

"Are you sure I'm not getting married?" Caitlin planted her hands on her hips and glared at Catherine.

"Why do you keep asking me that? Of course not."

Caitlin grabbed a slice of bannock from a small platter a servant had brought in. It was fresh off the fire and melted in her mouth. She truly didn't mean to badger Catherine but she wasn't about to be tricked into marrying a man, like Arianna had...especially if that man was the laird.

"Sorry," she said. "So what are we doing?"

Catherine took her hand and led her from the room.

"We're going to wash our faces in May's first dew."

Caitlin refrained from a burst of laughter. "Dew?"

The other woman ignored her and led her outside the castle. Many other women were gathering together and walking over the drawbridge to the wide meadow beyond.

"Mind if I join you?" Emma walked up beside them. Her skin looked flushed and her eyes bright. Caitlin offered the best smile she could. Had Ferchar put that look there? "You look well, Emma."

She winked and leaned in close. "Mission accomplished."

Irritating as the sensation was, relief stole her. Emma meant her boyfriend.

The women walked in companionable silence onto the field. Caitlin was surprised how comfortable she was with them. Where she came from these poor ladies were merely ghosts of the past. That thought bothered her more than she would've anticipated. They were so alive and young.

Mist rolled in graceful sweeps along the border of the forest. The watermelon sunrise ignited the distant mountains into gleaming marble statues. A salty wind whipped her hair and pushed her skirts against her legs. Pockets of golden buttercups and red and white clover mixed with the green grass and covered the ground far and wide.

Catherine and Emma knelt. They looked up at Caitlin and urged her to do the same. She did. The moment more peaceful than any other she'd ever experienced. Women everywhere ran their hands lightly over the top of the grass. The varied colors of their dresses swaying in the wind made them appear as flowers in the mist.

"Run your hands over the grass, Caitlin," Emma said. "Then run the dew over your face. It will ensure that your beauty flourishes throughout the year."

Odd as the process sounded, she did. The tender blades beneath her hands bathed her palms in delicate moisture. Though she truly questioned how clean this would make her face, she ran her hands over her cheeks. The wind blew against her damp cheeks and cooled them dry. Interesting custom.

She stood as the others did and they made their way back toward the castle. Two mammoth fires were being lit off to her right.

"You're here at a good time, Caitlin." Catherine smirked. "Beltane is the time of sensuality revitalized."

Caitlin glanced at Emma, who only grinned back. They were co-conspirators, these two. "I don't need my sensuality revitalized."

Emma leaned down and picked a blue harebell. "Apparently not."

She'd walked right into that one. No doubt they were referring to the avid attention she'd received from both Arthur and Laird Alan the previous night. Caitlin didn't have to lift a finger they were so adept at pampering her. Not that she was opposed to the attention. Arthur was a blast to be around and Alan was not only sexy but extremely intellectual.

At least with the two of them keeping her entertained she could overlook the fact that Ferchar ignored her, as if what had happened between them didn't exist. He spent his evening with a wide array of women, every one of them beautiful.

"Good morn to ye, lassies," said Euphemia.

Caitlin turned to the large woman stampeding their way. Her wide girth didn't slow her in the least. "Good morn."

The woman kneaded her ample hips with her meaty fists and eyeballed their surroundings with a look of disgust. "Damn goats keep getting into my kitchen causing havoc. You'd think Ferchar would just lemme hog tie em' but the man's a loose cannon when it comes to these beasties."

"What do you need, Euphemia?" Catherine's tone was gentle, yet firm.

Caitlin stifled a giggle as the one singular goat that Euphemia had aforementioned as multiple goats circled the cook with adoration.

"I need Ferchar to—" She made a grab for the elusive goat.

"To what?" Ferchar materialized right on time.

Caitlin's pulse kicked up a notch. He wore no tunic and hadn't bothered to wrap his plaid over his shoulder but only around his waist. A large claymore was attached to his back and a few skinny braids fell by his chin. Her eyes drifted down to his sweat slicked, well- muscled chest and she licked her lips.

"Aye, my lad." Euphemia beamed up at him just before she took another swipe at the goat. "I need the sacred berries. The ones only the MacLomain laird can pick if we want the food this eve to bring health to the people of this clan."

Ferchar frowned. "Nay."

Euphemia's eyes bulged. "But 'tis tradition!"

He shook his head. "'Twas started five years ago by you." He pointed at her. "And 'tis ridiculous."

She appeared wounded. "What says I can't start a tradition? You've got em' for me just fine every other year. And has this clan not been healthy? One satchel of bloody berries, that's all I—"

"Stop. I'll get them." Ferchar interrupted.

Euphemia beamed. "Now?"

"Nay."

"Please?" Her ruddy complexion sizzled with renewed discontent.

He sighed. "Anything for you."

Caitlin watched with fascination. Ferchar was going to pick berries? There was no doubt in Caitlin's mind that even the king of Scotland could order him to do such a thing and be unsuccessful. But Euphemia, with a flutter of her thin, sparse eyelashes, had Ferchar doing exactly what she wanted him to.

Good woman.

Ferchar turned to leave, his eyes passing smoothly over Caitlin. "Goodbye lasses."

"Ferchar wait. Why dinnae you bring Caitlin along? Let her see some of this beautiful countryside," Catherine said, the devil in her eyes.

"No. I'm fine." Caitlin ignored the frantic note in her voice.

"She wants to stay here." He turned away.

"No, she doesnae." Emma nudged her forward.

Caitlin watched him continue to walk away. What a rude bastard. What was so wrong with her tagging along, anyway? She hadn't been beyond the field since she arrived here. Maybe she would go.

"I would like to come along." Caitlin grimaced at her own announcement. She'd gone from a frantic no to a desperate yes in under a minute.

He stopped and turned. His gaze purposely raked down the front of her dress in warning. "Are you sure?"

She straightened her shoulders and narrowed her eyes. "Yes."

Ferchar turned away and gave her the small honor of a reply as he started walking. "Follow me, lass."

Rude.

Caitlin waved goodbye to the girls and pursued him. She could've sworn when she walked away that she heard a collective burst of muffled laughter behind her.

****

He rode his horse hard through the forest.

Blasted woman. She was having no problem keeping up with him. In fact, her horsemanship was superior. Her long chestnut hair billowed behind her and her dark- green dress whipped.

Ferchar didn't want her anywhere near him. Yesterday was a lesson in truth. He'd never wanted a lass more than he did her. He could still taste her lips, the sparks of magic burning between them eager to be free. It wrapped itself within his lust and drove the texture of her skin into his bones. Her eyes had shone like the sun when her legs wrapped around him. He'd been so close to true bliss for the first time in his life when Emma had interrupted.

Thank the gods she did.

He had no intention of becoming a slave to a woman. He'd rather be horsewhipped than chase her through time. Scotland was his home and he would not leave it behind as his uncle had. He would not commit another unwilling soul to deal with all he'd dealt with because Iain had to find his lass.

Absolutely not. Caitlin suddenly reigned in her horse and laughed.

He'd just continue on. This was not where he wanted to stop.

"Goodbye." Her word was a whisper. Furious, he swung his horse around, rode back and dismounted. Before she had a chance to comprehend his actions, Ferchar was on her. He pinned her shoulders against a monster pine tree.

Caitlin's nostrils flared with alarm. She grabbed his forearms. Her nails dug into his skin. Her thick lashed eyes locked with his. "What is your problem?"

He could smell her fear. Tangy and sharp. "Dinnae ever speak to me that way."

She tried to shove forward but he allowed her no leeway. "What way?"

"Through the mind. I dinnae talk that way to anyone. Especially not you." He tightened his grip on her shoulders.

"Through the mind? I don't know what you're talking about." Her cheeks were blazing red and her eyes turned a deep bronze.

"Dinnae you?" He leaned in closer until his mouth ran parallel to her soft ear. Her skin smelled sweet.

Her soft hair brushed his cheek. Suddenly, all he could remember was sitting behind her on a bench in another time. Her tight bottom nuzzled against his rampant arousal. The desperate need to push deep inside of her.

After too many years, he'd finally locked onto William's essence. He'd been taught well the art of magic and time travel. Especially after Iain left. He had reached out and stemmed his ability for a lifeline to his cousin.

It was her he had found.

"I don't read minds." Her assurance sounded false. "And I certainly don't know how to speak within the mind."

She turned her head slightly, just enough so that her cheek brushed his. Awareness tore through him. "Get away from me, Ferchar."

He caught her knee before it made contact. Hellion. Time to reposition her into a more submissive position. He grabbed her waist and swung her to the ground, covering her before she could fight him.

"No." He grabbed both her wrists and secured them with one hand over her head. She was breathing hard. Her flushed cleavage struggled against a weakening bodice. So sweet. So perfect. He licked his lips.

They lay in a blanket of grass at the border of the very field that Iain had lost Arianna in as she traveled back to the future. How ironic.

"What is it with us Ferchar?" Caitlin's calm words were in direct contradiction with her body language. "Is it sex you want from me? Is that it?"

He stared down at her. Sex? Aye, definitely sex. Hard, fast and non-stop. But his soul told him that just sex with her would not be enough. That merely being inside her body would invoke the imminent loss of all that he knew about himself.

"Berries. I need to pick berries." He shifted and used his lower half to spread her thighs, pushing his erection against her steaming hot center.

She licked her lips and her eyelids drifted. "Berries?"

Ferchar swooped down and seized her full lower lip lightly with his teeth. She pulled her arms against his grip and arched her body. Instinctively, he pushed her legs wider apart and tightened his grip on her wrists. He left her mouth and took her velvet neck. Inch by inch, first nipping and then soothing.

"Why are you doing this to me?" She groaned and rubbed against him. He released a sharp breath. Her scent tugged him steadily toward oblivion. A warm, honey-suckle-ridden wind wrapped them in springtime perfume. Sunlight poured over them and stole the shadows from the wood line.

Don't you know? Can't you sense it? Of course not.

"You chose to come." He trailed his lips over her ample cleavage. *I could taste you forever.* "What did you expect would happen?"

Her eyes rolled back when he lowered her bodice and seized one pebble sized nipple in his mouth.

"Let me touch you." Her impassioned, breathy plea made her thighs tighten, made his hips thrust without fulfillment.

He didn't want her to touch him as she had yesterday. For him to touch her, there still existed a small modem of control, and it was his. If he released her hands, she would take that control and he would lose it forever.

Kissing her was not an option either. Was it sex she had wondered about? Had she asked if that was what he wanted? He did well to hold his thoughts together but felt them breaking apart, piece by piece.

"Let me touch you," he murmured and flicked his tongue over the corner of her mouth. She turned her

Destiny's Denial

head to capture him with her sweet lips but he moved away.

Her legs lifted and wrapped around him. "But you are touching me." She ground against him.

Bloody hell, she was wanton.

Electric pulses pounded through him until he could hear nothing but the sound of his own heartbeat. Blood scorched his veins and pooled below. His erection had never been so full. "Aye, 'tis sex between us."

Panting, Ferchar offered the confirmation through clenched teeth and made to move her skirt aside. He was dizzy with need.

"A rainbow," she said, her voice suddenly too soft and feminine.

A rainbow? No. Sex. Now. He came up between her legs. She was hot and alive. Sensual and provocative. Now. No more waiting. *I need to feel the clenching heat of your body.*

An eagle screamed above them and the wind died. Bloody hell, no! His head snapped up. The forest was quiet and the trees still. He looked to the mountain and sniffed the air. Ferchar shot to his feet.

A rainbow.

"What the heck?" Caitlin lay on the grass at his feet, completely confused. Ferchar offered her a hand but she refused it.

"I don't need your help, again." She scrambled to her feet, fury evident on her face.

"We have to go." He whistled for their horses.

Caitlin strode over to him and shoved a finger into his chest. "Don't ever touch me again." Her words were oddly emotionless considering the violence of her finger.

Ferchar swung onto his horse. "As you wish."

She took a deep breath, ran a hand down her dress and swung onto her own horse.

As he led them across the meadow into the forest, his mind should've been flooded with trepidation. He should've been anxious about what that rainbow meant for him, what the eagle's highhanded alert implied. But none of what he rode toward fazed him in the least.

What Caitlin had said did. Don't ever touch her again?

****

Caitlin was furious.

With herself, with him and with whatever, exactly, had brought her to Scotland. She was even furious with Gram and Shane right now. Gram because she undoubtedly knew so much more than she ever said and Shane because he liked being here.

She averted her eyes from the sight of Ferchar's muscled back moving astride his horse. No more stargazing his way. Forget him. How dare he use her like that?

She grunted. Better yet, how dare he not use her like that? What sort of man took a woman as far as he had taken her and then just stopped? It wasn't as if he'd not been turned on, because he had, every long, hard delectable inch of him. It made no sense.

Caitlin followed him into a clearing. When she broke free of the tree line she nearly fell off of her horse.

A man and women sat together at the edge of a beautiful stream. Two horses grazed nearby, a huge black warhorse and a buckskin horse with a black tail and mane.

Caitlin's breath caught when the horse raised its head. A mark resembling a Celtic cross graced its equine forehead. Her gaze immediately swung back to the woman looking with adoration at the man beside her. Arianna?

Her long hair shone with streaks of gold. It couldn't be. It had to be! She wore a deep blue gown and was whispering something in his ear. He stopped and turned his head slightly.

Though he hadn't looked at them he spoke. "Hello, Ferchar."

Ferchar sat stoically. "Welcome home, Laird Iain."

"I believe you have that wrong." Iain stood and helped Arianna to her feet. "I believe 'tis I who should address you as laird."

When the couple turned toward them, Caitlin's breath caught. She didn't know which one of them she wanted to study more. Arianna was fabulous. The book did her no justice. Her lips were full and her bone structure perfect. Her eyes were captivating. They were the color of the Caribbean on a cloudless day, exactly the same shade as Shane's.

Her eyes drifted to Iain. Wow. He and Ferchar bore a striking resemblance. Their height and build were near replicas and their faces almost mirrored one another, save Ferchar's was slightly leaner. Iain's hair was lighter and his eyes a bold emerald. His eyebrows arched a bit more and his face bore no battle scars.

Ferchar dismounted and Caitlin followed suit.

The two men clasped hands, hand to elbow, before Iain pulled Ferchar into an embrace. "You've grown."

"You knew I would." Ferchar turned his attention to Arianna. "Welcome back."

She embraced him and smiled. "Thank you, Ferchar. You look wonderful." She slid a glance at Iain. "You look just like my husband now."

Ferchar held her at arm's length. "Well, eleven years will do that. Now you're younger than me."

Arianna laughed. "I know, isn't it bizarre? Yesterday you were a gangly boy of fifteen and now look at you."

Iain turned his attention to Caitlin. "And you are?"

When Arianna turned her way, she froze. Her complexion paled and she stepped forward. Her brow furrowed in confusion. "Annie?"

Caitlin took an uncontrolled step back and shook her head. "No, my name is Caitlin."

Arianna shuttered. "My God, you are exactly what I envision my cousin would look like as an adult."

Her eyes drifted to Caitlin's hair in awe. "Your hair is the exact shade and your eyes..." Her voice trailed off.

Iain placed a hand on her elbow. "Will you be able to do this?"

Arianna's uncertainty vanished when she looked at him. "Aye."

Caitlin's mind was twisting like a tornado. Arianna had just arrived back in Scotland from the start of the nineteenth century. She'd left her family behind forever, her Aunt Marie, Uncle Liam, her best friend Beth and her two little cousins, Coira and Annie. She'd just forfeited life as she knew it for Iain.

Ferchar's eyes stayed on Iain while he introduced her. "Iain and Arianna, this is Caitlin. She is from the twenty-first century and, I believe, a distant relative of yours." His eyes swung to Arianna.

Both Iain and Arianna seemed startled.

"You are a relative of mine?" Arianna's expression shifted and her eyes turned moist. "That would explain why you look like her, you must descend from Annie."

Caitlin nodded slowly. "So I've recently been told." The next thing she knew Arianna embraced her.

Arianna pulled back. "I'm so happy to meet you. To know I'm not alone in this century."

Caitlin searched her eyes and liked what she saw there. "Me too."

And she was. Though she had Shane, he wasn't a woman. Somehow that made a difference. Caitlin was not about to acknowledge yet the parallel of them being drawn to two men that were not only blood relatives, incredibly similar in appearance, but both lairds of the MacLomain clan.

"'Tis a pleasure to meet you, Caitlin." Iain brought the back of her hand to his lips briefly. Who would've ever thought the hero in a novel would kiss her?

"I have much to tell you, Iain." Ferchar turned to his mount. "You arrive home at a festive time."

"Beltane," Iain said, as he and Arianna mounted their horses.

"Aye." Ferchar and Caitlin did the same and the four of them rode their steeds back toward the castle.

The men rode their horses a ways ahead and conversed in hushed tones.

The instantaneous bond between her and Arianna humbled Caitlin. She couldn't help but like her. The woman was enigmatic and talkative without being overwhelming. She was polite, yet blunt. Curious, yet tactful.

Caitlin told her all she could of what she knew. That she lived in the very house that Arianna had just left. She spent the remainder of their journey back answering questions. Was the oak tree still there? What about the barn? What did Salem look like in the twenty-first century? What sorts of clothes did they wear? Were women allowed to work at gristmills still?

By the time they reached the edge of the massive field, Arianna appeared stupefied. "There's actually women and men running for presidency? That's wonderful."

Caitlin laughed. She definitely liked Arianna. As far as she could tell so far, colonial America would not have suited her well.

Late afternoon had set in and the bonfires burned bright.

"Iain." Arianna urged her horse forward. "I'm worried."

He stopped and allowed her to ride up alongside him. "There's naught to worry about, lass. We're expected."

Arianna brows drew together. "But we're still the same age."

"Aye, they know that. 'Tis my clan, lass. My family. Secrets don't keep well here."

He squeezed her hand. "Trust me."

Her bottom lip quivered, then gave way to a smile. "I do."

Caitlin stayed a distance behind. What would it be like to have a relationship like that? With a man who didn't allow you to doubt or be afraid. A man who looked at her the way Iain was looking at Arianna. She winced.

Wake up, Caitlin. She's an eighteenth century female and you are a twenty-first century female. Reality is just different where Caitlin was from. It was easier to get a divorce than stay married. Men and women alike didn't trust each other anymore. With the Internet, it was easier to cheat. The twenty-first century had a passive-aggressive way of promoting the idea that human beings were not monogamous creatures. Almost as if that line of thinking was becoming an undeclared law and excuse for promiscuousness.

Ferchar rode alongside them as they passed beneath the second portcullis. Caitlin was alone all at once as people swarmed around the three of them and she was pushed back. She dismounted and handed the rein off to a nearby stable boy. Arthur's laughter shook the air around her.

One bonus to being a waitress was the inept ability to filter through a crowd of people without disturbing any of them. Utilizing that skill, she made her way back to the three of them.

Ferchar stood tall and silent beside Iain. This must be an unusual moment for him. Arianna was embracing both Muriel and Emma, tears in her eyes. Iain had his arm wrapped around the back of Arthur's neck.

She was witnessing a homecoming of mass proportions.

Catherine stepped forward and Arianna's eyes rounded. "Catherine? You have grown up!"

Arianna embraced her and Caitlin swore that Catherine was preening. "Welcome back," Catherine said.

Shane had just stepped out of the castle and was watching everything with rapture. Caitlin guaranteed if she gave him a pen and a notepad right now, he'd be scribbling away.

Caitlin made her way to Arianna's side. "Arianna, this is my brother, Shane."

Arianna turned to him and swayed a little. Iain looked at her and then at Shane.

"He does bear a striking resemblance, aye?" He said.

Arianna took Shane's hand and nodded. "Hello, I'm Arianna. I apologize for my reaction in seeing you, it's just you look so much like my Uncle Liam."

Shane was smooth. "I'll take that as a compliment and might I add that you bear a slight resemblance to my sister, with the exception of your fiery hair and mesmerizing eyes."

Arianna burst out laughing. "And I'll take that as a compliment, not to say your sister's hair and eyes aren't magnificent as well."

Shane had met his match and swaggered down the steps. "So we are very distant relatives right?" He raised an eyebrow in Iain's direction.

Caitlin stepped forward. For all Shane claimed to know about medieval Scottish clans, he struck her too bold in the face of Iain's considerable size.

Iain, however, only quirked a corner of his lips in Shane's direction and then looked at Caitlin. "He has good taste in lasses."

Caitlin tried for a smile but failed. There were far too many lethal weapons within mere feet of them and she didn't like Shane taking chances. Flirt or no flirt. Each and every one of these men could kill him before Caitlin blinked.

When she looked his way, Ferchar's blue eyes caught hers. For a moment she felt a certain kinship with him. They were both on the outside looking in. He was the leader of a clan welcoming back to their breast the former Chieftain and she was a woman who didn't belong here, although a colonial woman did. It was bizarre and unsettling.

She looked away.

She didn't want to have anything in common with him. He was her enemy. There was no way around it.

Caitlin only hoped he fully understood that.

Chapter Nine

Ferchar stood, hands on the ledge of the window and searched out the pale, full moon in the time between twilight and eve. The air felt unusually warm and salt off the loch filled the confines of his chamber. From his viewpoint, the loch stretched deep and black, much like his mood. He'd known this day would come. Had hoped it would come much, much sooner.

His vision had told him the truth a long time ago, however. Eleven years. From the eve of the battle he'd fought in at fifteen winters of age. He leaned forward and breathed in the new eve.

He had increased the MacLomains' land to nearly double what it was before Iain left and allied their clan to many more highland clans as well as a few lowland clans. Up until now his life had been a fairly predictable, if not severely monumental, task. Now his purpose had changed. One part of him was eager, the other resentful.

A soft knock interrupted his thoughts. "Come in."

Emma slid through the door and walked over to him. "Are you planning to join the festivities?"

He wrapped his plaid over his shoulder. "Aye, I'm coming now."

She put a hand on his arm. "The clan still looks to you as their Chieftain. You have to remember that for those of us who are younger, you have been our laird just as long as Iain was."

Ferchar looked down at her. "I know that. Dinnae worry. I'm not up here sulking."

Emma walked with him out the door. "You do know that I explained our relationship to Caitlin, aye?"

They walked past the wall walk. "'Twas unnecessary but courteous. Thank you."

She followed him down the twisting staircase. "'Twas necessary. She has feelings for you."

Ferchar continued down the stairs to the great chamber below. "Lass, while I appreciate any regard you have for Caitlin and me, this discussion is over."

Emma scurried up beside him and walked with him out the door. "Dinnae tell me you dinnae find her attractive. I saw you two in the armory."

He stopped and scowled. "What are you hoping to accomplish?"

She grinned. "I'm naught but returning a favor."

Ferchar shook his head and continued walking. "The last thing I'm concerned about right now is my love life."

Emma sighed and followed him onto the field. Bagpipes echoed off the mountains and wrapped the MacLomain clan in Scotland's pride. The fire that normally burned on the great hearth in the castle lay in ashes as it paid homage to the two gigantic bonfires on the field spitting sparks into the sky. Children ran in all directions and men and women danced close, their bodies ushering in the Beltane.

His restless gaze raked over the crowd. Where was she? He scoffed at himself. It mattered naught where Caitlin was. No doubt she was well cared for. His fellow clansmen disgusted him. Arthur was a pompous fool and Alan a rake. Whomever she got, she deserved.

"You both look well this eve," he said as he approached Arianna and Iain.

"Thank you," Arianna replied, admiring her blue dress. "Muriel lent this to me. It was the very same one she wore the first night I officially met all of you. Do you remember my infamous trip down the stairs into Iain's arms?"

He laughed. "Aye, how could I forget? You had on the gown you wore earlier and were a vision. A clumsy vision, but a vision nonetheless."

Iain shook his head. "You have a good memory, nephew."

Muriel and William joined them. Iain took measure of the lad while he spoke to Muriel. "I'm glad he was returned to you."

Her smile was pure and welcome. "As am I. I never thought—" Muriel's voice broke, emotion evident.

William took his mother's hand. "Nor I, if it wasnae for Caitlin and Shane, I might have never found my way home."

Ferchar remained silent as his family reunited. It still seemed impossible to him that William had been flung into the future at the base of the waterfall. Water held a great deal of power but Ferchar had sensed no magic that day. Only despair.

What he hadn't known until recently was that William was a visionary. He confessed to Ferchar that he'd known of his vision for some time before he vanished. He was to travel to the twenty-first century. He'd had no choice but to follow it. Adlin had known, but had told William to remain silent so as to not affect fate. Devious wizard. The scrap of bloodied tartan at the base of the waterfall was from a knick William received on a rock before he plummeted forward through time.

Yet William had persevered at such a young age. When he found himself in a time and place so unlike his own he had acclimated with astounding grace. He cut his hair, changed his name and survived. Through his own magic he even managed to mask his accent.

The only person missing from the reunion was Hugh. Where was he now? Ferchar had tried to connect with him again through magic. Nothing. One year ago, Hugh's magical essence had vanished. Not even Adlin could locate him.

Iain's gaze shifted to their surroundings, his emerald eyes darkening. "It appears our heroes have taken well to our clans folk."

Ferchar followed his gaze to Catherine. She sat on a wide log near the fire, her head bent close to Shane's. The smile she wore spoke of female intrigue and her eyes sparkled.

"Aye. That they have." His eyes locked on Caitlin. There was no way she'd been within the fire's light before or he never could have missed her.

She was glorious, beautiful beyond compare.

She wore a flowing gown of shimmering crème. The low bodice only enhanced her full cleavage and the fitted waist accentuated her slim midline. The gold streaks throughout her hair sparkled in the firelight, a perfect match to the gold threads sewn into the fabric. Weaved into the shape of a delicate cross across the bodice, the threading drew forth the pale gold of her almond shaped eyes.

"Why is she wearing that dress?" He kept his voice low and careful.

Arianna gasped in delight and took Iain's hand. "Your mother's wedding gown!"

"Why is she wearing it?" Arianna repeated Ferchar's question.

"Beltane." Adlin's explanation reached them before he did. "'Tis the eve of fertility after all."

Problematic Wizard. He was up to something.

"Adlin!" Arianna embraced him and then pulled back. "You are a very sneaky wizard."

Destiny's Denial

His long, bony finger tapped her nose. "And you are still with Iain, just not where you thought you would be with Iain."

Her eyes turned to slits. "Well, it was you who implied just earlier today in my aunt and uncle's house that Iain would be leaving. There was no mention of me going with him."

Adlin snickered and winked. "Some things are better left unsaid."

Ferchar decided to interrupt their banter. "And why, again, is Caitlin wearing that wedding gown?"

The wizard turned his way and raised his eyebrows. "I believe I mentioned Beltane."

Iain perceived the contained anger rising to the surface of Ferchar's eyes and spoke. "Caitlin's a single lass. I see at least two men that will be chasing her into those woods tonight. The dress is suiting in its own way."

"She knows nothing about the extent to which this clan takes the old tradition," Ferchar said.

"She will this eve." Iain's verdant gaze narrowed on him. *"Why does this bother you so, nephew?"*

"I think that is fairly obvious." This from Adlin.

"Stay out of my head, both of you." Ferchar took a mug topped with whiskey from Emma.

Adlin's voice was tempered with probing magic. "Mayhap, this Beltane, you'll participate. That would gain you another year single in the eyes of God."

He swore under his breath. "But not under the eyes of the old gods." Ferchar stood his ground. "I won't be tricked."

Emma decided to join the conversation. "But how could you be tricked, Ferchar? Unless there's somcone you're likely to chase after this eve?"

"Be gone, lass," he muttered.

"As you wish, my laird." Her tone was the perfect combination of sarcasm and tease as she wandered away.

Caitlin danced with Alan now, their bodies close and complimentary to one another. The muscles in Ferchar's shoulders tensed when Alan's hand drifted down her back.

Iain pulled Arianna close. "Shall we go dance, luv?"

Her face flushed and she followed him into the night.

William and Muriel locked arms and headed for the fires.

Adlin's voice was soft, deceiving. "I can feel the shift in you. The warp of your soul."

Ferchar made to walk away but Adlin stopped him. His face had transformed to that of an ageless man who wielded great power. "You try to convince yourself that you have fulfilled the prophecy. 'Tis a risk only to you, Ferchar, to do so."

He looked down at the vein-filled hand that grasped his with the virility of youth. "Prophecy has become monotonous and tedious. My will is my own. I refuse to let visions dictate my life anymore."

Adlin's grip tightened. "You have no choice. Either you can face the truth or end in darkness."

"I have every intention of doing what is best for this clan." Ferchar met Adlin's eyes. Ice blue crackled off of ice blue.

"Then why haven't you?" Adlin's gaze shifted to Caitlin. "You should not have drawn her into this."

Power met power whilst they probed one another's intentions. "I had nothing to do with her coming here."

"Didn't you?" Adlin released his arm, but not his eyes.

"William has returned, has he not? I made a connection and brought him home." Ferchar would not back down.

"Through her!" Adlin's roar slammed into his mind so hard he nearly fell to his knees.

Ferchar took a moment to regain his composure and pulled his eyes from Adlin. He felt as though the sun had just seared the flesh from his body. His bones were stiff and fire burned his tendons.

Adlin turned away and vanished into the shadows of the meadow.

Was he forever to be a puppet of the gods? A warrior to the whims of ancient magic and tales foretold by ghosts long before he was born?

No.

His destiny now belonged to him.

****

Caitlin sat on a log in front of the fire. *I think I drank too much.* She was feeling pretty good. Between the endless ale and relentless dancing that she had finally succumbed to, she needed to sit down. Iain and Arianna sat near Iosbail who was surrounded by children. Emma swung in happy circles with a tall, blond Scotsman. Ferchar had disappeared a while back into the shadows with a buxom redhead and Arthur and Alan hovered within a group of clansmen, surely only giving her a brief respite.

What a day.

Shane plopped down next to her. "I'm truly blutered, lass."

She released an exasperated wisp of air. "Blutered?"

He smiled. "Drunk."

"I figured that's what you meant. You're really getting into this place, aren't you?"

His eyes wandered to Catherine across the way. "I am. Catherine's incredible. And smart. She has this obsession with words that just...well, it's very endearing."

Caitlin brows drew down. "No doubt. Be careful Shane, she's Iain's sister. Don't underestimate the man."

Shane yawned. "I know, sis. I won't do anything rash."

She took a swig of whiskey. "Don't. I'm convinced that Iain still sees her as his ten-year-old kid sister. That's really dangerous ground."

"Point taken. What about you? I see your fan club is keeping a close eye on you. They do know that I'm your brother, right?"

Caitlin laughed. Arthur and Alan were looking at Shane with nothing less than loath. "Yeah. But you better keep your eyes straight ahead anyways."

"Wasn't today incredible? So much tradition," Shane said.

She nodded and thought of their visit to the moor earlier. "I don't like custard."

He smacked his lips. "I didn't think it was so bad."

Caitlin scrunched her nose. "That was a strange custom."

She remembered how methodical the clan members had been as they cut a huge circular trench around their group, creating a table in the green sod beneath them. The women kindled a fire and then made custard out of milk and eggs. After that, they kneaded a cake of oatmeal and toasted it against a heated stone.

"I loved the oatmeal cake." He chuckled. "Leave it to you to have to leap the fire. The laird didn't seem too happy about it."

"Only because I didn't manage to go up in flames..." Caitlin had made all three leaps with room to spare. Well, that might be pushing it a bit.

Prior to, Catherine had taken the oatmeal cake and divided it as evenly as she could for the ten in their group, making sure each piece was similar in size and shape. No small task.

Then she daubed one of the pieces with charcoal until it was completely black. All the pieces were put into a bonnet and each of them were blindfolded and made to pick a piece from the bonnet. The person that picked the black oatmeal was made to jump the fire.

That's precisely why Caitlin never played the lottery or bought scratch tickets. She had no luck. According to Emma, her leaps over the fire were a means to implore one of the ancient Gods for a year of productivity. How her almost being burned alive achieved that, no one could or would tell her. The custom had been handed down through too many generations and not honoring it was out of the question. Scots, she'd discovered, were a superstitious lot.

The sound of a lone bagpipe drew their attention to Adlin, who had just stepped between the two behemoth fires.

His strong voice reverberated over the clan's folk when the pipes ceased. "We welcome the Beltane and worship the gods' hands as they cover the land with warmth and fertility. Your crops shall thrive beneath mother Earth's kiss. Her womb is ripe and ready for seed. Till the soil with your heart and welcome life with your soul. There will be boundless feasts and sweeter drink."

His arms spread wide. Caitlin blinked at the mirage before her. Adlin's white flowing robes made him appear a great white eagle with its wings spread wide. The two great fires created living, boisterous wing tips.

The wizard's arms lowered. A wiry grin consumed his face. It appeared the crowd was braced on the edge of a precipice as they awaited his words.

Shane leaned over and whispered, "You might want to get ready to run."

She whispered back. "Why?"

Her brother's face erupted into a devious smirk. "Because both of those men poised to catch you have long legs."

Caitlin frowned. "What are you talking about?"

Shane looked at Alan and Arthur. "I probably should've told you earlier."

Adlin was saying something about human maidens, seeds and sensuality. Apprehensive, she asked, "Told me what, Shane?"

He looked resigned and slightly sorry for her now. "In Scotland, on Beltane, all the single women are up for grabs."

Now the wizard was raising his cane as though it were a flag held between two cars getting ready to race each other.

"Up for grabs? Could you be more specific?"

Shane looked at Adlin and pursed his lips. "I'm pretty sure he's getting ready to give the go ahead to every single man here to chase you women down into the woods behind us, pair up and spend the night together."

Caitlin grabbed her brother's arm. "You mean sex?"

"Yep." Shane pointed at the forest behind him with his thumb. "In there, all night, no questions asked."

Caitlin's eyes whipped to Adlin. "Not me?"

Shane nodded. "I'd say you're part of the package."

She looked to where Arthur and Alan stood. They looked right back. Their bodies were locked and their expressions feral. This was ridiculous.

"Ah, Caitlin?" Shane shoved her to the edge of the log.

She looked at him, panicked. "What?"

"Run!"

Adlin's cane came down and the crowd burst with life. She didn't bother holding her ground or questioning the sanity of this.

She ran.

Chapter Ten

The night had turned moonless.

Black puddles of nothing swallowed Caitlin while she ran through the Highland forest as fast as she could. *Please don't let me run into a tree!* The pine needles underfoot muffled the sounds of dozens of feet behind her.

No. No. No. She ran harder, pushing her leg muscles to an impossible pace. All she could focus on was escape. She didn't want to sleep with either Arthur or Alan and knew with horrible certainty both of them were closing in.

"Slow down, lass." Alan's voice was right behind her. She banked a hard left and sprinted forward. After a three second count she veered right. Evade. Evade. She repeated the words in her head and prayed for sanctity wherever she could find it. Mid-flight a hard arm came around her midsection and pulled her back. She was lifted and flung over his shoulder.

Then he was running.

Caitlin couldn't breathe. Darkness pickled her vision and bore through coherent thought. Then water poured over her back briefly in icy sheets. She closed her eyes and tried to grab at the granite muscled back. As she worked to clear her muddled mind and find the words to get herself out of this situation, scent flooded her...male and sweet.

This was not Alan.

Flipped down onto a bed of soft grass, she opened her eyes. A single torch burned in a bracket attached to the wall of a wide cave. The air simmered warm and humid. A glass of silky white water crashed over the entrance like a magical door. Wild orchids grew in clusters everywhere, their scent potent.

A man kneeled over her, his features hidden in the shadows.

"You're a foolish lass, Caitlin." His eyes blazed blue as he pulled her forward. "You didnae run fast enough."

Caitlin kneeled. She didn't run fast enough? Did that mean—?

Her thoughts were cut short when he wrapped his hands into her hair and angled her head to look up at him. "Now, you're mine."

Ferchar. But of course it was Ferchar.

His hair and skin were wet. Drops slid onto his neck and whirled down his wide chest. Yellow dandelions and cat's ear bloomed beneath them and verdant moss covered the stone beside them in plush velvet.

Her eyes met his. The nerve of the man! "No, I'm not."

Ferchar's mouth took hers with such vengeance she leaned back. He guided her lips, allowing her no control. One hand kept her head and the other wrapped around her waist. Oh dear God! Her body suddenly felt weak and light and very, very needy.

Cool water dripped from above and mixed with the taste of his hot lips. Pull away. Say no to this! But she couldn't resist him. He felt too damned good. Caitlin wrapped her arms around his shoulders and held on. The man could kiss. When his tongue swooped in and twirled with hers, she moaned and ran her fingers through his thick hair.

The Devil's whip couldn't be as fiery as the searing burn that filled her veins. Magic. His magic. She didn't fight it but followed his lead. The grass steamed below and the torch flickered.

"Ferchar," Caitlin whispered as his talented lips trailed the length of her neck. His wet hair brushed her collarbone and ripples of pleasure raked her from head to toe.

"Just this. Us. This eve." His words scorched her skin, branding it.

She breathed deeply. The torchlight snuffed out and a deep green sprang from the grass. Cool spray blew off the waterfall and burst into a tie dye of blue light reflected over the ceiling high above.

He'd brought nature to its feet. Hell, he'd brought her to her feet.

Ferchar yanked down the front of her dress and clamped his mouth over one of her erect nipples. His teeth grazed and his tongue swirled eagerly. Her eyelids grew heavy and her center ached harshly with near painful desire.

"Ah, luv. Hurts, aye?" He murmured against her breast. His hand rode up beneath her dress, skimming her inner thigh until one of his fingers delved between her folds and hovered over her clit, touching it ever so lightly.

Damn, damn, damn. He knows what he's doing.

He grinned up at her. "Did you think I wouldae?"

Oh shoot, had she said that aloud?

It didn't matter as he slowly pulled the dress down over her hips, his lips brushing, his teeth nipping, as though he found her a delectable treat. Before she knew quite how he'd managed it, her dress was gone and she stood, while he still kneeled.

Caitlin loved the feel of the chilly cave against her bare, steamy skin. Loved the feel of his large hands cupping her backside as his lips explored. When his tongue licked where his fingers had been, she clutched his shoulders and arched. He groaned against her womanhood and the vibration made her inner muscles clench deliciously. Shaking her head, she tried to sink, pull away, anything, but he held her tight, his hands solid vices.

There was no escape.

Oh no, don't do that with your tongue! But he did. Caitlin's body started to shake. She dug her nails into his shoulders and couldn't hold back a keen as an intense orgasm ripped through her.

Pliant putty in his arms, he allowed her to slowly slide down to her knees. Icy pale blue eyes met hers. A knowing, albeit fairly arrogant smile graced his too talented lips.

Despite the fact she was half gone within the aftershocks of bliss, Caitlin was sharply aware of the fact that Ferchar no longer wore clothes. His muscles rippled down from wide shoulders and his rock hard stomach led to a startlingly impressive erection. She'd never seen a better specimen of a man.

Before he could make another move, she very lightly scraped her nails down the front of his chest. His mouth fell open. His pupil's flared. She ran the pads of her hands over his hips and brushed his arousal just enough to tease.

His guard was down.

She took his face into her hands and brought his lips back to hers. His body shivered as she guided him. Took his mouth and made it hers. She traced the contours of his high cheekbones and then pulled back.

Abandoning what he most wanted touched, she ran her thumb over his lower lip and then leaned forward. Slowly, inch-by-inch she sampled first his lips, then his jaw line until she ran her mouth over his shoulder blade. She adored the salty, sweet taste of his skin.

"Caitlin," Ferchar growled and brought her body against the moss cushioned rock. He ripped back control and lifted her further up the stone until he had her pinned against it. The moss beneath her warmed and vibrated. Drips increased from overhead, bathing her skin in moisture. His hands again gripped her backside, kneading the firm globes.

He had her laid out well for his inspection. *I've never felt so sensual or desired in my life.* Reaching her hands over her head, Caitlin stretched languidly like a kitten beneath a warm sun. She watched him watch her from behind her eyelashes. Primal arousal flared in his eyes and she swore she saw them glow.

Caitlin slowly moved, allowing his shaft to graze her soft center. Suddenly she felt eager. Impatient. Her sensitive skin prickled with a fine layer of electricity. What was he doing to her? Her body nearly exploded when he rubbed against her. Ripples of pleasure seized her and she grabbed his arms.

Her head fell back. Somehow she'd swiftly gone from the seductress to the seduced. Her body burned to such a degree she almost feared what it'd feel like if he penetrated her. "I can't," she whispered almost urgently.

His laugh sounded low and ruthless. "Aye, but you will."

And she did.

Helpless to stop him, Caitlin braced herself as Ferchar slowly began to push forward. Too much. Too big. Yet somehow he continued penetrating her inch by almost painful inch until pleasure started to rush in. With a low groan she didn't recognize as hers, Caitlin bit her lip.

"Bloody hell, lass." He slid back to his knees and took her with him. Fully impaled, she felt his strong arms wrap around her. "What are you doing to me?" He whispered.

Caitlin heard his words from far away. She was losing herself. With every fiber of her being she knew it to be the truth.

When Ferchar laid her in the grass one reality ended and another began. Renewed strength drove him forward. He kissed and touched her with a fevered pitch— his hands everywhere.

Everything snapped shut until there was only him.

Moving in deep, even thrusts he began to plunge slowly at first. With sharp little cries of need she lifted her legs and wrapped them around his waist. She gasped when he moved even deeper, his pace increasing. Caitlin reveled in the spider web shivers that'd already started to thread through her body.

Her eyes rolled back in her head. For a moment he stood within her mind, tall and overwhelming. Though his body was slick with sweat his mind was dry, searing heat.

Then, for a flicker of a second, she could see them entwined high on the cliff over a raging sea. His hard, dark body wrapped with her ivory form.

The vision swirled into a burst of color as he took her higher. Deep purple mist encased them and became his fingers on her skin, probing and thorough.

"Let go." His order was husky and demanding. Empowering.

She opened her eyes, locked on the fire swirling in his eyes and met him thrust for thrust. Blow for blow. His muscles strained. Sweat slicked his body. She struggled for air as a shattering orgasm tore through her.

His cry of ecstasy mixed with hers as he throbbed deep inside. Their bodies shook as pure rapture engulfed. Consumed. Brought them to a place unknown to either.

Nothing could have prepared her for this. And there seemed to be no end in sight.

****

Twilight crept through the waterfall and flooded the cave with dim light.

Ferchar sat on the moss-covered stone and watched her sleep. Translucent and radiant, her soft skin was flushed and pristine. She lay on her side, head cushioned on one arm. Her thick black lashes curved against her cheek. She struck him as an elemental. There was earth, air, water and fire, and then there was Caitlin.

He was an impetuous fool.

Magic existed within her. He knew that. Why had he let it come this far? Because he had not expected it to be so strong perhaps? The fact that she was his equivalent didn't bother him so much. No, that would be too easy. It was something far more mediocre. Something he was ashamed to face.

Jealousy.

The worst kind of evil. 'Twas a mortal emotion that brought nothing but trouble. He thought himself above it, or at least in control of it. When Adlin had released his clansmen on their easy prey yesterday, something in Ferchar had bellowed in rage. All he could envision was her body writhing in ecstasy beneath another man. He should have just let her be...subjected her to the throes of Alan or Arthur.

He should have. What had happened between them was irreversible. They'd soared to a level of passion he knew no other lass would ever be capable of provoking. She'd felt so bloody good, a sensual siren in his arms.

Caitlin's eyelashes fluttered and her eyes opened. She merely watched him for several moments before she murmured, "Don't you sleep?"

"Why bother, the morn is here."

Her eyes stayed on him. "So? We've been up all night."

"I dinnae sleep when the sun is up, lass." He wanted to go to her but knew if he did the day would pass, the eve, mayhap many, before they left this place.

She sat up and looked down. "I see that I'm dressed."

Regrettably. "Aye."

"I take it you're opposed to morning sex." A slow smile crept over her face.

Gods, she was blatant. She had no idea how many times he'd taken her again in his mind since they'd stopped. "Are you not fully satisfied, lass?"

She blushed. He liked that. "What do you think?"

He disregarded the urge to get up and pace. Looking at her sitting there all rumpled from their lovemaking was distracting. "We must return."

"Must we?" One side of her lips inched up.

He jumped from the rock and held down a hand to her. "Aye."

She frowned and took his hand. "Are you so eager to be rid of me?"

It was less of a question and more of a statement. As such, he gave her no response. They passed beneath the waterfall and made their way along the path back to the forest.

"How do I get home?"

His heart stopped. Of all the things he thought she would say after spending the night in his arms, this was not it. "I dinnae know."

She turned toward the river and he followed. "That surprises me."

"Why?"

"You visited me in the twenty-first century and we both know it." She spun back. "By the way, you were a real jerk."

He stood over her and held back a smile. "You'll not get an apology from me. I knew you were near

William. How was I to know that you meant him no harm?"

Her eyes narrowed as they searched his. "You are a liar." She turned away and continued toward the river.

"You have no idea what you're talking about," he said.

Caitlin stopped and eyed the water. "Yes, I do. It stands to reason that you pushed yourself right into my mind and saw the truth of things."

She flipped her hair over her shoulder and pinned him with that golden gaze. "Don't try to tell me otherwise, I felt you." Her words turned soft and capable. "Just like I did last night."

Caitlin began to remove her dress still facing him.

"What are you doing?" He refused to look below her jaw line.

Inch by inch, she pulled the fabric down her body. "What any woman should do after doing what we did all night. Bathe."

His breath hitched when she revealed her body. Denying himself the simple pleasure of watching her suddenly seemed preposterous. Self-control was second nature to him.

Until she had come.

He would do well to remember that. "I cannae fault your logic."

"Join me." Her lips curved into a sensual smile.

Fully disrobed, she turned and waded into the water.

Her arse was a masterpiece. He leaned against a tree and relished the moment. Her body brought back the eve they spent together. The way she responded to him and he to her. To join Caitlin now would be the end of him.

"Nay, lass. I swam earlier while you slept."

Her voice carried over the waterfall as she dipped under the water and then broke free. "This is..." She flung her head back. "Amazing."

To look away was impossible. Her hair was slicked back and wet, her breasts high and full. He drifted forward, hypnotized. "'Tis a good spot."

She laughed, the sound tugging him closer.

"I read about it but never thought it would be like this." She leaned back into the water.

Read about this? "You have read about what it feels like to bathe in a highland stream?" His feet were at the river's edge now.

Caitlin's expression changed, became apprehensive. "Yes. We have history books."

She lifted out of the water and walked in his direction. Ferchar didn't move. "Aye, so you are interested in Scottish history?"

"All history." She wrung the water from her hair.

"Now you lie," he said, memorizing every dimension of her lush body. What wasn't she telling him? He could crawl into her mind now and find his answer but he abhorred the magical intrusion that was one of his gifts. When they made love it'd been impossible to avoid. She had taken him against his will.

Caitlin walked within inches of him, teasing Ferchar with her scent. "Believe what you will."

He turned and watched her dress. It was a shame to see all of that flesh covered. "What aren't you telling me, lass?"

Caitlin headed into the forest alongside him and disregarded his question. "What's going to happen to Shane and I? We don't belong here. We need to get home."

"I have no answer for you. I traveled to your century merely as a phantom through a ripple in time." He matched her pace, which was casual.

"A ripple in time," she repeated. "Like a vortex?"

The woods were quiet and attentive. "You've been talking to Arianna?"

Caitlin stopped at the base of a pine and picked up a small stone. "Yeah, Arianna. She'd mentioned that the rock back home had a vortex and she traveled back and forth at that location."

Ferchar contemplated her words. "Aye, some stones can do such a thing. There are many of them in Scotland."

She rubbed the rock in her hand. "Good. Is it possible that if Shane and I travel to one of those stones, we can get back to New Hampshire?"

New Hampshire. The word sounded strange on his tongue. "'Tis plausible."

Her eyes brightened. "I think I'll talk to Adlin."

He shook his head and stopped. "Dinnae do that."

Caitlin turned to him. "Why not? He's a wizard, right?"

Ferchar searched her face. "Aye, he is. And it strikes me you're very comfortable with that fact. Too comfortable. Again, I ask you Caitlin, what aren't you telling me?"

She resumed walking. "Nothing. Don't you trust anyone?"

"No."

"That's a shame. Maybe if you started trusting, you could form a solid relationship with a woman."

Ferchar seized her arm and pulled her back. "You're too bold by half. When I find the lass that I want to be with, trust will be one of many traits that I favor."

She yanked away her arm. "I say what I think, would you prefer I didn't?"

"I'd prefer you focus your attentions on finding a way home." He watched her flinch with grim satisfaction.

"Hence, Adlin." She whipped the rock into the forest. "It only makes sense to seek his guidance."

She was trying to goad him. So be it. "You might be right. If anyone can get you there, he can."

"Reverse psychology doesn't become you, Ferchar. Give it another try." She laughed in his face.

Reverse psychology? Her strange way with words was starting to grow on him. He wondered if she realized that the magic within her was softening her strange accent and transforming it one hour at a time. "I only wish to see you happy, Caitlin. If Adlin can get you home, you will be."

"You're really starting to get on my nerves." She stopped and came nose to chest with him, her eyes a well- utilized weapon. "You don't say what you mean, you use your fear of commitment as a knife of rejection against women and your arrogance is a bit much."

Where was this coming from? It didn't matter. His temper flared. He met her challenge. "Shall we cross swords, lass? I'm not half the lustful creature you have the potential to be, yet where I am honest with my opponents, you lead yours to slaughter. In addition, you're forthright to the point of being obnoxious."

Speechless, Caitlin's mouth dropped open and then snapped shut. "Get the hell away from me."

What had she expected? No woman spoke to him like she had. "Och, lass, are you truly that offended? What right was it of yours to speak to me as you did?"

She whipped around. He caught her hand inches before it struck his face but not the knee that drove into his groin. Ferchar drew forth his magic to soothe imminent pain and drove her back against a thin birch.

He pulled her hands around the back of the tree and tied them there with bonding magic. Stepping away, he breathed deeply and willed away the intense rage flowing in his veins. "You go too far."

She stood straight and proud. "As do you." She cocked her head. "What gives me the right to speak to you as I did is the fact that you had sex with me. Where I'm from that gives a woman the right to say what she feels. No, you know what? Where I'm from, women say what they feel to a man whether they've had sex or not."

Composure under control, he walked back over to her. He said nothing at first but let her feel the contempt he pushed her way. "I am not from your time and find I'm grateful for that. Women are less trying here."

"Do you like that, Ferchar. Really like that?" Her eyes were leaden and deceptive.

"Very much so." He kept his hands at his side.

"I think." She ran her eyes down his front. "That less trying is not the description you were looking for. Perhaps submissive is more accurate."

What kind of game was she playing? Time to shock her. "So be it. I enjoy lasses for what they are, lasses. Beneath me, against me, clasping me."

Her lips quirked and her calm tempted him. "I see. So women are good for one thing only, is that right?"

"No. You misunderstand. Lasses are good for two things-"

"Don't tell me," she interrupted him with a laugh. "Friends and lovers."

He brought his body up against hers, enjoying the firm globes of her clothed breasts pressed against his chest. "Aye, which do you prefer?"

For all he tried to keep up with this pointless banter, his body knew she was near and slowly licked at his intellect.

"I prefer both," she said and tightened her legs when he grasped them, fighting him.

He knew she felt it too. Her body vibrated and her skin glowed.

"I dinnae." He lifted her dress and forced her legs apart.

"You lie again," she whispered. Her lips parted in invitation. Sweet gods, she was beautiful. He swore he smelled her arousal. He cupped her face in his hands and rubbed the pads of his thumbs over her cheeks. "Do you want me to stop?" Why had he given her the option?

No. "Yes." Her eyes had glazed over.

"Which is it, Caitlin?" *Get out of my mind.*

"You tell me, Ferchar, that which I tell you from my mind or that which I tell you from my mouth?" Her tone was seductive, like soothing lava on his taut nerves.

His erection felt so heavy it nearly hurt. I want you. Now. He grabbed around her back with one arm and cupped the whole of her chin with his other as he spread her legs further and moved into her with one sharp, deep thrust. She gasped and her eyes widened.

Oh, sweet bliss.

"I dinnae play games," he whispered against her ear.

A wild wind whipped through the trees and rained pine needles over them. Her mind pressed against his and her heart thrummed heavily. Thump. Thump. Almost as hard as his own heart. He closed his eyes and ran his lips over her cheek until he found her lips. They were hot and eager against his.

He thrust harder. Once. Twice. On the third thrust her body went rigid and she screamed in pleasure. The sound was rapture to his ears as her body went where her mind was unwilling.

Panting, he brought his hands up and clutched the tree for support as he thrust one last time. An orgasm rushed through him so hard his knees almost buckled. Many near paralyzing minutes past before she spoke.

"You don't play fair." She breathed hard against his neck.

This lass was so different. A battle ram to the walls he'd built long ago. She need not know that though.

"I don't play, lass." He released his magical hold and caught her before she slid to the ground.

Caitlin steadied herself and met his eyes. For a flicker of a second he saw raw emotion in her eyes but it vanished. "Let's just leave good enough alone. It's obvious we're very different people. What we've shared so far is great sex. Let's leave it at that, okay?"

She turned away and smoothed her skirts and hair.

Ferchar rolled the sudden tension from his shoulders and walked to her side. She was right. It was better this way. "I'm sorry."

Caitlin introduced a quick chirp of laughter that died as fast it began. "Don't be. We had...fun?"

They resumed walking and Ferchar gave his answer to her closed off countenance. "Aye."

Neither said another word but walked toward the edge of the forest leading to the great field beyond. To the castle and clan that was his.

He wished he had more to give her.

But he did not.

Chapter Eleven

The glory of springtime in Scotland should've blinded her, but it didn't. The sun shone pink off of the castle and the loch sparkled sea-green. Tall, rounded clouds were in sharp contrast to the spiked mountains underfoot.

Regrettably, the memorable view wasn't able to push past her brooding thoughts. What did manage to penetrate her ridiculous stupor was the eruption of cheers that burst forth when they stepped onto the field. What time did these people wake up?

Dozens of clansmen and women cheered their arrival. The fires were gone and the wide expanse of grass stretched far and wide. "What's going on, Ferchar?"

He didn't meet her eyes but continued to stride forward. "We'll soon find out."

She didn't believe him. Thankfully, Shane was striding her way. The last time she'd seen the particular expression he wore was when he had told her, years earlier, that he had crashed her beloved Pontiac into a telephone poll. He was fine. The car was totaled.

"Caitlin." He cast a wary glance Ferchar's way. "We've got problems."

She was well aware of Ferchar's inquisitive ear. "And that is?"

"I've learned some new things this morning." He pulled her closer as they walked toward the sea of happy faces. "It seems I may have not had all the facts last night, at least not about this clan."

"What facts?" She hissed.

Again he glanced at Ferchar and spoke softly. "I can't believe you're coming out of the woods with him. He's the damn Chieftain for Christ's sake."

She reined in her temper. "What's your point, Shane?"

"His point," Ferchar said and grabbed her hand. "Is that our clan takes Beltane more seriously than others."

Shane shook his head and kept his mouth shut.

She stopped dead, halting both Ferchar and Shane. "How seriously?"

Neither said a word as Adlin broke from the nearby crowd and approached them with a wide smile. "Good morn to ye, lass."

Caitlin looked from Shane to Ferchar and then to Adlin. The wizard's face was the only one that held any inkling of humor.

"Good morning, Adlin. I'm surprised to see so many of you here to greet me."

He appeared sympathetic at best. "No doubt you are." His blue gaze swung to Ferchar and one eyebrow shifted up a fraction. Mirth was evident in his resolve. "Of course, you didnae tell her. Afraid she might dart away?"

Ferchar's face turned hard. "If that was the case, I would have never sought her to begin with."

Adlin snorted. "So you say."

The wizard took her hand and urged her forward. "Come, come lass. The clan is eager."

Caitlin let him lead her forward. She had a bad taste in her mouth. Ferchar strode alongside, head held high, haughty as ever.

Emma was there, as well as Helen, Arianna and Iain. Alan and Arthur were nowhere to be found. Iain was grim and Arianna aggravated as she shot a frown at Ferchar.

It was Helen's countenance that disturbed her the most. The woman's eyes were red-rimmed and her small frame looked ready to topple over in the light wind.

"I believe everyone has arrived that needs to be here," Adlin said and turned back to Caitlin and Ferchar. "And we have the pleasure of our laird joining in the celebration this year."

The clan's folk seemed thrilled and many men clasped Ferchar on the shoulder in welcome.

"What celebration?" Caitlin looked at Ferchar. His features were emotionless, his eyes a fathomless hue of evasiveness.

Adlin answered and swung to the whole of at least thirty couples. "'Tis the morn of the handfast, as you all knew." His gaze stole Ferchar's. "In this clan, to seek the women in the woods on the eve of Beltane invokes the handfasting."

A ripple of warning drove her spine straight. Handfasting? That sounded awfully familiar. She looked Shane's way and he offered an almost indiscernible shrug. His lips compressed and his eyes shifted from her to Ferchar. She looked down at the dress she wore. The dress that Emma had so painstakingly convinced her to wear. Oh no.

Adlin handed a scrap of the MacLomain plaid to Ferchar.

"Would someone care to enlighten me?" Caitlin asked. Ferchar clasped her wrist and began wrapping the cloth around it.

"What are you doing?" She tried to pull her arm away but Ferchar already had the other half of the material wrapped around his, locking them together. He said nothing but did not evade her eyes. His black hair shone in the sunlight and his brilliant blue eyes ignited.

Adlin diminished any hope she had of a response when his voice cut the air with sharp, precise, binding words. Power radiated from him in waves of warmth and absolution. "The sun greets you over Scotland's green and bids you the bond of the ancient gods."

Using the tip of his staff, he sprung forth from the earth a pentacle of long stemmed white roses that encompassed everyone. Their buds remained closed and patient.

"The Gods offer you and yours the protection of the old ways. From a time when the church lived and billowed within the trees and the angels thrived within the bed of the land underfoot. They give you opportunity and welcome thee into their breast for one year and one day. As such, the bond between you and yours is sacred. Old and powerful yet new and fragile. I give you my blessing as well, the children of my clan, may all that is natural spring forth from within you."

"You are handfasted," Adlin pronounced and smiled.

The rosebuds unfurled and thickened the air with sweet musk.

"We're what?" Caitlin echoed. She looked around from her own self-induced fog to find all of the other couples with their wrists tied together kissing and smiling.

Ferchar didn't move. "Handfasted, lass."

She hissed through her teeth. "Would you care to elaborate?"

One eyebrow shot up and he began untying the scrap of material. "Were you not listening?"

She yanked her arm free. Sarcasm was all she had to give the swine. "I was and it sounded like we were just sucked into some sort of agreement with each other. Forced is more like it."

Caitlin turned to Adlin and held her hand up like a child in a classroom. "Excuse me? Not undermining your custom or anything but I'd like to formally request a pardon due to the fact that I was duped."

"Damn woman," Ferchar said and grabbed her hand. He pulled her after him toward the drawbridge.

Caitlin fought him every inch of the way. "Release me!"

He said nothing to her numerous demands but continued to draw her after him into the great chamber where a fire burned again. When she fought him at the stairs he lifted her into his arms and continued on, past the second floor and past the third up a narrow, winding staircase.

At last, he set her down, shut the door behind him and spoke. "Have at it, lass."

They were in a small chamber without any furnishings. Only a single window rounded on the top and flat on the bottom relieved the lifeless room. Damn man. "Why did you bring me all the way up here?"

"Because I am the laird of this clan and you..." He pointed a finger at her. "Are loud."

Caitlin pulled back. "Can you blame me at this moment? I was completely swindled. What were you thinking? I don't want to be *handfasted* to you or anyone else for that matter. What does this mean exactly?" She breathed heavily from her nostrils. "It better not mean marriage. If it does, I want a divorce. Immediately."

He pulled himself into a sitting position on the window ledge. "Marriage is too strong of a word and even if such was the case, divorce would not be an option."

"Why did you do it, Ferchar? Why did you chase me down last night, knowing the result?" Caitlin leaned back against the wall, shaken.

His legs were spread and the muscles in his arms pressed heavily against his flesh as he leaned back and looked up at nothing. "Because I was thinking with my body and not with my mind."

Wrong answer. "Oh, my fool of a Chieftain, that is the oldest excuse in the book. Regrettably, I don't believe you. That would be too easy. No, everything you do is methodical and calculated. Now, my question is, where do I fit into whatever scheme you've surmised?"

His head slowly dropped forward until his flippant gaze settled on her. A wisp of a chuckle settled in his chest. "I dinnae want to marry. You just allowed me another year of blissful freedom."

Caitlin was careful to keep her emotions from her face. Damn, was she furious. "It's that simple?" She pushed off the wall and casually made her way in his direction. "No strings attached?"

A relaxed, heart-stopping smile brought his eyes to her chest. "Nay. 'Twas just a formality in the eyes of gods that no longer exist. A Beltane game, if you will."

She leaned against the wall beside him. "Then, tell me, why have you not handfasted before? Chosen sooner to dwell in your own private cage of safety?"

He leaned forward and sifted his hand through the strands of hair that fell over her shoulder. "Ah, that would be because of Alan. He seeks me out to marry his sister and I'm not ready."

A small shudder ran through her and his eyes met hers. Amusement danced in their depths. Just as Emma had said, Alan's sister. So many thoughts bubbled beneath the surface and Caitlin wasn't sure how to proceed. She lowered her eyes and contemplated her next move.

"I won't be here to play the part," Caitlin said.

"So you hope."

Destiny's Denial

She fingered the edge of his plaid. The fabric was rough beneath her fingertips. "So I hope."

His thigh tightened where her fingertip skimmed the edge of the material and touched his skin. "'Tis not such a burden being handfasted to the Chieftain. You will be highly respected," he assured.

She placed her hand on his thigh now and slowly ran it upward beneath the kilt. His eyes drifted down to her hand. "Burden? I would expect not." She pushed up further.

"Respect, not such a bad thing," Caitlin murmured. Salty, loch-driven air blew into the chamber and pushed back her hair. A vine wrapped around the ledge of the window and crept along the wall.

"And other privileges as well," he said softly and ran his hand up her arm.

She ignored the swell of sensation that crawled down to her belly. Ignored the fact she was more than ready for him to be inside her again. "Privileges are good."

Ferchar's breathing stopped when her hand found him, alive and pulsing beneath his plaid. She ran her finger ever so slowly along its steely length, knew that his restraint was pulled taut. The perfect planes of his face had gone rigid and unbendable. His lips parted and his eyes burned a frigid sapphire.

"Whenever you require them—privileges that is." A deep growl escaped him as he allowed her hand to wander.

She pulled back her hand suddenly and smiled. "I appreciate your generosity but find that the obvious relief of burden being handfasted to a Chieftain and the respect due me for such a position will be more than enough. You can take your privileges and shove them up your—"

Such a shame, she thought. Caitlin had managed to make it to the door and had to slam it shut in his face before she finished her sentence.

At least she had the hellish look on his face when he nearly caught her at the threshold, to give Caitlin even a fraction of the revenge she sought.

That would have to be enough for now.

****

Arianna and Iain stood on the wall walk together, hand and hand. Ominous clouds rolled in from the west and rallied the mountains to loom dark. In their own world, where more than a decade had passed in a moment, Scotland bore a stake of change through their hearts. He wrapped his arm around her waist and pulled her close. She rested her head on his chest.

"I did not tell Ferchar about the book that Caitlin read. That she knows our story and his part in it. How talented and inquisitive Beth must have been to glean so much. Having said that, the level of inquisition Aunt Marie must have withstood is...admirable," Arianna said.

Iain stroked her hair. "'Tis good you told Ferchar nothing. If you had it may have altered fate."

"I know." Arianna looked up at him. "It's so strange, everyone being older. I feel misplaced."

He cupped her face. "We are together. That is your place."

Her eyes stayed with his. "I know, and for that I'm eternally grateful. Do you not feel a loss of footing somehow? Mere days ago you ruled this land."

"We will take each day as it comes to us." He leaned down and kissed her. Tender. Soft.

Many minutes later they pulled away from each other. Arianna became speculative. "You hide something."

He stood beside her and watched his homeland swagger in the wind. "Luv, there are so many things that can only be told to you with time. 'Tis not my right nor my place to tell you all of the things I know."

Iain smiled. "I will teach you magic and year by year, show you everything in my mind. This is my promise to you."

Arianna breathed deeply. "I worry about Caitlin. She's much different than me but a match for that nephew of yours. He's so different than you. So different than the lad we left behind."

Iain's eyes were shuttered. "He is still of the mind that life shapes him, not the other way around. In time, he will learn the truth."

"Are you sure?"

"No. But I hope. He has led a very unique life thus far. If he can peel away the layers of bitterness, he will." Iain ceased talking and turned his head to the north. His emerald eyes turned nearly black and his stance became defensive.

"Iain?" She touched his arm and felt the darkness. Trouble.

A lone horseman broke free from the distant forest. Within moments, four more horsemen followed. The clouds overhead rolled and spit cool rain into the wind. The loch retreated into a gray shadow and the mountains puffed their massive chests in defiance.

Iain's jaw hardened before he turned away. He took her hand. "Come."

A warning of change crawled through her soul and Arianna shivered against the twists that ruled her very existence.

Would their life ever be normal?

****

Ferchar stood before the fire in the great chamber and waited. He sipped his ale, his eyes never leaving the door. Details sharpened.

Emma sat at the trestle table nearby flirting with her boyfriend. Shane avidly watched Catherine stitch a tapestry to his right. Sixty-four torches burned, three had snuffed out. Nine warriors drank whiskey five tables down. Three maidens crowed over a baby seven tables down. One mouse scratched away in the far corner.

The door whipped open and wind driven rain ushered in a stranger, followed by four MacLomain clansmen. His gaze latched onto Ferchar and he strode forward. The Chieftain put one hand up and halted not only his four clansmen but also the nine off to his left.

"Where is she, MacLomain?" The Scotsman came before him. He had no need of weapons. His plaid of yellow and green wrapped over his wide shoulders and he stood, legs apart. Magic swamped his aura and shoved at Ferchar.

"She's here, as you know. Your lack of manners astounds me, Ewan." He lifted his ale and drank.

"Manners will be implemented when such is shown to me," Ewan said.

Ferchar lifted an eyebrow. "Such impatience." He motioned to a servant.

Ewan surveyed his surroundings and received a mug of ale from the servant. "Why haven't you brought her to me yet?"

"Why bother when you traveled with such a magically enhanced pace to me?" he said. The silence of the chamber was deafening.

"Where is she?" Ewan surveyed the hall and frowned. "I want to see her."

Adlin appeared behind the man, his robes silent against the animal fur underfoot. "Ewan MacLeod, I expected you sooner."

The wizard passed him by and stood between Ferchar and the clansman.

"I should not have had to come at all." Ewan's stormy gray eyes narrowed on Adlin.

Adlin clasped his hands over his robes. "But you did. Did you not think we would honor an old pact?"

Ferchar kept his contempt deep inside. "The MacLomains stay true to their promises. Our apologies for the delay."

Ewan's eyes turned silver as they tried to cut through him. "I want to see her, now."

A wry chuckle shifted Adlin's shoulders. "Eager, are we?"

"Now." Ewan spit the word.

Adlin shrugged and looked up. "Iain, go get the girl."

Ferchar knew his uncle had stood on the balcony above all along, waiting for the inevitable. Villains, the lot of them. Hatred seared his soul. If he could wrap one hand around Adlin's throat and one around Iain's, their end would be upon them. He would pour every bit of power into crushing them both for what they were about to do.

Ewan's shrewd eyes swam overhead until they caught what they wanted. His muscles locked and a slow smile slithered over his face. Knowing eyes fell back to Ferchar.

"Muriel?"

The feminine inquiry teased him. Such Innocence. Ignorance. A lamb being led to slaughter.

"Aye, we have a visitor," his aunt said as she led Caitlin down the stairs.

Adlin stepped forward. "Caitlin, I would like you to meet Chieftain MacLeod. He travels here from the northern most tip of Scotland. The crux of the highlands."

Caitlin walked forward, her eyes avoiding Ferchar. "Hello."

Ewan licked his lips and nodded his head slightly. "Greetings, lass. I have looked forward to meeting you for some time."

"Really?" Caitlin smiled. "For some time?"

"Aye." The MacLeod laird made a bold appraisal of her.

Ferchar didn't move. He'd already dismembered the man a million different ways since Caitlin had appeared. "Would you like something to drink, Caitlin?"

She still refused to look his way though he had spoken to her. "No."

Muriel forced a mug into her hand. "Just in case."

Caitlin took the mug, her expression guarded. "Thanks."

Ewan emptied the contents of his mug. "We leave in the morn. I will await her at your border."

He drank in one last appreciative eyeful of Caitlin, turned and left the hall. Ferchar was well aware of the fifty MacLeod clansmen camped at the Northeastern tip of his land.

"That went well, I think," Adlin said as the door slammed shut.

Iain and Arianna stood at the bottom of the stairs, morose. Muriel, Emma and Catherine glared at the wizard. His mother, who had arrived in time to catch the interplay, burst into tears and ran upstairs. What had happened to his happy, carefree mother? He knew too well and pushed regret aside.

Caitlin obviously saw everyone's reaction and was naturally curious. "Who is he waiting for at the border?"

Emma made to stand but sat back down. Arianna stepped forward but Iain caught her arm. Catherine and Muriel both opened their mouths but nothing came out. Adlin, of all things, appeared tongue-tied.

Ferchar inwardly cursed the gods and spoke. "You."

"Caitlin?" Shane shot to his feet.

"Why me?" A flicker of alarm crossed her face.

Adlin took her arm and led her to the fire. "Please sit. We need to talk."

He turned back to the people in the hall. "Iain, Arianna, Shane and Ferchar stay. Everyone else must leave."

The hall was empty in under a minute. Shane moved to Caitlin's side. Ferchar stayed where he was. Arianna and Iain sat down before the fire. Adlin's eyes narrowed on Ferchar as the wizard sat down beside Caitlin.

"What's going on, Adlin?" Caitlin said. Her calm voice did not deceive Ferchar.

The wizard was silent for a moment while he studied her. "A long time ago a young, beautiful woman found herself in a most unusual situation; trapped in a land so different from her own and within the thrall of a highland clan. The clan's folk were kind to her and welcomed her though she was foreign indeed. The laird of the clan wanted her for his own but she would not have it."

Caitlin glanced briefly at Arianna. "Obviously, you're not talking about Arianna though the story sounds similar."

Adlin's small smile was rueful. "No, not Arianna. You see this woman's tale did not end as happily, at least not in the sense that theirs did."

Ferchar bit back a curse as Adlin continued.

"This woman did not love the clan's laird. She fell in love with a visiting Chieftain from another clan. This made for an uncomfortable situation. Well..." A mournful sound escaped Adlin. "A horrible situation, really."

Iain interjected. "The visiting Chieftain, who also fell in love with her, would not allow the woman to be married to a man she did not love. A man who would marry yet keep multiple mistresses to pleasure himself."

Caitlin frowned. "But what does any of this have to do with me?"

Adlin sighed and the firelight swamped his sunken eyes. It seemed for a moment his magic had abandoned him and left in its wake a sad, lonely old man. "The visiting clansman did not want to go to war, to spill so much innocent blood, simply to assuage his own desires. There was no doubt there would be a massive clan war over this woman because the laird that wanted to make her his wife was a righteous, warring man, as most men were then. Still are."

Caitlin looked horrified. "So did the visiting Chieftain leave her to her demise?"

"No," Adlin said, sadness enveloping him. "He made a terrible bargain. He promised unending support of his clan in all future wars and all of the land he had so recently obtained south of this clan's border."

"That doesn't seem so bad," Caitlin said, compassion edged her response.

Adlin took her hand in his. "And the visiting Chieftain's release of this woman back to whence she had come, their love to be no more, as well as a woman of her bloodline to a man of his."

Confused, Caitlin bit the corner of her lip. "I don't understand what you're getting at."

Ferchar wanted to interject. Throw her over his shoulder and take her away from the idiocy of what Adlin was about to say.

The wizard straightened. "The pact was never supposed to be. A woman of her bloodline was never supposed to be available, period."

"Available?" Caitlin shifted, her expression cautious.

Ferchar's frustration peaked. "You, lass. You."

She gasped, her gaze shifted to his. "Me? I'm of this woman's bloodline?"

"Aye," Adlin said and shook his head. "And Ewan MacLeod is the descendant of theirs."

"But what about Arianna? How has she escaped this inevitable pact?" Caitlin stood and moved closer to Shane.

Adlin stood as well. "Because, Arianna's bloodline led to this woman's birth whereas your blood is a result of this woman's birth. The dynamics are different."

Caitlin took a deep gulp from her mug. "You do talk in circles, don't you?"

Both Ferchar and Iain made inaudible sounds of agreement.

She raised a hand to stop Adlin from speaking. "So this woman, relative, was born sometime between Arianna's time and mine?"

"Exactly," Adlin said. "I did everything possible to ensure you didnae come here. I am so sorry."

"This explains, perhaps, why you have not sent us home yet?" Caitlin said softly.

Adlin merely nodded. "Aye, lass."

Caitlin touched his arm. "You could not control the pull of William to his homeland any more than I could've guessed that a stick would bring me back in time."

Adlin shifted his attention to Ferchar but spoke to Caitlin. "If we are to deal in truths, lass, neither William nor the wand brought you here."

Guilty rage bubbled beneath his skin as Ferchar met Caitlin's eyes—golden eyes that bore through him. "You?"

He had expected this of Adlin and was not surprised to have the blame handed him. Two could play at that game. "Aye, you were linked somehow with William. 'Twas easier to have you here, on my territory, then there. Before you give all your compassion to Adlin and your hatred to me, however, you may want to ask him who the visiting Chieftain was in the little tale he told you."

Caitlin turned back to Adlin but said nothing, waiting for him to reveal his truth.

Adlin was honest. "'Twas I, lass. I was that blackguard, with youth and arrogance at my disposal. And 'tis also I who will protect you, one way or another, to atone for my misdeeds."

Her face looked ready to crumble but held its ground. "I appreciate your honesty and as far as I can tell, it was just your young heart at work."

Ferchar braced himself when she swung back to him and issued one lethal word at a time. "What would truly make all of this cruel was if you knew about this before you yanked me here."

It was in that moment, through the accusation in her eyes, that Ferchar finally broke free from the man he'd become and saw the true damage losing William had wrought on his soul. The damaging length he had been willing to go to save his cousin. To bring him home to Muriel and restore her lost spirit. To give back to her what he felt he had somehow taken from her that day at the waterfall.

Though Adlin had made the pact, the wizard had fallen in love and vowed to protect the unknowing bloodline. Iain had but kept his secret.

It was Ferchar's place to deliver the final blow, to acknowledge his sins. To tell Caitlin that he was her ruin.

"Aye, I did."

She stayed that way, looking at him, for far too long. The accusation and regret in her eyes trailed a thick path into places within him he didn't know he possessed. The hall screamed with silence and the fire seemed silent with melancholy.

It was Shane who finally broke the tormented silence. "Well, he can't have her. What are you going to do about it?"

Ferchar met eyes that were so similar to Arianna's. "I'm going with her."

"No, she's not going. You're all nuts." Shane wrapped a protective arm around her shoulders.

"She must," Adlin said. "Or there will be a war unlike any other Scotland has seen in a very long time. I would not have it then and I will not have it now. Besides the MacLomain clan, the MacLeod clan is one of the most powerful in this country. They count a staggering amount of clans as their allies and every one will fight for them. I must think about this. As I do, she must go."

Shane pulled her closer. "I don't care if all of you zap me down with magic, you're not taking her."

Caitlin regained her wilted composure. "Adlin, can you get Shane home, back to twenty-first century New Hampshire? Can you, if I agree to this?"

Shane's eyes went wide. "What do mean, Caitlin? I'm not going anywhere without you!"

Her eyes stayed on Adlin.

"This time period is unpredictable and now it seems the clans may prove to be as well. I don't want him here if something bad happens. You're one to bargain and make pacts. Make one with me. If you get him home, I'll do what you want."

Ferchar watched the wizard with amusement. The lass had integrity. He was impressed with both her courage and her devotion. The laird also knew that her refusal to go with the MacLeod Chieftain would be futile regardless.

Adlin smiled and cocked his head. "You have a deal. This is something I can do."

Ferchar met Adlin's eyes.

It had been a long time since he'd looked at the man as anything more than a thorn in his side.

Mayhap it was time to change that.

Chapter Twelve

She liked the way Scotland looked at this hour.

The sun sat so low behind the distant mountains that a passive orange glow ignited their bases in muted fire. A half-moon dropped from the sky and tried to hook small, wispy clouds.

Caitlin's future was unpredictable, but not Shane's. At some point during the long night she'd conquered her fear. What choice did she have? Her emotions needed to stay tucked safely away if she was going to face this day with even an ounce of courage. Funny, just yesterday she was irate about being handfasted to Ferchar. Now, that appeared to be the least of her problems.

Wind blew in from the west and eased her discomfort. She couldn't change what was. Caitlin had to go forward and place her faith in Adlin.

"This is the hour my country tells us of the dreams she had the night before." His words were soft as he sat down in the grass beside her.

Caitlin traced the mountain peaks with a watchful eye and tried to ignore the masculine scent of him. "How poetic."

"It's true," Ferchar said.

She looked his way. His profile stood strong and steady against the living darkness of the loch beyond. "I don't know what to say to you, Ferchar. You've disappointed me."

His light blue eyes darkened when he looked at her. "I have disappointed myself as well. Please know that you were not my intended victim."

Caitlin studied his handsome face and sought signs of insincerity. She found none. As though the moment deemed it necessary, she was back at that waterfall. Diving into the water after him...surfacing and searching. Drowning in the pain that had haunted them both for so long...

"Is that your way of apologizing?" she asked.

He didn't look away. "Aye, 'tis just that, lass. I am sorry. I should have never pulled you here. 'Twas wrong on so many levels and I have only just realized that."

She said nothing, so he continued. "I dinnae expect your forgiveness. What I am guilty of cannot be undone and the wrong of it 'twill be with me always."

He may be gorgeous and an incredible lover but Caitlin doubted she would ever be able to voice forgiveness. Even knowing as she did the pain he felt at the waterfall. To use an innocent, unknowing woman from another time to achieve his goal was impossible for her to grasp.

"I think it's better if we just let things lie as they are. Your being sorry for what you've done isn't going to change what I've got to face today." She picked a blade of grass. "I noticed last night that nothing was mentioned about the fact that you and I are handfasted."

He looked to the mountains. "Ewan MacLeod cannae know about that."

"So the whole custom really is just a farce?" Caitlin said.

"It depends on who you're asking. If you asked someone who still truly believes in the old gods, aye, 'tis blasphemy to marry within a year and a day."

"Do you believe in the old gods?" She twisted the grass between two fingers and kept her eyes from him.

"What I believe doesnae matter. A pact has been made."

Something uncurled in her belly and she swung her eyes to his face. "I would think if you didn't believe, you would've just said so. Are you pagan or Christian? Who were you devoted to when you went into the forest after me on Beltane?"

He took the tormented blade of grass from her fingers and held it in his palm. Chills ran through her when the blade returned to its original form and glowed a soft, healthy green against his skin.

His voice was guttural and male as he lowered the blade back to the earth. He released it and the grass stood upright in the air. Slowly, it lowered itself until it took root in the soil. "I am pagan."

She couldn't take her eyes off the replanted grass. "You don't believe in God?"

A shadow of wisdom softened his features. "I didnae say that. I do believe in God, just not in the sense that Christians do. For me, he cannae be found in a church or bible, but in nature and her many facets. In the wind as it turns the sun within the leaves of a tree; in the water churning with emotion and everything born of the Earth."

He took her hand, palm down and ran it over the blade he'd just magically replanted. "Do you feel that?"

She turned her attention from the feel of his hand on hers to the grass. It was warm and alive, pulsing with energy. Caitlin was enthralled. If she ever made it home she wasn't going to be able to look at a lawnmower the same way again.

"They like pruning, and sound," he said.

She pulled back her hand. "How often do you read my mind, Ferchar?"

He remained expressionless. "Never, if I can help it. With you, when magic is implemented, 'tis impossible not to."

"Why?" she said.

Ferchar went to touch her cheek but she pulled away. "Because our magic is so alike that we become one."

I have magic? She found that it didn't really surprise her that much. Not after all she'd learned about Arianna. "I don't want to talk about magic and I certainly don't want to learn how to use it. It has no place where I come from."

He looked skeptical. "I dinnae believe I've ever met anyone who discovered that they possess magic yet have no desire to learn more about it. You are very unusual, lass."

"I try my best," she responded.

He laughed. "And you're very good at it."

"You don't laugh much, it's a good sound."

As if caught in his own folly, Ferchar's expression clouded over. "I know that we all discussed what today would be like for you, but I'm worried, Caitlin."

Her name on his lips flowed like wine in her veins. "Don't be. I'm a big girl."

"You are very brave in this venture but 'tis important to me that you ken the kind of man Ewan MacLeod is," he said.

"Yeah, he's the kind of man that's going to try to sleep with me as soon as I step across your border." Caitlin kept her tone light.

"Aye, he is." Tension brought Ferchar forward so that he rested his elbows on his knees.

"Adlin said that part of the pact included a legitimate marriage in front of the whole of his clan before he could," Caitlin said.

Ferchar visibly bristled. "So we must hope the man is honorable."

She pushed a false laugh through her teeth. "Well, if he isn't there's nothing we can do about it. I'll deal."

He grabbed her arm with too much force and she froze. "You won't deal. You've already sacrificed enough because of me."

On impulse, she covered the hand strangling her arm with her hand in reassurance. "He'll honor the pact."

His eyes glowed a soft, mesmerizing sapphire. "I'll be there. I won't let him hurt you."

"I know." She tore her gaze away. Why she trusted him after all he'd done she didn't know, but she did. The sky exploded with crimson and the moon vanished. "Do you really think he'll allow you to come?"

"He has no choice." Ferchar's face was cast in a timeless bronze. "'Twill be war if he doesnae."

"I don't want that," she said, too aware that he hadn't removed his hand from her arm.

"You have no choice, lass. I got you into this and I'll see you safely through it."

She drank in the salty air and ignored her growing fear. "So Iain will lead the clan while you're gone?"

"Aye." Ferchar's expression grew distant. "'Tis his place."

She removed her hand and he released her arm. "Do you resent him that?"

He returned to her face. "Nay, lass. While I'm gone, the clan is his. When I return, 'tis not."

She smirked. "If all goes according to the plan Adlin has yet to formulate, I will not be returning with you. Your handfast mate will be no more and you'll be painfully available."

Ferchar shrugged. "I'll just have to suffice."

Oddly enough, Caitlin had hoped he would look crestfallen, disappointed. But, no, he looked, if anything, contemplative.

"No doubt you'll survive unwed as long as you wish it," she muttered.

"I should have told you about the handfasting. Again, I was wrong. I'm sorry." He rose to his feet and pulled her up with him.

"Don't sweat it. It's over. All of this will hopefully be over soon," she said.

He leaned in quick and kissed her cheek. "Just be careful."

Caitlin walked with him back toward the castle. Her cheek burned where his lips had been so briefly. After all the distress the man had caused her she still wished he had kissed her lips.

One last time.

****

"I won't do it." Shane stood on the shores of Loch Holy and glared at his sister.

Catherine touched his arm gently. "You have to Shane."

"No, I don't," he said.

"It was agreed last eve. 'Tis the only way." She reached up and pushed back a lock of hair from his forehead.

"How can everyone ask me to leave my sister in Medieval Scotland to be married to some unknown barbarian? It's ridiculous." He ground his jaw.

"Adlin will return her. There is no one more powerful than him. You have to believe me," Catherine said.

Shane looked down into her warm, brown eyes. He would miss her. How eager he'd been to chase her into the woods on Beltane only to discover that she didn't participate. Probably a good thing, considering. Walking out of the forest with Iain's sister the next morning would have undoubtedly resulted in the loss of his manhood.

"I feel like a coward leaving her here."

Destiny's Denial

"Nay, if anything you're a hero. As it stands now, her leaving with the MacLeod Chieftain prevents war. If you stayed, she wouldn't go." Catherine cupped his face with her delicate hands. "I will miss you, Shane." She stood on her toes and gave him a long, thorough kiss.

Warmth flooded him and he wrapped his arms around her. There were no women back home like Catherine. They were abrasive where she was gentle. She was a true lady with an inquisitive mind that matched his.

"I wish I could bring you with me." He whispered his heart into her rose scented hair.

She pulled back and wiped the tears from her eyes. "I know. Just remember me, that's all I ask. Have children and find a woman who loves words as much as we do. Maybe another author?"

Shane laughed. "Not likely."

"She's waiting for you. Go." She nodded toward Caitlin.

He kissed the back of her hand. "You're the closest I ever came to finding love, Catherine. Please take care of yourself."

She nodded and smiled as he turned away. He hadn't expected to feel so sad leaving her. He now knew exactly what he wanted in a woman.

Caitlin met him halfway and wrapped her arms around him. He held onto her with all his strength. What was he doing? Leaving her to deal with all of this on her own?

"I love you, bro. Stop being such a wuss." She pulled back. "You're not going to lose me."

"How the hell do you know?" Shane searched her face. "For all I know, I'll never see you again. I lost mom and dad. I don't want to lose you."

She stood up straighter and held her head high. "You're not going lose me, kid. Remember when we were little and made that pinky swear?"

His lip twitched. "Yeah, I remember. You made me promise I would never leave you, no matter what."

"That's right." She took her pinky and wrapped it around his. "Now I'm making the same vow. You won't lose me no matter what."

He pulled her close again. "Promise?"

"Promise." She took his hand. "Come on. It's time."

They walked in Adlin's direction. Caitlin had one last request. "Remember what I told you to tell Gram last night?"

"Yeah."

"Repeat it back to me," she said.

Shane rolled his eyes, but smiled. "I found a note on the table saying that you had to jet down to Virginia on short notice to help our cousin, Debbie, deal with a crisis."

"And what was the crisis?"

"You didn't say."

Caitlin nodded. "And why don't I have my cell phone?"

"That's a good question. You must've forgotten it because I found it on your bedside table." Shane frowned. "She's never going to buy that. You don't go anywhere except her house without your cell."

"That's where you improvise and do your best to convince her I must've been in a real rush." Caitlin winked.

Shane shook his head. "I'll do my best. I hope Adlin took care of Sean or else I'll be going home to a mess. God knows who will be searching for us."

Caitlin shrugged. "Adlin said he did. He said that Sean will only remember being asked to search out garden equipment in the barn, group them together and then head home. All memory of Gordon, also known as William, is wiped from not only Sean's memory but anyone else that knew him."

"That's amazing and very convenient for me," Shane replied.

They stopped before Adlin. Iain, Arianna and Ferchar were walking toward them.

"Are you ready, lad?" Adlin said.

Shane grimaced. "If it feels anything like it did getting here then no, I'm not."

Iain caught Shane's sentiment and spoke. "This is where I traveled forward to find Arianna. No doubt, 'tis uncomfortable but the feeling passes quickly."

"That's what I figured." Shane frowned. "I've done it before, I can do it again."

"This will bring you to Mystery Hill, Shane. Make sure when you get home that you take care of C.C.," Caitlin said and swallowed hard.

"I will." Shane hugged her again. "Are we sure about this?"

"We're sure. Remember the pinky swear?" Caitlin wiggled her pinky finger.

Shane turned to Adlin. "If you don't bring her home, I will hunt you down."

Ferchar laughed, stepped forward and clasped his arm in the way of the Scotsmen. "Good lad. But know this, if he doesnae get her home, I will."

Shane looked up at the man and became as serious as he was willing to when it came to a Chieftain with a battleaxe strapped to his back. "You better."

Arianna stepped forward and embraced him. "It was wonderful meeting you. When you get home, see if you can't locate an old family picture of Liam O'Donnell. You might be surprised."

He stepped back and grinned. "I'll do just that."

Adlin looked at Shane, his wise blue eyes crackling with magic. "Are you ready?"

Shane took one last look at Caitlin and then to Catherine. She was gone. "I suppose so."

The wizard urged him to follow and he did. The two walked slowly along the loch's shore. Adlin's white robes and hair billowed back in a sudden gust of wind. The choppy water swelled and a black cloudbank rolled forth from a pinpoint on the horizon.

"I will stay with you." Adlin's words were now distant and comforting though he stood right beside Shane. "Dinnae stop walking."

Shane wasn't about to dispute anything Adlin said as the cloud began to circle into a tornado. The funnel of clouds stayed attached to the sky but released from the water and swung toward them. Lightning crawled within and the wind increased.

Then it swallowed them and encased him in a massive storm. Adlin's white robes beckoned him through a haze of gray invisibility.

"Keep walking," Adlin said from very far away. Shane did.

A maelstrom of dark gray and black sucked him forward. Silence and thunder mated in vicious persuasion until he longed to cover his ears but could not. Still, Shane moved forward.

Then, as though a vacuum sucked him down, all footing was gone. The smell of melting sugar and smoke choked him and a deafening crash resounded. Instead of panic, he felt the wizard all around him. Reassuring. Calm.

Everything went black and Shane slammed into a state of sleep he'd never achieved in the mortal form. He dreamed about Scotland and Catherine. About the way she'd felt beneath him the night following Beltane's eve—her skin white and her soul delicate.

And then she was gone.

Slowly, he opened his eyes and saw oaks swaying in a warm breeze overhead. Shane's head throbbed for but a moment before it dissipated and left him whole.

He sat up and leaned against the monolith that'd been Arianna and Iain's at Mystery Hill. Adlin was gone and he was home. It all felt like a strange dream.

But it was not. Not any of it. His sister was still there. Shane laid his head in his hands and stayed that way for a very long time.

Would he ever see her again?

What struck him the most inappropriate was that he was not thinking that about Caitlin...

Chapter Thirteen

She wasn't going to cry. Not an option.

Caitlin turned away from her brother's transparent form on the horizon and strode away from the shoreline. Tears were now, officially, a pointless venture.

"Caitlin, wait, please." Arianna ran to catch up with her.

She didn't stop. "I have to get back to the castle and get ready."

Arianna strode alongside her but kept her distance. "I know how hard this is for you."

Caitlin stopped short and channeled her sadness into anger. "Do you? According to what I read, you were flung into the past, married against your will, had great sex and then conveniently got flung back home. All of this with a man who chased you down because he was in love with you. You didn't give up your brother and have to stay so that you could fulfill another person's obligation with nothing but rape and God knows what else on the horizon."

Arianna kept her posture submissive. "You're right. It was a tidy little package for me, wasn't it? What with being tormented by the same dream for ten years, shot in the shoulder with an arrow, thrust alone into the past, the near rape by the enemy clansman and having to give up my family forever."

Though she drew an admirable parallel. Caitlin was in no mood to affiliate. She continued walking. "I just need some time alone."

"Do you?" Arianna strode after her. "When I first came here I had no one to talk to that could possibly understand what I was going through, no one who even believed that I wasn't the pre-arranged lass meant to marry Iain from the distant shores of East Lothian. You do have someone to talk to. Please, Caitlin, talk to me."

Caitlin slowed her stride slightly. "Arianna, you're from the colonial period. That's a little different."

"How so?" Arianna caught up with her. "Because I don't speak with the same slang as you, though you try to mask it? Because the America I knew was less progressed? No, in light of the circumstances we have both experienced, I don't see as how we could be anything but devout allies. We're American after all. And even in your time that means we come from a young, though incredible country. Have you no pride in America?"

Caitlin chuckled. "You were born in Scotland, around about the time of the Highland Clearances, right?"

Arianna nodded, obviously unsure where Caitlin was going with this.

"Well, not to shock you, but I'm more of a mutt," Caitlin said.

"Mutt?"

"Yeah. I've got your Scottish blood in me but I've also got Irish, English, French and German bloodlines as well." Caitlin enjoyed the amazement that crossed Arianna's face.

"Really? That's wonderful. So many nationalities all in one person." Arianna nodded her head in confirmation. "That is America."

Oh please. Caitlin continued to walk. She wasn't in the mood to chat nationalities.

"What did you do back home?" Arianna asked. "I know you told me you served food to people for income, but what was your pastime, your passion?"

Caitlin walked slower as they crossed the field. Her pastime? Shopping, hanging out with her friends, reading, these were pastimes. She knew what Arianna was wondering about though. "Design."

"Design?"

"Yep, I liked to design both clothes and home interior," she said. "In fact, I sell my information through my website. I offer downloadable e-books. I have a lot of great ideas. Eventually, I intend to do both in home consultations as well as start my own clothing line."

Arianna appeared stumped but optimistic. "So you sew clothing?"

Caitlin smiled. "I can. That's not the crux of it though. Where I'm from my field is very competitive. My hope is that I obtain a financial position that allows me to have others do the sewing for me."

"You sound very passionate and independent, Caitlin. Not that I understood half of what you just said to me."

Arianna's expression shifted to one of concern and her line of inquisition changed. "I'm curious about your state of mind. Will you be all right?"

"I will and I'm sorry I snapped at you before. This hasn't been easy on you, either." Caitlin turned her face away and wished she could break down on this woman.

"I'll do what I have to do."

"Do you love, Ferchar?"

Caitlin almost choked. "No. Why?"

Arianna was blunt. "It would make your situation easier."

She was too curious. "How's that?"

"Well, to start with, it might make it easier to put up with your current endeavor."

Caitlin stopped again. "How would being gang heisted by another Chieftain prove to be any easier if I was in love with Ferchar?"

Arianna probed her eyes. "Honestly, I'm not sure. Perhaps a higher level of comfort in that he will be alongside you?"

Caitlin made another mental note that Arianna was from the colonial period. "No such luck. Where I'm from, it's inbred in women to be self-sufficient. We try our best not to rely on a man when we're in a tight spot. It doesn't pay."

"It doesn't pay?" Arianna looked confused.

Caitlin touched her arm. "In my time, chivalry is not a predominant factor with most men. Women are equal and having attained such a standing they had to forfeit many old fashioned values. Most men don't open the door for women anymore and you'd be hard pressed to find one that helps you on with your jacket. Women are just tougher, I guess."

Arianna cut right to the heart of the matter. "And do you like being tough, Caitlin?"

No. "Right now, yes. It's helping me through this."

"Ferchar will watch out for you," Arianna said.

"He doesn't need to. I'll watch out for myself."

Caitlin didn't wait for Arianna's response but whipped away to the castle. She was on her own now. Shane was gone and Scotland still had her. Well, technically, a MacLeod had her.

****

A hundred men were horsed and ready behind Ferchar when Caitlin made her way down the steps of the castle.

"I made these for you lassie," Euphemia said, her rotund figure carrying her in a steady pace toward

Caitlin. "It's my best of everything except fish and meat. They wouldnae hold well."

Caitlin received the two heavy satchels from the woman and attempted a smile. "I'm going to miss you."

Euphemia waved away the sentiment and scowled. "Ye shouldnae be leaving, ye just got here. But 'tis none of my business, no. If the laird says you have to go, you have to go. But then again, he says a goat isna a hindrance so maybe he's got a portion of his head up his arse."

"Euphemia, you're a wise woman, don't let anyone tell you different," Caitlin said.

The woman's wide cheeks spread into a grin. "Aye. I told Ferchar from the get go about you. That's a smart lassie, that one!"

"You just keep running that kitchen like you have been." Caitlin grinned. "And start taking inventory. There's a good chance you might discover why you're always coming up short a barrel or two on wine."

Euphemia's lips pursed and she narrowed her eyes. "You're not going to tell me what you know, are ye?"

"Not a chance, just start doing a nightly count and post a man to watch over things." Caitlin wasn't about to make an enemy out of herself with the other clansmen.

"Point taken, lassie. Point taken." Euphemia wrapped her up in a bear hug she thought would be the end of her before she shoved Caitlin on her way. "You keep an eye on my lad, Ferchar, you hear?"

Caitlin nodded and smiled over her shoulder.

William met her next. "Caitlin, I'm so sorry about all of this."

"I see you've lost your brogue for my farewell William, or is it Gordon?" Caitlin teased him and gave him a quick hug. "You're one of a kind kid."

A small, secretive smile played at the corner of his lips. "Well, I did spend three years in your time. It was an enlightening experience."

She shook her head and met his eyes. "I can only imagine."

"Take care Caitlin, you're in good hands." William nodded once, backed away and faded into the crowd.

Arianna met her outside the stables, her horse, Fyne, beside her. "I want you to ride her."

Caitlin was incredulous. "You can't be serious. This is your horse, Arianna. Your cherished friend."

"Please." Arianna stroked Fyne's forehead. "It would mean so much to me. She'll keep you safe."

"I can't guarantee her safe return," Caitlin said. Touched.

"I know." Arianna smiled. "Did you know that she had a colt?"

Caitlin's eyes locked on the cross on Fyne's forehead.

"No, I didn't."

"In the year 1797. I believe she was sold to a family by the name of Irving." Arianna's eyes turned moist.

Caitlin smiled and touched Arianna's shoulder as a warm flutter encompassed her heart. "My grandmother's maiden name was Irving. She gave me my horse, C.C., a couple of years ago."

Understanding brightened Arianna's eyes. "Then you are as lucky as I am. Take Fyne with you. She knows that you share my blood and will treat you as such."

Caitlin hugged Arianna tightly. "It has been so great meeting you. Take care of that handsome Scotsman of yours. I'm so happy you found true love."

"Thank you," Arianna said, her turquoise gaze drifting to Ferchar. "And I hope you find the same, someday, as well."

Caitlin swung onto Fyne's back and turned the horse toward the waiting clansmen.

"Caitlin." Catherine and Emma walked out from the armory. Emma came up beside the horse. "We want you to have this."

Caitlin received the small, black handled dagger handed to her. Tiny bits of blue sapphire sparkled within the metal as she flipped it back and forth in the sunlight. "This is amazing."

Emma offered an un-dainty snort. "You bet your arse it is. Catherine added a little extra protection to it, if you ken my meaning."

Caitlin looked to Catherine. "Magic?"

Her brown eyes turned demur. "Not that you know of. If Ewan MacLeod thinks the dagger is touched he'll take it from you. It being a simple dagger, he willnae. The man doesnae perceive a knife in a woman's hand as a threat."

"Doesn't he possess magic as well? Won't he sense the dagger is not just what it appears?" Caitlin said.

Emma ran her hand down Fyne's mane. "Those sapphires in the blade are made for your eyes only. No one else will be able to see them, let alone sense them. 'Tis a gift from one lass to another."

Caitlin tucked the blade into a satchel and chuckled. "Not that I'm not extremely grateful, but I've never had to use a dagger on anyone before."

Catherine grabbed her hand. The pretty planes of her face grew serious. "My thought is that if a situation does arise, you will wield that dagger with efficiency. Any lass would."

Her eyes traveled from Catherine to Emma. "Thank you both. I'll miss you more than you know."

Emma nodded and one corner of her lip lifted. "I'm glad Ferchar handfasted with you. He has good taste."

Catherine giggled and her words turned shy. "When you see Shane again, tell him I miss him and—"

Her words broke off and Caitlin squeezed Catherine's hand. "I'll tell him."

"Caitlin, 'tis time." Ferchar's deep voice took her from the women and turned her attention to what lie ahead.

She steered Fyne alongside him and they made their way beneath the first portcullis, over the moat, and under the second portcullis onto the field beyond. The horsed clansmen followed behind them.

"Where is Adlin?" Caitlin said. She refused to allow worry to burden her inquiry.

Ferchar pointed to the sky. "He chose to travel in comfort."

Caitlin looked to the tree line. A huge white eagle soared in lazy circles on the wind. The day was bright and clear and far too cheerful for her mood. She thought of Arianna's recount of flying in Adlin's shape-shift form. What would it feel like to be a bird? To soar over the problems below, flap your wings and leave it all behind. What she wouldn't do to be that beautiful eagle right now.

Ferchar remained silent as they entered the forest. The fierceness of the great warhorse beneath him couldn't compare with the demeanor of the Chieftain as he scanned the trees. Muscles rippled through his chest and arms in steady pace with the beast beneath him. More braids than usual fell by his strong jaw line as his blue- black hair brushed against his tanned skin.

Caitlin straightened her back and scanned the trees. "Will they cross your border and intercept us sooner?"

"Not without me knowing." He moved his horse closer to Fyne.

Unease brought her eyes back to him. "I'd swear the woods are too quiet even though there are hundreds of hooves behind us."

His eyes met hers and their blue depths became still and crystalline. "This land worries for you, lass."

A strange peace passed from his eyes into hers and spread calming warmth throughout her.

"I would've never thought a week ago that I'd be traveling by horseback through a highland forest with a hundred clansmen at my back and you by my side." Her gaze dropped. "To see you separated from me, a whole person."

His gaze became more intense. "What do you mean?"

She hadn't told him about the dream but had assumed that he must have known she was there that day. Must have. Why else would he have sought her? A part of her mind wondered why three years had passed before he did. "I have dreamed many times, from your viewpoint, of the day that you lost William."

His eyebrows slammed together. "I dinnae ken."

Ferchar's thick brogue burned both her ears and her conscience.

Why she confided now, Caitlin had no idea; possibly to assuage her mounting panic. "I dove after William with you. Surfaced and saw Muriel on the rock. Felt the extreme fear you felt when you discovered he was gone, the guilt and pain."

One eyebrow drew up over the ice in his eyes. "Why didnae you tell me this earlier?"

"Because I thought you knew—hoped you did. I figured it may have had something to do with why you pulled me back here."

"Yet you have thought since that it was odd that I only pulled you back recently, though you had been in my mind so long." Ferchar locked onto her eyes and pushed through her defenses.

Caitlin felt his blatant intrusion into her mind as a warning. Not in such a way that he was going to hurt her but in a way that would reveal too much of herself to him. The way she saw him, felt him and fought him in all ways mental and feminine. It was as if she was afraid he would see something inside her she could not yet see.

"You who hates to intrude on others thoughts... please get out of my mind, Ferchar. It frightens me and I'm trying hard not to be scared in general right now." Caitlin put the back of her forefinger to her forehead and looked away.

"You should have told me sooner." Ferchar spoke soft, yet firm. "I had no idea that our bond was so strong."

A shiver of awareness tore through her when his mind released hers. "Our bond?"

His eyes moved over her form, though his disclosure was directed toward the mental aspect. "It appears our minds formed a link within my trauma. A unification of souls caught within a singular moment when the heart wishes to no longer beat, cease to exist."

Caitlin kept her eyes on the path ahead of them. "You sound like Adlin."

Oddly enough, Ferchar didn't comment on the comparison but entertained a ghost of a smile. "Somehow, Caitlin, you saved my soul."

Her stomach did a somersault and she looked at him. His eyes devoured her face and left her breathless.

No way. Not right now. He could not do this do her. "You're melodramatic, Ferchar. We didn't link or bond or—" She wasn't going to say it. Put the old, overused sentiment into a voiced conclusion.

He did it for her. "Soul-mate."

Because Caitlin didn't know any other way to handle him, she looked down her nose at Ferchar and unburdened any too heavy thoughts he entertained. "That's ridiculous. I don't believe in that and neither do you."

He gave a loose shrug. "Relax, Caitlin. I'm not declaring love for you, just analyzing all the facts based on an upbringing of magic and strange occurrences."

A flourish of activity ripped her attention from Ferchar. Arthur and Alan rode through the woods toward them. When they reached Ferchar they turned their steeds around and kept pace alongside him.

Amazing as it was, Caitlin hadn't seen either of them since Beltane two days ago.

Arthur leaned over and grinned at her. "You would have been better off with me."

God, she loved this guy. He obviously had no use for uncomfortable moments. "I know."

A hearty laugh shook his chest and cleared a lighthearted path to her morbid destination. He winked at Caitlin and then turned his attention to Ferchar. "They're eager, impatient bastards, the lot of them."

"Can you blame them?" Ferchar said. "Look at how the three of us have behaved."

Caitlin hadn't expected the casual humor in Ferchar's voice. She had, however, expected the lack of humor in Alan's tone when he added further comment.

"You are full of surprises, MacLomain. First, the rejection of my sister as your bride and then the theft of the lass I sought for my bride."

She had a lot to say about that. What was Alan thinking? His bride? No way. They had only just met. She conveniently set aside the fact that she slept with Ferchar after knowing him less than forty-eight hours.

A vein in Ferchar's neck became more pronounced when he met Alan's accusation. "We've made no formal agreement in regards to your sister and Beltane dictates that whoever catches the lass gets the lass. You were not the only one who wanted her, Alan."

Caitlin felt her face burn. This was uncomfortable. It was one thing back home to know a guy might be attracted to her. But to have three very large, heavily muscled medieval Scotsmen debating the policies of not just a mere date, but sex and marriage, in regards to her, was disorienting. The fact that they discussed her as though she wasn't there was typical of any man from any time period. Yet, medieval highlanders? Please.

"Did it ever occur to any of you that I might not want to be made to spend the night with you, let alone be handfasted?" She threw out the question in the midst of their banter.

It was met with laughter, even from Alan.

Arthur spoke for them all. "No."

"What do you mean, no?" She repositioned herself on Fyne and glared at them. "I did nothing to provoke any of you."

Alan's deep brown eyes slid her way. "Lass, I've yet to meet a Scotswoman who can flirt as well and thorough as you."

Ferchar and Arthur nodded in agreement. "'Tis true, lass. You've a way with men," Ferchar said.

He was supposed to be on her side. Lout. "Flirting is one thing. What all of you animals accuse me of promoting is another."

"Is it?" Arthur's massive barrel chest heaved with yet another round of laughter. "All you made clear to me was that you were willing and able."

Caitlin growled at him. "I did not!"

"Aye, lass, you did."

"Me, as well." Alan nodded.

Ferchar's light blue eyes were merry and ruthless when they met hers. "And me."

She shook her head. "Definitely not you."

"Aye."

"When?" Caitlin would love to hear this.

"In the armory." His tone matter of fact.

He had her there. Darn, she'd forgotten about that. "So you had nothing to do with my lack of modesty?"

"Oh, I'm sure I did. But most lasses would have shunned me for my forthrightness." Ferchar's eyes fell to her cleavage.

Doubt it. "Be that as it may, my actions were that of a woman under the throes of duress. After all, I'd just found myself eight hundred years in the past."

Humor faded from Ferchar as he turned his face forward. His posture changed and carved his features to stone. He breathed in the wind from the north. "We're almost there."

Caitlin felt the tension saturate the men around her and then sharpen into a weapon. There would be no more joking. Where she was and what she was about to face had reared its ugly head. It occurred to her, as a wall of clansmen rose up out of the forest in front of them, that Caitlin had been given a reprieve. The MacLomain clan had found her before the MacLeod clan.

Ferchar before Ewan.

****

He drifted over the forest of pines and pulled the whole of Scotland into his breast. The sun shone through a filter of regret overhead and shied away from his feathered body.

His purgatory was impregnable. Heaven and Hell both could not relieve him of the intricate webs he had woven. The salty wind whipped his body and he yearned for the pleasure of new beginnings. When the clouds still swelled with rain and their cool drops held him enthralled within the glory of nature. When the sound of a newborn flower bursting free from the Earth brought tears to his eyes.

It was all so very far behind him now. Lost to a magic he had allowed to consume him. A level of power that bound him to a path he alone controlled, or at least he had.

The clansmen below him were coming together now. What would he do? How would he save them? This puzzle should have been solved by now. He'd had ample time.

With a renewed beat of his wings, Adlin screamed at his fate and flew up into the mountains beyond.

He'd had ample time...

Chapter Fourteen

The two clan fronts met at the border. Animals and nature together were nonexistent but for the sound of the Eagle overhead. The tree trunks were silent giants at his side and the golden carpet of pine needles cushioned the sound of nervous hooves.

Ferchar could feel the beat of Caitlin's heart in her chest. Too fast and unsteady, her fear threaded through each vein in his body and tugged at his resolve. He had to release her from the heart of him, let her flow back into her own body, inch by inch.

Her strength in itself was admirable but only he knew how much he held her together. How he worried for her. What she had to face. Ewan would sense their tie immediately and demand retraction. Could she stand on her own?

Ferchar had formed a channel of strength to her that morning as they sat overlooking the mountains. The idea of her going through this alone, without the aid of his magic, sickened him.

Ewan approached on his black warhorse. His eyes were alert, yet arrogant. "'Tis late in the day; I expected you sooner."

Ferchar pushed his mount forward and met the laird between the two clans. "We're here, that's all that should concern you."

The MacLeod Chieftain's eyes drifted to Caitlin. "Where's the wizard. Does he not wish to see his promise fulfilled?"

The way Ewan's words drew out the word fulfilled as he covered Caitlin's body with his eyes, churned Ferchar's nerves. "He will do that when you two are wed."

"Will he, then?" Ewan urged his horse closer to Caitlin.

"As will we," Ferchar said.

Caitlin's horse stepped back at Ewan's approach. The clansman's response to Ferchar did not veil his irritation though Ewan stalked his intended and did not remove his eyes from her. "You may send five of your men to aid her in the journey."

"I will send one hundred of my men, no less," Ferchar replied.

Ewan pulled alongside Caitlin and met Ferchar's eyes. "No, unacceptable. Five."

Ferchar did not look at Caitlin, despite her discontent. "This is an old pact. One made before both of us was born. One that will tie half of Scotland into a force of power she has never seen before. Five of my clansmen to witness such a thing and escort Caitlin is not fathomable."

The MacLeod Chieftain appeared to weigh his options. Tally the potential wealth the MacLomains and all of their affiliated clans would bring him. "I will allow twenty-five of your clansmen to travel north with us."

Ferchar was gaining ground, as he'd intended. "Seventy five of my men are acceptable in this endeavor."

Ewan brought Caitlin's horse forward. Her eyes stayed on Ferchar as she swallowed. He pulled his eyes from her delicate throat and waited.

"No," Ewan said. "Twenty five, that's it."

Ferchar straightened and ran his eyes slowly over Ewan's men. "Then you cannae have her."

The MacLeod laird raised his eyebrows. "Really?"

Ferchar held his ground. "No."

"Then we go to war?"

He looked at the men beside him, allowing a moment of weakness to cross his face. "Then we go to war."

Ewan narrowed his gaze, which was already drifting back to Caitlin. She met his eyes and a small smile blossomed on her face. Slowly, she brought her hand to her breast and lowered her eyes submissively.

The MacLeod Chieftain leaned over and ran his hand over her collarbone. Ferchar stayed steady and waited. Waited while every excruciating breath he pulled into his lungs matched the leisurely stroll Ewan's hand made over her breast.

He kept his eyes cold when Ewan's met his. The man could see nothing of Ferchar's thoughts when he searched his face.

"Fifty men," Ewan said. He cupped Caitlin's face with one hand. "To match mine, fifty men."

Ferchar sighed. "Seventy five."

The MacLeod Chieftain pulled his hand away from Caitlin. His mouth turned hard and his eyes harder. "Fifty, or we go to war."

"Fine. Fifty. I'm not pleased." Ferchar scowled and turned his horse. With a hand signal, half his men disbursed into the woodland. He'd brought one hundred men into this forest, knowing full well he would need less than half of them. Ewan had been swayed easier than he had anticipated. Thanks to Caitlin. She had played her part well.

Arthur and Alan stayed with him. When Ferchar turned back, the MacLeod clan was making ready to depart.

Ewan looked Ferchar's way. "Not you."

"We agreed on fifty. Nothing was said in regards to who those fifty were. I go." Ferchar gave the signal to his men and they continued forward.

"What purpose does this serve you, MacLomain?" Ewan was suspicious and his tone dangerous. "You cannae leave your clan leaderless."

Ferchar ran his hand along the hilt of the sword at his side. "As I said before, this marriage will tie two of the most powerful clans in the Highlands together. As Chieftain, 'tis my obligation to be present."

He kept his eyes locked on Ewan and rested his hand, palm down, on the sword's hilt. His voice was low and even, a sharpened promise. "If you cannae see the logic in this, we've a war on our hands; a war that will start here, now. If you deny me the honor of escorting such a woman as Caitlin, who is at the heart of this tie, I will show you no honor by waiting for the rest of your warriors and provisions before I attack."

"With such words said to me now, I'm doubly surprised that you would choose to leave your clan unattended. I've many allies that would gladly attack once we leave," Ewan said. A muscle leapt beneath the thick hide of his neck.

Ferchar felt the fury of Ewan's magic seeking entrance to his intentions. He did not like the feel of the man's essence. It was corrupt and manipulative.

"Every one of my men is trained in strategy for battle and can thrive as an independent unit without a leader to protect their clan, their family. However, my third in command is available to lead them and achieved his current status due to the fact that he personally killed the Cochran's wizard back in the war between clans in eleven ninety-nine. Do not question the MacLomain clan's ability to defend itself in the absence of its Chieftain," Ferchar said.

He delivered his final warning. "I also have seven allied clans to the north ready to move at my command. A command they will receive whether I'm here or at the peak of Scotland."

"So you say. Your reputation precedes you." Ewan said. One corner of his mouth curled up with contempt. "So be it. Come, then. It will give us an opportunity to further acquaint ourselves. After all, 'tis history our clans will make together."

Ferchar removed his hand from his sword. He had to give Caitlin credit for not noticeably slumping with relief. The gods had truly favored him this day. As it stood now, everything was going as planned. But Ferchar was not one to believe it would continue to do so.

Though there were weeks yet before they arrived amongst the MacLeod clan, the outcome of this pact presented too many errant possibilities. Adlin had little time left to formulate a plan. If he did not, Ferchar would. To whatever end, he would get Caitlin out of this and home safely.

Sunset quickly ushered in dusk as the forest thickened and the two clans trekked northeast. The MacLeod laird and his clan had fallen in behind the MacLomains. A strategic move that kept Ferchar in front of him rather than at his back with a dagger.

He longed to turn and check on Caitlin but would not risk Ewan seeing something useful in his eyes. It was important that he only think Ferchar an innocent party to an old agreement between a wizard and a now deceased MacLeod Chieftain. Whether Ewan speculated that the current MacLomain laird was anything like Adlin and capable of falling party to the same mistakes, Ferchar did not know. But he would not fuel the warrior behind him with doubt.

Steering his horse around a thicket of whortleberry shrubs Ferchar turned his attention to Alan and entered his mind. *"When will you branch off for home?"*

"I've decided against it," Alan said, his essence a wall of support.

"Now, you surprise me." Ferchar returned.

Alan's forgiveness warmed him. *"I cannae truly hold your recent actions against you. I can relate with your trepidation to take a wife, even if she is my sister. Bloody hell, I'm eight years your senior and I've yet to take a wife."*

Ferchar felt the flicker of mild resentment thrown at him.

"It just so happens that when I found one I truly wanted, you got to her first," Alan said.

"If it's any consolation I only intended the match as long as the handfast."

"Nay, lad. A year and a day would not have been enough for you. Not with her." Alan's internal chuckle brought a smile to Ferchar's face.

"And that is the benefit to getting older," Alan said. *"I know what I want and would have married her right away. Not hidden behind a handfast."*

"Point taken." Ferchar swallowed a morsel of regret. *"'Tis good I didnae do as you would have. For war it would be now for sure."*

"She is a strong lass, that one. I sense your worry and can assure you no harm will come to her," Alan said.

Ferchar stilled his heart. *"I welcome your optimism and appreciate your devotion to both Caitlin and myself. Mayhap, I would have not shown the same support if I was in your position."*

"Aye, another bonus to my age," Alan returned. *"You would have been viciously jealous and a bloody blackguard to the bone."*

Ferchar almost shook his head in response but caught himself. *"Nay, I would've just ordered you to leave wifeless."*

"Exactly," Alan said. *"And to me, the Chieftain of a clan that has been your ally for hundreds of years.*

Destiny's Denial

Unbelievable. Some would say no lass is worth the disintegration of two such clans."

"*Would you?*" Ferchar was soft with the tone of his interest.

"*Aye. I would say that Caitlin is a lass worth taking life-changing risks for,*" Alan said.

"*Then you love her that quickly?*" Ferchar steered clear of probing Alan's mind.

"*I know that I could. I know that since I first laid eyes on her, she's all I can think about. The way her golden eyes capture the highest point of emotion and transform it into a man's innermost desires...the way her forthrightness leaves no doubt of her intentions and keeps no secrets from the hearts of others. Having known her mere days, some part of my soul is already hers,*" Alan said.

"*I cannae be sorry for taking her from you but I am sorry you lost your heart so quickly. 'Twas not my intention to hurt you in any way.*" Ferchar pushed forth compassion and reined in his own unsteady response to Alan's honesty.

"*I know, lad. I know.*"

Ewan interrupted their exchange with a sharp bark. "We camp here for the night."

They'd stopped in a wide thicket of trees at the base of a mountain. Ferchar swung down from his horse and searched out Caitlin. Her legs wobbled as she unseated Fyne and grabbed the horse's mane for support. Both Alan and Arthur scowled but kept their distance. Ferchar felt their desire to go to her ripple through him. He experienced the same urge.

"She camps with us," Ferchar said and met Ewan's look of disbelief with unwavering eyes.

"You're gall is endless, man." The MacLeod Chieftain took her arm. "The lass is my wife."

Ferchar stepped forward. "Not yet. Until such legalities have been observed, she is a MacLomain and will camp with her clan."

"You push me too far." Ewan wrapped the MacLeod tartan over her shoulders.

The sight of the possessive endearment shot a tsunami of bloodlust into Ferchar's veins. "She sleeps amongst her clan until you are bound in matrimony. No sooner, so says the pact made between yours and mine, long ago."

He held his breath.

Ewan's lips twisted into a sneer. "There are many aspects of this pact I find unfavorable. As it stands, her virtue is not intact. I believe the pact referred to a virgin."

"What she did before she came to the MacLomain clan has no import to my order," Ferchar replied.

Ewan's ferocious eyes warred with Ferchar. "She reeks of MacLomain lust."

He called the MacLeod's bluff. Ferchar had ensured that any trace of himself did not remain on her skin. "Dinnae insult me to champion your own cause."

Caitlin looked up at Ewan, her eyes sultry and promising. "My misdeeds are in the past, not here. When we arrive at your home, my past is no more. You will become my future."

The MacLeod Chieftain stood taller and his eyes fell to her lips. "Show me the truth behind your words and I'll grant MacLomain his request."

Ferchar should have looked away. But he did not.

Caitlin rose to her toes, cupped his face and kissed him. Kissed him with the passion of a woman eager for more. Ewan seized her and pushed her back against Fyne. The horse whinnied in protest but didn't budge.

"Ferchar, dinnae move." Alan's order staked his mind and held him captive.

The Stewart laird's magic was strong.

Not as strong as his. "I can push you aside, Alan."

"Dinnae be a fool. She's only doing what was asked of her. If Ewan doubts her desire in any way, she sleeps alongside him this eve."

The MacLeod Chieftain had his knee between her legs and her head in his hands. Caitlin's hand had fallen to his chest and gripped his tunic. A low moan swam in the depths of the highland Chieftain as he deepened the kiss. Caitlin was receptive and allowed his body to push further against hers.

Bloody lass was acting the part too well.

After a near century passed, Ewan pulled away and caught his breath. He stepped back and ran his hand through his hair. "Caitlin will sleep with her clansmen until she is my wife. We leave at dawn."

Alan released him and Ferchar stepped forward. Caitlin breathed deeply as she turned to Fyne and removed one of the satchels of food Euphemia had given her. Her hands shook slightly yet her stance was that of a warrior.

He stepped beside her and took the satchel from her without meeting her eyes. A ridiculous amount of rage burned rational thought from his mind. 'Twas impossible she'd felt nothing when she'd kissed the MacLeod Laird as she had. Some unattainable recess of his mind told him over and over again she had simply done what he, Adlin and Iain had requested of her.

Do what you have to do to stay with our clan. Do not allow Ewan MacLeod to have you under his care. We cannae protect you that way.

Ferchar squelched reason. "You are good at what you do."

When her teary gaze met his, Ferchar's gut clenched. Would his potential apologies to her never cease? He despised his lack of control, both physical and mental, when it came to her.

She went to speak but stopped and shook her head. Instead she turned back to Arthur and Alan. "Where is it proper for me to sleep?"

Alan stepped forward, smiled warmly and held out his hand. "Come, lass. My thought is in the very center of your clan."

Trying to control his raging emotions, Ferchar followed and searched his mind for an answer to their plight.

Regrettably, nothing came to mind.

****

A week and a half later, Caitlin was raked with doubt and fear. *I am strong. I can do this.* She recited these words again and again, like a prayer, as they traveled deeper into the mountains. She saw fewer lochs with their Bog- Ban, pale blue water Lobelia and white water Plantain. Vegetation had become scarcer in the past few days and trees a treasure. The wind blew cold and direct through her soul and bit-by-bit, broke her down.

Why would anybody willingly live in this climate?

Darned if she knew. She equivocated the chilly lower highland, Argyll, with Aruba compared to this harsher climate. The uncomfortable, scratchy wool tartans were beginning to make more sense by the hour.

Ewan's white blond hair blew back and drove his granite profile forward. Unlike Ferchar's long, lean muscles, the MacLeod laird was built more like a wrestler. Stocky and weather worn.

"We make camp soon lass. This will be one of the last eve's we sleep apart." Ewan's baritone voice interrupted her reverie.

She bit back a million terse words and nodded with eagerness. "This is good."

His pewter eyes swallowed her cleavage. "Aye."

Caitlin had endured his stolen kisses with stellar patience. What she'd found harder to handle was Ferchar's response to her when Ewan had kissed her the first time before them all. The MacLeod had tested her with his mouth and mind. She could still remember clearly the way he'd felt inside her head. Like a spider with a machete. Prickly and lethal. Searching her innards for clues.

She cringed at what he'd planted there. His body taking hers in every position imaginable. He sought to swell her dreams with desire. Instead, she woke up sick in the morning, day after day.

Hers was a living hell with no end in sight.

Ewan announced the end of their day's journey. Time to rest. She came down off Fyne with relief. Her legs were becoming used to the long, hard riding and she was finally able to gain ground without pricks of fire burning her calves and thighs.

She yawned and stumbled after the MacLomains. Her clan. Whatever. Not in a few more days if Adlin didn't make his wizardly appearance known. She was freezing and way past the point of needing a bath.

Ferchar walked up beside her and took her elbow. "Are you well, lass?"

She pulled away. "Well enough."

"I'm not your enemy," he said under his breath.

"Everyone's my enemy right now." She went to flop down on the ground but he stopped her.

"You've done well so far, lass. Is there anything I can do for you to ease your comfort?" His eyes were subdued and genuine.

She sighed. "Just let me go to sleep."

He released his hold and allowed her to drop into a moderate patch of grass next to a cluster of wintergreens. Ferchar covered her first with her tartan and then his own.

Her eyes drifted shut before he could speak another word.

Chapter Fifteen

An imploring whisper teased the corner of her nightmares. It flung Ewan back and pushed peace into her subconscious. "Caitlin?"

She swam through a tidal wave of multi-colored prisms to reach him. To touch him. "Ferchar?"

"Wake up, Caitlin." He whispered into her ear, his warm breath brushed her cheek.

She cracked her eyes open. It was nighttime. Clouds rushed past the full moon. Ferchar crouched beside her, a finger to his lips and held out his hand.

Without hesitation she allowed him to help her to her feet. He pulled her after him, away from the wide circle of clansmen asleep around them. The men posted to watch were nowhere to be seen. He said nothing but continued to lead her to some unknown destination. Was he reneging on Adlin's pact? Was he taking her home? Had Adlin made contact? Had they figured out a way? Excitement and trepidation muddled her thoughts.

Was it time to say goodbye?

A soft glow warmed the path ahead. When Ferchar pulled her around the edge of a rocky wall, her insides melted. Like well-molded clay under a heat lamp, her legs liquefied and she would've dropped to the ground if he hadn't caught her.

"For you, lass. A bit of luxury in the midst of chaos. You are safe here. Ewan cannot hear you nor sense you." Ferchar's voice wrapped her in a safe cocoon of peace.

"It's so beautiful," she whispered.

He'd led her to a simple cove carved at the base of a mountain with nothing but sheer cliff as a balcony. The walls glowed as though thirty candles licked its edges. In its center was a steamy pool of water the size of ten bathtubs. The water shone a Caribbean blue from within.

"Someone will see this, it's not safe." Caitlin held onto him but couldn't tear her gaze from the tempting water.

"Caitlin, no one can find you here. You are safe." He led her forward.

The air smelled of sun lilies and roses. How was that? Up here, as they were, above the whole of Scotland, why did she smell flowers? He brought her in front of him and slowly removed her dress, careful to keep his eyes on her face.

Wary, she stopped his hands. "I can undress myself."

He stepped back and nodded. "So be it."

Caitlin averted her eyes. He was too handsome, standing there with his kilt low on his waist and his hair blowing in the wind. Though it was cold, he wore no tunic and his broad chest was hidden in the shadows. A strange vision of him in long black wizard robes with his blue-black hair flowing around him and his icicle eyes glowing filled her mind. Her eyes snapped back to him.

Nothing had changed. He stood silent and unwavering.

Shaken, she removed the rest of her clothes and waded into the pool. The water was blissful, the perfect heat for her tired bones. She sunk down against the side and leaned her head back. As warmth penetrated her muscles, she shut her eyes.

Magic lapped at the edge of her mind. It slid over her as though it were a strip of the softest silk. It had to be magic, it felt so good.

Then the magic had hands.

Hands that sifted through her hair and rubbed her temples, skimmed against the taught skin of her cheekbones and like a whisper over her eyelids. Beneath her earlobes and along her neck, gentle and soothing. She released air from her lungs and kept her eyes closed.

"Where do you end and I begin, Caitlin?" His whisper was far away and hypnotizing.

She said nothing as he pulled her hands above her head, kissing and tasting each finger. His mouth was hot as he brushed her hair aside and brought his lips to her neck. They rode up over her chin until they rested against the corner of her lips. "Can you feel me inside of you?"

Caitlin breathed harder but didn't answer. He had not moved but she could feel him cover her, move against her, his hard body pushing against her soft skin. It was the picnic table at the restaurant all over again, but much, much more acute.

Somehow she felt him enter her. Stretch her. In and out, faster and faster in a split second. Her inner muscles rippled and gripped, eager and hungry. Without warning, her body quaked and she arched. She turned her lips into his as the orgasm rocketed through her limbs.

Even as ripples of pleasure tore through her, she sought more. Needed more. Her hands wandered to his face and traced his jaw line as he kissed her.

"Please," she said against his lips. "Give me more."

He traced her lips and his blue eyes looked lost. "I cannae."

Caitlin closed her eyes against the sting of his rejection. "Why? You said yourself I was safe here."

He nodded and moved away from her. "And you are. But if I was to take you this eve, he would know it on the morn."

She sank beneath the water and resurfaced. "Then why did he obviously not know for certain you had already had me back in Argyll?"

"Because that is the homeland of my ancestors, my magic could protect you from deeds done there. Not here. My scent on you now would annihilate the pact." Ferchar leaned against the wall, tormented.

Caitlin rose from the water and made her way to her clothes. "Deeds done? My scent on you? You make me feel half whore, half dog, do you realize that?"

His eyes followed her as she dressed. "'Twas not my intention."

"What the hell is your intention, Ferchar? Really, you take me physically when it's safe and mentally when it's not. All and all, I think you're just a coward and a tease."

She'd just finished dressing when he grabbed her arms and pulled her forward. "Go to sleep, Caitlin."

"What?" The single word became a struggle to say as his face blurred before her eyes.

"Go to sleep." The last thing she felt before she drifted to sleep standing before him was Ferchar's thumb moving in small circles over her palm.

****

Ferchar caught Caitlin before she fell and pulled her into his arms. He sank slowly down against the wall and cuddled her in his lap.

He should not be doing this, had no right.

But he did.

He'd never needed a lass more in his life. He felt desperate for her, to the point of taking chances. Dangerous chances. Her chestnut hair fell over his lap and her full lips drifted open in light slumber. He'd never attempted what he was about to do with another human being but could not let her leave him without this, without taking it to this level.

He placed the pad of his thumb just above and between her eyes and traced the outline of a pentacle. His mouth wove the ancient tongue and requested admittance into another's soul; sought guidance along the planes of another mortal's existence.

His eyes drifted shut and his body relaxed. His world shifted beneath him and the air condensed with humidity. The sound of a bagpipe echoed on the wind and the thick scent of roses permeated the air. Harsh energy compressed around him, then released.

When he opened his eyes her eyes were open.

On this plane they were white gold. The streaks of gold and flaxen in her hair were electrified and blinding. Her skin color was indiscernible and her lips smooth planes of dewy satin. Neither he nor she wore clothing.

"You dream, Caitlin." He lifted her and brought her into the water. "Just dream."

The fluid moved around them in slow motion swirls of deep, consuming royal blue. The rock walls sparkled with diamond clarity as it buffered a wind that one could see more than feel. The wind was silver and black, moonlight and darkness. It blew bits of eve's ash over her high cheekbones and dusted her temples with moonlight.

"I'm so scared. What if Adlin abandons me? What if you do? I don't belong here. Why did you do this to me? Why did you really bring me to Scotland? Was it only because of William? I don't believe that."

Her heart was free within her dreams and he covered it with his lips. Hearing her soul was not why he had brought her here. He remained silent.

She returned his kiss and wrapped her arms around his shoulders. Her mouth tasted sweet and urgent. He lay back and pulled her onto him.

"I read about you, Ferchar." Her feather-light words drifted against his neck.

Read about him? Her mind reminded him of a summer meadow. Warm and welcoming. He ran his hands down the soft skin of her back and trailed his fingers over each small vertebra.

"In a book about Arianna and Iain. When you were younger. So noble and brave. Living your life with a vision of such proportions. One withheld from everyone save Adlin."

She moaned when he instinctively brought her tighter against him. What the bloody hell was she talking about? What book? Why had he seen nothing of this in her mind previously? Adlin, no doubt.

Caitlin brought her lips back to his. His thoughts split apart at the feel of her lush, responsive body. Her hands were everywhere and, even caught in this place of broken moments and continuous snippets of her thoughts, sensation drowned him. It was becoming harder and harder to keep her from entering his mind.

Ferchar had thought he was strong enough to keep her at bay. Why, after she had been in his mind so long, he thought he was capable of that only proved how obsessed he was becoming, sloppy.

He chuckled. No doubt he'd let his body rule his mind once again. Ferchar turned her, pushed her back against the edge of the pool's wall and took control.

Caitlin's eyes had drifted shut and her head was flung back. Her lean thighs ran up and down his provocatively. "Why would I see you in black robes? That strikes me rather sinister. Like a dark angel, an unholy wizard."

Ferchar's erection swelled even more if that was possible. He slammed his hands down on the rocky surface on either side of her body. His gut clenched. Anger, fear and lust blazed within. Silence was no longer an option. Through clenched teeth he asked, "What do you speak of lass?"

Then he saw himself through her eyes. Felt the awe and confused perception of him that she held in check by a thread. Only Adlin, Iain and one other knew of what she had witnessed in her mind's eye. How had she seen him so clearly? The answer was simple. She was a victim of visions as well. It explained so much about their link.

He would not allow her to misunderstand and fear him so he voiced his secret. "I balance our circle, lass. Adlin and Iain are white wizards and I am a black wizard; not evil, just the shade to their light."

Her eyes opened and ran the length of his torso. "You don't look like shade." She grinned and licked her lips. "Definitely don't feel like shade."

Ferchar reined in his heart. For the woman to have a sense of humor now only added to her character. "Shade is the best way I know to describe it to you, lass. Where their lives are predominant and self-controlled, mine is dictated by a higher power."

She ran one hand along his jaw line and the other around his neck. "You have control over your life, Ferchar. You can't tell me you don't."

"I only have the control to follow my visions." He did not want her to know the extent of his discontentment nor the content of his visions.

"You're wrong." Her concern slid through him. "I'm new to this but my thought is that a vision is more of an insight then it is an obligation. If—"

Enough of this. Now wasn't the time. Her words died on her lips when he lifted her onto the ledge and came between her thighs. Urgency in a dream was different. The subconscious consumed and magnified his desire. Took her away from his eyes and then brought her back without moving her. Made him far more desperate to take what he had brought her here for lest she awaken too soon and deprive him.

"You've a beautiful soul, lass, but you talk too much." Ferchar ran his hands up her thighs until he covered her backside with them. He loved the feel of her smooth, taut skin.

"But you alone, one black wizard, would not even the balan—" She gasped into his mouth when he gave her in a dream what he could not in reality. Not anymore. Caitlin sank into him and he groaned.

Bracing himself, he held onto her the best he could and moved quickly. Her nipples clenched into tight little knots. Leaning forward, he took one into his mouth and rolled his hips.

"Ohhh!" She raked her nails down his back and pain mixed with pleasure.

Wild with lust, he grunted and rolled the other way while thrusting sharply again and again. When her tongue licked her lips in anticipation, he slowed, nearly stopping and leaned forward and twirled his tongue with hers before slipping it into the deep recesses of her warm mouth.

Caitlin's hands clenched his sides when he ran his fingers lightly up her vertebrae and cupped the back of her neck. One hand still guided her bottom, the other her neck as he tilted her head and kissed her harder. He plunged once more, filling her so deeply she squeaked and squirmed then released a sharp bark of pleasure.

Eyes closed in near agony, he thrust again and was amazed when her mind suddenly transported them. Quickly. Northbound. On a fierce wind born of the soul and free of the body. Faster and more free than the gods, she moved against him until they lay on a cliff. The one he had seen in her mind the night in the cave.

Why here?

What was it that drove Caitlin's mind to a place unknown to her? To him. A storm raged overhead and sleet drove against his skin. Her eyes glowed white and her lips were frantic. He met her passion with his own and warmed the frozen pellets of pewter to heavy drops of azure blue. Her hair shone with the glow of an absent sun as her nails desperately raked down his back.

'Twas her magic; free and rabid, without direction and lethal. Her soul twisted around his heart and squeezed. Sucked the air from his lungs and flung it to the winds. Brought him so far into her he didn't recognize his own essence. He could do nothing to stop her. Slow her. Not when he was already so deep within her.

"Caitlin." He used her name like a battle-axe against her. Well aimed and deadly.

Tears poured down her face in ringlets of white fluid. It was too late. She was lost to him, her anguish too deep. He fought the images rushing at him.

The look on her grandmother's face when she told Caitlin her parents had died.

The first time her heart was broken by a man. Her grandfather dying. The news that her grandmother had had a heart attack. A younger Shane lying in bed ravaged with fever.

Ewan forcing her to his will in a nightmare, again and again.

Ferchar swung his tongue into action and viciously chanted the ancient language. Free her. Release us from this dream bond. At eam. Libera nos a vinculo somniu. He'd been a fool to have done this. He knew full well that her soul was the mate to his. Arrogance should be a sin. As fate would have it, they were at the peak of finding release within each other at the exact moment he pulled them apart.

He knew immediately that such a thing was very bad. The dream shut down and reality burst open. A poisonous thorn of caged lust barred him from her. His muscles retracted with venomous precision and his groin pulled tight.

Bloody hell. The pain was intense.

He pried his heavy eyelids open and instantly brought his thumb back to her forehead, tracing the pentacle to return her to the slumber she fought so hard to pull free from. Her lashes fluttered and the turmoil ravaging her exquisite features calmed.

Ferchar sat there against the wall with her curled asleep in his lap well into the night. He'd thought himself immune to another's pain. That if he had managed to conquer his own through the course of his life, then others should as well. And she had. He had taken her innermost demons and made them available for his evaluation. Had confiscated without permission what she kept locked inside and walled from others.

It amazed him how levelheaded and unaffected she portrayed herself to those around her. How vulnerable she really was. He leaned his head down and brought her head to his chest as the last vision she'd released in her dream state overwhelmed him.

It had been of him when she'd awoken in the cave the morning after Beltane. The irrevocable change that had shifted within her when she looked up at him sitting on the moss covered rock.

Now he knew the truth.

She was in love with him.

Chapter Sixteen

Caitlin had one thing on her mind when she woke up.

Sex.

She opened her eyes and peered at the early dawn forest. To say she was simply aroused was a massive understatement. What on Earth had happened? The last thing she remembered was Ferchar telling her to go to sleep.

Caitlin sat up quickly and scanned her surroundings. What had he done to her? She threw aside the tartans that covered her and stood. Her legs were sore. Used in a way that had nothing to do with riding a horse. Where was he? She strode forward and searched the men. Some were just waking up and some sat in circles around small fires.

"Good morn to you, lassie," Alan said and offered her a cup of water. "Are you all right? You look eager for an easy kill."

"Where is Ferchar?" She continued to scan the clansmen around her.

"Aye." He shook his head. A dry grin grazed his face then vanished. "I should have known. The lad has always had a trail of angry lasses at his heels."

Caitlin stopped, planted her hands on her hips and studied Alan. He was tousled and handsome. One of those men who looked even better the next morning than they did the night before. "What do you mean by that?"

He shrugged one broad shoulder and touched the bridge of her nose. Cedar sidled past dark chocolate brown in his eyes. "I think you know exactly what I mean."

She threw back her shoulders and smacked her lips together. "No, no. Whatever you're thinking is wrong."

His brows rose. "Now lass, do you think me born yesterday?"

"I didn't sleep with Ferchar last night, Alan. Do you think I would be this uptight if I had?" Caitlin rolled her eyes and sighed. Why had she just said that?

He said no more about it but instead removed a small satchel from his side and handed it to her. "This is for you."

She peered inside. "Berries?"

"Aye. I picked them this morn. They will give you strength." He pushed back a wisp of hair from her cheek. "Much lies ahead of you."

Caitlin fought back a wave of emotion. "Thank you, Alan. You're so thoughtful."

"We will reach the MacLeods' land this eve," Alan said.

"What? Ewan said yesterday it would be a few more days!" Caitlin reached into the satchel, grabbed a berry and chewed it with vigor. It was tart and electrified the inside of her cheeks.

"He meant his castle. His land is vast and will take time to travel across." Alan's gaze narrowed with concern.

"Once we are on MacLeod land, things change."

Caitlin popped another berry into her mouth. "I know. I remember what I was told. Both you and Ferchar's magic becomes weaker."

Alan nodded and moved a step closer to her. "Be careful, Caitlin."

She looked to the north. "I know. From the pot into the frying pan"

He swiped a bit of berry juice from the corner of her mouth with his finger. "Your phrase is foreign to me but I gather you understand my concern."

She stared, mesmerized, as he brought the drop of juice to his mouth. Caitlin clamped her gaping mouth shut and cursed Ferchar. What had he done to her? She knew he did something and whatever it was had her ready to drag Alan into the woods for a little morning rendezvous.

Not to say Alan was innocent. He made quite obvious his desire. He brought his hand to her cheek. Sadness betrayed him and he swallowed hard. "I would have made you happy, Caitlin."

Shame humbled her. He was serious, in so many ways. What she saw in his eyes reflected what she'd looked so long for back home. Love. Alan's heart was in his words. She placed her hand over his. "I know you would have."

She longed to lighten the mood with a joke. A declaration that she felt the same way, but she couldn't.

He leaned forward and brushed his lips over hers. When he spoke his voice cracked. "The MacLeod will not know I touched you. Have no fear."

Caitlin shook her head and whispered, "That was the last thing on my mind."

"Not mine." Ferchar appeared from nowhere, his steady gaze on Alan.

The Stewart Chieftain met him with a smile. "Intrusive bastard, aren't you?"

Ferchar wrapped his plaid across his tunic and over his shoulder. "More like vigilant in my endeavor. You just took a risk that even I would not have taken."

Caitlin's blood boiled anew. Brazen liar. She strode right at him. Skip the knee to the groin. A slap would have to do in mixed company. She drove her palm against his cheek with all the speed her arm allowed. His head didn't budge an inch.

"You." That's all she could say through clenched teeth.

Alan chuckled. "Ferchar, you've a way with the lassies."

He ignored Alan's comment and stepped around Caitlin. "We leave soon."

She swung back and walked alongside Alan and Ferchar as they headed toward the horses. He was not getting off that easy. "How do you feel this morning, Ferchar?"

He allowed her a brief, sidelong glance. "Well enough."

"Do you?" She touched his arm and felt the electrical charge. "How convenient, because I'm feeling rather unsatisfied."

The muscles in his jaw clenched.

A wave of lust swamped her as dreams pushed forward. Dreams of him. In a pool of water tucked in the corner of a mountain. His hands as they roved and tormented her. Incredible need.

Then nothing. But there was more. Much more. She knew it but could not find it.

"What did you do, Ferchar?" She shook her head and backed away. When his eyes swung around to follow her departure a heavy weight crushed her. "What did you do to me?"

Alan moved faster than Ferchar and wrapped a supportive arm around her shoulder. He brought her quickly to her horse and leaned Caitlin against Fyne.

He pulled away and looked in the direction of the MacLeod clan. "Ferchar, you have been foolish. Of this I have no doubt. Fix it. Now."

Caitlin ground her teeth and swung onto Fyne's back. She looked down at Alan. "He cannot fix it.

Destiny's Denial

What's done is done. Ewan will be none the wiser. I promise."

Not bothering to look at Ferchar she swung Fyne around and rode into the MacLeod camp. Ewan was just swinging onto his warhorse. His eyes scanned her face.

Caitlin turned flirtatious. "Good morning."

He sat back and contemplated her. "You look fresh this day, lass."

Do I really? I've been betrayed, used and am ten types of aroused, do I really look refreshed?

"Thank you." She pushed back her clean hair. "I bathed."

"Where?" Ewan rode alongside her.

Please let some grain of truth mark her words.

"Beneath a small waterfall." She pointed in a random direction. "Not far from here."

He stopped their horses, leaned over and cupped her chin. His fingers were firm on her jaw. Caitlin concentrated on keeping her breathing even and her eyes submissive.

Whatever he discovered pleased him. "Very good. You needed to bathe."

Caitlin smiled. Jerk. He needed to bathe still. Smelly bastard. "Aye, it had been too long."

He released her face and urged their steeds forward. Caitlin fell into the pattern of travel. Single file, Fyne followed directly behind Ewan's horse as they followed a trail carved into a mountainside. She refused to look down at the steep drop off to her right but focused on her anger at Ferchar.

One upsetting thought followed another while the sun rode the sky in a wide arch overhead. Icy wind whipped her face and she pulled her plaid tighter around her shoulders. Had he raped her last night? No. What was she missing? Why did she feel so incredibly unsatisfied sexually? She struggled with a muddle of shapes, sounds and smells locked within her mind.

She struck on something. A dream, one that she desperately needed to remember. Frustration only magnified her animalistic needs. Sex. The word was at the bow of her mental ship. It made every other potential thought dwindle to a flicker caught in the shadows. Shadow. Shade. A wizard of shade. She straightened and narrowed her eyes.

Ferchar.

A black wizard. One that balanced four? It had to be four.

"Welcome, lass," Ewan said and broke her thoughts. She'd been so close to something. They left the narrow path and entered onto a plateau of rock and pockets of moss. "To my homeland."

Caitlin felt like a flag on the end of a pole as cold, salty wind drove into her. "It's beautiful"

It wasn't a lie. Though the landscape was far more barren here, it was powerful. There weren't the secrets of a forest but the harsh honesty of rock and sky. Hundreds of shades of noble gray and so much blue. Pockets of pine trees huddled together in the distance, their tops needles and their bases longer and tougher.

She'd read her share of Scottish Highland romance novels and could understand when the authors wrote of the men's countenance being made of steel. Hard reality against a woman's soft curves. How else could it be? Living on this land, a man would have to be born with a heart encased in platinum.

In her opinion, Argyll was a nice medium. A better place to fall in love and rationally live out a life with a man. Good for Arianna. Irrelevant for her.

"Soon, you will see better." The pride behind his words hinted at the first inkling of nonviolent emotion she'd ever depicted from the MacLeod clansman.

"I am eager," she lied as they made their way over the harsh terrain.

Ewan said no more but called camp a short while later. He'd chosen a glen with more plant life than she would've expected. Miraculously protected from the wind, nature struggled for springtime. Sturdy bushes held tight to new blossoms and grass grew in desperate patches underfoot.

As the two clans moved into their individual positions for the upcoming night, Caitlin prayed again for Adlin's appearance. Where was he? They were running out of time.

Arthur approached with a wide smile and rubbed his stomach. "Not much food to be had here, lassie."

Caitlin had bypassed hunger about four hours ago. "No doubt. Any ideas?"

He sat beside her on a wide rock and shook his head. "If I had one. You'd know it. It's too bloody desolate up here."

She bit the corner of her lip. Of all the MacLomains, this land suited Arthur the best. He was as large as the mountains. She was convinced that if he just reached up and swiped one aside the ancient rock would come crumbling down.

Caitlin kept her voice low. "Any idea where that wizard of yours is?"

Arthur leaned back on his elbows and shook his head. "Damned if I know. No sound of an eagle overhead in days."

She leaned back beside him. "I'm getting nervous."

His long red hair blew back and his blue-green eyes met hers. "I know, lass. Me too. But you're not alone, remember that."

"Those two." He nodded in the direction of Ferchar and Alan, who were deep in conversation. "Are combining their abundant intellect to save you."

"Lucky me." She shook her head. "You know what I figure though, Arthur?"

He cocked an eyebrow in her direction. "What's that?"

Caitlin frowned. "If Adlin had so long to formulate a plan just in case a woman of this doomed lineage came to be here and he hasn't, in all his infinite wisdom, done so yet. What can any of them, Ferchar, Alan or Adlin, come up with now? Really, it's fairly obvious to me that this is a no win situation. I just happen to be the misfortunate victim."

He sat forward and took her hand. A friendly gesture, nothing more. "But you're a victim and that's what matters. I've known the men you speak of a very long time and my faith in them is thorough. If it wasnae, I'd toss you over my shoulder, pull free my axe and battle the whole of the MacLeod clan here and now. But I know that they'll come through. You will not be married to Ewan. You will not be left here alone."

Caitlin squeezed his hand. "I hope you're right."

"I am."

The two sat together in companionable silence and shared the last of Euphemia's generous bundle. A single crusty piece of bannock.

"You only want me for my food," she said through munches.

He laughed. "Aye, aren't you grateful?"

The fit of giggles that seized her had many clansmen looking their way, most pointedly Ferchar and Alan.

"Darn straight. Scotland has managed to make me feel like some sort of esteemed virgin princess with the body of a goddess. It's ridiculous." Caitlin pushed the words out past laughter that had her grabbing her sides and wiping her eyes. Her muscles eased with the long overdue release of tension and stress.

Arthur smiled and popped the last of the crusty bread into his mouth. "You underestimate yourself. There's more to you than your body, which isna half bad."

He licked the crumbs from his fingertips. "You've a spirit that attracts a highland male like bees to honey."

She shrugged. "So be it. I have the spirit of a twenty-first century female."

"Nay." He shook his head. "You're wrong about that."

"Explain yourself." She sat forward alongside him, her eagerness for insight and simple, friendly conversation intense.

Arthur nodded toward Ferchar and Alan. "Those two are Scotsmen. They have dealt the whole of their lives with Scotswomen."

"Your point?"

"My point is, Scotswomen, especially that of the highland breed, are hellcats. They have always and will always think themselves equal to their male counterparts."

Caitlin thought of what Emma had said about Alan's sister and her submissive attitude in regards to Ferchar. "That's not true. What about Alan's sister? Is she a hellcat?"

Arthur balked. "Highest form of. With any other man but your lad, there. Lasses have taken all sorts of approaches with Ferchar and come up bereft. That lass just tried another tactic. It didnae work."

"He's not my lad," Caitlin murmured before getting to the point. "How am I different than a highland woman, then?"

He stretched his barrel arms over his head and yawned. "'Tis the way you go about it. You're bold like a highland lass but deceptive and mysterious."

"Give it up, Arthur. I'm not asking for a fortune cookie reading."

He cocked his head at her, baffled. "Fortune cookie?"

"Get on with it." She laughed.

Arthur's expression suddenly turned deadly serious. A formidable thing. "Have you Muriel's dagger?"

"What?" She clenched her fists and dug her nails into the rock.

His eyes locked on hers. "The dagger of Sapphire's. Do you have it with you?"

He jumped off the rock and pulled her after him. "The one that Emma and Catherine gave me? You know about that?"

"Aye." He moved no further but nodded his head in Fyne's direction. "'Twas made by Muriel. She alone has the power to make such a thing. It was agreed she not be the one to give it to you."

"Why?" A ripple of warning dripped down her spine.

"Irrelevant, lass." Arthur lightly shoved her away. "Go retrieve it and then act nonchalant. Ewan is coming."

She did not question him further but obeyed. Where was she going to put it? Why did Arthur want her to get it?

Push fear aside, Caitlin. Just do as he says.

She made her way to Fyne's side. The horse bent her neck and blew a stream of moisture into the air as Caitlin tucked the dagger into a satchel which she then threw over her shoulder. She moved away from Fyne and walked back in the direction of the rock.

Calm. Stay calm.

"Caitlin." Ewan's voice boomed across the way as he passed by Alan and Ferchar.

She turned to face him and smiled. "Aye?"

Destiny's Denial

"I want to show you something." He took her forearm. Caitlin didn't make the mistake of looking over her shoulder when he led her away from both the MacLomain and MacLeod clans. Until Adlin made contact, she was at the whim of this man. The whim of an old pact and the prevention of hundreds of lives lost to war.

Ewan said nothing while they walked for at least ten minutes along a narrow goat's path. Eventually they stopped at the base of a small waterfall that streamed into a shallow pool of water. Water trickled down the walls of the cliffs on either side of her.

The spot was secluded and intimate. The only sound was that of an eagle screaming overhead. She went to look up but was caught against the MacLeod Chieftain instead.

Her body was sandwiched between his and mountainside. He ripped the front of her dress down and ran his mouth over her breast. Caitlin closed her eyes, kept her palms against the rock and disregarded her terrorized heart.

As he roved her with his lips, one hand slid down and squeezed her wrist tightly until she released the satchel.

"You willnae be needing that," he said.

She allowed him to grip her wrists and willed herself to relax. He didn't know what was in the bag. Of that she was sure.

"We are not married, my laird," she said. Play the part. Do not waver. "What are we doing here?"

"I think you know." He pulled her dress lower. "We are on my land now. The pact is as fulfilled as it needs to be. Do you not think so, lass?"

She kept her hands back against the rock and pondered her next move. If she went against him, would he see the crack in the MacLomain's pledge? It was just he and her alone and she had done nothing but lead him to believe she wanted him. So, yes, if she turned away from his advances now his suspicions would be justified. What woman would not want to cheat a bit and take the object of her desire sooner than anticipated?

It'd finally come to this. Caitlin was a whore to an old Highland agreement.

She could just walk away. She should. But some inbred devotion kept her still and silent as Ewan returned to her lips. Her allegiance was to herself, not Adlin or Ferchar. Not anyone. What was she doing?

The MacLeod laird spent little time on formalities before he whipped her around and bent her forward. Caitlin flattened her palms against the wet stone and bit back a sob. Not like this. She didn't deserve this. Damn it, she did not belong here.

"My laird, are you there?"

Ewan's hands ceased their insistent exploration and paused on the backside of her hips. "Aye. Leave me," he barked.

A brief silence ensued while he ran one hand over her belly and the other up under her skirts.

"Your brother has traveled to meet you." The voice sounded neutral.

With a grunt of frustration, Ewan pulled away and grumbled, "Bloody hell."

Released, Caitlin pulled her dress up, turned and thanked any God willing to listen. "We will wait then?"

"Aye. Angus is an impatient bastard." Ewan strode back the way they'd come.

So the MacLeod Chieftain bowed to his brother? Not that she was complaining. This stranger had just saved her hide.

When they returned to the glen, Ewan grabbed her wrist. "Come with me, lass."

Alan, Ferchar and Arthur sat on the wide rock now. Deep frowns etched their faces.

Ferchar tossed a dagger up and down in the air, first catching its blade and then its hilt. His eyes never left hers. Though his posture was relaxed, contained rage chiseled the light sapphire of his eyes into fire. That rage was not directed at her. Good thing. Had it been, she would've ended this charade here and now.

Two MacLeod clansmen approached. One of them was very handsome and the other fearsome.

"Brother, I grew restless." The man who had to be Angus spoke. Caitlin tried not to flinch when she looked at him. He terrified her. Taller than Ewan and thicker, his face was craggy and his hair a deep red. His eyes were sinister and intense, black, evil orbs that flickered over her with disgust. Her bones turned brittle and tightened in defense.

"That doesnae surprise me," Ewan said. He didn't bother to make introductions

Angus's eyes narrowed to obsidian slivers when he looked at the MacLomains. "Why are they here Ewan? Why is Ferchar here?" His thin lips flattened with repulse. "You always were too pliable."

Caitlin was shocked when Ewan didn't defend himself. Who was in charge here?

"You have been replaced," Angus said.

Ewan's eyes widened and he reached for his axe one second too late. A dagger hit the center of his forehead and he fell forward onto his knees.

Oh my God! What the heck! Caitlin covered her mouth with her hand and stepped back. Bile rushed into her throat as Ewan slowly fell forward and slammed down, face first, onto the hard rock floor. What the hell was going on?

The MacLomain clan surged forward like a tidal wave. Ferchar at the front, sword drawn.

"Nay, all's well." Angus held a hand in the air and stopped both the MacLomains and the MacLeods.

Ferchar halted his men mere feet from Angus. "Explain yourself."

A horrible shutter of laughter plucked his gut as Angus reached down, cracked Ewan's head to the side and removed his dagger. "My brother had turned mutinous and had to be dealt with."

Angus wiped his dagger on his tartan and met Ferchar's eyes. "'Twas his intention to attack one of our allied clans within the week and take their land for his own. 'Tis not the way of the MacLeods to abide such betrayal."

Ferchar's reply sounded well measured. "I take it his decision was in direct correlation with the numerous new allies that come with this marriage."

Angus nodded his head once as though he allowed a child a boon. "Precisely."

"How convenient for you that you take his place at such a time." The octave of Ferchar's tone sounded dangerous.

"Aye, 'tis rather unnerving." Angus cocked his head, mirth evident on his face.

"How easily you murdered your own kin," Ferchar remarked almost too casually.

Angus slowed his hand and his dagger shone bright in the sun. "I have no use for betrayal."

Caitlin tried not to shrivel when his black eyes found hers. "Such a treasure you bring me, MacLomain."

Ferchar smiled and eyed her like prized cattle. "Aye, 'tis good to fulfill this pact. Adlin has created too many problems. She's used but a beauty. A good tie of clans."

Caitlin trembled beneath Angus's stealthy appraisal.

"She'll do."

Apparently he didn't care when or by whom she had been used. Terror struck anew at the thought of

Destiny's Denial

this man touching her. She was his now and Caitlin was actually starting to entertain suicide as a last resort before becoming his wife. Whatever it took to get her out of this place.

With a signal from Ferchar, the MacLomain clan backed away and returned to their camp. The MacLomain laird remained silent.

Angus turned to the clansman alongside him. "Stephen, the whiskey."

The man pulled a makeshift flask from his satchel and handed it to Angus. "Where do you want the wench?"

Caitlin studied the man while Angus tipped back his head and drank. Stephen was of a more average height and his frame slighter compared to the other men around her. He was, perhaps, six foot one. His hair was a deep and glossy brown. Deep set sky blue eyes held the experience of a man twice his age.

She had to give Scotland credit. It put out some fine looking men.

Which should be the very last thing she should be thinking about right now; but no, sexual tension rose to the surface again in the midst of the most frightening experience of her life. It made no sense.

"With us." Angus declared his specifications regarding Caitlin's sleeping arrangement without removing his eyes from Ferchar's.

Stephen walked over and took her elbow. "Come lass."

Her eyes pleaded with Ferchar to say something, anything. But he didn't. Instead, he turned and walked back to his own camp. Oh no.

She'd depleted the last of her courage when Ewan almost did what he did. Bravery was fast becoming a distant memory as she was led into the heart of the MacLeod clan.

Not one single man dared to look at her. It was apparent that they feared Angus. Her legs became wobbly but she continued to put one foot in front of the other. *I have to get through this. I have to make it home somehow.*

"Here, lass." Stephen stopped and pointed to the ground by a small fire. "Are you hungry?"

She shook her head, surprised by his concern. "No."

He sat cross-legged on the other side of the fire, removed another container of whiskey and surprised her again. "Dinnae be frightened. We MacLeods dinnae bite."

The octave of his Scottish burr soothed her nerves and her own honesty shocked her. "I've never seen someone killed before."

His blue eyes stared into the flames between them. "I'm sorry you had to today. There was no other way."

Stephen's eyes rose to hers with deadly calm. "Dinnae cause trouble for my new Chieftain, lass. You will find yourself on the other end of his dagger if you do so."

The seriousness of his promise sent a downpour of warning through her blood. "I have no intention to."

"Good." He handed the whiskey across. "Drink. Please."

She didn't hesitate but took three deep gulps. It burned her throat and heated her belly. Caitlin closed her eyes and breathed deeply. She needed this. When she opened her eyes, Stephen watched her intently.

"Thank you," Caitlin said.

"You are of the Broun clan."

His words startled her. "Through my Scottish heritage, yes, so I've been told."

"You have the sparkle in the eye that is theirs." He leaned forward and took back the whiskey.

Was that nostalgia she detected?

"You know of the Broun clan, then?" She pulled her tartan so that it covered her neck.

"Aye. A long time ago." He drank the last of the whiskey, lay down on his side and propped himself up on his elbow.

"Your clan is allied with them?"

"No. We are not." His eyes drifted to the fire again.

He was about to say something else when Angus approached.

Her veins contracted and Caitlin struggled to breathe. Night had fallen and the firelight carved his face into the Devil. He sat, placed his feet on the ground and rested his elbows on bent knees.

"Come here, lass."

She squeezed the satchel by her side. There was no way she could remove the dagger without being seen. Time to deviate. "I'm so tired, my laird, surely you can—"

"Come here." The threat behind his order shredded her potential denial to shreds. This man was different than Ewan. He would be swayed by no one. Period. He was a man who was obeyed without question.

Caitlin rose slowly, pulled her tartan tighter around her shoulders, walked forward and stopped by his side.

"Here." He pointed to the area directly in front of him.

Her heart beat so hard it hurt. Where was Adlin? Why were they all allowing this to happen to her? She walked to the spot he'd designated and froze.

With lightning reflexes he grabbed her wrist and tugged down. She fell onto her knees. His free hand came up and ripped the plaid from her shoulders.

"Now we will see if you were worth the wait."

Chapter Seventeen

The sky was as gray as the rock and spit shards of icy raindrops. Water ran in rivulets through crevices and formed puddles. Wind whipped the warriors from slumber and drove them to their horses.

Ferchar kept his dark mood well hidden as he made his way through his clansmen and ensured that each man was provided for to the best of his ability. He smiled at them and preached false reassurances.

Sturdy to the bone, none complained. Not about the weather or the lack of food, nor the potential hell they were about to enter. He'd chosen his men with specific criteria in mind.

None had children.

There would be no wee bairns left without a Da. He knew they were aware of that. Though their mission was not of the caliber of war, its perils were endless. That had been proven yesterday.

Had Adlin known this would happen? That Angus would make such a move...callous son of a bitch. Ferchar should've seen this coming. The twisted lad he met only once as a child had grown up into a monster. Ewan had been a problem but nothing compared to what Angus presented.

It had killed him to let him have her last night—to give her over to him. He'd gone from the torment of watching Ewan disappear with her to the madness of Angus taking her with one question devouring his innards: Why was he allowing this?

Destiny's Denial

Was the welfare of his clan worth the horror Caitlin was going through? If he could ask each and every lass and lad of his clan if they thought so, what would they say?

Alan's face was hard as he approached. "They're making ready to leave."

Ferchar swung onto his horse. "Aye. Let's go."

The MacLomain clan fell in behind him and Alan.

"She's all right," Alan said. "You had no choice but to let him have her last eve. 'Tis the whole of your clan at stake here."

"I know," Ferchar snapped.

The MacLeods were horsed and anxious. He located Caitlin beside Angus's mount. Her wet hair was plastered to her head. Wrapped in the MacLeod tartan, she sat straight with her head held high, a testament to her pride. Her eyes did not meet his but stayed steady on the northern horizon.

He rode up alongside Angus. "I take it she met your expectations."

The new MacLeod Chieftain spit to the side and moved his steed forward. "Aye. She will make a good wife."

Ferchar kept his thoughts closed even though the man made no attempt to infiltrate his mind. "So we unite."

Angus snorted. "So we do."

The man was vague and evasive. Two traits Ferchar knew well. "We'll stay a fortnight and then return home."

"You'll stay three days, enough for your men to rest and then leave." Angus didn't bother looking his way. "I am the descendent of a man deprived of his love and swindled by a MacLomain wizard. I don't like you nor your clan. My only concern is how our clans can better one another in the future, to strengthen Scotland."

Ferchar contained a smile. Angus purposely tried to disarm his enemy with too much knowledge. He was telling Ferchar what he expected to hear, what made sense. But Angus's mind was quicksand—deceptive and deadly. The man longed for war. He wanted every last MacLomain dead. Caitlin was of little import save a means to an end, a spider web thread that enabled his clan access to Cowal.

"We'll stay seven nights," Ferchar said, if only to humor himself.

Angus yawned. "Three, that's final."

Ferchar nodded. He wouldn't bother wasting his breath bargaining. There were more important things on his mind. "When will you marry?"

"This eve."

With the effort of a man carrying a hundred year old pine on his shoulder, Ferchar pushed a burst of laughter from his chest into the air. "For a man recently come into leadership and obligated to marry, your eagerness is well received."

Angus didn't smile. "Be careful, MacLomain. I have the ability to make her wedding night a dour thing, indeed."

"Take her in whatever manner you choose." Ferchar felt his edge slipping. He wanted to run his dagger across the man's throat, watch his blood pour over the smooth highland rock beneath.

Angus shuffled his features. "Enough with your patronizing, MacLomain. Your care for the lass does not escape me. I'm not my brother."

So be it. Diplomacy was a lost cause on evil. "Hurt her, and I'll kill you."

Now Angus laughed. "I thought at first you might be worthy of my respect. Now I know that I was wrong. Why jeopardize your men for a lass?"

The loath Angus shot Caitlin locked Ferchar's intention with the force of an oceanic whirlpool. "Because that lass is a MacLomain."

And she is mine.

"Are all of the MacLomain men here willing to die at the end of the blade that marks your words to me now?" Angus's eyes smoldered with contempt.

Ferchar carved his words with the pride of a clansman. "Is your clan willing to forfeit such a massive tie to the south if you act upon the order your tongue is ready to deliver?"

A smirk ruined Angus's face then departed in deliverance. "You know the answer to that."

"Do I?" Ferchar looked to Caitlin's stern profile.

Angus appeared thoughtful. "As of this eve we will start anew, you and I. On a journey I'm not eager to take, but a journey nonetheless."

Ferchar said nothing more. They'd run out of time. Every step forward brought them closer to a doom he was unwilling to accept. He knew nothing of what Caitlin had endured the previous evening. Knew nothing of what she thought about him at the moment.

That it was bad, he was sure.

Many hours passed and the smell of sea salt grew stronger, the climate more ferocious. Ferchar and Alan rode directly behind Angus, Stephen and Caitlin. Her slender frame shuttered on occasion but her back never slumped and her head stayed high in the wind and rain. He longed to pull her down off of Fyne, strip the soaked clothing from her body and warm her in any way possible.

Eventually, Angus interrupted the silent travelers. "'Tis your new home, lass, just beyond the next bend."

"I welcome it after such a long, strenuous journey."

Ferchar cringed at the submissive waver heavy in Caitlin's response. What had he done to her last eve? In the case of Angus, rape may have been the lesser evil of possible scenarios. It had come too far. It was time to stop this. Gods forgive him. He was about to pull forth his magic when Caitlin spoke again.

"Save for last eve. That was pleasurable."

Angus cocked his head in her direction and narrowed his eyes. "I'm glad you thought so."

Ferchar tightened his fists and glanced at Alan. His expression was grim as the Stewart Chieftain raised his eyebrows and lifted one shoulder. What was she saying? That she had, indeed, taken him into her bed willingly? That he had been kind to her? Ferchar cut through a wave of emotions in an instant before he hardened to reality. One that had been created for her by him; a place of agonizing lust.

"Your castle, my lady," Angus said.

Through the driving rain, a fortress stood stoic on a cliff. Unlike his concentric castle, this one was square. Like their surroundings, it was jagged and roughly strewn. Tall and steep like the mountains, it was as old as the MacLomains' but far less inviting, a lone warrior with a bad attitude.

"It's beautiful." Caitlin peered forward, her voice wistful.

Did she really think so? Unlikely.

Angus looked over his shoulder at Ferchar. "There's room in the stables for your men's horses and room enough in my clansmen's quarters for all of you."

Ferchar offered a crooked grin. "You trust my warriors amongst yours?"

"My warriors will sleep in the castle." Angus smiled thinly. "Because I don't trust my clansmen amongst yours."

"'Twould appear your clansmen are at an advantage anyway, what with sheer numbers." Ferchar nodded and lost all humor. "But I appreciate your attempt at hospitality, it intrigues me."

Angus's smile widened. "As it should."

Unlike Cowal, this castle had one surrounding wall, portcullis and drawbridge, which lowered at the approach of the clans. The huts on the outskirts of the castle were weather worn and the metal on the portcullis rusted.

The villagers were thin and their expressions guarded. Dogs kept their tails between their legs. Children didn't laugh and play, but stood gaunt, like silent statues, their eyes nervous and dull from both malnutrition and servitude.

Angus rode his warhorse like a king by his people, barely sparing them a glance. Ferchar made eye contact with as many of the men as he could; sought revelation in their murky depths. What he saw did not surprise him but enlightened. This clan was unsteady, unhappy and afraid. What was the story of these people? What had they endured here, sitting alone at the pinnacle of Scotland?

As they entered the courtyard, Angus swung his horse around and nodded at the stables. "They'll take your horses there." Then he looked at a large abode behind him. "Tell your men to refresh and stay out of trouble. The celebration begins soon."

Ferchar swung down from his horse. He doubted their horses would be returned to them. Not under Angus's charge. His focus now, as his men knew it had to be, was to get both Caitlin and the whole of his clan back in Argyll, safely out of this situation.

To do that he had to anticipate the new MacLeod laird.

****

Caitlin lay curled up on the meager cot and fought off pointless tears. The room was windowless and damp. One torch burned from a wall bracket and illuminated the unadorned room. Not a rug, tapestry or piece of furniture could be found.

She'd been so strong, yet where had it gotten her? Nowhere. Tired and defeated, Caitlin wiped at her eyes. She'd never been one to cry. It went against her nature. What else was she supposed to do at this point? Ferchar and Adlin were miscellaneous pegs in a forgotten game as far as she could tell. She was on her own now.

"Caitlin." The feminine whisper startled her and she peered into the dark recesses of the room. There was no one there. The chamber was empty.

"Who's there?" Caitlin pulled her satchel closer to her. A very faint coolness covered her skin.

"Dinnae be frightened." The voice was a whisper in her ear now.

Caitlin jumped up and searched the chamber again. Fear made her veins go icy. "Who said that?
"Me. I did."

She stumbled back when an apparition formed. It sat on the cot and appeared to be a small woman with bright red hair.

"Who are you?" Caitlin said and shook her head. A ghost? Hadn't she been through enough already?

"Dinnae be frightened. Adlin sent me. My name is Marie. Marie O'Donnell." The apparition didn't move.

Marie O'Donnell? "I know that name. You are... were, Arianna's aunt. From New Hampshire?" Caitlin backed into the wall.

"Aye, that's right. Have you seen her? Is she well?"

Caitlin worked to relax and tried to disregard the fact that she was talking to a transparent woman. "Yes, she's with Iain back in Cowal."

Marie's icy hand touched her own cheek and her voice was wrought with emotion. "You look exactly like me Annie. So beautiful."

"So I've heard." Safe answer. Out of pure instinct, Caitlin sidled along the wall toward the door. One would think she wouldn't be afraid of a ghost after meeting a Scottish wizard.

Marie stood. "I have little time. Adlin could not come, for the MacLeod would have sensed his magic. You must listen to me, Caitlin."

It was hard to listen to a floating Colonial period relative and focus. "I have to get out of here. Angus is about to marry me. Where is Adlin?"

Marie nodded and a midnight-blue glow emitted from where her eyes should be. "He waits for you. You cannae stay here, lass."

"No, really?" Caitlin said.

Her sarcasm was lost on the ghost. Marie pointed at the wall. "That way. West. As soon as you can. The MacLomains are no longer your concern. You must go."

Caitlin pulled her satchel tight against her chest. She was finished with the MacLomain clan and her conscience was clear. "How? There are MacLeods everywhere at the entrance."

Marie vanished before she answered. Caitlin lurched forward. No! Where was she? Oh crap.

Tap. Tap. Tap. She spun. "Who's there?"

No response, just another knock on the door.

Super. Maybe she would open the door and find a dragon or even an elf. Nothing would surprise her now. Caitlin squared her shoulders and flung open the door.

Stephen stood in the doorway holding a dress over his arm. "Good eve, lass. I've brought a change of clothes for you."

She unchained the muscles holding her head on straight and stepped forward. "Thanks."

He handed her the dress and a comb. Before she could shut the door and turn away he held up a finger to halt her and turned back around. When he turned again, he carried a big barrel of water. He passed her and walked into the center of the chamber where he set it down. When he turned his face had changed. A deep frown lined the corners of his mouth and his eyes were intense. "I am sorry about last eve, lass."

Caitlin turned away and threw the dress on the bed. "Don't be. It wasn't your fault."

He ground his jaw. "Be that as it may, I am still sorry. You didnae deserve such as that."

"You bet I didn't." Caitlin ran a finger through the lukewarm water in the barrel. "What's done is done."

Stephan reached a hand forward to touch her face but stopped. "Aye. Here."

She took the crude bar of soap he held out to her and nodded. "Where should I go when I'm ready?"

"Down to the hall below. We celebrate for awhile yet." Before she had a chance to respond, he turned and left. Caitlin didn't give herself time to think but did the best she could with a keg of water and dressed. The deep violet gown was simple in design, with a scooped neckline and long bell-shaped sleeves that trailed nearly as long as the hemline. Not a good garment to try to flee in. She made a mental note to tie and roll the sleeves when the time came.

What she wouldn't do for a pair of jeans and a sweater right now. Oh well, pretty soon. She felt revitalized and optimistic. Adlin had made contact.

The hallway outside of the chamber was what she would have envisioned a medieval castle to host. Wide with high ceilings, the passage was lit by random brackets of torchlight and pockets of black. The ocean's salt mingled with the stone walls in ancient musk. A servant passed her at the top of the spiraled stairs leading to the main chamber below. The young clanswoman kept her eyes averted and her head down.

Caitlin had a brief glimpse of her profile as she passed. Iosbail? It couldn't be. She turned back to confront the servant but no one was there. Oh well. Her mind was bound to play tricks on her at this point. After all, Iosbail was old.

"Lass, over here." Angus's words greeted her the moment she entered the hall. Fresh rushes covered the floors. A single, wide fire overlooked the room, much like in Cowal. The tapestries were more severe, done in black, silver and gold. They spoke of war and violence on the sea. Viking ships climbed walls of black water with warriors breathing fire in defiance. Caitlin swallowed and made her way toward him.

"My laird," she said, when by his side.

Angus wore what looked to be high boots, a black tunic and his plaid wrapped over his shoulder. His hair hung free, save for several dozen small braids. A monstrous claymore was strapped to his shoulder and three daggers that she could count were visible on his person.

"You may drink this eve, lass." He handed her a heavy mug and turned his attention back to the men by his side.

Caitlin took a sip and nearly choked. The whiskey tasted like gasoline. Different distillation process evidently. As much as she needed to escape, it wasn't within this cup. She would pretend to sip from this point forth and be alert for a way to get out of here.

She scanned the faces around her and stopped on Ferchar's. He sat, back to the wall, with his clan at a long trestle table in the far corner. His intense blue eyes bore into hers with enough force, she was shocked she didn't fall back into the fire. Caitlin tore her gaze from his and focused on the cup in her hand. He had no right to even look at her.

What next? Caitlin located the door to the chamber. Just run? Not such a good idea. Tempting, but no good. She needed to get out that door. What possible reason could she have for just walking out? Caitlin bit back a smile.

Feminine necessity.

She turned to Angus and touched his arm. "My laird?"

He didn't acknowledge her at first. Arrogant bastard. "My laird?"

Angus frowned at her. "Aye?"

"I'm afraid I have need of some privacy." She nodded to the door and kept her voice discreet. "You understand."

His lack of concern was evident. "Stephen."

Stephen came alongside. "Aye."

"She requires assistance. See to it." Angus nodded his head in Caitlin's direction and then turned back to his conversation.

Caitlin breathed in and out slowly as Stephen led her through the crowd toward the door. Almost there, almost. When they left the hall, Caitlin contained a sigh of relief. Now she had to deal with Stephen and them…she looked to the numerous highland warriors who guarded the way out. But how?

"Back there." Stephen pointed to an area behind the armory.

"Much thanks." Caitlin went in the general direction that Stephen had pointed. The rain had stopped and a full moon shone bright overhead. Not the best for stealth in the dark. She navigated the rocky terrain until she reached what looked to be a trench dug along the wall. It stunk.

Twenty-first century plumbing, here I come. She veered away from the smell until the tall fortress wall loomed lonely before her. Caitlin leaned back and studied the night sky. The bright moon diminished the brilliance of the stars overhead save the one she was looking for. The North Star. She held her hand up, pointed at nothing and whispered to herself. "If that's north, then that's west."

Caitlin smiled and shook her head. This is what stress did to a person, made them daft. Obviously, if the castle stood at the northern tip of Scotland, then going to the left of the castle would be heading west.

She surveyed her surroundings. The only plan Caitlin had was to try to sneak past the men at the front, swim through the moat and then decide what to do next. One step at a time. She looked to her right. It was dark here and she was fairly confident her form would stay in the shadows. Time to move.

She made it ten steps before she slammed into a wall of chest. "Where do think you're going, lassie?"

Caitlin looked up into Stephan's face. "Nowhe—"

He put a finger to her lips and shook his head. "Not another word from you."

He grabbed her wrist and pulled her after him. Caitlin stumbled forward, past the trench and the route back to the castle door. The next thing she knew they were following the fortress wall into the blackness beyond. Where was he taking her? She started shaking as he pulled her deeper into the unknown. Not again. This was too much. No more.

Caitlin stiffened her legs and stopped walking. He didn't miss a beat but swung around, gagged her with a cloth, lifted her over his shoulder and plodded forward. She kicked and flailed but was held tight. Before she completely lost it, he descended a steep path, flung her down to her feet and pushed her back into the crevice of rock.

"I'm not going to hurt you, Caitlin. We have little time before Angus follows us," he whispered close to her face, his voice low and urgent.

She shook her head and fought a wave of tears. "I'll take you to Adlin, Caitlin. Do you ken? Adlin."

His eyes were lost in the darkness. "I'll remove the gag if you promise not to scream."

She nodded vigorously.

The moment he removed the gag she coughed but he covered her mouth with his hand. "Quiet."

Caitlin removed his hand. "Adlin?"

"Aye, come." Stephen grabbed her arm and dragged her after him. Neither spoke as they made their way down further until the path changed and they began to climb.

She believed him. Why, she couldn't fathom. Maybe because there was no one left to believe. Twenty minutes later they were on flat rock again. Caitlin glanced back while she was dragged forward. The MacLeod castle was behind them, studious and condescending in the moonlight. The ocean stretched as wide and far as the eye could see, silver and molten.

They veered away from the ocean into a meager stretch of sturdy pine and larch. "Why are you doing this?" Caitlin asked.

He didn't look back. "'Tis a favor I owe the MacLomain clan. To right the wrong I did them."

"What?" Caitlin was running out of breath. "Stephen, I can't keep up."

He slowed slightly. "Come, as quickly as you can. He follows now."

Forget lack of breath, she increased her speed again and questioned him through ragged gasps. "What wrong did you do the MacLomains?"

"I took Arianna from their former Chieftain." Caitlin tripped but he caught her. "Arianna?"

He nodded and urged her on. "She was to marry their Chieftain, many years ago, but—"

The emotion in his explanation was evident when he broke off. Her mind imploded. This was Stephen Broun from the novel? It had to be. The mysterious clansman who'd run off with the Arianna Broun from this time, the one intended to be Iain's bride. The defective Scotsman who defied his clan and an old promise for the love of a woman. Incredible. And here he was saving her life.

"Where is she Stephen? Where's Arianna Broun?"

She was met with silence and he pulled her forward faster. Caitlin was about to speak again when Stephen yanked her down just before an arrow whizzed over her head. Caitlin contained a scream, gripped the mossy rock and looked back. Angus appeared a demon as his horse thundered through the tree line.

"Stephen!" She turned her head back but he was gone. Where was he? Hooves vibrated beneath her fingertips. Go. She had to go forward.

If it was her time to die, better here with an arrow in her back than years of hell with the man behind her. Caitlin sprinted forward and broke free from the trees onto an open cliff.

Time sped up and slowed down at the same time.

Adlin stood tall at the edge of the cliff. Against the fierceness of the wind, his white robes rose and slowly flapped in the wind like a bird ready to take flight. His eyes glowed blue against the backdrop of black whirlwind behind him.

"Stop." Angus's one word shackled her legs together and she dropped to the ground.

Caught betwixt them, Caitlin lowered her head. Adlin had one hand raised in the air behind him and one in front of him.

"Release her." Adlin's voice sounded young and powerful.

"Nay, old man." Angus swung down from his horse. "This time, you willnae win."

The MacLeod clansman stopped short when he hit an unseen barrier. Caitlin tried to stand but her legs were still mysteriously bound together so she began to drag herself toward Adlin. She was going home, darn it.

"I willnae give her to you, Angus." Adlin curled his fingers and Angus was pushed back.

The clansman chuckled. "Aye, but you will." He removed a satchel from his side and released the cinch. A small, black, metal pentacle dropped into his palm.

Caitlin felt the power shift unfavorably.

"How do you have that?" The pain in Adlin's gaze turned the power in his eyes a murky shade of blue.

Angus smiled and brought the pentacle to the unseen shield that barred him from moving forward. It dropped and he laughed. His lips straightened and his eyes died when he looked at Adlin. "I suppose you could say I've good acquaintances."

"Very good." Caitlin swung her gaze to the sound of the deep voice.

Ferchar. He stood, legs apart, about ten feet from her. Alan was beside him.

"Ahhh, MacLomain. You've come properly attired." Angus massaged the pentacle.

Caitlin closed her eyes to Ferchar's beauty and looked away. His plaid was gone and black robes billowed around him. Though his eyes were the magnetic sapphire of Adlin's, his black hair made him appear an archangel. A non-mortal who understood Angus's sinister heart better than Adlin ever could.

The MacLeod Chieftain held the black pentacle by its heart and ran one of its five points along his cheek. "Where's yours, MacLomain?"

There was nothing in Ferchar's face to acknowledge that he'd heard Angus's taunt, nothing to prepare her for what happened next.

"Go, Caitlin. Go." Ferchar's voice crashed into her mind as he removed from his folds a black pentacle identical to the one Angus held. *"Go!"*

Caitlin looked back to him but he didn't look at her. Go? Her eyes drifted over his face in that moment. Leave you? She looked back to Angus and saw the sudden resolve and fury overtaking his features.

"Home, Caitlin. Go home." This time it was Adlin who filled her mind. Slow motion overtook Caitlin as she stood, and her legs were freed.

"Dinnae move, lass," Angus snarled.

Underwater. She remembered how that affiliation was made in the novel about crucial points between Arianna and Iain. As though movement was nearly impossible, time pushed against them, hindered their every move.

That's how everything happened.

She took a step back toward Adlin and Angus shook his head. He raised his hand and whipped the black pentacle at her. At the same moment, Ferchar threw his and it intercepted Angus's, mere feet in front of her.

Rage engorged Angus as the pentacles froze midair above them in a war of magic. He pulled his axe free. Caitlin reached into her cleavage and withdrew the sapphire dagger.

As Angus thrust his axe at her, she whipped her blade at him.

"No!" Alan jumped between them, his back to Caitlin. Ferchar caught her head on and pushed her back.

All Caitlin could see as she fell backward was Alan falling to his back, an axe handle protruding from his chest and Muriel's dagger lodged in Angus's heart, swamping his shocked form in flames of intense sapphire.

Then it all fell away.

Everyone and everything faded as she fell off the edge of the cliff—into blackness and wind, heartache and regret.

An end. Finally.

Chapter Eighteen

The day dawned bright and clear, warm and inviting. She threw back her head and relished the sun's rays on her face. Glorious...Scotland in the spring.

Cowal in the spring.

"Well, now or never," she said and narrowed her eyes. With all the power she had in her legs, she ran forward and plummeted headfirst over the waterfall. As the water rushed at her, she shut her eyes.

But she never hit the surface.

Instead, she floated, her skin massaged by the crashing waterfall. First, slow and patient, like a lover, careful and talented; then, aggressive and eager, impatient.

She curled into a ball as it became cruel. Unknown. Overwhelming. Hurting her.

"No!" She curled tighter and shook her head. "No."

"Caitlin."

The waterfall drained away and a voice pushed past fear to reason.

"Caitlin."

She lay still as her soul sank into her body.

Caitlin shook her head and opened her eyes. It was so dark. Wherever she was, whatever was meant for her next, he was here. She couldn't see him, but felt him. His hand skimmed her cheekbone. His scent surrounded her.

"Did you die, too?"

Destiny's Denial

His warm lips touched her forehead. "Do I feel dead to you?"

Caitlin blinked. Not dead? She wasn't dead?

She ran her tongue over her lips. I'm alive!

Thunder roared overhead and lightning flashed. The interior of the barn appeared and then disappeared. Another flash of lightning revealed C.C. looking down at her from the stall above. Tears welled and poured over. I'm alive! Caitlin scrambled to her feet and wrapped her arms around the horse. A blood and flesh horse that was more than a bit disturbed.

"C.C., I'm home!" She wasted no time but flew in the direction of the barn doors and flung them open. It was torrential and storming. Wind blew in all directions. She ran outside and blinked at her house. The outside light was on as well as the kitchen light.

"I'm home! The twenty-first bloody century!" She screamed at the sky and spun in circles. "Thank you, Adlin."

Rain soaked her as she jumped and twirled in more circles. Shane. Where was he? Caitlin ran for the front door as a clap of thunder roared overhead. She slid in mud to the front door and swung it open.

"What the—?"

She heard him from the kitchen and sobbed. "Shane, I'm home."

Her brother flew around the corner and froze. "Caitlin?" His dog, Nakita, was right behind him wagging her tail.

"Yeah!"

He ran forward and pulled her into his arms. They held each other for a few moments before he pulled back and studied her. Shane shook his head. "You're really home?"

She smiled and wiped tears from her eyes. "Yeah."

"Wow, come in. Shut the door." He slammed the door and ushered her into the kitchen where he sat her down at the table, plunked a beer in front of her and shook his head. "You're really home."

She downed half the beer and looked around with vigor. "Electricity. I didn't realize how much I missed electricity."

Caitlin took another sip of her beer and encompassed the bottle with her hands. "And cold beer."

He laughed, shut his laptop and pulled his chair closer to her. "How are you? You okay?"

She sat back and drank in the sight of modern appliances. "Good. I'm good. I'm here!"

"I know." Shane looked incredulous. "I was so afraid for you."

She grew serious when she met his eyes. "Me, too."

Caitlin pushed away the beer and stood. "How long was I gone?"

"About two weeks." He stood as well.

They looked at one another, caught in a moment of perplexing indifference. Shane took her hand. "But you're really okay?"

"Yeah. I went through a lot after you left but in the end, Adlin and Ferchar—" The words died on her lips.

"Adlin and Ferchar, what?" Shane frowned.

"Oh no." She turned and headed for the door.

Shane was right behind her. "What Caitlin?"

She flung open the door and they both froze.

Shane's words trailed in a long blaze of disbelief. "Caitlin, is that who I think it is?"

Ferchar leaned casually against the old oak with his legs crossed. He wore the MacLomain plaid as rain sluiced over his muscular chest.

She was speechless as his blue eyes met hers. No wizard, just a beautiful Scotsman standing in the rain without a care in the world.

A sharp jab to her ribcage prompted a response. "Yes, Shane. I'm pretty sure that's who you think it is."

Her brother smiled in Ferchar's direction, pleaded a moment alone with a gesture, ushered Caitlin back into the house and shut the door. "You took a handfasting that serious, Caitlin?"

"A what?" She went to open the door but he stopped her.

"You do realize you're not legally married to him, right?" Shane's eyebrows slammed together and he shook his head.

"I still don't—" Caitlin allowed a small smile. "Oh, you think I couldn't possibly leave my husband behind."

Her brother shrugged and his voice became a masculine warning. "Well, that seems to be one possible reason you would've brought home an eight hundred year old Scottish Chieftain."

She gave a weak laugh. "He's twenty-six, not eight hundred years old, to begin with."

Caitlin put a hand up before he could speak and crushed his theory. "And I did not bring him home. Think about it Shane, I've never wanted to be married and still don't. Do you honestly think if I did, I'd do it with him?"

"Never mind. He's here and we can't let him stand out there in the rain. Can we, Caitlin?"

She narrowed her eyes. "No, I suppose we can't."

He shook his head and opened the door. Expression grim, Ferchar hadn't moved. Caitlin stepped out the door into the rain and stopped.

Lightning flashed and suddenly everything that had happened snapped into vivid detail.

Alan. He'd died for her. Ohhh nooo. Her chest squeezed painfully. Her body shook violently and she dropped to her knees. How could I have forgotten? Oh dear God. No. No. No. She hung her head. No. Bile rose fast and she threw up over and over again.

Eventually, nausea started to fade. She held her stomach and kept her head down.

"Caitlin, hon. Talk to me." At some point, Shane had knelt beside her, a strong arm of support around her as he held her hair back. "What's going on?"

She rubbed her sweaty forehead. "He saved me." Caitlin's voice broke on a sob. "He was too young to die."

"Who?"

She said nothing for a period of time before sitting back on her heels. Ferchar stood over them now, his eyes like steel.

"Alan." She whispered. Shane carefully pulled her to her feet. "Come in the house. Obviously, you've been through a lot."

Caitlin nodded and stood. She met Ferchar's eyes. Her anger with him was irrelevant at the moment. He'd suffered a loss as well. "Please come inside. Dry off."

His eyes shifted to the house behind her and a muscle leapt in his cheek. Still, he said nothing and didn't move.

She held out her hand. "You can't stay out here, Ferchar."

"Please," Shane said as well. "Unless you have to return now."

Ferchar's eyes swung to Shane's and then back to Caitlin's. "I cannae return."

She dropped her hand as her heart-rate increased. Caitlin turned and nodded at the door. "Of course you can. Iain did. Come inside. We'll discuss this where it's dry."

Ferchar's eyes lingered on hers for a few more moments before he nodded and followed them in. His large body shrunk the foyer and made it seem a closet.

Destiny's Denial

Caitlin and Shane glanced at one another. Who would've ever thought they would have a medieval highlander standing in their house?

Shane shook his head at his dog. Nakita eyed Ferchar warily but didn't bark. "You're really not much of a watchdog, are you?"

Nakita lowered her ears, wagged her tail and smiled.

"What time is it, Shane?" Caitlin asked. While she still didn't feel that well she could at least function.

He looked at his wristwatch. "Eight-thirty."

"Good. The mall is still open. You need to drive over and buy some suitable clothes for him until we get this sorted out." Caitlin grabbed a couple of towels from the linen closet and handed one to Ferchar.

Shane frowned. "Now? Are you sure you're well enough for me to leave?"

"Yes. But before you leave, grab a pair of your sweatpants for him." She towel dried her hair.

"You're serious?" His eyes took in Ferchar's size and then he looked down at himself. "They're not going to fit him well."

She gave Shane a pointed look. "Hence, the trip to the mall."

Caitlin offered her brother a weak smile. "Or you can stay here with Ferchar and I'll run to the mall."

Shane narrowed his eyes. "Point taken." He dashed up the stairs and returned with navy blue sweats.

"Here." Shane handed them to Caitlin, put on his jacket, grabbed his keys and dashed out the door into the rain.

Before Caitlin had a chance to speak, the door reopened and Shane stepped back inside. He looked Ferchar up and down. "You don't happen to know your size, do you?"

Her eyes slid to the Chieftain's tall frame, wide shoulders and well-muscled everything. "I'd say hit the tall and big store."

Shane nodded and yelled over his shoulder before he shut the door again. "I'll see what I can find."

Then they were alone. No MacLomains. No MacLeods. No Scotland. Caitlin's heart skidded in her chest. *I'm not ready to be alone with him. I thought I was but no.* The air suddenly became sparser and a wave of dizziness had her grabbing the banister.

"Are you well, lass?" Ferchar's hand shot to her elbow.

Heat sizzled up her arm, down her torso and lodged below. Arousal flared. Hell, he still managed to turn her on despite the circumstances. No. Not good. She closed her eyes and breathed deeply. "Yes. Please release my arm."

His fingers briefly skimmed her forearm then pulled away. The urge to let him have her here at the base of the stairs nearly made her howl like a damned animal. Forget that. "Follow me, I'll show you to the bathroom so you can get out of those wet clothes."

"I'm fine, Caitlin. We need to talk." He moved closer.

She held up a hand and shook her head. "No. You're not staying in that wet plaid and we don't need to talk about anything. You gave up that right when you let Angus have me."

His voice stayed low and flickered with regret as he followed her up the stairs. "I had little choice, lass."

Little choice? Sonofabitch! She swung around and pointed a finger at his chest with each and every word. "You. Had. A. Choice. You just chose wrong. And when you did, you lost any inkling of respect I may have had for you prior."

He seized her wrist. "Your respect for me was not at issue. Your life meant more."

"My life?" Caitlin wanted to punch, smack, then kick him. She tried to pull her wrist free but he held it firmly. "Or the lives of your clansmen?"

"Both." He ground his jaw. "And I have succeeded in half of my endeavor."

Furious, she twisted the knife in the wound. "You mean Alan succeeded in half of your endeavor."

In the blink of an eye, Ferchar pulled her to the top of the stairs and had her back against the wall. His face drew close and fury flared in his ethereal eyes. "What Alan did was love you, and die for you." Ferchar's words dripped venom as he held her tighter. "Twould be ill advised for you to mention him to me again. Do you ken, lass?"

An errant, unwelcome tear slid from her eye. "And it would be equally ill advised for you to accost me in my own home."

"I would have to agree with that." Ferchar ignored the warning from below but leaned in closer. "You are home, Caitlin. The whole of it is over for you."

"I'll use this if you don't back away, now."

"It's all right, Amanda." Caitlin took a deep breath and pushed his slackened hands away. She saw clearly how much he hurt. How losing his friend ravaged his good sense. She peered down the stairs at her friend.

She stood at the bottom with a small, black object held high. Her hands shook. "I don't believe you."

"Is that a stun gun you're holding?" Caitlin cocked her head.

"Yeah." Amanda nodded. "I got it last summer."

"Well, you don't need it. Put it away."

Her friend's eyes drifted to Ferchar when he turned around. Her arms lowered slowly. Her mouth moved but nothing came out.

Despite the tension between them, Caitlin took Ferchar's hand and led him down the stairs. Her mind worked fast. This should be interesting. "Amanda, this is my cousin, Ferchar. He's from Scotland."

Amanda stepped back but kept the gun handy. Her eyes traveled from his hair, over his chest and straight down to his plaid. "I never would've guessed. What part of Scotland, exactly?"

An extinct part. "Cowal. He's an actor."

Amanda met Caitlin's eyes. "And he's in costume now, why?"

Ferchar smiled. Caught off guard, Amanda couldn't help but smile in return. When he spoke his Scottish burr was thick and sensual. Caitlin watched her friend melt before her eyes. He stepped forward, took the back of her hand and raised it to his lips. "This is the United States, is it not, lass? The land of opportunity? For any level of success I must sharpen my abilities. Caitlin was gracious enough to allow me to practice my skills on her."

Amanda's mouth hung open as she stared up at him. Though she spoke to Caitlin, her eyes remained on Ferchar. "I didn't know you had a Scottish cousin, Caitlin. Family secret?"

Caitlin was dumbfounded. Had he just said The United States? And this is instead of 'tis? A murmured consent was all she was capable of offering Amanda. "A family secret. Yeah, I guess so."

"You guess so?" Amanda was still riveted on his face. Caitlin rolled her eyes and walked into the kitchen.

She bypassed the beer and went straight for the tequila. She hated lying to Amanda but had no choice. "He was visiting Deb down in Virginia. I managed to convince him to come here before he headed for California. What're a few more weeks?"

"I like your thinking," Amanda said. Ferchar stepped back and allowed her to enter the kitchen first.

Amanda received the shot glass full of liquor Caitlin handed her and looked back at him. "Ferchar. I've never heard that name before."

Caitlin downed her tequila and kept her eyes from him.

"It's rather old fashioned. Handed down through the generations," he replied.

"Ahhh." Amanda nodded and frowned at Caitlin. "Aren't you going to offer Ferchar a refreshment?"

Actually, she'd fully intended to drink the whole bottle on her own. Reluctantly, she removed one more shot glass from the cabinet and filled it. "Aye."

Amanda looked at Caitlin. "Aye? You're really in part right now, aren't you?"

Caitlin gave an inward curse. "You could say that."

Her friend's eyes ran the length of her. "I like the dress. It's very..."

"I know, old fashioned." Caitlin poured another shot.

"And you're wearing it, why?" Amanda smirked.

"That would be because of me." Ferchar downed his shot and rolled the glass between his fingers. "I insist on my heroines being in full costume as well."

Caitlin almost choked on her second shot. His heroine? Let him keep on fantasizing.

His words were deeper and smoother than the finest liqueur. "It makes the whole interplay so much more authentic, heightens the actor's ability to imagine a romance left behind in a far off place and time."

Amanda released a sentimental sigh, grabbed a shot glass and poured both of them another round. "I can understand that."

She handed him his glass and raised her brows. "And your era would be?"

Caitlin looked his way. He made a suave study of the liquid before he shot it back and his eyes locked on hers. "I would imagine that's fairly obvious. Medieval Scotland." His sapphire eyes swung to Amanda and he offered a brilliant smile. "Early thirteenth century to be precise."

Amanda's hand fluttered to her chest. "Before Robert the Bruce and William Wallace."

Caitlin's heart slammed into her throat and she poured a third shot.

"Aye, lass. Before the Bruce."

Her eyes shot to Ferchar. His expression was unreadable. He knew of Scotland's history. From the cut of his features and distance in his eyes, she would swear he knew all of it—including the eventual downfall of the MacLomain clan. That possibility hurt beyond reason. Could it really be that he already knew the eventual fate of Scotland? The ruination of the clan structure that was his? Caitlin sipped from her shot glass this time.

"I've always wanted to go there." Amanda handed him another shot. "What's Cowal like?"

Ferchar leaned against the door jam. Again his eyes drifted Caitlin's way. "Beautiful. Like a lass."

One corner of his mouth drew up and his gaze fell somewhere beyond her. "With soft, curved rolling hills and proud, noble mountains. Her eyes are golden in the morn and her skin as delicate as the mist in the eve."

Caitlin's mouth turned dry when his eyes found hers.

"She's forthright, Scotland's Cowal. Unafraid of stinging your eyes with the wind's sea salt and gracious enough to give you shelter in a waterfall's cave or beneath a faithful birch."

Amanda's eyes went from Ferchar to Caitlin. "You speak well of your homeland."

"Aye." His blue gaze dropped briefly to Caitlin's lips before he consumed the shot in his hand. He turned a devilish grin Amanda's way. "This is good but you dinnae happen to have a wee bit o' whiskey?"

A smile creased her gray eyes and she pushed away from the counter. "Will scotch do?"

Ferchar grinned and handed his glass back to her, his gesture answer enough.

Amanda nodded and headed for the cabinet.

Caitlin stepped aside. "I take it you have tomorrow off?"

Amanda grabbed the bottle. "It's Sunday, of course I do."

"Speaking of work." Amanda untwisted the cap and opened another cabinet. "Do you still have a job?"

Caitlin sat down at the table. Good question. She'd given the restaurant no notice of her departure and left no instructions for Shane. "I have no clue."

Amanda winked. "I'm just playing with you. They called and I covered for you, though I'm surprised you didn't call them yourself."

Caitlin leaned her elbow on the table and covered her eyes. "Thanks, sweetie. I owe you."

Amanda's hand touched her shoulder. "Go run upstairs and get out of that wet dress. Why it's wet, I won't ask."

Caitlin nodded slowly and stood. "Yeah, I'll do that."

Ferchar's form filled the doorway. What about his clothes? When she brushed by him her hand grazed the wool fabric of his tartan. It was nearly dry. She looked up at him and her knees almost buckled. He was too good looking by half. Caitlin climbed the stairs, stumbled into her room and sat on the bed. Her bedroom seemed bereft and distant. A place that had somehow remained the same though she'd completely changed. She lay back and stared at the ceiling. A multitude of thoughts and emotions crushed the surface of her awareness. She was so tired.

Pure exhaustion settled over her and she shut her eyes. She needed to rest for just a moment. To try to sort everything out. To plan her next move. Then, as slumber stole Caitlin, it occurred to her that she was home. Safe.

There was no next move to plan.

****

Eventually, the thunder receded and left in its wake flashes of misplaced lightning. Raindrops slid free from the wind and fell in straight sheets on the roof overhead.

He sat in the corner of the dark room and watched her sleep. Her arms were flung up over her head and deep chestnut hair fanned out in a halo on her pillow. Peace enveloped her rest.

When he'd come in earlier, Caitlin had thrashed with restlessness. He'd shut off the light, removed her dress, pulled the blanket over her and pushed calm into her soul. He owed her that and so much more.

Now he was here.

He'd traveled forward in time to ensure her safety, nothing more. Ferchar was not Iain—lovesick and foolish. He had pledged to bring her home and he had, or so he kept trying to convince himself. Iain and Adlin were fully prepared for what lay ahead of them. For what Adlin's pact had meant for their clan if not fulfilled. Ferchar had done all he could.

Caitlin knew, he knew, hell, they all had. That if Adlin was bereft of a plan to begin with, one would not surface in such a short amount of time.

But they'd hoped. In the end, their problems had been solved.

Ferchar leaned forward and clasped his hands. There would not be a massive clan war. Thanks to Caitlin's quick thinking, Muriel's dagger had destroyed Angus. He knew who the next Chieftain would be. The MacLeods would release Adlin from the pact and the people would flourish under their new laird. So Caitlin had been wrong, both endeavors had been accomplished.

What an incredible woman she was. Who would have thought she could throw a dagger like that? But then again, Caitlin had proven herself capable of most anything. Now he understood why her dreams and their lovemaking had brought them to that cliff.

All along it was but her vision of the cliff that should've taken her away from him, which would have been the case if he'd not been in a position where he thought to save her life. Nothing had mattered but her safety. Not even his aversion to traveling to the future.

Ferchar sat back and closed his eyes. What had she endured that night with Angus? Boundless speculation overwhelmed him. Her pride was fierce and her mental wall higher than any he'd come across. He knew why. The moments in her mind within a dream had laid a map. Made him understand how adept she had become at setting aside the past and offering the world a face devoid of her inner torment.

But he would not let them go forward without the truth. Years could unravel before she told him. Years that would eventually drive the pain of that night deeper into her soul. Change her irrevocably.

Ferchar could not allow that.

As was taught to him by his mentor, he would do something he'd done only once before for Arianna when she was nearly raped by the enemy. He would erase the memory from Caitlin's mind. He was not fond of magic used this way but the idea of her living with something so horrible hurt him physically.

Ferchar got up and crossed the dark room. Sitting on the edge of the bed, he whispered the words of the ancients. Release the memory. Make it mine. Release memoria. Satis mihi. He lightly skimmed his fingers over her forehead and closed his eyes.

It was the obligation of whoever took the memory to witness what they erased. That was the hardship of it. The memory became their own for all time. A secret they brought to their graves, for to talk about it to another irrevocably brought the memory back to its owner with a force that crippled the mind and ruled his or her existence.

As he chanted, a slow light burned in the distance of his mind. Like a black wave rolling away from the sun, it blinded him and then faded until a campfire surfaced. Her memory became his, her thoughts his. Caitlin knelt in front of Angus as he ripped the MacLomain plaid from her shoulders.

His low voice said, "Now we will see if you were worth the wait."

Caitlin cursed her shaking bones and said nothing. Stephen was silent behind her but she felt his tension. Angus's black gaze roved over her shoulders, then fell to her midsection.

"My brother didnae even have the balls to take you." Angus offered a sadistic chuckle and reached for his whiskey.

She tried to swallow but couldn't. The fear pushing the blood through her veins blurred her vision.

Angus nearly had the whiskey to his lips when he paused. "What do you think of that, lass?"

Words. She needed words to speak and grabbed for any she could find in her terrified mind. "Do you really care what I think?"

A grin that would've made the archangel Gabriel flinch broke his horrid visage. "No. But aren't pleasantries wonderfully useless?"

Caitlin threw up a mental wall and sat back on her heels. What point was there in the horror that flooded her now? It wasn't going to change anything. A strange, blissful calm enveloped her, or maybe just the resolve of a woman who had already been through too much, one who had become used to living with fear day after day.

When she spoke her words were level. "Let's just skip the formalities and get right to your so called pleasantries. I haven't the use for your antagonistic banter."

The berserker entered his ebony gaze as one of his large hands shot forward, seized her throat and pulled her forward. Mildew breath soiled his threat. "Dinnae play brave with me, lass. You stink of buried panic and false pretension."

He slammed her back onto the rock and moss. "And arrogance in a woman is equivalent to a Scottish lowlander mating with a Sassenach whore."

Caitlin didn't bother fighting him, but lay still and baited him further, as though she had a death wish. Maybe she did. "Regrettably, I've both lowland Scot and English blood running through my veins."

"Have you?" Angus sneered. "How corrupt."

He lowered himself over her. "Luckily for you, I need a breeder."

Caitlin turned her face away and suffered through his lack of foreplay. He didn't touch or look at her but simply pushed her dress up.

She crawled inside herself and tried to ignore the man who was becoming more and more frustrated above her. As reality began to slowly sift back into place she kept a small smile well hidden. Eventually, he rolled off of her, growled with irritation and dismissed her back to the other side of the fire. Though slumber did not find her that night, relief did.

Angus was impotent.

Ferchar released Caitlin's mind and opened his eyes. A swell of intense relief nearly doubled him over. She'd been so courageous. Ready to do whatever it took to ensure his clan's safety. His safety.

This twenty-first century lass had the heart of a hero, the soul of a warrior. Alan was right, he should have made her his wife immediately. Ferchar studied her. She was so lovely. Perfect.

His heart turned his eyes from her and he sighed. Could he marry her now? Would he? Yes. If given half the chance, he would be honored. But would it be that easy after everything they had been through?

Ferchar was not such a fool to think so.

Chapter Nineteen

"Caitlin, you have company!"

She rolled and pulled the comforter over her head. Company? Of course I do. A hundred Scotsmen warriors and three temperamental Chieftains. Why Shane felt the need to yell that to her in the middle of the forest baffled her. In fact, Shane went home, so how was he—.

Caitlin bolted upright.

Bright sunlight streamed through the windows and a warm wind blew the curtains inward. Home. Not a cold Highland forest. She looked at the clock. Ten already?

"Caitlin!"

"Yeah, I'll be down in a minute," she yelled and swung out of bed. Caitlin frowned. She was naked. When had she removed her dress?

The night before was a blur. Shane had left to get clothes and Amanda came home. She closed her eyes and shook her head. Ferchar was a Scottish actor.

Shots of tequila…coming upstairs to change…

Caitlin groaned. Oh no. She'd fallen asleep and left Ferchar on his own. Panic made her move fast. Where was he? How was he? She threw on a pair of black sweatpants, a baggy white T-shirt and flew downstairs.

When she rounded the corner to the kitchen, Caitlin almost dropped dead at the sight that greeted her.

Shane leaned against the counter, coffee cup in hand and shot her a devilish smirk. "Would you like a cup of coffee, Caitlin?"

She was speechless. Ferchar sat comfortably at the kitchen table with an adoring Nakita by his side and a cup of coffee in hand. He wore a pair of stonewashed blue jeans and a black sweater. His braids were gone and his blue-black hair was brushed. She'd thought him unbelievably handsome as a highlander but this transformation was incredible. He wore the twenty-first century as though he had always been a part of it—an elite, super sexy part of it.

His light blue eyes were that of a predator as he watched the man across from him.

Of all the people she expected to see, Rick was not one of them. She leaned against the counter for support and took the proffered cup of coffee from Shane.

Rick stood but didn't move forward. "Caitlin."

"Rick," Caitlin said, bereft of further comment.

"I heard you were home so I popped over. You left so unexpectedly." His eyes shifted briefly to Ferchar, then back to her. "Is your cousin okay?"

"My cousin?" Caitlin tried to sip her coffee but lacked the power to lift the mug to her mouth.

Shane crossed one leg in front of the other. "Yeah, Deb, down in Virginia. Remember her?"

Caitlin blinked. Pull it together girl. "Oh, of course. Deb. She's okay. Thanks."

"Rick happened to be at the mall last night and was worried about you, Caitlin," Shane provided.

She nodded absently, still unable to introduce a steady stream of dialogue.

"I've already introduced our cousin, Ferchar." Shane met Caitlin's eyes over the top of his mug.

"Good." Caitlin gripped the edge of the counter with her palms. "That's good."

"I didn't know you had family from Scotland." Rick leaned against the counter beside her.

Neither did I. She kept her eyes on Rick. "Yes I do. He's distant, well, kind of."

"Really, lass. I'm only twice removed, aye?" Ferchar's talented tongue rolled his R's and a smile was evident within his Scottish drawl.

Her eyes met his and her stomach flipped. "That's right."

"Are you coming back to work soon?" Rick touched her arm.

Caitlin almost pulled away before she remembered she was supposed to be dating this guy. Though she nodded, she said, "no."

Rick brushed the back of his hand against her cheek. "Is that yes or no?"

Ferchar's eyes narrowed at the intimate gesture, but he said nothing.

That alone brought Caitlin out of her stupor. How dare he presume a fraction of possessiveness when it came to her? He was on her territory now.

She smiled at Rick. "Pretty soon. I'll call Jessie and see what I can work out. I'll be back by Wednesday at the latest."

He leaned over and brushed his lips across hers. "I missed you."

"I'm sorry I didn't tell you I was leaving, it was sudden." Caitlin sipped from her mug. She had missed coffee. Enough with watered wine first thing in the morning.

"No problem." His deep blue eyes twinkled. "We've only just begun, after all."

"Nonetheless." She took his hand in hers. "It was rude."

He stared down at their entwined fingers for a moment. "I've got to go to work. Can I swing by later?"

Caitlin was playing a dangerous game with Ferchar here. So be it. She squeezed his hand. "Absolutely, I'd like that."

"Great," Rick said.

"Let me walk you out."

"No, you have company." He smiled. "I can see myself out, thanks."

He waved goodbye over his shoulder to Shane and Ferchar before he left. "Bye guys."

Shane sat down at the table as the door shut. "It didn't take long for him to show up, huh?"

Caitlin refreshed her coffee and pulled herself up into a sitting position on the countertop. "I was gone a while."

"You've a way with men, lass." Ferchar's tone held a sharp edge of humor. "In any century."

Her brother snorted. "She always has."

Caitlin wasn't amused. "Neither of you are saints from what I've seen."

Shane winked at Ferchar. "Did she tell you she's already turned down one marriage proposal?"

Her mouth hit the floor. "Shane!"

"I can believe that." Ferchar's eyes slid the length of her legs.

When had these two become so chummy?

"He was crushed when she said no." Shane laughed and refilled Ferchar's coffee mug.

She slammed down her cup in retaliation. "I was only eighteen. That's way too young for marriage."

A smug smile managed to only magnify Ferchar's sex appeal when his quiet voice speared her. "I would have wed you at fourteen."

Instinct prompted her to squeeze her thighs together. "And that, MacLomain, is just nasty."

"You would not have thought so."

The confidence in his statement burned her womb and beads of sweat covered her skin. Bloody Scotsman.

Shane cleared his throat and stood. "I've got things to do."

Caitlin glared at him. "No, you don't"

"Actually, I do." His grin turned sheepish. "I've got an appointment with a New York publisher here in town."

"What?" She went to jump down, but he stopped her.

"Easy there," he said. "Don't jinx me with congratulations. Not yet."

She grabbed his wrist. "Well, you have to tell me something."

Shane chuckled. "Let's just say I've been busy writing since I got home and I've finally got something that interests the ridiculously selective world of publishing."

"That's great." She tried not to tear up. He'd been trying so hard for so long. "Good luck."

He clucked her under the chin. "Thanks."

"Bye, Ferchar. Keep an eye on her," Shane said.

Shane shouldered into a light jacket. "By the way, Caitlin. You better go visit Gram. I told her everything you wanted me to, but you know how she is. Worried."

She nodded. "I'm all over it."

He gave a quick wave and flew out the front door.

"He's a good lad, your brother." Ferchar unraveled himself from the chair and stood.

Her mouth went dry and she clamped her teeth. His long legs looked great in jeans and though the sweater was a looser fit, his muscles defied the fabric.

A steady, nonchalant voice was key here. "Yes, he is."

Like a panther, his movement forward was slow and deliberate. "And I like Amanda, as well."

She should've jumped down but her reflexes pushed her in the opposite direction until the back of her kneecaps hit the edge of the counter. "So you enjoyed each other's company last night?"

"Very much so." He was mere feet from her now. "She has a good sense of humor and a quick intellect."

Caitlin brought her coffee cup to her mouth, a barrier of sorts between him and her. "I didn't think a sense of humor was your thing in a woman."

He stopped. "Why does everyone think that?"

She laughed into her cup and offered him no explanation. Caitlin had far more important things on her mind. "You have adjusted well to my time period, Ferchar. Why is that?"

Nakita came up beside him, sat down and eyed him with worship. Ferchar ran his hand over her head. "Why do you think, Caitlin?"

She shook her head. "No, don't do that. Don't answer my question with a question. That sort of thing tries my patience."

His eyes locked on her. "Patience? Somehow, that word doesn't suit you."

"Excuse me? I've been nothing but patient since I was flung back in time, handfasted and made to ride horseback for over two weeks to the tip of Scotland to marry a man who was killed in front of me in cold blood by his own brother." Caitlin had so much more to say but felt her emotions starting to bubble over.

"Aye, you have been amazing," he murmured. "But that is not what I was referring to. Your thinking is—"

She frowned and interrupted him. He better be careful. "Is what?"

One eyebrow shot up and he shook his head. "Do you see how easily I took you away from your original question? A more patient person would not have been swayed so easily."

She bit her lip and cursed. "You don't have on your robes so don't speak in circles as if you do."

Caitlin sucked in a ragged breath as her words brought to mind the visual of him standing on a cliff in black wizard garb. She'd gone somewhere she wasn't nearly ready to go.

"My apologies." He made a slight movement with his hand and Nakita happily went and lied down in the foyer. "It was not my intention. I was only going to say earlier that your thinking is accurate. In all of those cases you were very patient."

"There it is." She sat forward. "You said it was, instead of 'twas. Your words are very modern now, Ferchar."

He straightened and sighed. "I'm just trying to make this easier for you, Caitlin."

"Easier? That's the least of my concerns. What I think is a more pressing matter is how you've adapted to the twenty-first century with such ease, as if you've been here before."

Ferchar closed the distance and braced his hands on the counter, caging her with his arms. "Well, I did visit you before William was returned."

Caitlin went to push him away but decided against physical contact. "You did, that I'm sure of. But I don't think you stayed long beyond that. I think there's a lot you're not telling me."

He shrugged. "Does it not make sense to you that I would study the time period in which I found my long lost cousin whom I thought dead?"

Caitlin didn't pause. "How, precisely, does a wizard from the past research the future?"

Ferchar's even, white teeth appeared behind his mischievous grin. "Now, that I cannae tell you."

"Of course you can't." She polished off her coffee and used the willpower of a saint to ignore his close proximity. "And you can add that secret to the universal gap that's grown between us."

She dropped her mug when his hand shot up, buried into her hair and tilted her head back. "I feel no gap now, lass, do you?"

Caitlin's lip quivered but she kept her gaze locked on his. "You come on too strong, Ferchar. Does what you've learned about the twenty-first century allow you to understand what it means when a woman says that?"

He spread her thighs and stepped closer. "Aye, but your eyes and your body dinnae agree with your tongue, Caitlin."

His free hand rose to her face and the pad of his thumb brushed her lower lip. "I can feel what you want."

"You have no idea what I want." She tried to turn her head away but he grabbed her chin. Caitlin brought her hands to his forearms. His muscles flexed beneath her fingertips.

Ferchar's eyes disarmed her when they fell to her hands. Before she could savor any small victory he swooped forward.

Her lips were caught before she had a chance to retaliate. Not demanding like she thought they'd be but gentle and exploratory. Almost like a first kiss. His hands released her and his arms wrapped around her lower back, pulling her tight against him. Ferchar's head tilted further and deepened the tender exchange.

She should stop him. He had no right to do this. Caitlin fought to keep all the reasons she despised him at the front of her mind but his lips cracked the foundation of her will and everything slipped away. She moaned and raised her hands to his shoulders.

It wasn't a slow and easy burn that overtook her, but a raging inferno of need. Caitlin gripped his hair and pulled him tighter to her. Ferchar's hands seized her backside and he ground his raging erection against her.

"Oh, my gosh!"

Both of them froze at the feminine exclamation.

Caitlin pushed him away and tried to regain her breath. A stream of curses sat silent in her mouth.

Amanda stood in the doorway, bleary eyed. "I've heard of kissing cousins before, but I've never seen it." She swallowed. "Not to this extreme."

Caitlin jumped down from the counter and faced her friend. What choice did she have? "We're not cousins, Amanda. I'm so sorry. I lied last night."

Amanda eyed first Caitlin, then Ferchar and at last, the coffee maker. "Surprise, surprise."

Caitlin stepped aside as Amanda reached into the cabinet for a mug. "You don't seem that shocked."

Her friend filled her cup with coffee and poured a level scoop of sugar into it. She added some creamer, stirred and turned back to them. Amanda's hair stood up at odd angles and her eyes were slightly bloodshot.

"Do you think I'm completely blind?" Amanda took a long sip from her coffee.

Caitlin didn't bother to look in Ferchar's direction as he sat down at the table. "What do you mean?"

She lifted one shoulder. "Anyone, especially a woman, could see the way he looked at you last night. If I'd truly thought you two were even remotely related, you and I would've been sitting down and having a heart to heart chat. The kind of talk that would have ended with me convincing you to go on medication, immediately."

Amanda sunk into a chair and pillowed her head in her arm. "Remind me to never try to out drink a Scotsman again."

A deep chuckle rumbled in Ferchar's chest. "You're half the size of me, lassie, but your spirit is equal. You met me drink for drink."

Amanda groaned. "Don't remind me."

Ferchar might be calm but Caitlin's nerves were shattered. "Again, I'm sorry I lied."

And she was about to do it again. "We met down in Virginia. It happened so fast. I wanted to show him where I lived. I didn't tell you because I knew how you would've responded."

Amanda sat back. "Caitlin, you don't have to explain yourself to me. In fact, at the moment, I'm in no mood to be upset with you. Why I even got out of bed, I've no idea."

With that final statement she rose, grabbed her coffee cup and headed for the stairs.

Caitlin stepped aside. "We'll talk later."

"Yep. Sounds good. Much later." Amanda trudged up the stairs and disappeared down the hallway.

"You're turning my life upside down." Caitlin mumbled more to herself then to him.

She looked at Ferchar. His eyes said nothing of what he felt. As usual. "I have to go take a shower."

His steady gaze stayed on her. "I'll be right here, luv."

She rolled her eyes. "I'm not your luv."

"Figure of speech," he said and sipped his coffee.

Caitlin put her cup in the sink and nodded. The last thing she needed to affiliate with this man was love. God help her if she did.

Things were already complicated enough.

****

Ferchar leaned against the tree and looked to the east, to the Atlantic and further on to his homeland. He had known it would hurt. The distance. What he hadn't known was that the wound would be so minor. That being near her would ease the ache.

The leaves overhead whispered kinship in his ear and the life sprouting from the earth below promised solace to his misplaced soul. A young cluster of wild ferns grew at his feet. He leaned down and ran his hand through their length. A warm, spring wind whipped up from the south and carried the smell of commerce. Ferchar stood and touched the weathered base of the thick oak tree behind him.

The world had changed so much. Modern conveniences saturated this land. He could feel it in the seemingly white clouds that tumbled overhead, tired and polluted. By the way the sound of nature was muted, overused and scarcer by the day. He would have never placed her here.

A Greek Goddess with Hates at her command, extremely plausible. Engorged in the Roman times, a royal concubine, aye. A creature of renaissance France, a painted nymph that demanded the king's attention, most certainly. Even the queen of Scots. But never this. Not a woman of the twenty-first century.

His musings failed when she walked out the front door of the house. Bloody hell. Maybe this century did have its benefits.

Caitlin's hair fell free and she wore a dress that would not have been decent in any of his scenarios. The top was fitted, low cut and had no sleeves, leaving her slender arms bare. The bottom was looser and short. So short it made his mouth water. Her slender legs went on forever. Strappy high-heeled sandals graced her feet. She had a swing to her hips as she strode toward him.

"Now, you have to be on your best behavior because I'm not leaving you here to wander around," Caitlin said.

He released the breath he didn't realize he was holding. "Easy lass. I'm not a child."

"Aren't you?" She breezed past him and headed for her vehicle.

"I take it we're not traveling by horseback." He followed her.

"Heck no." She opened the door and climbed in, her skirt rising even higher up her thigh.

Ferchar smiled and walked to the passenger side. He knew well what a car was but had never ridden in one. It was too small by far. He wedged himself inside and frowned. "Dinnae they make these things larger?"

She laughed. "Yeah, I just can't afford one."

Her hand gripped the shift and pulled it down. Why hadn't he continued to seduce her earlier in the kitchen? He should have. Every movement she made tightened his groin further.

When they lurched forward he grabbed the door. This was incredible. The power in this machine impressed him. "I would like to drive one of these."

Her beautiful profile broke into a smile. "And I'd love to see you do it. Problem is, you don't have a license."

"And is that mandatory?" He didn't care if it was.

Caitlin turned her head slightly, eyes devious. "It doesn't have to be. But you could get in big trouble and without proper citizenship, if you got pulled over, it would be catastrophic."

He almost reached out and touched her tempting thigh. "And how do I obtain proper citizenship?"

"You don't, sweetie." She pulled up in front of a house three quarters the size of the one she lived in. "Because you're going home. Even if you weren't, an illegal immigrant is all you could ever be."

From the Chieftain of one of the most powerful clans in Scotland to an *illegal immigrant*. Somehow, that sounded like a massive drop in status.

"Now." She turned to him and grew very serious. "You need to be the perfect gentleman. I've seen you do it so I know you're capable. Just follow my lead."

He put his hand on her firm thigh and enjoyed the change in her expression. "Wasn't it my lead that saved you last night, lass?"

She pushed his hand aside. "Come on."

Caitlin opened her door and was halfway to the house before he caught up. Wide, paneled windows glistened to their right as they reached the front door. She pulled open the outer door and was about to knock on the inner door when it swung inward.

At first look he saw an elderly woman with a cane. Then he looked again. She fought her years and stood tall. Her hair was snow white and her eyes a shrewd, youthful shade of blue. Beautiful. He could see that in an instant. A woman who had surpassed all others in her day.

"Caitlin." She pulled Caitlin into her arms. "I was so worried."

Emotion caught in Caitlin's response. "I'm so sorry I didn't call you, Gram. I should have."

"Yes, you should have." The woman held her tighter. "I missed you."

When they unlocked, Caitlin wiped an errant tear aside and nodded. "I missed you too. It was all so sudden."

The woman's eyes studied Caitlin for many moments and then moved to him. "And who is this?"

Tension poured off Caitlin in crisp, precise waves. "This is Ferchar, Gram. A friend of mine."

Caitlin looked to him. "Ferchar, this is Mildred. My grandmother."

He lowered his head slightly and smiled. "Hello, Mildred, it is a pleasure to meet you."

Caitlin's grandmother remained silent for several moments before she spoke. "So you're Scottish."

Ferchar nodded. "Aye."

The woman seemed undecided for a moment and then she stepped back. "Come in, both of you."

They walked into the house and waited for Mildred to seat herself. An incessant yapping drew his attention to the back of the house.

"Do you want me to let the dog in?" Caitlin asked as she disappeared into the other room.

"Please do." Mildred motioned him to a plush chair across from her. "Please sit."

He lowered himself into the chair just as a small dog rounded the corner and ran his way. A foot from him, it sat and stopped barking. God love the Tibetans. They were a spiritual people and this dog was one of their reincarnates. He murmured a greeting in his mind and the dog cocked his head. Nakita had been slightly more difficult. An American with Japanese blood. A dog who's soul mixed both well preserved oriental tradition and the hellion nature of a new breed.

Mildred unwrapped a hard candy and shook her head. "Well, I've never seen him do that."

She popped the sweet in her mouth and eyed Ferchar. "That's quite the talent you have."

He met her blue eyes. "I get along well with animals."

"So you do." She studied his face before turning her attention to Caitlin. "He's very handsome. Wherever did you two meet?"

Caitlin pulled a chair from the kitchen table and placed it beside her grandmother. "Virginia."

"Really?" Mildred's eyes sparkled with interest. "You found this Scotsman in Virginia?"

He declined an offered hard candy.

"Yes. He was visiting. He's an actor, Gram." Caitlin crossed one leg over the other.

"I'm sure he is."

Ferchar's eyes flew to Mildred's and found nothing alarming in her gaze, only simple curiosity. Regardless, his instincts told him something was off. Against his better judgment, he pushed into her mind. Nothing prevalent stood out save five happy children and two husbands. The first husband had been a bad marriage for her, unwelcome and dark. The second husband, named Jim, a businessman and horse connoisseur, remained a white light in her heart, though he was deceased. Caitlin's grandfather.

"He will only be here a short time and then he's leaving for California," Caitlin said and looked his way.

She mesmerized him with her golden eyes. The woman she became in this small, low ceiling abode. Her vulnerability surfaced, she was innocent and open. Ferchar stared at her lips, enchanted by the way their fullness narrowed and rubbed, upper lip against lower lip.

"California?" Mildred shook her head and made herself more comfortable. "Why bother when you could stay more local. With your looks, New York City would welcome a new model."

Ferchar peeled his eyes from Caitlin's crossed legs. "The acting offers more of a challenge."

"Ahhh. So this is a casual fling you're having with my granddaughter," Mildred said.

"Gram!" Caitlin rode to the edge of her seat. "We're just friends."

Ferchar met Mildred head on. "I assure you, there's nothing casual about the way I feel toward Caitlin."

Caitlin fell silent and he continued to do battle with her grandmother's worldly demeanor.

"Then don't go." Mildred's voice was as stern as her countenance.

With every instinct that made him a great warrior, Ferchar knew that this woman was more informed than she let on.

His eyes shot back to Caitlin. She appeared uncomfortable. Her eyes shifted too much and that delectable tongue kept her lips far too moist. What was he missing?

Ferchar's eyes swung back to Mildred. "Your concern and welfare for your granddaughter is duly noted. But I wonder." He sat back and enjoyed Caitlin's skirt riding further up her thighs as she squirmed. "What is amiss?"

The woman didn't flicker a lash. "What do you mean, Ferchar?"

Caitlin stood at that moment, a look of relief evident on her face. "Is that Uncle Dan and Aunt Vera?"

Mildred's eyes didn't leave his but narrowed. "Is it dear?"

It took all that was left of him to keep his eyes locked on the woman across from him and not Caitlin who now leaned forward to look out the window, her skirt riding dangerously high.

"Did you know they were coming to visit?" She looked down at her grandmother and purposely swung her backside in his face, blocking their view of one another.

"Aye." Mildred leaned around Caitlin to look at him again. "As they would say in Scotland."

What was this woman about?

Ferchar reached out and touched Caitlin's waist.

Startled, she looked down at him.

"I'm thirsty, lass. Have you nothing to offer me to drink?"

Her eyes narrowed and she straightened. "I'll see what I can find."

When she turned away and headed for the kitchen he took careful measure. The couple that arrived had just opened the trunk of their car. That gave him less than a minute alone with Mildred.

He leaned forward, positioned himself to go to war, and spoke.

Chapter Twenty

Caitlin stood, hands braced on either side of the kitchen sink and stared out at the backyard. No birds visited the feeder, as though they sensed the oddity of time warping around them. Ferchar and Gram spoke quietly in the other room, their words muffled.

Gram's cat nudged her hand but said nothing. She looked down into his green eyes and suddenly wished Arianna was here. For backup perhaps. Confirmation, definitely. But she wasn't. This battle was Caitlin's. Arianna had had to deal with Iain coming face to face with her family, now it was Caitlin's turn.

She'd hoped to talk to Gram, had hoped that introducing Ferchar to her would somehow be normal. Caitlin turned on the tap in the sink and splashed water over her face. It may have been wiser to call him by a different name. As if Gram wouldn't find it peculiar that she brought home a man with such an unusual name. Bloody hell. Gram had given her the book, she would obviously relate the name.

Where was her common sense? Had it totally abandoned her?

Aunt Vera's voice drifted from the living room as she spoke to Gram. "I didn't realize you had company besides Caitlin. Hello..."

Caitlin tuned out the rest of the words, opened the cabinet, pulled down a can of coffee. She measured out the grounds, poured water into the coffee machine and hit the on button. Her shoulders slumped. She was exhausted.

"Did you just pour eight scoops of coffee grounds into a maker made for twelve cups of coffee?"

Caitlin almost cried when she turned. "Gram likes it strong."

Uncle Dan stepped into the kitchen and shook his head. "That's just not good for you."

Then, unwittingly, the tears fell and she shook her head. "Nothing's good for me anymore."

Her uncle made Ferchar look a novice when it came to showing no emotions, so when he stepped forward and took her into her arms, Caitlin had no choice but to let it all go in silent tears. All of it—the book, traveling back in time and finding so much more than her mind could've ever been ready for. So much pain, good and bad. Suppressed, yet awakened. Old pain mixed with new.

At last, after minutes of blissfully uninterrupted anguish she pulled away and wiped her eyes. Dan's gaze was compassionate and unsure. Thankfully, he didn't ask her what was wrong. They'd always been close and he knew that if she wanted to share she would.

She bit her lip. "You didn't happen to bring one of your ever handy candy bars with you, did you?"

Relief flooded his eyes as she offered him something more substantial than a broken down niece. He shrugged his shoulders and his brows shot high with resolve. "I've got beer."

Caitlin liked the way a smile felt as it split her face— real, genuine and too foreign as of late. She nodded emphatically. "That'll do."

They reentered Gram's living room. Funny, Caitlin hadn't worried about leaving Ferchar once she knew her aunt and uncle had arrived. Whatever tension had so quickly arisen between her grandmother and him would have to have dissipated, and she was correct.

Gram was still in her chair, Aunt Vera in the chair Ferchar had left. Her misplaced highlander stood in front of the pellet stove. They all held a beer and the small room was at ease. Not a shred of tension to be found.

"We've been thinking of visiting Scotland for some time."

Aunt Vera's words trailed off when Caitlin and Uncle Dan reentered the room. Caitlin leaned over and gave her a hug.

"Are you all right?" Vera studied her face with concern.

Caitlin only nodded as Dan sat down on the couch, retrieved a beer from the cooler at his feet and handed it to her. She stood beside Ferchar, undecided what to do next. When his thickly burred voice rumbled across her contemplation, Caitlin closed her eyes.

"Well, before you go to Scotland. Seek me out."

Vera looked at him. "We will. Thank you." Her verdant green eyes locked on Caitlin. "This is quite unexpected. Wherever did you two meet?"

Gram's eyes twinkled with amusement. "Virginia. He's an actor."

"Really?" Vera said.

Ferchar stood straighter which was a nearly impossible task in this house. "Aye."

Out of nowhere, anger infused her. She hated lying to her family. Caitlin tipped back her beer and relished the minuscule amount of comfort it offered her. She should have never brought him here without talking to Gram first. But her blame naturally swung to the root of the problem.

Him.

She didn't want him here. Since he'd come into her life it had been a slew of negative events. Well, almost. She pushed aside memories of Beltane. Perhaps, there had been a few other good times, but not nearly enough to atone for the whole.

Caitlin set down her barely touched drink and nudged him. "We have to go."

Vera looked from Gram to her. "So soon? We haven't seen each other in a while."

She stepped forward and hugged her petite aunt again. This woman had always been like a mother to her after Gram, but what she needed right now was a savior. Someone who could wipe Ferchar off the face of the planet and ensure that Caitlin would never set eyes on him again. "I'm sorry, we have to go."

They all stood at the door as she and Ferchar left. Caitlin waited until Ferchar had closed the door to the SUV before she turned on the radio. She wished she could leave him here. That she could shift the vehicle into reverse, then forward and drive away from him forever.

But she could not.

****

Ferchar remained silent as Caitlin pulled into the driveway of her house. It seemed he was not going to see civilization beyond her grandmother's house today. She brought the SUV to a stop, got out and slammed the door. He got out as well and watched her cross to the barn without looking his way. Cruel emotions slammed into him like well-aimed arrows.

She was angry with him, surprisingly enough, more so than she'd ever been before. He strode after her. A battle of words might just ease the tension

Destiny's Denial

between them. The sun slid behind a massive cloud and eased the barn into the shade. The doors were open and Caitlin stood in the stall next to her horse. She held a brush by her side but didn't move.

"Do you mean to groom the horse, lass?" He leaned his arms over the stall door.

She set the brush back on a shelf. Her golden eyes scolded him with burnished bronze. When she addressed him, her tone was feral. "What happened to Fyne, Arianna's horse?"

So she aimed to ease into this confrontation. Ferchar shrugged. "I know naught."

"And what about Arthur and your clansmen?" She was still, her body stiff and contained.

He spoke low and lit the flame from beneath. "They became a secondary concern to you for me. I cannae say how they fare."

Caitlin's eyes welled for a moment then turned dry and lethal. "It's time for you to leave."

"I told you already. I cannae leave."

She swung a saddle onto her horse and nodded vigorously. "Yes, you can. I'll bring you to the Stonehenge now. You obviously have the power to travel through time. I'll bring you to the door and send you off."

He moved to her side and grabbed her wrist before she could mount the horse. Caitlin's skin heated beneath his touch and her heartbeat increased.

"I cannae travel back, lass."

She tried to pull away but he held tighter.

Her breath came faster and she shook her head. "That makes no sense! Iain could. Arianna could. Hell, even Shane and myself. What are you talking about? Aren't you supposed to be a black wizard? You can't stay here, Ferchar!"

"Do you honestly think I intended to be here? Stay here? I have no choice. Iain knew it. Adlin knew it.

Bloody hell, my poor mother knew it." He released her wrist but not her eyes as a wave of pain tore through him. His poor Ma, first her husband gone and now her son.

Caitlin blinked several times. "You're serious?"

He kept his roaring response to a whisper and walked out of the stall. "Aye, very."

"But why would you—" She broke off and stared at him.

"Why would I have come here willingly, knowing I couldnae go home?" He bit back an oath at what he saw in her eyes. "Because I owed it to you. Adlin's power had been weakened by the black pentacle and he would not have been able to get you here."

Caitlin slowly, methodically, removed the saddle from the horse. "He would have eventually."

Ferchar ground his jaw. "I didnae know that Alan would do what he did. That axe would have killed you."

She hung the saddle, walked out of the stall and shut it behind her. Her expression was devoid of emotion. "And I appreciate your gallantry. I do. But do you realize what you just told me? The gap in your plan to stay here for whatever reasons you feel the need to?"

Ferchar reached up and twirled a lock of her hair around his finger. He knew what some part of her longed to hear. "Aye, you speak of Adlin's temporary weakness and my strength. I was able to push us forward through time."

"Very good." Her breath was ragged. "So why don't you push yourself back, Ferchar?"

He cupped her chin and tilted back her head. One type of fire was being replaced with another. "I must fulfill my vision."

Her eyes did a lazy survey of his face. "And the twenty-first century is part of your vision?"

He leaned forward and kissed the corner of her mouth, teased it with promise of little talk. "Since Iain left, I knew that when he returned I would leave. Hoped, somehow, I wouldnae."

Her head fell back as his lips swooped down her neck.

"But you can't stay here. You can't."

Caitlin's words drifted away when he pushed her against the outside of the stall. A bright burst of sun streamed into the barn and lit her hair as golden as her eyes. With that burst of brilliance came the urgency left behind in a dream...abandoned and unfinished. Lips, tongues, hot skin, burning desire.

It was unavoidable. He had to be in her again, had to feel her tight center, her moans of pleasure. Painful need tightened his hold and drove coherent thought away. Jeans didn't slow him down any more than a plaid would have, nor did a short little dress.

Jeans down, Ferchar shook with need as he ran his hands up her smooth, silky thighs and under her skirt. Tearing away her panties, he pulled the skirt up, gripped her backside and lifted her against the stall door. He loved the sweet smell of her skin and hair and breathed deeply.

No time. I need her now.

Caitlin barely had a chance to grab his shoulders before he moved into her with one sharp thrust. He only managed to groan when he heard her breathy little gasps. Driven, eager, almost mindless with the need for release, he moved in and out, in and out, faster and faster, pushing her up the stall door with each well measured thrust.

"No. This. Us. Stop," she panted but seemed to crawl up him as she met him thrust for thrust, her heels digging into his arse.

She released little cries, each louder and louder.

Her nails dug so deeply into his back she drew blood.

He couldn't get deep enough, close enough.

As was the way with them, her mind flooded his with images of him and her caught in a sizzling stream of sunlight. Her slender legs long and wrapped high.

Something akin to passion but much more violent and sensuous drove them together, buried them in twists of steaming gold sparks. Mated them in a fusion of opulent power and lust so strong it nearly ripped the ground from beneath them.

Gods, he couldn't even breathe, only feel.

It felt like she alone kept him alive.

Caitlin screamed and bucked against him. He ground his teeth and continued to ride her sweat slicked body up the wall. More. More. More. His body shook so violently he barely held on. She moaned low and guttural, her orgasm so powerful it made his world flip over. Rapid shudders clenched his cock so tightly he gave one final harsh plunge and cried out. He didn't recognize the deep keen that came from his mouth.

In that moment, when their bodies swept each other to another place...when moans became screams and release so intense it was painful, he could imagine doing this a million more times with her. Knew that he wanted to and with no other.

As he lowered her to the ground, a familiar bitterness curled around his heart. He should have had a choice. Chosen to be with her because it was his desire; not made to be by a vision.

She was everything and more.

Then, as if the old God's mocked his very thoughts, another vision rocked him with the force of a thousand storms.

****

Caitlin leaned back against the stall and closed her eyes. Her legs wobbled but managed to keep her upright when he pulled away. Her heart thundered and she breathed as deeply as her lungs would allow.

She'd never experienced anything so amazing. He'd outdone himself. Quivers rippled through her body in slow, delicious waves. Shaking her head, she kept her eyes closed. If she could hold onto this moment for the rest of her life she would.

Thoughts slowly reformed in her mind. He'd said things, shared things. Her muscles tensed. His vision had led him here? How had she never known that? Opening her eyes she looked around. The sun sat lower in the sky and she had the sudden impression that though they'd made love for what seemed mere minutes, it'd taken much longer to assuage their needs.

Caitlin ran her hand down to her stomach, still quivering with ripples of pleasure. She was taking far too many chances with him without any form of birth control. Something warm unraveled within when she realized she wasn't bothered by that fact. What was the matter with her? Was it because he said he had to stay? She had the potential father right where she wanted him? No. Even if he was leaving she would feel this way and that scared her.

Ferchar stood at the barn doors, his back to her. The wind blew through his hair and the doors bumped lightly off of the barn walls. Though a kilt may be his natural attire, jeans did the man some extra justice. Her heart tightened when his head turned slightly and his profile became clear. Something inside let go and Caitlin knew for certain.

She was in love with him.

After everything they'd been through, her heart wanted him. She'd never felt this way about anyone and searched for some reason to explain why this man was the one. The excitement? The chemistry? Had they even accumulated enough conversation for this feeling to be real?

Adjusting her clothing, she went to his side and shoved emotion aside. She had more questions. "If you all have the power of time travel then why did Iain need Adlin's assistance to travel forward in time but not to travel back?"

He leaned against the threshold of the barn door. If he was affected by their sexual encountered he hid it well. "'Twas Adlin's request that I not tell Iain of my vision of his fate with Arianna. It was his decision, as Iain's mentor, to keep vague the concept of time travel. You see lass, Adlin is a planner and 'twas his wish to control Iain's arrival in New Hampshire. He knew well enough that when Iain traveled here he would instantly learn the magic that it took to get him home."

"Why don't you ignore your vision? It won't offend me if you go." Every word was a struggle to say but necessary. Within a matter of minutes it'd become obvious to her that she didn't want him to leave. That if he did, some part of her would leave with him.

His eyes searched hers. "Because, lass, one way or another, it would ill effect the course of too many. Iain's and Arianna's, my clan, and many others. That is the sole purpose of one who has visions—to travel in the foreseen direction in order to ensure the correct course of so many lives. We who foresee give aid to the gods of old and new. Nudge fate in the right direction."

What a terrible way to live. Caitlin swallowed a lump of sudden remorse for him. He wouldn't appreciate it. But she had to understand one more thing so she said softly, "And me? How are you supposed to affect my life?"

He appeared ready to say something but his attention turned to the driveway and he spoke, his brogue thick and contemptuous. "You've company, lass."

Caitlin ran a hand through her unruly hair and smoothed her dress. A black sports car had just pulled into the driveway. Oh no. Not Rick, not right now. She walked forward and met him when he stepped from the vehicle. His smile wavered as he took in her appearance and then looked past her to Ferchar.

He leaned back against the car. "Hey."

"Hey." She leaned back beside him and looked at Ferchar. "Could we have a few minutes alone, please?"

"Not bloody likely." Ferchar held his ground.

Incredulous, Caitlin narrowed her eyes. Who did he think he was? Yeah, they'd just had incredible, mind-blowing sex but as far as she could tell that didn't mean much to Ferchar. If anything, he'd fulfilled an obligation to his gods. She was just about to tell him what she thought of his response when Rick touched her arm.

He kept an eye on Ferchar, but spoke to her. "I take it he's not your cousin."

Oh hell. She met Rick's eyes and felt like such a jerk. But no matter the circumstances, she knew she'd come too far with Ferchar. That continuing anything with Rick would be wrong no matter the Scotsman's feelings toward her. *I'm so sick of lying. I have to tell the truth.* "No, he's not. I'm so sorry."

Rick sighed. "I had a feeling that was the case this morning."

She didn't know what to say.

"It's serious?" Rick said.

"Aye, or I wouldnae be standing here, would I?" Ferchar said, his tone a little dangerous.

Her breath caught when she met his eyes. Her irritation with him suddenly vanished. Did he feel the same way she did? Did she really want him to? Yes. Without a doubt.

"Caitlin?" Rick pushed away from the side of the car and nodded at the door she leaned against.

She stepped aside. "I'm so sorry, Rick. Really."

"I know. Don't worry about it." He squeezed her hand before he got into the car.

Caitlin was without words as he shut the door and left. Better that they finished it before anything really started. She swung her attention to Ferchar. "So what now? You just ran off the only man I was dating."

Before he could respond, Gram's white Lincoln Town Car rolled down the drive. Caitlin felt a twinge of annoyance. She needed to talk alone with Ferchar, to figure out so many things. She opened the car door for Gram and took her elbow as she stepped out. "Gram, what's going on?"

"I didn't want to be left out." Mildred squared her shoulders and walked toward the front door.

"Left out of what?" Caitlin trailed her into the house. Gram walked into the living room and sat down on the couch.

"Me leaving." Caitlin whirled at the sound of Shane's voice. His eyes were sad and serious.

Her heart hit the floor when Ferchar walked into the room behind him. What on Earth? Why? A terrible ache of denial crept into her chest at his attire. No jeans. No kilt.

But black robes.

Gram clapped her hands together in childish delight. "Unbelievable."

Caught between one astounding moment and the next, Caitlin narrowed her eyes at her grandmother. "Gram?"

"Yes?"

It took nearly more than she was capable of not to yell. "Does it not strike you unusual that Ferchar is dressed like an evil wizard?"

Mildred's eyes rounded in astonishment and a thimble of laughter dribbled from her lips. "Evil? You really are dramatic at times, sweetie. Ferchar and I had a little chat earlier. I know who he is, silly girl. The lad from the book!"

Caitlin's eyes rounded. "How could you possibly know the book was based on truth?"

"Oh, come now child. You must have put two and two together when I gave you the novel after you told me about your dream and bizarre visitations."

Though Gram hadn't entirely answered her question, Caitlin was more concerned with her brother at the moment.

Shane passed her and walked over to the fireplace where he proceeded to build a small fire on the hearth. Stunned, Caitlin questioned the horror show she'd walked into a thousand different ways, yet nothing came out of her mouth. Ferchar touched her arm but she jerked away.

"Lass, why dinnae you sit with your grandmother," he said.

His tall, hard body encased in black robes at this vicinity swamped her senses, and not with fear, as she would've expected, but lust. Caitlin felt lightheaded and propped herself on the edge of the couch.

Somewhere in all of this she found her voice, weak as it was. "Shane, what are you doing?"

Fire lit, he stood and turned. Remorse both dulled and brightened his eyes. "I have to go back, Caitlin. I love her too much to stay."

"Love who...oh. Catherine." Caitlin's chest tightened. She met his eyes and shook her head, pleading for a mere glimpse of a joke held at bay. "You can't. What about... about—"

"About what, Caitlin? My only loss in this venture is leaving you and Gram." His eyes pleaded with her to understand.

Tears welled in her eyes. "But you pinky swore."

His eyes turned moist. "And I'm keeping that promise, Caitlin. Though I'm not here, I'm still with you."

She shook her head in denial and the tears started to overflow. "That sort of sentiment doesn't work and you know it."

Gram put her hand on Caitlin's arm. "He deserves to be where his heart is. We all do."

She wiped away the tears and looked into Shane's eyes. There was so much worry and regret in their depths. All for her, not for the twenty-first century nor all the modern conveniences he would be leaving behind. Had he truly found a love that powerful? That he was willing to give up everything for it? If so, who was she to keep him from that?

Caitlin took Shane's hands in hers, completely dumbfounded. "I'll miss you so much."

He pulled her into a strong embrace and said nothing more. She found it odd that when it was time to say goodbye to someone you loved, there were never any words available that said everything in your heart. No words seemed more efficient than a hundred. Maybe it was the soul's defense mechanism. Do not over-talk the moment and make it harder.

Maybe it was just the fear of hearing that person's voice for the last time.

****

Mildred took Shane into her arms and held him. Her grandson was going back to Scotland, the living, beautiful beast that ripped the Brouns wherever they may be, back to its breast. The medieval heartland of the MacLomains. A clan that no Broun could ever deny.

She closed her eyes to the sound of robes brushing the hardwood floor. Her heart pounded and long forgotten heat flooded her face. He was here, again, after so very long.

"Mildred."

She was not a young woman any more and when she opened her eyes she saw that he was no longer a young man.

"Adlin." She met his light blue eyes and felt young again...as though if she looked down at her hands, the skin would be smooth and supple, her body lithe and firm and vibrant.

He knelt before her, his heart in his eyes. "You are still so beautiful."

She ignored Caitlin's gasp and offered him her shaking hand. He kissed the back of it. Suddenly, she was running through tall, highland grass again. Both frightened and thrilled by the avid pursuit of this man. His dark hair shone in the sunlight and his blue eyes burned with sapphire intent. So many years ago, she had been so young and innocent, alive and eager.

Incredibly in love with the visiting Chieftain.

"Thank you for bringing Caitlin home, I was so afraid for her." Mildred eyed his hair. It was the same alabaster white as hers. She regretted never having had the chance to lay with this man. They were torn apart too soon. Funny thing, fate.

Adlin looked as if he wanted to lay his head in her lap but he did not. "I didnae, lass. 'Twas Ferchar and his mentor, Iosbail."

She chuckled. "And how is your sister?"

"Wizened, frail and very old I'm afraid. However, she still makes her presence known within a throng of attentive children by the fireside. She loves to tell them tales of the past and instill as much superstition in them as she can." Adlin shook his head. "She claims her visions have left her in peace, alas."

"No?" Mildred had always loved their easy gossip. "Say it isn't so. A pessimist forever plagued by the gods' whims. Are you sure she hasn't just finally chosen to ignore her visions?"

Adlin leaned in closer. "Always so wise, my Mildred. Indeed, she still does follow her visions or else I would have had to kill her."

Her old heart set to flutter at his closeness. "No?"

"Aye." He winked. "I thought she had betrayed me. But she didnae. It turns out when she gave a certain black pentacle to a very bad MacLeod laird, it was with the foresight of Ferchar doing just what he did."

Ferchar muffled a curse but Mildred ignored him, young blood that he was. "I have missed you, Adlin. More than you know."

"And I you, lass." He steepled his fingers over her hands in a lover's worship. "It's over now Mildred. Your bloodline is safe. The new MacLeod laird has terminated the pact. Come back to Scotland with me. Live out your days there."

Her heart did a somersault. What she would have done to hear those words sixty five years ago. But now she was tired and everything that her and her husband had built was here. All of her memories. It was too late to go back, to leave everything she knew.

She sighed. "Oh, Adlin. I can't do that. My life is here. The only traveling I will do at this point is straight on to Heaven to be with my Jim again. I'm sorry."

Rueful, Adlin gave a sad nod. "You found love again, of course."

"Didn't you?" She whispered and touched his wizened face.

A flicker of regret darkened his eyes. "Aye, but as is the way of things, I lost her as well."

A tear nearly escaped her eye. "Life is not easy, is it?"

"Nay." He leaned forward and kissed her cheek. "'Tis not."

He stood then and turned to Ferchar. "You've done well, my great-grandson. Your Da would be proud, as am I. Will you need any assistance?"

Mildred tensed. Caitlin looked miserable and confused. She didn't blame her. She wished she could've told her more from the beginning, made things easier. The book was all that she could offer her. Nothing else would have been believed. As was the way, in the grand design of things, once she had heard about Caitlin's reoccurring dream and her strange visitations, Mildred's hands were tied.

There was nothing she could do to stop her granddaughter from traveling back if that was her destiny. In fact, she aided Caitlin when she'd had those garden tools brought up to the attic. Her faith in Adlin was the only thing that had made the past weeks bearable. She had known that Shane's explanation was bogus.

Like Mildred, Scotland had brought Caitlin back. A MacLomain to be specific. That brought her attention again to Ferchar.

Who would have ever thought?

The moment she'd seen Ferchar, she knew he was related to Adlin. Those icy sapphire eyes, his self-confidence and arrogance nearly as tall as his frame. What was the pull between the Brouns and MacLomains? Only God knew.

But now it was time to say goodbye to her grandson. She would not cry. Caitlin would need her strength. Tears were better left for late at night, tucked in her bed.

She wondered if her poor, sodden pillow could handle many more.

Chapter Twenty-One

The room spun and then straightened one too many times in the brief exchange between Adlin and her grandmother. Gram was the mysterious woman at the root of everything? She was Adlin's love and the reason for the pact that had shaped Caitlin into an entirely different person?

Shock had her numb on so many levels.

"Caitlin, take this." Shane handed her an envelope.

"What's this?"

"It's the backup disk that has my completed manuscript on it. My publisher will be contacting you soon. They know that all royalties are to go to you." His smile was reflective and his eyes proud.

The full impact of what he was leaving behind staggered her. "Your book is getting published?"

He laughed. "Yeah, can you believe it?"

Caitlin nodded. She could definitely believe it.

He had accomplished his goal and was ready to go back to an era that had always fascinated him. She could already see him finding a way to write again there. Anything was possible.

"You're going to have to learn to use a sword and ride a warhorse, you know. Medicine is primitive and times are perilous where you're going. You could be called to war at any time—"

He put a hand over her mouth. "I know fully what I'm getting myself into. I'll be okay, I promise."

Ferchar stepped forward and put a hand on Shane's shoulder. "We must go."

Caitlin stood and hugged Shane again. She pulled back to give Gram a look of reassurance and stopped cold at the look in her eyes; a look that had little to do with Shane and everything to do with Caitlin. Her mind grew fuzzy with comprehension.

Ferchar had said, "we."

Her eyes met his. "What do you mean, we must go?"

She'd never be able to define the emotion that twirled silver in his eyes. His hand rose to her forehead and his finger grazed the area just above and between her eyes. Like a firefly in her peripheral vision, a sapphire pentacle blazed in the darkness and then vanished.

"I had another vision, Caitlin. I have to return," he said. His heart and soul were in his eyes. "I'm sorrier than you could know."

Her legs gave out but he caught her and pulled her against him. He felt so good, so right. What twisted game was this? After everything they'd been through, he was leaving? Had some God been listening earlier when she wanted him gone? No. It had to have been the Devil.

She hated the plea in her voice. "You don't have to. I lied earlier. Illegal immigrants, with the right forged documents, can run multi-million dollar businesses in this country, especially via the Internet. You're resourceful and intelligent. The twenty-first century suits you. I'll even let you teach me magic."

He buried his face in her hair. "Dinnae do this, Caitlin."

She couldn't stop the tears if she tried. "I don't understand, you just said out in the barn you had to stay."

Ferchar pulled her body tighter against his. "The vision came after we...after our time together."

"You could've told me that before I sent poor Rick on his way." Not that Caitlin cared. She would have ended it anyway. She knew that now. Now that she knew what love felt like...

He offered her nothing more than his lips on hers. So sweet and soft, a last touch of passionate heat that would leave her spirit dehydrated. When he pulled away, his eyes roamed her face one last time. "I'll not forget you, lass. Your soul is part of mine now, for the rest of my days."

Desperation flooded her but she pushed it aside. To beg was not her style. But to regret was not either. She would never forgive herself if she did not tell him. "I love you."

Pain drew his brows together. "I know, lass."

She closed her eyes to the sight of him turning away. When she opened them again he was already pulling forth his magic. Caitlin had never seen him do such a thing. He used the fire burning on the hearth as Adlin used the wind and clouds.

The flames licked and rolled forward like a tidal wave. Desert heat blew back his robes and his eyes shone a bright, blinding sapphire. As it was on the cliff in Scotland, Ferchar's beauty was frightening.

She went to reach for Shane's hand but he'd already walked forward. They were both leaving her. The fire roared to an inferno that twirled around the room but left both humans and house safe and unscathed. Deep crimson and orange swirled and danced around Ferchar and Shane. As the flames consumed their forms in a tornado of fire, his eyes met hers one last time.

Then they were gone.

A low fire crackled on the hearth and the faint smell of sugary smoke tainted the air. He was really gone. It was over. Numb, she leaned against the side of the couch.

"Oh, Caitlin." Gram's voice broke.

She looked at her grandmother as though she was far away. Tears soaked Mildred's cheeks. Adlin was gone.

"I need to be alone, Gram." Caitlin turned and walked on wooden legs up the stairs. The house vanished as she entered her bedroom and sat on the bed. The world turned black and white.

How could they have left her? How could he have? She lay back on the bed and stared at the ceiling. Time ceased to exist along with rational thought. The lonely sun moved from window to window until it gave up and disappeared into the night. Still she stared at the ceiling. Why couldn't she have a happy ending? Arianna had.

Caitlin jumped up from the bed. Arianna had! She could too. It was the twenty-first century, after all. Women didn't wait for a man to rescue them anymore. They went out and got what they wanted on their own.

Caitlin flew down the hall, fumbled for the key above the door, inserted it and flung open the attic door. She turned on the light and ran up the stairs. Wasn't this where the women of the Broun clan came to be with their magic? The sanction to a bloodline of powerful witches? Wasn't she a witch? She didn't care before, but now she did.

She wasn't surprised to find the piano gone. But the bucket of canes was still there, sitting in the middle of the attic like a beacon. Caitlin dumped it upside down and searched frantically through it. With everything she'd witnessed in the past month, the possibility of the wand being here was favorable.

"You're not going to find it, lass."

Caitlin's head whipped up at the familiar voice.

Marie O'Donnell, the ghost from the castle in Scotland, Arianna's aunt, sat in a small wooden chair. She was not transparent but whole and her hair was bright red under the light bulb. "It is not meant for you anymore."

Caitlin disregarded the woman's words as new hope flared and she rose to her feet. "I need to go back. How do I go back?"

Marie remained seated. "You cannae go back, luv. Your place is here with your grandmother. His is there."

Caitlin stood her ground. "I'll come back for Gram. My place is with him. How do I go back?"

Marie shook her head and stood slowly. "You dinnae ken. Only the wizards can accomplish such a feat, and none will bring you back, lass."

"Bloody hell!" Fury filled her. "Why not?"

She raised a hand when Marie started to explain.

"No, don't tell me. It wasn't part of a flipping vision," Caitlin snapped. "Right?"

Marie went to speak again but Caitlin stopped her. "I'm still confused how Ferchar had a vision of ultimately traveling here with me to stay yet he was never supposed to bring me back in time to begin with."

"Visions aren't always perfectly clear." Marie touched Caitlin's arm. "They tend to leave the shaded areas to the follies of the human heart."

Caitlin cursed. "Trust me, I didn't exist in any shaded area within Ferchar's heart."

"But you did." Marie's smile was faint. "Or you would have never ended up in Scotland. Don't you see? That's the only way it would have been possible. A Broun woman or man can only make the leap if they are pulled there by a MacLomain man or woman and that person can ever only be their one true love."

Caitlin scowled. "Then explain my grandmother's little visit."

A cloud crossed Marie's face. "A sad story, that one. Theirs was a true love but Adlin had to forfeit it to save her."

"So you're trying to tell me that Gram never loved my grandfather as much as she did Adlin?"

Marie sighed. "No, she loved your grandfather just as much, I'm sure. You see, Adlin had to erase the link between their souls. This left her with an open heart. The chance to forge a new link with whomever he chose."

Caitlin swallowed hard. "You mean Adlin chose my grandfather?"

Marie shrugged. "Aye. And made sure your grandmother found him."

She was stupefied. How powerful were these MacLomain wizards? A bizarre twist of fear clutched her chest. "Ferchar's going to do that for me, isn't he?"

Marie took her hand and squeezed. "Aye."

"I don't want that." She didn't mean to yell but she was furious. "I don't want him controlling my heart. I just want him. Why is that so difficult?"

With that, the light bulb overhead flickered out and a lone candle on a three-pegged wooden table sparked to life. Caitlin fell to her knees as a long, oak chest materialized beside them. Hundreds of gems encrusted its surface. The trunk from Arianna's tale, the one that'd held her mother's wedding dress. It had to be.

But instead of hundreds of Emeralds coating it, there were sapphires.

Marie knelt beside her. "Aye, it's the same trunk, lass. But the stones reflect your story, not Arianna's."

She shook her head and ran her hands over the surface. "I take it there's not a wedding dress or a crown of jewels in here?"

Marie smiled. "I'm afraid not."

"Why are you here, Marie? Why don't you look like the ghost that you are?"

"I'm here because Adlin sent me and I'm not transparent because I'm in this attic. The magical forum of my mortal existence. When you leave the attic, I will vanish once more." Marie took Caitlin's hands and placed them on the metal-shaped rose petal handles on either side of the trunk.

As Caitlin went to lift the handles they turned to real roses in her hand and the sound of a distant bagpipe could be heard on a warm gust of air. The trunk clicked then and opened of its own accord. She peered inside. There wasn't a glimmering display of wedding gown glory but the hard, crisp colors of blue and green wool tartan.

The MacLomain plaid.

She pulled the rough fabric from the trunk. One scene after another accosted her. The first time she'd seen Ferchar approach her in the highland forest. The way he'd sat regally upon his horse when confronting Ewan MacLeod at his clan's border. Him standing, kilt low on his waist, in the magically enhanced crevice of a mountain. His arrogant, casual form leaning against the old oak tree in the pouring rain.

She brought the fabric to her face and breathed deeply. It smelled of him. Masculine and potent. Her word was muffled in the fabric. "Why?"

"Adlin wanted you to have it."

When Caitlin pulled the tartan away she was shocked to see tears glistening in Marie's eyes.

She failed to lighten the mood. "Why, so that I never forget what I almost had?"

"No, lass." Marie leaned forward and placed her hand on Caitlin's stomach. "So that what you do have, who you have, will have his Da's plaid."

The deep throated sob that rumbled within Caitlin's chest sounded foreign to her own ears. She grabbed Marie's wrist, shook her head and asked a question she already knew the answer to. "What are you talking about?"

Marie's blue eyes softened. "I think you know."

"Does Ferchar?" She should not have asked because the wrong answer would cut like a knife.

"I dinnae know," Marie said.

"Somehow, I highly doubt that." Caitlin stood, plaid in hand, and stared down at Marie. It was a wonder she wasn't crying her heart out in the woman's lap right now. But she was not and would not. There was no Cinderella and Fairy Godmother moment to be had here.

She put a hand to her womb. Ferchar was gone. Caitlin would not play this scene out with Marie. All emotion had fled.

"Thank you for coming, Marie. Your kindness means a lot."

Caitlin turned and descended the stairs calmly. She walked into her bedroom and flicked on the light. In one swift movement, she grabbed the book, Fate's Monolith, off of her bedside table, walked over to the open window and flung it as hard as she could into the night. Every last character in that book could go to hell as far as she was concerned.

Most of all, Ferchar.

Chapter Twenty-Two

The book was very good.

The ending was Shane's, of course. A happily ever after in Cowal, Scotland, living out his days with his one true love. The book hit print last month and sales were staggering.

Caitlin pushed herself back and forth slowly on the swing that hung from the old oak tree branch. She'd been compelled to have another hung after reading Fate's Monolith, to reinstate a nostalgic portion of the colonial period, a part of the family that'd lived in this house so long ago.

As she swung, Caitlin rubbed her stomach passively. Late September dusk blew through the copper dusted leaves. Her four feet tall garden of dahlia's were sturdy and still in full bloom. The deep purple petunias had passed and would need to be replanted next spring. Within the month, she'd be pulling up the dahlia bulbs and storing them for the winter.

Caitlin had changed so much in the past five months. Once she'd confirmed her pregnancy, her priorities shifted. She'd turned her focus to her online endeavors with her design books, improved her website and had spent ample time learning how to direct traffic there. Her list of affiliates was growing and more people were buying her ideas. College would have to wait until she had the baby.

Amanda had moved out in July. Though she'd been concerned about leaving, Caitlin had urged her to go.

She'd received a job offer down in Florida that was too good to refuse. Overall, it was better for Caitlin. She and Gram set to designing a nursery for the babe. The walls were light crème with cherry wood furnishings and the fabrics were a mix of slate blue and dark blue.

Gram had even hired an artist to come in and paint an elaborate portrait that covered the whole of the wall behind the crib. It depicted a long, sparkling loch with Scottish highland mountains looming beyond.

Caitlin wasn't lonely. Not really.

Every day she went to work and was surrounded with familiar faces and routine. She spent most of her time with her grandmother and waited patiently for the healthy baby boy inside her to be born.

Regrettably, the pain of losing Ferchar had neither vanished nor waned. She dreamt of him often, as if he had inflicted her with the same horrible stigma that Ewan MacLeod had. Except the dreams were dreams, not nightmares. He made love to her and told her he loved her. Showed her love in more ways than even she, a woman of the pornographic era, could've ever fathomed existed.

Yet, somehow, she knew that they were just dreams. Not magic. Caitlin stood and stretched. The baby had just gone through a growth spurt. She stood straight and looked down. Nope, her feet were nowhere to be found. Closing the front door behind her, she made a cup of decaf tea and walked upstairs. Four more months and she could have a blissful cup of coffee again.

A rumble of distant thunder broke the silence as she removed her clothes and slipped on a long oversized T- shirt. Caitlin opened both windows and allowed the eager wind admittance. She was hot all the time and the fresh, cool autumn air was welcome.

She checked her email and crawled into bed with a highland romance. That was all she could read lately. Even though they tended to fuel her memories and add to the hormonally charged state she was in, she continued to read them. As always, her eyes grew heavy quickly and she drifted off to sleep.

The dream came swiftly.

Catherine met her in the land of slumber, her brown eyes twinkling. Her voice was soft, feminine and as clear as a dream was capable.

"You're going to have a niece, Caitlin."

She tried to catch the pregnant girl's hand as she ran through the meadow ahead of her. "Shane's?"

A tinkling of laughter drifted through the air. "How else would you be having a niece?"

The dream fragmented and both Emma and Catherine ran ahead of her with a young child running between them. Emma tossed a smile over her shoulder before both women disappeared and Caitlin fell to her knees in the warm grass.

The child turned and stood before her. She had jet black, curly hair and large, curious chocolate brown eyes. She held out a small hand to Caitlin and her freckled face broke into a wide smile. "Hello, Auntie Caitlin."

As she went to embrace the child, the little girl became Shane. His hair was longer and small braids were sewn into his hair. The MacLomain plaid wrapped over a more muscled shoulder and though his eyes were harder than she remembered, he looked happy. So happy.

"I love you, sis." His endearment was a whisper on the wind.

Then he was gone and a stretch of grass lay before her. Highland mountains loomed crisp in the distance yet the castle beneath them was fuzzy.

A hand came out of nowhere and she took it. Helen stood before Caitlin, her long blond hair free in the wind. She looked to Caitlin's stomach and smiled. "You hold my grandchild."

The dream slowed as Helen moved forward and touched Caitlin's belly. "No other woman could have been more worthy."

Humbled, Caitlin tried to speak but couldn't. She met Helen's silver gaze and knew that no matter what had happened, Ferchar's mother approved of her, liked her.

Silver eyes turned green and Muriel linked her arm in Caitlin's. Her dark hair floated around her and her dress continued to shift colors. "My dagger served you well."

Why didn't you say goodbye at the castle? Nothing came out of Caitlin's mouth but Muriel responded regardless. "Because, lass, I was the one mind that you would have caught snippets of thoughts from. Though you may not have realized it, and I did not until you arrived. You and I were bonded throughout all of those dreams you had of the day William disappeared. Ferchar had the strength, most of the time, to keep you from his thoughts. I was too weak and would not have been able to. Why do you think I stayed away from you so much? You could not know your potential fate, as I did."

Muriel's explanation faded as did her form. Caitlin grasped air as she reached for her.

Thunder crashed and lightning flashed. Caitlin sat up. Her shaking hand went to her stomach and she attempted to settle her nerves. She knew the baby could sense her emotions.

The dream had seemed so real, but so had all of the dreams since she became pregnant. Colors were more vivid and textures more intense.

Another clap of thunder roared overhead and shook the house. Caitlin went to turn on the light only to find the power was out. Super. She fumbled with the drawer in the bedside table, found the handle and pulled it open. She grabbed a votive candle and lit it with a small lighter.

Calm at last, she took the candle and went downstairs. Heavy rain pelted the roof and drove her tormented thoughts to the surface. Why had she dreamt of all of them? Now, after so many months. Emotion clogged her throat as the vision of her brother rose in her mind. He had a little girl? Why would her subconscious fabricate such a thing?

Caitlin grabbed a small plate from the cabinet and rested the votive candle on it. As she reached into the refrigerator for some milk it occurred to her that the rain had ceased. An eerie silence filled the house. Milk forgotten; she turned and walked over to the kitchen window. Bright moonlight flooded the yard. The swing hung unmoving in a wind that made the Dahlia blossoms sway back and forth. What was going on? Fear infused her but she shoved it aside.

Caitlin sucked in a ragged breath, walked to the door and opened it. The air was warm and humid. Large drops of water dripped from the eve overhead. She'd never known a storm to vanish so fast.

Leaving the house, she walked down the steps and stood in the warm, wet grass. Too warm. It felt like mid-summer. The wind blew her shirt around her legs as she walked forward. Caitlin had to touch that swing, felt oddly compelled to make it move. She should be afraid, but she wasn't.

The air was even warmer around the swing. She reached out and touched one of the ropes. It was cool and flexible. Caitlin was sure it would have been stiff and flaming hot. Her eyes wandered the yard bright with lunar light. The full, swollen moon overhead filled every shadow for her appraisal.

The Rhododendrons and Boxwoods lining the house shook the raindrops from their leaves and stood taller. The house was crisp and clear, the small field and numerous trees beyond, silent. C.C. was quiet in the barn and a flash of lightning lit a far off, retreating cloudbank.

The air held the sweet tang of an abandoned summer storm. Caitlin leaned against the old oak. Its bark was warm and soothing. Its trunk sturdy and supportive. She closed her eyes and remembered Ferchar's words. *I do believe in God, just not in the sense that Christians do. For me, he cannae be found in a church or bible, but in nature and her many facets. In the wind as it turns the sun within the leaves of a tree. In the water churning with emotion and everything born of the Earth.*

She flattened her palms back tighter against the bark and whispered to the night. "Please give me strength."

"The oak is the most powerful tree known to Scotland. It will give you all of her strength."

Caitlin opened her eyes as his words drifted through her mind. Strong and magical. Ferchar? No one was there, just rays of moonlight and a wide splay of curious stars. Hope died instantly.

Not anger.

She pushed off the tree and yelled at her desolate surroundings to appease her own weakened sanity. "I'm not insane. You're here. You have to be. And if you're not, never speak within my mind again, no matter where you are. If I can't do it to you, you can't do it to me. I'm not yours anymore!"

"I never was," she whispered.

"Are you sure about that, lass?"

Caitlin spun and grabbed the rope of the swing. Her knees weakened but she stiffened them with pride born of disbelief.

Ferchar?

He leaned against the trunk of the oak, arms crossed. As self-assured as she'd ever seen him. His broad, muscled chest was bare above his kilt. He was as painfully handsome as she remembered but his eyes looked different. They held something new in their sapphire depths. Was she still dreaming? That seemed a logical explanation for the weather.

"You're not real." She didn't dare to step closer to him.

"Look at your ring, Caitlin." His well-formed lips curved slightly.

"My ring?" What was he talking about? She looked down at the claddagh ring on her finger and gasped. The small encrusted sapphire at its heart glowed a soft blue.

She shook her head in awe. "I don't understand."

"It's one of the first three ever created, Caitlin. It can only shine at its heart when your true love is present in body, not spirit."

"No." She continued to shake her head but met his eyes. "It never has before when I was around you and Arianna's doesn't."

He stepped away from the tree. "It has, lass, you just refused to see it, as did I. Arianna's ring glows for her and Iain's eyes only."

Caitlin took a step back as he drew closer. "Please, if you are real, you have to go. I can't go through losing you again."

His eyes dropped to her hands resting protectively over her rounded stomach. "You never lost me, Caitlin. You've had me your entire life." He closed the distance before she could bolt. "And I you."

Ferchar lifted her into his arms, swung around and sat her on the swing. He knelt on the ground before her and grabbed the ropes on either side of her. "Caitlin, I have loved you my whole life."

She was still shaking her head no. The time for lies and truths was well past for them both. "That's impossible. Please go away, Ferchar."

His intense gaze bore through her. "'Tis possible, Caitlin. Though I refused to acknowledge it, through William's connection I was drawn to you, your essence. I could never see the whole of you when I visited at both the picnic table and in your bedroom. 'Twas William's vision to bring us together."

He shook his head, remorse evident on his face. "The moment I saw you in the woods when you arrived in Scotland, I recognized you. You were the mysterious girl I had dreamt of since I was a wee lad. The little girl with thick chestnut hair who visited me in my dreams after my Ma and Da tucked me into bed at night. The golden eyed lass who tortured me with her visage. Hidden, masked and brutally familiar in the face of Iain's beloved."

He took her face in his hands. "I also knew the first time I saw you that you were the lass from my vision. The one I would have to leave Scotland for. I should have never left you once I found you."

"You make no sense." She tried to push his hands aside but he wouldn't allow it.

"Look, Caitlin. Look at what your soul so easily chose to forget."

Before she could stop him, his finger touched her forehead and waves of forgotten images flooded her mind. Childhood dreams that her conscience had locked away.

A little black haired boy sat cross legged across from her on a bed of golden pine needles. His blue and green kilt a hindrance on his bony frame. Blue eyes danced with delight as he showed her how he could make the needles dance a jig in the air between them.

That same little boy cried in her lap at the edge of a small stream when he had lost his father, his big blue eyes sad and confused.

A teenager, perhaps thirteen, showed off for her as he stood in two feet of loch. He braced a sword on his still slender shoulder, created a water spout with the flick of his hand and then cut it in half with his blade.

Then a young man, taller and thicker, cradling her tight. Hungry for the support and strength only she could offer him as he slept just beyond the hundreds of men, dead in a war that had taken so many countrymen and left him Chieftain of a powerful clan.

Caitlin opened her eyes as more images flooded her mind. Her hand shook as she brought it to a face that had always been so familiar to her. A face she'd watched grow and change. How had she forgotten so much?

"You went through everything I went through as well, Ferchar. Why didn't you say something sooner? Why put us both through so much?"

He turned his face into her hand. "Fear. Pride. I was tired of visions ruling my life and therefore tried to deny my destiny. There are a hundred other reasons and not one of them worthy of you. I thought my life was not my own and put my rage on you. In mortal form, you were an ignorant target. I knew you did not remember and took advantage of you."

He spread her thighs and moved closer. "I have used you as a buffer to assuage my own demons."

She brought her other hand to his face and ignored the endless stream of tears running down her cheeks. "To put a more modern twist on it, Ferchar. It sounds like you did what all couples in love do. You took your aggravations and imperfections out on the one person that you knew could handle it. Your soul-mate."

He brought her hand down to his heart and a small smile stole his lips. "Who would have thought the witch wiser than the wizard?"

He was here. This was real, gloriously, perfectly real. She laughed. "A passive-aggressive feminist, that's who."

"There's very little that's passive about you, lass." His eyes dropped to her stomach and caressed it.

She took his hands and brought them there. The baby gave a hearty kick and more laughter bubbled from Caitlin. "It seems he knows you."

Ferchar's eyes glowed sapphire for a moment then dulled to that of their everyday brilliance. "Aye, lass."

Caitlin wavered. "Are you here because of him?"

Ferchar's eyes returned to hers. "Nay lass, I'm here because of you. Not to say my lad doesnae need his Da, he does. But I didnae return for that reason. I returned because I love you, Caitlin."

His lips drew closer. "And because I dinnae want to live without you." He touched her stomach. "Or him."

"But what about your visions? I cannot lose you again." Caitlin held her breath.

Ferchar's features never wavered and his eyes gave her the core of his heart. "Any visions left for me in this lifetime include you and the baby or the gods can look elsewhere."

Caitlin brought her hands to his face and said, "But you said so many lives would be affected if you did not fulfill your visions."

"Aye." Ferchar's eyes again dropped to her stomach. "But what of your life? And his? Are not both of you part of my existence?"

Caitlin stifled a wealth of new tears and eased his distress. "Yeah, I suppose we are."

She brought a finger to his lips before he could speak. "But are we bigger than however many other countless lives? Bigger than whatever the gods have foreseen?"

"To me, you two mean more than anyone in any era," Ferchar said softly.

Caitlin held her weak heart at bay. "The problem with your rationalization is that it includes me. Your eventual guilt would be mine as well."

There was not fear, but interest in his eyes. "Then what do you propose, Caitlin? Because I willnae be without you."

"A promise." She kept her eyes steady on his.

Ferchar's breath escaped and his mouth curved. "Anything."

"Promise that if you ever have another vision you'll bring the baby and I with you, no matter what."

Pleased, Ferchar didn't pause. "You have my solemn promise that no matter when or where, I will not leave you or our son behind."

He told the truth. She could feel it in every recess of his mind, every corner that'd been kept from her before. When his tender lips finally met hers, there was nothing left but him and their child.

And a future Caitlin had forgotten within dreams she had been having all of her life.

Epilogue

As Ferchar carried his one true love and son into the old colonial house, the stars winked at one another and the moon rolled across the sky.

The old oak bristled with pride and spread her branches further. Her trunk glowed green and her leaves grew protective fingers over her new family. A white eagle cried with triumph and swooped down to land on the swing.

It spread its feathers until it possessed the hands of a mortal man. Adlin pushed himself sideways and patted the old oak. At its base he dropped a satchel that contained a birth certificate and social security card.

Ferchar had done the right thing...the inevitable thing. He'd followed that last vision and gone back to Scotland where he rescued Hugh from a small skirmish with another clan far east of clan MacLomain. How the man had gone magically undetected for so long, Adlin would never know. Regardless, Ferchar had brought Hugh back to his wife, Muriel and son, William, then returned home to New Hampshire.

Like a child, Adlin swung back and pushed his legs off the ground, moving the swing until his white robes brushed the Earth beneath with speed. When the swing met its highest point he laughed and spread his arms that turned back to wings. He flew high over the house and howled with delight once more.

Then he shifted his wings until his fluid body flew due east. Scotland waited. Time to go home.

SNEAK PEEK …

Sylvan Mist (The MacLomain Series-Book 3)

Prologue

"Flesh and blood?" The devil chuckled. "You give yourself too much credit."

She didn't bother struggling. "Do I really?"

He leaned in close until the edge of his mouth skirted hers. "Aye, and I've little use for those such as you."

"I doubt that." She remained still.

"Dinnae doubt, lass." He ran his tongue along her jaw until he seized her earlobe with his teeth. He growled, released his hold, and threw her to the ground. In a flourish of precise, deadly movements, he lodged a knee into her back and withdrew his sword. She felt the satisfaction in the steady draw of his breath, the purr of domination.

So she was to die like this? With a sword driven through her back? Fear rose sharply. She tempered it. What good would it do?

He lifted her dress, straddled her backside, and whispered in her ear, the words more efficient than his blade. "Did you think your death would be so swift?"

To speak would be a waste of time. He'd only become more violent. Again, fear threatened to overwhelm. God, please don't let this happen. No. No. No. His hands traveled up her thighs.

"Release her."

It was a dark and dangerous whisper on the wind. She struggled to see, but blinding snow made it impossible. Her teeth began to chatter.

The brute above her chuckled, the sound evil and warped. He threw his words at the unseen stranger. "Interesting that you chose words over action. Do you ken the difference? The result of such foolishness?"

He shoved her face against the ground and leaned back. Then his large hands squeezed her neck. She gasped, arms flailing.

She tried to fight the horrifying fear of helplessness. The clutch of strong fingers dug deeper into her windpipe and made reasoned thought impossible. The alabaster snow released black flecks into her vision. Panic seized. She fisted the icy moisture beneath and struggled for air. Her body grew heavy and leaden.

Milky white ground became foggy gray. She struggled to see, not to lose the last of this reality. Yet fate was not that kind.

Blackness descended.

Chapter One

Salem, New Hampshire, 1816

"No more!" Coira jerked awake, slammed her hands down on the secretary, and shook off the dream. Flame still curled in the lantern, the papers she'd been working on scattered about.

Ridiculous, this nightmare of hers, it had started on the first of the year and was nothing but a thorn in her side. She knew well what it meant and wanted none of it. She'd done just fine for herself thus far and had no intention of being lulled into the oddities that plagued her bloodline. Besides, what did he mean "no use for those such as her"? And how did she seem to know what to answer?

She walked to the window, and pulled back the curtains. The moon was a wide eye overhead and sparkled off the oak leaves beyond. Why her? She closed her eyes and banged her palm again the glass. She couldn't deal with this, not now.

"Coira?" She turned and offered her mother a steady smile. "Mama, why are you up at this hour?"

Marie stepped into the room, and candlelight flickered off the traces of silver in her red hair. "It's not that late, child. I thought I heard something."

She walked back and straightened her paperwork. Her mother knew. Secrets such as this did not keep well in the O'Donnell family. "So you know. I'm surprised it took this long."

"I've known for some time." Marie placed a hand on Coira's arm. "There's no shame in it. Let me help you."

"No." She pulled away. "This makes no sense. Remember, I'm the only child who carries no magic. And thus far I've been content with such."

"That does not mean you are immune to the MacLomain call. Magic is not necessary to feel their summons," Marie responded.

Coira sighed and sat. She was an odd being, the child of a witch and sister to two more. Only her father shared her plight, her normalcy. Sixteen years ago, her cousin Arianna vanished. She'd traveled back in time to medieval Scotland, never to return, all because of a MacLomain.

Not her. Coira would not be pulled. "I've a love for England and all things English. Somewhere, somehow, someone miss-stitched. No offense, Mother, but Scotland would not appreciate me on its soil."

Marie's back straightened. "Lass, you're half Irish and half Scottish. Will that ever mean anything to you?"

"Of course it does. It's just not my passion." Coira took her mother's hand and squeezed. "Come now, I merely mean that I'm an English history teacher. It's highly unlikely my fate would carry me in such a direction."

Her mother had fled Scotland during the Highland Clearances but remained fiercely proud of both her homeland and her clan, the Brouns. Liam, her father, was proud to be from Dublin, Ireland.

Marie's expression saddened for a moment. "Aye, it does seem unlikely, but fate is a funny thing. There's always a lesson to be learned in its design."

She nodded her head once. "But not a lesson for me. My lessons are only what I teach here in Salem."

Her mother's eyes turned hard and wise. "So you think. I'll leave you to your rest now. Remember, your sister and brother will be visiting tomorrow for the festivities. They will not leave you be about this dream you've been having."

She watched Marie depart and frowned. No doubt they wouldn't. Calum would be returning from overseas having studied in France for the past year, and Annie lived in Hampstead working as a housekeeper. She'd not seen Annie since Christmas, because she was thoroughly engrossed in writing one novel or another when not busy with her duties.

Though twenty-four, Coira remained with her parents. The siblings had decided that one of them would stay to help their parents and watch over them. She didn't mind living here for the most part. Spinsterhood had suited her fine until recently.

Now things would change.

At tomorrow's gathering, Coira and James would announce their betrothal. Her friend would become her lover. She ignored the ripple of apprehension that stole down her spine. There was no reason for it. James was dashing and as British as they came.

She retired to bed and snuffed the candle. As darkness surrounded, she wondered yet again. Who was the stranger who meant to save her in the dream? Did she really care?

After all, he was but a Scot.

****

"Come here, you!" Annie lifted her skirts and flew across the drive.

Coira braced for impact. Never was a more spirited woman born than her sister. Annie swooped in for a tight embrace.

"Oh, how I've missed you!" Annie laughed and pulled back.

"And I you." She smiled. Where she'd inherited their father's black hair and blue eyes, Annie possessed the glorious chestnut hair and golden eyes from their Scottish blood.

Immediately, Annie's eyes narrowed. "No?"

Coira grimaced. Not this fast. Annie had only to take one look at her to know about the dream. "Shush."

Her sister's eyes were saucers now. "You? Who would've thought? My Lord, this is incredible!"

"Shush!"

Annie waved away Coira's insistence. "People are only just arriving, and nobody's paying attention anyway. This just astonishes me. Aren't you getting married? Oh no, that's a bad idea. You should break it off right away. You know how these things—"

She clamped a hand over Annie's mouth and leaned in close. "If you don't stop talking now, I'll tell everyone about what you always wondered and were determined to find out."

If it was possible, Annie's eyes rounded further, and she shook her head.

"That's what I thought." She removed her hand and offered a serene smile. "We'll talk about this later, and I am announcing my betrothal."

Annie rolled her eyes and shrugged. "Who am I to argue when you blackmail me?"

"And how have you blackmailed your sister this time?" James had approached unseen.

She welcomed the intrusion. "Would I do such a thing?"

James laughed and took her hand. His sea green eyes twinkled. "In a heartbeat to get your way."

She loved his accent, so crisp and English. Defined and articulate. His sunkissed brown hair was wavy and his height substantial. They had known one another for years, and both taught at the same school.

They'd finally decided to marry in that neither had found another who suited. They would live nearby and be available to help Marie and Liam with whatever they might need.

"James, how are you?" Annie gave him a big hug.

"Excellent, now that I've nearly secured your sister as my fiancée."

Annie shot her a look of aggravation. "No doubt, and it's about time, too. She's not getting any younger!"

"You should talk." Coira arched an eyebrow. "You're but a year younger than I."

"And you're still both unmarried, me daughters?" Liam announced on arrival.

Annie rushed to their father and mumbled a tearful greeting into his chest. Liam beamed and held her tight. When they pulled apart, he looked Coira's way.

"My girl, today is a big day for you!" He was a beautiful man, her father. Tall, big boned, and as black Irish as they came.

"I've some sad news, lassies." He frowned and shook his head. "Calum will not make it home for the day. I've received a post that his ship has been delayed. I'm sorry to bear such news."

Both girls deflated. How they missed their brother.

"I'd say everyone else is here. Are you ready?" Liam directed this at James.

"Of course." James pulled her toward the tables where people were gathered. Theirs would be a casual announcement.

She pasted a smile on her face as James gathered everyone's attention. Suddenly, her feet felt like lead. A newborn trepidation swallowed her.

Or was it so new?

James hailed the crowd and smiled widely. "I'm certain you all know why we're here." He turned to her but spoke to them. "I have an important thing to ask of Coira."

The women smiled knowingly from beneath their bonnets, and the men nodded their approval.

James fell to one knee and took her hand in his. His green eyes gazed up with both approval and finality. "Coira, we have been friends for so long. Would you do me the honor of becoming my—"

His lips continued to move, but something shifted. Time slowed, his form faded, blurred. His hand in hers became a death grip, a force. A fever stole up her arm and wrapped her body in mist. Verdant lightning blinded her with images: diamond eyes, sensual lips, incredible, unattainable, foreign beauty. But where was he? She fell to her knees.

The world was gone. He was not. Moisture prickled her skin and dampened her pores. She was light and alive, alone yet not. Arms of nothing wrapped around her waist and pulled her close. Then there was lust. Like a roll of flaming ice, it churned her womb with potent agony. She reached out and grasped male flesh.

His voice roared, yet whispered. "You are safe."

Her mind rebelled against the thick Scottish burr, but her soul clutched him tighter and pleaded. "I'm not safe. Not from you. Leave me be."

He pulled her close. "Who are you?"

She closed her eyes yet images continued to bombard. Hard skin, thick lashes. "I am no one."

Rich laughter buried her defiance. "Aye, you're someone."

She opened her eyes, and daylight blinded as James embraced her. They knelt before one another on the grass. Applause saturated the lawn full of townsfolk. She pulled away from James and accepted his hand as they stood.

She shuddered at the chill that swept through her. God no, it really was happening.

One look at Annie more than confirmed it.
****

Annie met Marie's eyes in mutual understanding. Coira was being called back. They were both surprised. It was obvious in the distress blatant in her mother's eyes. Coira? Prim and proper and all things English.

This was bad.

They could all have understood it happening to Annie. After all, she loved all things Scottish. The obvious difference between the siblings had always been a bit of a joke between them. When they were children, they would battle with sticks in the woods. Annie would be the Scotsman defending his country, Coira the Englishman determined to bring order and surrender. Yet when the call came from Scotland to a woman of the Broun lineage, it was impossible to ignore.

Literally.

Annie knew the moment she touched Coira she was doomed. Doomed in Coira's eyes, not in hers. Why couldn't she have been called? Blast it! When her sister fell to her knees, she'd seen the magic swamp her. Felt it in her bones. What had Coira just experienced? How she longed to find out. But she knew her sister. She would be tight-lipped to the end. She was determined to marry her Englishman, come Scottish plague or no.

Her mother made it to her side. "We will bring her to the attic, Annie. We must show Coira her wedding gown."

"Do you really think that's wise?"

Marie's expression darkened and she murmured, "Aye, it is. Though I wish it were not the case."

She knew the pain her mother was feeling. "Oh, Mama. I'm so sorry."

"No, no." Marie shook her head. "Don't be. This is the way of things, I know that."

Coira walked in their direction, face pale though she smiled for the neighbors. She suddenly seemed to want to avoid them and veered toward the barn. When they caught up with her, Annie linked an arm through one of Coira's and Marie did the same.

Annie spoke softly. "Are you well?"

Coira stopped short, a blank expression on her face. They saw the crisis coming and led her forward a few steps before they closed the barn stall doors behind them.

Then, like a candle flame beneath a heavy downpour, Coira crumpled to the ground.

****

He swirled before her. A man made of mist, beautiful, hypnotizing, and without a face. A hand held out to her in offering through a fog of barn ceiling and hay. Though reluctant, Coira was curious, and she lifted a hand in welcome.

"Sweetheart, are you well?" Her mother's voice drifted through the enthralling haze and sharpened her senses. Am I well? Am I engaged? Her eyes felt heavy and overused, as though she'd been correcting papers for centuries. She spoke yet nothing came out.

"Coira, it's Annie." Her sister's cool hands brushed back the hair from her forehead. Slowly, she opened her eyes. Oh, but the dim light of the barn blinded. She shut her eyes and pushed herself to a sitting position.

"I'm fine." She whispered the reassurance more to herself than to them. At last, she opened her eyes and saw her mother and sister kneeling in front of her.

"Are you?" Marie worried.

"Coira?" Annie frowned with concern.

She shook her head and smiled ruefully. "If you could both stop looking at me as though I'm some sort of anomaly, I do believe I would feel much better."

They appeared momentarily chagrined but smoothed their expressions. Her eyes drifted to her left hand. The engagement ring was exquisite, a shimmering diamond that overtook her slender finger. The stone shone brightly in the dim recesses of the barn.

But not nearly as brightly as the small diamond chip within the ring that Annie wore. She again cursed her envy of the ring given to her sister by their parents years ago. Two hands coming from separate directions holding a diamond-centered crowned heart between them.

Why she should envy the Irish heirloom was beyond her. Perhaps because it was one more stone in the wall between her, with no magic, and her mother and sister. An Irish ring would not suit her any more than the Scottish plaid her mother so favored.

She brushed her thoughts aside and stood. "I'm fine."

Marie shook her head. "Nay, lassie. You're about as far from fine as I've ever seen you. Annie?"

Annie nodded. "Aye, Mama's right. You just had a moment with him out there, didn't you?"

A painful rumble of laughter rose in her chest and she waved them away. "You're both mistaken. I had a moment with no one."

Lucky them, witches that they were, that they could so easily see. Still, she didn't mean to give them an ounce of assurance or confirmation.

"Come, lass, I've something to show you." Marie looped her arm through Coira's and reopened the barn doors.

Sunlight overwhelmed and she squinted. Townsfolk filtered around and offered smiles. The smell of apples and cornmeal filled her nostrils, the grass underfoot lush and suddenly so green it was all she could see. The oak overhead flipped its leaves in passing. A light wind caressed her cheeks. Compelled, she stopped a moment and looked up past the tall sturdy trunk to the many branches that forked against the afternoon sky.

"I'll protect you."

She stared at the leaves overhead and heard his voice, clear, intense, and horribly Scottish.

"No, you won't!" She screamed at the oak and shook her head. Through the red haze of anger, she heard her mother command Annie to get her inside, up the stairs into the attic. It was happening too fast.

She tried to speak, tell them nothing was happening too fast. That she was newly engaged, and all was well. All was normal. But they didn't listen, because they couldn't hear her. She saw the doors to their home. Saw the foyer and the stairs, knew that James was behind them but being told to go away.

Then the attic stairs loomed before her, steep and foreign, a place where she'd never been invited for she carried no magic. Breathless, she was led up, yet was so outside herself that she stumbled and fell.

But he broke her fall.

Of mist and muscle and flesh, he cushioned the blow of the sharp wood. His concern washed over, and his words echoed in her ear. *"I'm here, lass."*

She pushed away from nothing and stumbled up the stairs. Everything was happening too quickly. She couldn't get her bearings. The attic rose up, and nausea brought her to the flat planks underfoot. Before she could vomit, Marie brought her to her feet and pulled her close.

The nausea receded. What on Earth was going on? She was shocked when Annie bit off a sob.

Marie pulled back slowly and stared into Coira's eyes. She'd never seen such a sad look upon her mother's face. "I must show you something."

Destiny's Denial

She slowly released her breath. "What do you wish to show me?"

The sunlight streaming through the small windows receded when Marie flicked her wrist, and a candle sputtered to life. It rested on a small three-legged table and cast a glow on what looked to be a tree stump sitting alone in the middle of the attic. On that stump sat the most amazing thing she'd ever seen.

A crown of gold, so glorious it was hard to look at.

Marie lifted and held it out to Coira. "This is a family heirloom."

Instinct shot her hand forward, and she grasped the circular piece between the sharp spikes. Reluctant, Marie released and the crown's full weight took her by surprise. She studied it. "How beautiful!"

Marie appeared confused as did Annie.

Annie spoke first. "So it's not as it seems?"

Marie shook her head, mystified. "It has to be, the wedding dress was not right yet."

Her eyes snapped to attention. "What are you two talking about?"

But they were already too deep in debate.

Annie's eyes narrowed. "Well, why is nothing happening?"

Marie's brow furrowed and distress crossed her dainty features. Before she could utter another word, Annie sprang into action, as was Annie's way.

"May I?" she said to Coira, and wrapped her hand around the crown as if to inspect it more closely.

Coira gasped when the golden headpiece turned to ice. Her arm numbed, and her legs liquefied. Oh dear God, what was happening? Annie was falling, a look of both horror and wonder on her face.

Marie screamed in denial from a great distance away. Coira could barely see anyone or anything as a whip of green moisture encased her body. It crawled over her calves, up her thighs until it encaged her torso. She tried to push it away, but her hands slid through the weightless cocoon. The verdant mist took her torso and head.

All turned white and peaceful.

Then hell was unleashed, and everything fell away. A horrible roar filled her eardrums, and a sugary smell filled her nostrils. The floor let loose, and she fell hard and fast. But she had no fear, only wonder. Was she finally a part of magic? Had she been allowed entrance?

When terror should have seized her, wonder turned to anger. Why should she be shown magic now after all this time? She locked her muscles and flailed in defiance. Darn them all, she was an English teacher, and as such this plight held no interest. As she fought the maddening rush of energy and harsh whips of power thrown, she had only one thought.

She did not want to go to Scotland.

About the Author…

Best-selling author and New Hampshire native, Sky Purington writes a cross genre of paranormal/fantasy romance heavily influenced by history. From Irish Druids to Scottish Highlanders many of her novels possess strong Celtic elements. More recently, her vampire stories take the reader to medieval England and ancient Italy. Enjoy strictly paranormal romance? Sky's latest novels follow three haunted houses and the sexy ghost hunters determined to make sense of them. Make no mistake, in each and every tale told you'll travel back to another time and revisit the romanticism history holds at its heart. Sky loves to hear from her readers and can be contacted at Sky@SkyPurington.com.

Find out Sky's latest news at SkyPurington.com
Twitter @ SkyPurington.com
Facebook Sky Purington

Made in the USA
Lexington, KY
10 February 2012